Tame the Restless Heart

Tame the Restless Heart

F
Mat

Patricia Matthews

BANTAM BOOKS
TORONTO · NEW YORK · LONDON · SYDNEY · AUCKLAND

Published simultaneously in the United States and Canada

Bantam Books are published by Bantam Books, Inc. Its trade-
mark, consisting of the words ''Bantam Books'' and the por-
trayal of a rooster, is Registered in U.S. Patent and Trademark
Office and in other countries. Marca Registrada. Bantam
Books, Inc., 666 Fifth Avenue, New York, New York 10103.

PRINTED IN THE UNITED STATES OF AMERICA

There are some people who love reading, and who believe that books possess a certain magic. One such person is my friend, Chelly Kitzmiller, and it is to her that I dedicate this book, with great affection. May the magic always be there for her.

AUTHOR'S NOTE

In this book, the author has written of several historical characters. The boy comics Fields and Weber, who went on to become one of the most famous vaudeville teams of all times; Phineas T. Barnum, the world-famous showman, and his second wife, Nancy Barnum; James Bailey, Barnum's partner in the Barnum and Bailey Circus; Adam Forepaugh, Barnum's chief rival; the world renowned midget, General Tom Thumb, and his tiny wife, Lavinia; the so-called Wild Men of Borneo; the connected twins billed as the Two-Headed Girl; the huge elephant, Jumbo, and the midget elephant Tom Thumb; all existed, and the author has attempted to portray them as accurately as possible.

The descriptions of Pacific Grove, California; the traveling show offering culture and entertainment, called the Chautauqua after its town of origin; and the Barnum and Bailey Circus as it existed in the late 1800s, are all based on fact, as are the stories told by P. T. Barnum; however, the incident involving Barnum's discovery of the "Forest Creature" is completely fictional.

The remaining characters, other than those mentioned above, are entirely products of the author's imagination. In the case of most of the circus performers, the author has made no attempt to portray the actual employees of the circus at that time, but has instead tried to present a collection of typical performers of the day.

Welcome to the world of the circus!

CIRCUS PARADE

—Patricia Matthews

Here they come;
the calliope
hooting and shrilling its wild song
through the still afternoon air,
shattering the ordinary day
so that it fractures into magic shards
that reflect a fantasy.

Here they come;
the clowns, stilted eight feet tall,
and two foot three,
painted smiles and jumble-sale clothes,
tumble-jumping, horn-honking,
carrying laughter
like a banner.

Here they come;
the acrobats and men who are shot from guns,
bareback riders,
and daring young men from the flying trapeze,
spangle-caped and tighted,
the lion-tamer,
marching hand in hand with courage.

Here they come;
the animals,
golden-maned lions,
tigers, lushly striped,
and bears.
The elephants, ponderously graceful,
stately walking head to tail.

Here they come;
their footsteps smell of tanbark,
and their clothing of wonder,
the band blows excitement over the crowd,
stirring old dreams,
and brushing us with
a touch of magic.

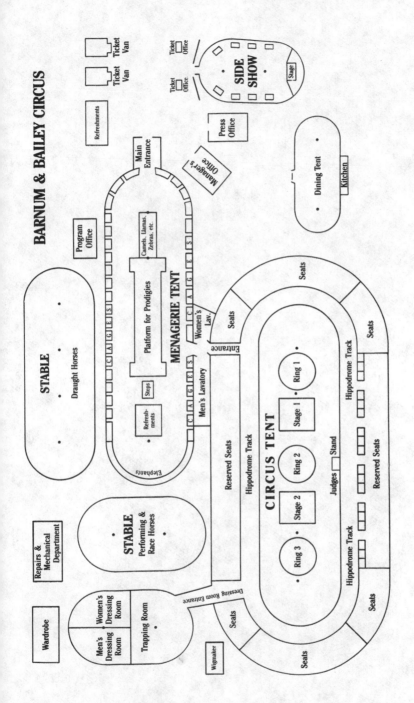

BARNUM & BAILEY CIRCUS

Ticket Van

Ticket Van

Refreshments

SIDE SHOW

Ticket Office

Ticket Office

Stage

Program Office

Main Entrance

Press Office

Manager's Office

STABLE

Draught Horses

Camels, Llamas, Zebras, etc.

Platform for Prodigies

MENAGERIE TENT

C A G E S

Women's Lav.

C A G E S

Entrance

Men's Lavatory

Steps

Refreshments

Elephants

Dining Tent

Kitchen

Seats

Seats

Seats

Ring 1

Stage 1

Reserved Seats

Hippodrome Track

Ring 2

Judges Stand

CIRCUS TENT

Stage 2

Reserved Seats

Seats

Ring 3

Hippodrome Track

Hippodrome Track

Repairs & Mechanical Department

STABLE

Performing & Race Horses

Wardrobe

Women's Dressing Room

Men's Dressing Room

Trapping Room

Dressing Room Entrance

Wigmaker

Seats

Seats

Seats

Part One

1881

Chapter One

Pacific Grove Retreat

SAMUEL Purcell's heavy hand hit the flimsy table with
a crash that made the tent quiver and caused his daughter
to wince; but when he spoke his voice was low and controlled, as it always was when he was in a rage.

"You are not to go! You know my views on such matters!" His cold gray eyes were fixed on hers, and Laura
was conscious of a force as physical as if he were manhan-
dling her.

Her own anger was as icy as his, but she did not dare
let it show in her face or eyes, for that would only prolong
the abuse. She could never win an argument with him,
the only thing she could hope for was defeat with dignity;
and so she struggled to keep her expression calm, for he
seemed to enjoy it when he could reduce her to tears or
an obvious display of her feelings. And always, despite the
knowledge that she could not win, Laura felt compelled to
try to talk to him reasonably.

"Father, would you just listen to me?"

He folded his arms on his chest. "I always listen to what
you have to say, daughter. Never let it be said that I am
not a fair man."

Fair? Laura would have laughed if she dared, but she
plowed stubbornly ahead. "I know your feelings concern-

3

ing frivolous entertainment, Father, but this is not entertainment as such. The Chautauqua is put on by the
Methodist Church. It's educational. Why, they even use
it to train their Sunday-school teachers. They . . ."

He raised a hand, palm toward her. "I know very well
what they do, and as far as I'm concerned it is frivolous. I
do not want my wife and daughter exposed to play-actors,
musicians, and charlatans, and that is my final word upon
the subject."

Helplessly, Laura looked over at her mother, who was
sitting in the rocking chair on the other side of the tent;
but her mother's head was turned away, and Laura knew
that she could expect no help or support from her.

"You are a selfish girl!" Samuel's voice was soft now,
soft and very cold. "You know that I will be away for
several days during the time that devil's show is here, and
you also know that your mother will have need of you, in
her condition. Even if you have no respect for my feelings, how can you ask permission to attend such a function
knowing that your poor mother would be left here all
alone?"

Laura turned away to hide the burn of angry tears. He
well knew that there was nothing really wrong with her
mother, except illnesses that she concocted in her mind.
Why did they have to go through life pretending that her
mother was frail?

She heard him move, behind her. "Now I must go out
for an hour or so. I will be back in time for supper, and
when I return, I want to hear no more about this foolishness!"

Laura waited until she heard the wooden door of the
framed tent slam, then whirled on her mother. "Mother,
why don't you ever help me? If you would only say
something, take my side just once. You *know* he's
unreasonable!"

Mary Purcell would not meet her daughter's eyes. "He's
the man of the house," she said in her lifeless voice. "He's
my husband and your father. He knows what's best for
us."

Laura gave a sob of anger and frustration, and reached

for her gray wool shawl, which was draped over the back of a straight chair.

"I'm going out to the point. I'll be back in time to help with supper. You might at least start it while I'm gone."

Wrapping the shawl tightly around her, Laura angrily pushed out of the tent and down the wooden steps to the ground, her anger expressing itself in her hurried stride as she headed away from the Grove, down toward Jesus Lover's Point and the sea. The afternoon sun was lowering toward the horizon, and the wind had come up, but the chilling air felt good on her hot cheeks.

When she reached the point she climbed out on the rocks until she could look down on the sea moving below her. Clasping her knees with her arms, she lowered her head and let the tears come, but they brought her no comfort.

She always came here, to the point, when she was unhappy or angry, which seemed to be more often of late. The sight of the sea and the rocks usually soothed her; and as she watched the wheeling gulls above her and the frolicking sea otters below, she could usually attain a measure of calm. There was such beauty here, in the Pacific Grove Retreat—the pines, the sand and the sea, the fresh, salt-tinged air, and the summer sun. Laura had been so pleased when her father had decided to buy a lot here and erect a semipermanent tent so that they could spend the summer months in the cooler weather of the coast; but it had not really changed anything. The location was lovely, yet her father and mother remained the same. They had merely brought their problems to a different site. And today even the magic of the sea failed to work. Laura's anger and hurt were too great.

Why should she be required to live like this, without love and almost without hope? She often felt that she lived her life like a squirrel caught in one of those wheels, where the poor creature ran and ran and never got anywhere. She was a prisoner, with her father the jailer; and if she was ever to have any kind of life at all, she must escape, must get away.

And yet, it always came down to the question of how.

Many women escaped unhappy families by marrying, but
her father had somehow managed to turn away every man
who had expressed the slightest interest in her. Those
who were not as strong as he, Samuel Purcell bullied and
badgered until they gave up trying to see her. There had
been some who were stronger, but they, too, had finally
given up, and she knew that her father had found some
way to get to them, as well. It was clear that he did not
intend for her to leave by that exit; and yet he seemed to
enjoy taunting her with the fact that at almost twenty-five
she was still unwed.

Laura had never understood her father. His motives
were incomprehensible to her; but she had often been
conscious of something in him that frightened her—an
unnatural possessiveness that went beyond paternal concern, that made her fear and—yes—hate him.

Of course, she could just walk out. Pack up her belong-
ings and leave. But where would she go, and what would
she do? She had some money, which she had squirreled
away over the years, but she had no skills, except a flair
for figures, and some talent for playing the piano. Still,
something must be done. If this was all there was to life,
all she had to look forward to—life as a caretaker and
companion to a dominating, overbearing father and a weak
and spiritless mother who suffered from feigned illnesses—
life was not worth living. She might as well fling herself
down on the rocks and let the sea take her!

"Hello there!"

Startled, Laura raised her head and looked around.
Standing on the rock beside her was a tall, slender man, a
stranger, clothed in a light sack coat, a vest, and brown
trousers. He had a straw boater in his hand, and the wind
tossed his head of curly black hair and tugged at his
waistcoat.

Laura's first reaction was annoyance at this invasion of
her privacy, and then curiosity. The Pacific Grove Retreat
was a small enclave, and after being there for several
weeks, most of the campers were familiar to her, at least
on sight; yet, she had never seen this man before. She
was certain that if she had, she would have remembered

him, for he was extremely attractive. He appeared to be in his late twenties or early thirties.

Brushing her hair back from her face, and hoping that her tears had not made her eyes red, she tentatively returned his open smile.

"Hello there," he said again. "I hope you'll forgive me for being so forward and speaking to you without being introduced, but I am badly in need of some information, and you, ma'am, are the only person around."

His voice was deep and quite pleasant, and he pronounced his words in a rather pedantic fashion—rather like a teacher, Laura thought—but the effect was elegant. He certainly was not a local.

"What is it you wish to know, sir?" she asked in a low voice.

"Do you mind if I sit down first? I had to walk all the way from the gate. It seems that the whole retreat is fenced around." He sat down without waiting for her response, his smile broadening. "Well now, are all the young ladies in Pacific Grove as pretty as you?"

Laura felt a hot flush warm her body. He was being very bold. If her father could hear him, he would be even more enraged than he'd been that afternoon. At this thought, she lowered her head and smiled to herself.

The man leaned toward her. "And what a lovely smile! I've embarrassed you, I do believe. I shouldn't have spoken out so openly, but somehow I feel as if I've known you for a long time. That may strike you as strange, but that does happen with people sometimes, you know." He shook his head ruefully. "Of course, I shouldn't make the assumption that the other party is experiencing the same phenomenon. Do you wish me to go?"

Laura glanced up quickly. That was the last thing she wanted this handsome stranger to do. He certainly *was* forward, yet he did not seem to mean his words in a bad way, and his friendliness was contagious. It was not often that she got to talk to a man alone. She might as well make the most of it.

"You said you had a question of me?" she prompted.

"Ah, yes. You see, I am new in the area, having just

arrived this morning, to be exact, and someone told me that there was a drugstore somewhere in the retreat."

"Yes, there is." Laura turned and pointed behind her. "On Lighthouse Road. It's called Seaside Drugstore. It's only a short walk."

"Thank you. You are most kind. I think I'll rest a moment before looking for it, if you don't mind. It has been a long day!" He turned to look at the beach, to their right. "That's a lovely bit of beach, isn't it? I'll bet it's grand swimming there."

He fixed Laura with his dark eyes, one of which was slightly cast; however, it seemed only to add to his attractiveness. "I'll wager you look smashing in a swimming dress. Oh, there! I've embarrassed you again, haven't I?"

His tone was rueful, but the twinkle in his eyes said that he was not a bit sorry, and Laura found herself relaxing. It was difficult not to like this friendly stranger.

She started to laugh as she thought of her swimming dress, which was heavier and bulkier than her everyday clothes. She felt a wave of recklessness rising in her; she did not want this very cosmopolitan man to think her a rustic.

She said, "I'm afraid that you would not find our style of bathing dress terribly exciting. This is, after all, a religious retreat, and most of the people here are devoted to a very moral way of life."

He nodded. "Yes, I've read 'God's Kingdom by the Sea.' " He leaned toward her. "Have you heard it?"

Smiling, he began to recite:

"P is for Pacific, the name of a Grove,
Not far from Del Monte where Methodists rove,
And hold their camp meetings, and sing, shout, and pray,
And have a good time keeping Satan at Bay.
Here no requirements of fashion restrain,
And satins and swallowtails all may disdain."

He declaimed the words in such an amusing manner that Laura could not help but laugh. She knew that she should be getting back to the house, but she was feeling so good that she could not bear the thought of going.

"Where did you hear that?" she asked, curious.

"A friend in Monterey sent it to me. It was written by Major Ben Truman and was published in the *Del Monte Wave*."

"Have you lived in Monterey?"

He shook his head. "No, this is my very first trip to California. I live in Buffalo, New York. That is, when I'm not traveling."

"Are you a salesman of some sort?"

He laughed. "I suppose some might say so, but it is not an ordinary product that I sell. I sell enlightenment and education. I'm a lecturer with the Chautauqua, and I've really forgotten my manners. I haven't even introduced myself." Gracefully, he rose from the rock and bowed low, formally. "Nickolas Orlando, Chautauqua lecturer, at your service. And with whom may I have the pleasure of speaking?"

Laura, feeling gay and lightheaded, rose also and curtsied. "Laura Evangeline Purcell, sir, although I'm afraid that I don't have any title that I can give you."

He reached out and took her hand; although she was startled, she did not remove it. Slowly he raised it to his lips. The touch of his mouth on her skin filled her with a glorious warmth.

"Charmed, I'm sure," he said. "And you don't *need* any titles, my dear Miss Purcell. Your beauty alone is more than enough."

Flushing, she snatched her hand away, feeling both pleased and extremely awkward. "You're early," she said abruptly.

He looked puzzled. "I beg your pardon?"

"For the Chautauqua. It doesn't start until next week."

He shrugged. "I had some spare time on my hands, and as I said, I've heard about your piney paradise. I thought I would spend a few days looking around. Once the Chautauqua starts, I won't have much free time. It's very beautiful here. Are you staying at the camp?"

Laura nodded. "My father just bought a lot and tent in the retreat. We've been here only a few weeks."

"And where is your home?"

"Sacramento."

"Ah, yes. I was there once, with . . . on business. It was in July, as I recall, and I found it very hot there, although it was a drier heat than New York."

She nodded. "That's why I love it so here. I don't really think I was meant for hot, dry places. I much prefer the ocean breeze, trees, and water."

His appraising look was so patently approving that it sent a slight shiver down her spine. "Ah, yes, with your fair skin and blue eyes, you should shun the sun. I presume you live in Sacramento because your father has a business there?"

She nodded again. "Yes, he is in farm equipment, and such. Even here he keeps working, making contacts with farmers in the surrounding communities and over in the valley. He travels quite a bit." *And thank goodness for that*, she thought, for it gave her a brief respite from his constant surveillance.

Nickolas laughed. "Well, he must be a successful man, your father. A man with his nose to the grindstone may not enjoy many pleasures of the world, but they usually make money."

"Yes," Laura said scornfully. "Father's very good at that."

Nickolas stared at her quizzically, and she flushed. Why had she said that? She did not want him to think her a shrew.

Looking away from him, she became aware of just how long the shadows had grown. She had to be getting back, and yet she wanted to prolong this meeting. It had been so long since she had chatted like this with a man. She was certain that she had smiled more this afternoon than she had all the rest of the year. Just thinking of going from this to the depressing atmosphere of the family tent made her feel like weeping; and yet she must get back, or risk a worse scene than that which she had faced earlier.

Slowly she rose, and he looked up at her questioningly.

"I really must be going," she said. "I had no idea it was getting so late. My mother will be wondering what has happened to me."

He stood also, an expression of comic dismay on his face. "But you can't go now! Why, we're just getting acquainted. There are at least a hundred things I want to ask you."

"I'm sorry," she said, thinking those words did not nearly convey what she felt.

"But just a minute or so more, please. As I told you, I want to look over Pacific Grove and the rest of the peninsula. There is so much to see. I want to see Monterey, and the Chinese village my friend told me about, and I have also heard of the beautiful Seventeen-Mile Drive through the Grove and along the coast. I badly need a guide, Miss Purcell, and I can think of none I would rather have than you. Will you allow me to call upon you and make myself known to your parents?"

All of Laura's happiness faded, as if a plug had suddenly been pulled, draining her of good feelings. So here it was again. If this man came to call, her father would want to know where she had met him. Then her father's usual campaign of intimidation would begin.

All at once a tide of anger replaced her depression. No! By heaven, this time she would not let it happen. This handsome, seemingly kind man had come into her life like a gift. If he was single—she must determine his marital status—she meant to try to get him to marry her. It was a sudden, audacious thought, considering that they had just met, but she was desperate, she realized; and desperation called for bold measures.

She gazed down at her hands, which were tensely holding the edges of her shawl together. Her decision made, she looked up boldly into his eyes. "I don't think you had better call on me at our tent, sir. My father is . . . well, he's a very rigid man, with very strong religious views. For some reason, he disapproves of all things which smack of the theater, or what he considers frivolous activities."

Nickolas's expressive face registered his surprise. "But

surely he doesn't think of the Chautauqua as theater? He
must know that it offers educational programs—"

"I know it's unreasonable of him," she broke in, "but
that's the way he is."

Nickolas made a wry face. "I see. And if he disapproves
of the Chautauqua, then he certainly would disapprove of
a Chautauqua lecturer."

She nodded. "That's exactly right. He would also disapprove of the way we met. I mean, since we were not
properly introduced."

Nickolas looked melancholy. "Then you won't be my
guide? I won't see you again?"

She raised her chin. "I did not say that."

His expression brightened, and he stared at her expectantly.

"For once, I am going to defy my father. I am a grown
woman, and I can't let him tell me what to do all my life. I
just want you to realize that I may have to be home at
certain times, and that it might not be easy for me to get
away. Also, there is something else you should know."

He looked dismayed. "You're not going to tell me that
you're married?"

"No." She laughed. "And I should like to ask you the
same."

He shook his head, his laugh echoing hers. "No. No, I
am free and unencumbered. Uncaught as yet!"

Mentally, Laura gave a sigh of relief. "No, what I
wanted to say is that I haven't been here very long myself,
and since my father is so restrictive, I haven't yet seen
any of those things you mentioned, except for the Seventeen-Mile Drive. Do you still want me for a guide?"

His smile was dazzling. "We shall brave the unknown
together, then; and I could not, and would not, ask for a
more charming companion. Would it be possible to start
tomorrow?"

Laura thought quickly. Tomorrow morning her father
would be leaving for a trip inland, where he had to see a
potential customer; he would be gone at least two days.

"Tomorrow would be fine," she said, smiling. "Will ten
o'clock be all right?"

His answering smile was so full of frank delight that she felt completely disarmed.

"Capital! I'll order a carriage of some sort in Monterey, and a lunch. I'll meet you at the retreat gate."

Laura turned away, feeling very strange indeed. At last she had taken a step toward living her own life, and it filled her with a sort of fearful pleasure.

Chapter Two

NICKOLAS Orlando stood gazing after the young woman as she walked away from him toward the main body of the campground, admiring the fine swing of her stride and the movements of her tall, well-proportioned body, which even her drab gray bodice and skirt failed to hide.

Despite her rather unfashionable clothing she was quite a beauty, with her fine, pale skin and dark blue eyes. Her hair might not be elaborately dressed, but it was a rich, deep chestnut, and she had masses of it. In smart attire she would be devastating. He was fortunate to have met such a promising beauty on his very first day at the retreat. Perhaps his luck was turning!

Nick smiled ruefully to himself as he watched her disappear into the trees. He hadn't been quite honest with her when he had told her that he had arrived early for the Chautauqua simply to see the Monterey Peninsula, the fabled "Circle of Enchantment."

It was not entirely a lie—he was interested in the area, as he was always interested in anything new and intriguing. But there had been the matter of the young woman back in New York State, and her angry family; and it had seemed expedient to leave Buffalo a bit earlier than he had planned.

Smiling, Nick put on his hat and turned to look toward Monterey, three miles distant, thinking that it was lucky that he was strong and enjoyed walking; for it was apparent that he was going to have to do a good bit of it here.

When he had arrived, he had discovered that no horses or wagons—save for the broken-down cart that rattled from tent to tent and cottage to cottage to collect trash— were allowed within the precincts of the Grove, except when delivering retreaters and their luggage to their tents or cottages. There were wagons that plied a passenger trade between Monterey and the Grove gate—in fact, he had come to the Grove in one such, for two bits; but they had no regular schedule, and to catch it Nick would have had to walk the width of the retreat again.

He smiled to himself, thinking of the list of retreat rules he had been given at the gate, rules that banned the buying or selling or giving away of any intoxicants, gambling in any form, dancing of a social or public nature, and profanity. Assemblies and public parlors must be closed by ten at night, at which time all shades must be drawn. Interestingly enough, there was another rule that stipulated that until that time, all shades must be up!

Nick shook his head, snorting. Blue laws. The bane of man's enjoyment. Still, it was an extraordinarily beautiful spot, there was no gainsaying that. Nestled among the pines and cypresses, close to the Pacific Ocean, it really was the Eden that people claimed it to be. The coastline, with its rugged piles of rocks and pounding surf, was something to inspire the soul and the spirit.

But in Nick's opinion there was more to man than spirit, and the nearby town of Monterey was better equipped to cater to that side of the human animal. Right now he was in the mood for a good stiff whiskey or two, and, after meeting Miss Laura Purcell, for a rousing tumble in the hay with a willing woman. Of course, he had no illusions that the kind of woman he would find willing in Monterey would be as attractive as Miss Purcell; however, since Miss Purcell was obviously a "good woman," it would take some time and some fast and smooth talking before he could hope to take any liberties with her. The time was in short supply, but smooth talking was his stock in trade; and unless he was very much mistaken, Miss Purcell, cautiously guarded by a possessive father, was not only eager but ripe for seduction by a man of his charm. Nick was well aware of his attraction for women and that his smooth talking had worked to his advantage often in the past. Miss Purcell clearly was desperate to escape from her father's domination; and Nick, with his poetic good looks and intellectual leanings, was the sort of man to appeal to her.

He grinned wryly at his thoughts. Dr. Nickolas P. Orlando might not be the most honorable of men, but at least he saw himself with reasonable clarity. Born William Shugg, in Rochester, New York, in 1851, the youngest son of Richard Shugg, a drayman, and his wife, Mabel, a laundress, Nick had, early on, decided that he must be adopted, for it was impossible that two such plain, hard-working, but mentally limited people could have produced a son such as himself. He had absolutely nothing in common with his parents or his brothers and sisters; even their physical appearance was dissimilar—his brothers and sisters were composites of their parents, with varying shades of mouse-brown hair, sturdy bodies, and blunt features, while Nick was tall and gracefully built, with fine features and large, dark eyes. There was the slight cast in one eye, of course, but Nick had learned over the years that this imperfection only added to his attractiveness.

Once, when he was small, he had even asked his mother if he was her natural child. He would never forget her shock and dismay as she assured him that he was indeed flesh of her flesh.

Given this assurance, he began to search for other explanations, and even went so far as to surmise that his mother had dallied with some handsome aristocrat and that he was the child of this union—although it was difficult to understand how his plain, dumpy mother could ever have attracted the attention of such a man. Still, there were those stories about serving maids and gentlemen, and such a supposition offered a solution of sorts.

Finally, when he was sixteen, and still asking his mother embarrassing questions, she began to realize how his being different sorely puzzled him, and she showed him an old family portrait of his paternal grandmother, Eugenia Lavalle. There at last were the dark hair, the narrow, intelligent face, and the large, dark eyes; and Nick finally admitted to himself that he must be a throwback, not a by-blow. Well, it was not quite as romantic, but it still set him apart; and he consoled himself with the thought that he had inherited from this exotic grandmother a finer and more sensitive nature than had the other members of his family.

Feeling as he did, it was no wonder that he left the bosom of his family early. The aristocratic nature and tastes that he was so proud of seemed far less desirable to his parents, who valued hard work, honesty, and family loyalty above imagination, a poetic nature, and reluctance to engage in any form of manual labor.

At seventeen, feeling misunderstood, a silk purse in a family of sows' ears, Nick left home to join a group of traveling actors who had just lost their juvenile lead.

He had absolutely no experience in acting, but then, as now, lack of experience in a certain area did not deter him from convincing prospective employers that he had the necessary credentials for the job. His youthful good looks were a further incentive, especially to the leading lady of the troupe, who had a sharp and hungry eye for attractive young men.

He had proved quite successful as an actor, having a natural bent for the theater, and had gone on to larger troupes and more lucrative positions with other companies. But there was not much money in acting, and as soon as he found out how convincing he could be, Nick branched out into other areas. He had, he decided, a gift for appearing skilled at whatever he chose to do. In a very short time, he could convince anyone of anything—that he was a doctor, a stockbroker, or a college professor— and was able to carry it off with dash and flair for as long as he cared to.

Women, in particular, found him believable in whatever role he chose to play; and although Nick was not overly proud of this aspect of his life, he had taken in a great deal of money from older women, who were usually willing to pay handsomely in cash and gifts for his company and his favors.

However, he thought ruefully, women were also his downfall. He could not resist them, particularly when they threw themselves, so to speak, at his feet. The more mature women were not the problem. Often they had husbands and reputations to protect, and they were relatively realistic in their expectations, for, as Benjamin Franklin had so cleverly stated in his "Advice on the Choice of a Mistress": a young man should prefer an older mistress, because an older woman was more knowledgeable, there was less chance for begetting children, and, lastly, they were so grateful.

However, the young ones were often so adorable, and frequently just as willing, although they had an annoying tendency to expect marriage in return for sexual favors.

Of course, Nick was not actually opposed to marriage. It was a sterling institution and a steadying influence; also, it meant that a man had a steady sex partner as well as someone to look after his other creature comforts. It was just that most of the young women he had dallied with were not suitable material for marriage. In bed, it did not matter how stupid a woman was, but if one must live with her, it would be preferable to be able to converse with her on a sensible level; after all, one could not make love twenty-four hours a day. A suitable wife would be an intelligent woman with some money, good to look at, a good housekeeper and cook—in short, someone who would be an asset to her husband. Somehow, in all his years of bachelorhood, Nick had not come across a woman with all these qualities.

Of course, his way of life was an obstacle to marriage. So much traveling—but he did not really regret it. He had done rather well financially, although admittedly he spent the money as fast as it came in, and he had enjoyed himself. It was only occasionally that he wondered what and where he would be today if he had channeled his intelligence and energies into a respectable career of some sort. Yet, these introspective moments did not occur often, or for very long, for in his heart of hearts Nick knew that he could never have endured the boredom of a regular career.

At any rate, here he was on the Monterey Peninsula, one of the country's loveliest locations, he had just met a charming and evidently intelligent young woman, and he was now on his way to refreshment and relaxation in Monterey. What more, for the moment at least, could a man ask for?

It was evening by the time he reached the town of Monterey, and the setting sun had washed the darkening sky with great splashes of orange, rose, and gold.

The town itself was not large, only two or three streets paved with sea sand, but the white adobe houses with their red-tiled roofs made a very attractive picture. Below the pines and the graceful rise of ground that supported the town lay the magnificent bay, large enough to hold several naval fleets. To Nick, the place seemed a relic of bygone times, sleepy and pleasant and quite Spanish in flavor.

He had no trouble finding a place to dine. A passerby whom he stopped on the street referred him to the newly built Del Monte Hotel for food and lodgings if he wished something gracious, and to Simoneau's Restaurant for supper if he wished something less grand.

After looking over Simoneau's, which proved to be part barber shop and part bar as well as restaurant, Nick decided to try the hotel. After all, there he might find a lonely lady of quality who would appreciate his company. If he did, it would save him the price of a prostitute and her possible diseases. It was worth a chance, and he had ample money in his pocket.

The Del Monte proved to be a huge and elaborate hotel, near the railroad, a seemingly strange and out-of-place edifice for this sleepy village. But when Nick climbed the low rise of steps onto the deep, covered veranda and entered the lobby, he saw that the hotel was well patronized. Seated in the lobby, and passing through, on their way to no-doubt fascinating activities, were scores of well-dressed men and women. A string quartet was playing somewhere out of sight, and the whole effect was one of graciousness and privilege. It was, Nick thought, his kind of place; the type of establishment in which he felt comfortable and at ease. Now, to see if he could get a reservation for dinner, and a room for the night.

He had been assigned lodgings in the large dormitory at the retreat, where all of the Chautauqua members would be staying, but for this one night he decided to indulge himself. Also, after a night of drinking and, he hoped, romance, he certainly would not want to face a return trip to Pacific Grove and the walk in from the gate.

An inquiry at the desk determined that there was indeed a single room available, and the desk clerk promised him that a reservation would be made for him for dinner. Nick explained his lack of luggage by simply stating the truth—that he was residing at the Pacific Grove Retreat but had come to see Monterey and had decided to spend the night. Since he looked a gentleman, there was no problem.

After several drinks in a cool and comfortable bar, Nick felt refreshed and eager to see what might be available to him in the way of women. He began by idling through the hotel lobby, looking over the seated groups of guests, returning smiles when he received them, initiating them when he did not.

There were many lovely women scattered about, but most of them appeared to be accompanied by male escorts; and then he saw them, two women seated alone on the veranda, both attractive and both of that certain age— young enough that they still retained their looks, yet old enough to be sophisticated players at the game of seduction.

For a while Nick simply watched them, as he stood at the veranda railing, ostensibly looking out at the grounds, but in reality waiting to see if they were waiting for escorts, and also making sure they had a chance to get a good look at him. He noticed that there were only two glasses on the small table between their chairs. After about fifteen minutes, when no men joined them, he felt it safe to assume that they were alone.

As he approached, he gave them his most charming smile. "Good evening, ladies. You look so lovely and

restful sitting there, I wonder if I might be permitted
to join you?"

The taller and more voluptuous of the pair studied him
speculatively, while the other woman gave him a friendly
smile. Nick waited calmly for their response, already sure
of what it would be.

The shorter woman, who had dark hair and pink cheeks,
looked at her companion. "The gentleman looks quite
lonely, Eloise. Don't you think perhaps . . . ?" she said in
a rather high-pitched voice with an eastern accent.

The tall blonde let her gaze linger on Nick's face for a
bit longer; then she smiled, showing large white teeth
between full red lips that he was certain had obtained
some of their color from paint.

"I agree," she said in a deep voice that had in it something of the purr of a great cat. "It would be a pity to let a
gentleman remain alone on a lovely evening such as this.
Won't you please take a seat, Mister . . . ?"

Holding his hat across his chest, Nick bowed. "Dr.
Nickolas Orlando, ladies, at your service."

"Oh, a doctor!" The shorter woman clapped her hands.

"Of philosophy, dear lady," he said, as he pulled up a
chair and sat next to the blonde. "And with whom do I
have the pleasure of speaking?"

"I am Mrs. Barbara Hudson," said the short woman,
"and this is my friend and traveling companion, Mrs.
Eloise Warren."

Nick smiled at them both, and waved his hand to attract
the attention of a passing waiter. It looked as if it was
going to be a delightful evening, and his pulse quickened
in anticipation.

"Mmmmm! Yes, dear boy, yes! That's it, my love,
touch me there, and there. Oh, yes, my love, I'm ready,
I'm ready!"

Nick took his mouth from Eloise Warren's ample breast
and removed his hand from the warm nest between her
thighs. He was throbbing with passion, but still he took a
moment to look appreciatively at the sexual feast spread
out below him.

Eloise was turning out to be everything her appearance had promised—full figured, with large breasts and ample hips and thighs; her body was as white as cream, and just as delicious.

Watching her writhe beneath him, ready and eager for his penetration, Nick felt a certain sense of power. He had brought her to this point, and this gave him a power over her. At this moment, despite a no-doubt stuffy husband at home, despite children, even despite other lovers, she was his and his alone, to do with as he pleased.

"Please, please," Eloise moaned softly; and with great pleasure he plunged into her, feeling her moist heat encase him as her arms and legs went around him.

No need to be gentle here, he knew. Women like Eloise Warren liked their sex a touch on the violent side. When it was over, they wanted to feel as if they had been thoroughly used, as well as pleasured.

So, not holding back, Nick drove into her, letting his body grind against hers, enjoying the wet, slapping sound that ensued as their perspiring bodies met, enjoying her gasps and moans of rapture as he brought her to climax once; and then again and again, before his own pleasure reached the unbearable stage and he experienced his own climactic satisfaction.

Gasping, he relaxed on the soft, white cushion of her body, and she stroked his back and sighed deeply.

"My, my. And I thought it was going to be a dull evening, just me and Barbara. You're very good at this, you know?"

Nick laughed, his breath rasping. "It was you, Eloise. Your body inspired me. It was made for love."

She gave a deep chuckle. "That may very well be, but it has been a long time since any man has pleasured me three times in one lovemaking. Can you always go so long?"

He nodded drowsily. "One of my many talents."

"Do you want to spend the rest of the night? We're leaving Monterey tomorrow."

He roused himself slowly and moved off her body. "I would love to, dear Eloise, but I cannot. I must rise early in the morning and return to the Grove, but I will always remember and cherish this night."

Nick could see the full curve of her smile in the moonlight that came through the window. "Likewise, I'm sure," she said.

As he pulled on his clothing, his mind was nearly blank, awash with pleasurable images. He had had a fine dinner, paid for by Eloise, and a rousing tumble with a very attractive woman. A perfect evening's entertainment.

Dressed, he kissed Eloise a lingering farewell, carefully closed her door, and headed down the hall.

A few moments later he knocked softly on another door, which was opened by Barbara Hudson, looking very fetching in a sheer nightgown revealing a slender but well-formed figure.

"I thought you would never get here," she said, and drew him into the room.

Chapter Three

THE Purcell tent was constructed much the same as the other tents in the Grove: centered on the thirty-by-sixty-foot lot, a wooden floor and a few uprights and pieces to top the roof, covered with blue and white stripes—the stripes there to eliminate the shadows that could be seen from outside the tent when lit from within.

The inside was lined with clean white canvas, and just beyond the entrance were four wooden chairs and a small table, for the family and their guests. Behind this hung a full-length curtain of muslin, trimmed with a border of bright blue calico, which shielded the area reserved for bedchambers. This area was divided by a similar curtain. The larger area contained a double bed and a large chest and a wooden-frame clothe rack. The smaller area held Laura's camp cot, a clothes rack, and a small chest. In back of the tent was a board-and-bat kitchen containing a woodburning stove, a table, chairs, and a huge washtub that served for bathing as well as for laundry.

It was in the smaller "bedroom" that Laura now stood, looking over the dresses hanging on the flimsy rack. Plain and dowdy, all of them—the result of her father's strictures against frivolity. She thought longingly of a dress she had seen in a pattern book belonging to one of their neighbors, Mrs. Thompson, a woman her father called "that Godless wench," and who was actually a very nice woman, and quite religious, although not in the same way Samuel Purcell was.

24

But that dress in the pattern book! The overdress, made of fawn-colored cretonne, fastened in front. The matching skirt was swept back into a swag at the hips and knees, forming a low bustle. The dress was edged with braid and a small ruffle, with a double ruffle at the sleeve cuffs. It was to be worn over a blue silk bodice. The dress required twelve yards of cretonne and two yards of silk, which, of course, her father would never let her buy.

Laura sighed again and looked through her skimpy collection of clothes. The most fashionable thing she owned was a pale blue summer basque and matching skirt. It was also the coolest thing she possessed, although the basque's tight sleeves and high neck resisted all but the most insistent breeze.

It would have to do. The sun had already burned off the morning fog, and it promised to be a warm day. Strangely, here in the Grove summer days were not always hot. The warmer inland valleys drew in the fog, which sometimes lasted for days. However, since many of the campers came from those hot inland valleys, there were few complaints.

Laura arranged her chosen outfit on the narrow camp cot, then placed next to it her sailor hat—her father had made her remove the flowers and ribbons—and her cream-colored bag and parasol. She stood looking down at the ensemble for a moment, then rummaged in the drawer of the small chest in the corner of the sleeping room. In the drawer, under her bloomers, were the artificial flowers and the ribbons that had been removed from her hat. Getting out her sewing basket, she began to reattach the band. She saved one cream-colored ribbon and one flower to tie at the neck of her basque.

Her father had left early that morning, while it was still cool. After he had gone, Laura had told her mother that she would be out during the afternoon to visit friends and acquaintances in the Grove. Her mother, as Laura had expected, complained about being left alone but did not offer to accompany her. The older woman seldom left the tent except for church services.

Laura frowned. There was nothing wrong with her mother, Laura was convinced, at least nothing the doctors could find. Privately, Laura was certain that her mother's illness was her husband; and it was an illness to which Laura was no longer going to cater. This man, this Dr. Nickolas Orlando, was her chance to get out, to escape. He was handsome, he was single, and he seemed to be attracted to her. Now all she had to do was to make him fall in love with her and want to marry her, within a very short period of time. The thought brought a wry smile to her face.

Well, it was not a sure thing by any means, but at present it was her only chance.

At eleven o'clock sharp, Laura was at the wagon gate of the Grove, hoping that Nick Orlando had arrived before her. He had not. There were a number of people there, but Nick was not among them.

Laura prayed that she would meet no one she knew before Dr. Orlando arrived. Or *would* he arrive? Had he, perhaps, forgotten their appointment? Or had something more important come up?

Her high anticipation began to wane, and she swallowed hard to hold back the threat of angry, frustrated tears. Turning away, she walked a short distance along the fence.

A sound behind and above her caused her to turn and look up into the grinning face of a small boy, arms outspread as he catfooted his way along the board that went along the top of the fence.

"Henry! You get down from there right this minute, before you fall and break your neck! How many times do I have to tell you?"

The child's angry, red-faced young mother shot Laura an apologetic look before plucking her reluctant child from the fence. Normally, Laura would have smiled indulgently at this homely vignette of family life, but now it only made her feel more depressed. Would she ever have a family of her own, a husband, a child?

The woman hustled the child away, the two voices fading, one scolding, one crying.

Laura turned and walked back toward the gate, and at

that instant she saw him. He was driving a rather shabby but sturdy-looking buggy drawn by a trim bay mare.

Happiness swept over her. He had come, after all!

Jumping down from the buggy into the mist of dust his arrival had created, Nick said, "Laura! You're here. I'm sorry I'm late, but I had trouble getting any equipage. I was afraid that you might not be here—that you had forgotten or that your father would have forbidden you to come."

He was near her now, smiling in open delight, his hands held out, and Laura felt her face lift to his like a sunflower.

During the night she had wondered if he could possibly be as handsome and attractive as she remembered; for she had noticed that occasionally, upon meeting a man for the first time, he would seem attractive and appealing, only to seem entirely different at a second meeting.

But with Nick Orlando this was certainly not true. He seemed even handsomer and more charming today; his springy dark hair and long sideburns formed an attractive frame for his pale, sensitive features, and his dark eyes had an eager expression.

He did, she thought, look a bit tired. Probably some late business to do with the Chautauqua.

He took her hands and led her toward the buggy. "This rig was all I could get. Everything else was out. It's not fancy, but it seems serviceable enough."

"It's fine. And it looks as if you got a good horse."

He patted the mare's dusty flank. "Yes, she seems strong but gentle. I had the hotel pack us a basket for lunch. Their food is quite good."

He helped her up onto the high buggy seat, then climbed up beside her.

"The hotel?" she asked curiously. She had assumed that he was staying in the Grove, in the dormitory area set aside for the Chautauqua personnel.

He laughed. "Yes, I decided to treat myself last night and went in to Monterey. That new Del Monte Hotel is really very grand. Have you been in it?"

"Not yet," Laura said, impressed that he spoke so casually of staying there. "I've heard of it, of course. People here talk about it all the time, and some have even stayed there, but Father . . ."

Nick cocked an eyebrow and flicked the reins. "Yes, I don't suppose it is the kind of place your father would approve of. A pity, since it is something to see. It's huge, you know, and very well appointed. I had a good dinner, a nice stroll around the grounds, and then a good night's sleep."

The mare was moving off at a gentle trot, leaving the gate behind.

"Now," Nick said, "tell me about yourself."

Laura smiled and shook her head. "First, where are we going? Yesterday you named several places you wanted to see."

He flicked the reins again, and she noticed that his hands were long and narrow. An artist's hands, she thought, or a surgeon's.

"I thought we'd do the Chinese village today," he replied. "From what my friend says, it sounds fascinating. A real bit of old China. But now back to my question: What about you?"

Laura shook her head again. "You don't really want to hear about me. There's nothing to tell. I've never done anything, been anywhere. It would be very dull."

Nick laughed, and gave another flick of the reins, goading the mare to go faster. "Suppose you let me be the judge of that." He turned to her with a wide smile. "You are a beautiful, obviously highly intelligent woman, Miss Purcell, and I would like to know you better."

Laura shrugged, feeling both flattered and ill at ease. No man had ever wanted her to talk about herself before.

"Well, I was born in Sacramento in 1857. I'm an only child. I've already told you something of my father. He's very religious and very strict; and my mother is what I suppose you might call a professional invalid, although I don't believe she's really all that ill." She looked over at Nick.

"Go on, you're doing just fine," he said with an encouraging grin.

"I didn't have much fun as a child. My father didn't like

me to play with the neighborhood children, so I was quite lonely. I used to mope about and wish that I had brothers and sisters to play with. I think that if there had been other children, my father's attention would not have been focused so exclusively on me. Because I was alone so much, I became a great reader, a daydreamer, and I had my music. That helped. I was a good student, and obedient at home."

She laughed self-consciously. "I make myself sound the paragon, don't I? But actually I was good because it was easier than being bad and having my father punish me. I really wasn't very brave."

He gave her another reassuring smile. "It takes a kind of courage to put up with the kind of life you've just described. I haven't known you long, but I sense a strength in you. You're no coward, of that I'm positive."

She felt herself warm under his words of praise. "Well, I intend to be braver! I have decided that I'm going to leave my parents and go out on my own. I don't know just how, yet, but I'll find a way!"

Embarrassed and startled by her words, Laura flushed, and turned away so that Nick could not see her face. "I don't know why I told you all those things. It's not the sort of thing I usually do."

He reached out and patted her hand. "I take it as the highest compliment that you consider me friend enough to confide in me. And I agree with you: you certainly don't want to spend the rest of your life in a cage. You're too beautiful and rare a bird not to be set free."

Despite her embarrassment, Laura felt a deep glow of pleasure. He understood and was sympathetic. It was a beginning. And then she flushed again, thinking of the trap she was attempting to set for him. But he seemed her only chance, and she was certain that she was falling in love with him already. Somehow this thought eased her conscience, and she was able to turn back to him with a grateful smile.

The Chinese village, located about a mile from the Pacific Grove Retreat on a point of land adjacent to a small

bay, was a quaint facsimile of the small fishing villages
along the Yangtze River in China. Malodorous but fascinating, the village consisted of about two hundred wooden
houses perched on rickety stilts, among which wound
crooked paths and roads. Laura was captivated. She had
never seen anything remotely like it.

"I suppose we'd better get down and walk in from
here," Nick said, reining the mare in next to a battered
hitching post at the edge of the village. "We'll be able to
see better if we walk. I hope you're wearing sturdy shoes."

Laura smiled. "With my father, what else would I be
wearing?"

Nick gave her his arm, and, laughing together, they
started down the crooked dirt road into the village.

There were so many things to see! Laura's head swiv-
eled this way and that. The doors to most of the houses
and shops stood open to catch the breeze, and Laura
could look right into their interiors, where she saw the
exotic-looking Chinese women, in their bright clothing,
playing cards or busy with their household chores.

Some of the older women walked with a lurching, crip-
pled gait, and it puzzled her, until she remembered reading about the Chinese custom of binding women's feet.
She grimaced.

"What's wrong?" Nick asked.

"The bound feet on the women. I guess I should be
glad my father isn't Chinese. He would certainly have had
my feet bound."

"That custom is dying out, or has died out in most
places, I understand. I've never been able to understand a
society that deforms themselves in some way, and then
calls that deformation a sign of beauty."

Laura nodded, then smiled. "Well, I have recently read
some articles that came out against the corseting of women.
The writers claim that it deforms our rib cages."

Good heavens! She was doing it again. For some reason, this man invited confidences of the sort she never
gave. While with him, she seemed somehow impelled to
blurt out her most private thoughts. She hoped that she
had not shocked him, but then was reassured by his burst

of laughter, which caused a passing Chinese fisherman, who wore his hair in a long pigtail, to turn and stare at them with an unreadable expression.

Laura resolutely turned back to examining this fascinating alien culture. She had a sharp and curious eye and noted and remembered all she saw: the brightly colored clothing hanging from crude clotheslines; the fishermen's odd-looking boats, moored so close to the shore that they served as front porches; the joss house that was the focal point for the village, hung about with bright banners and Chinese lanterns; the gambling parlors where men, women, and children gambled with dominoes and cards—which Laura found shocking, but was prepared to excuse because it was a different culture.

But the people fascinated her most, with their yellow-brown skin, slanted eyes, and exotic clothing. The village seemed industrious and, despite its flimsy structures, reasonably prosperous. She enjoyed everything thoroughly.

By one-thirty they had seen the entire village and Nick began to complain of hunger.

"Where would be a good place for a picnic?" he asked. "I'm starving!"

She thought quickly. The places she liked best were Main Beach and Jesus Lover's Point, but people who knew her would likely be there. Then she thought of Moss Beach. "I know a really pretty beach."

"Not in the Grove, I hope. I'd like to keep you to myself," he said with a sidelong glance.

His words brought her a flood of pleasure. "No, it's not in the Grove. I'd rather we went someplace where I'm not likely to meet anyone who might report to my father," she said quickly.

He nodded. "How far is the place you have in mind?"

"Not far. It shouldn't take long."

"Very well," he said, smiling. "Point the way. I am yours to do with as you will."

Her cheeks flaming, Laura accepted his hand up into the buggy, thinking that if she *did* have her way, Dr. Nickolas Orlando would soon find himself with a new wife.

*   *   *

Moss Beach was an ideal spot for a picnic. The beach was wide and white, backed by sand dunes. At low tide a person could walk out on the hard-packed sand for almost a half-mile and look for shells.

"I think that's the bluest water I've ever seen," Nick said.

They were seated on an old blanket that had been in the buggy, and the remains of their meal were spread out around them.

Laura, feeling pleasantly full and content, nodded in agreement. "It has so many colors. Sapphire, emerald, opal. It looks like it's made of liquid jewels."

Nick leaned toward her and took her hand. "That is an extremely poetic image, Laura. Do you do any writing, by any chance?"

Acutely aware of the touch of his hand on hers, Laura shook her head, but did not pull away her hand. "I don't really have a talent for it. The only artistic talent I have is an ability to play the piano."

He squeezed her hand and lifted it to his lips. "I'm sure you play beautifully!"

She was hardly aware of his words, for she was too bemused by the warm pressure of his lips against the back of her hand. She must say something, she knew, or he would think her a complete fool.

Trying to act as if nothing unusual were happening, she said as calmly as she could, "Yes, I play fairly well. It's one of the few things I do well."

"I should think that you do everything well," he said, moving closer to her and putting his arm around her waist.

Thrilled and simultaneously uncomfortable, Laura looked about quickly to see if anyone was around to see them; but the only people in sight were three Chinese gentlemen gathering seaweed into large baskets.

Nick pulled her tighter against him, bringing his face down to hers. "Don't be afraid, Laura. I wouldn't do anything to hurt you. I already care about you, you must know that."

Her heart was hammering, and she was filled with a

pounding excitement. Gently he cupped her face with his hands, then his lips were upon hers, soft, warm, and insistent. She was suffused with the most wonderful feeling she had ever known.

Her instinct told her to make the kiss last. She wanted nothing more than to stay like this forever; yet, her common sense warned her that she must break away. If she wanted him to fall in love with her, to care for her enough to propose marriage, she must not let things proceed too rapidly or too far. She did not have much experience with matters of the heart, but she did remember her mother's blunt words, spoken to her on the occasion of her first gentleman caller: "A man's not going to buy the cow when he's getting free milk!"

She had been shocked and embarrassed at the time— not that her mother needed have worried about her virtue, considering that her father never let any young man come around often enough to get past the first, tentative kiss.

But now she recalled those words, and, coupled with information from the few novels she'd managed secretly to read and the occasional magazine articles on love and marriage, it made sense. She must make him want her, but she must not allow him to get too intimate with her until they were man and wife. Besides, her own reaction so frightened her that as his kiss became more demanding, she instinctively pulled away.

She became aware that his heart, as well, was pounding, and that his handsome face was flushed.

He almost groaned her name. "Laura, my beautiful darling! Do you have any idea how tantalizing you are? I'm quite overcome with desire for you."

His impassioned words left her breathless. What should she say now? What should she do? She was unsure of herself and terribly callow.

Trembling, she gazed down at her hands. "Perhaps we should go now," she said in a low voice.

Nick reached for her again, and before she could stop him his mouth was once more upon hers.

She felt like syrup, slowly melting in the pan, and it

took a great effort for her to pull away. "I'm sorry, Nickolas, I—I can't. . . ." Oh, Lord, she was stammering like a schoolgirl.

Nick, very near her, was still for a moment, then he heaved a weighty sigh. "Of course. I apologize, dear Laura. We've only known each other for a day, and here I'm . . . I really am sorry. I didn't mean to offend you."

She could not meet his eyes. "I'm not offended. It's just that—"

"It's all right, I understand."

She looked up at him gratefully. He really *did* understand. He was amazingly sensitive; she had never known a man like him.

"I . . . I do care for you, Nickolas."

"Please call me Nick, Laura." His smile was dazzling. "And I care for you. We have a special rapport, you and I. I knew it when we met, but I shouldn't have pushed matters. It's just that my time here is so short!"

Laura drew a deep breath. Yes, that was the problem— too little time. If only it would be enough for her purpose!

As they drove back to the Grove, Nick shifted uncomfortably in the buggy seat. Despite his excesses of the night before, the pressure on his testicles was unrelenting, and this both annoyed and amused him. It had been a long time since he had suffered a case of "passion's pain," and here he was, uncomfortable as a sixteen-year-old with a case of unrequited desire.

Actually, of course, his desire was not unrequited; for if he was any judge of feminine feelings—and he was confident that he was—Miss Laura Purcell wanted him just as badly as he wanted her.

Naturally, with her background and strict upbringing, she had to fight it, had to refuse to admit it to herself. Experience had taught him that women of her type rarely gave in easily, no matter how much they wanted to. Her response on the beach had been both unexpected and welcome; and he had to admit that she aroused him more than any woman he had met in a long time. There was a depth of passion in her, repressed and never tapped, that was exciting to contemplate.

Chapter Four

CHAUTAUQUA was to start the day after tomorrow, and Laura was beside herself. She had to attend! But how could she manage to get away?

The two days her father had been gone had been wonderful. Besides visiting China Point, she and Nick had taken the Seventeen-Mile Drive, and had gone to Monterey so that she could see the Del Monte Hotel, which had greatly impressed her. Someday, she vowed to herself, she would stay in such places regularly, and it would seem natural to her.

After her father returned, Laura managed to get away one afternoon, telling her parents that she was going shelling at Moss Beach with a friend. Luckily, her father, weary from his trip, did not question her too closely.

But now there were no suitable excuses. Try as she might, she could think of none. She could not say that she was visiting friends or going with them to the beach, for they would all be at the Chautauqua. Also, knowing her desire to attend the programs, her father would be keeping a close watch on her.

Lying on her cot at night, she tried to think of various schemes that she might use; but her thoughts were always interrupted by feverish memories of Nick, of his mouth, warm and insistent upon hers, and of his hands upon her breasts—for he had finally touched her there, when they had stopped to admire a view along a secluded portion of the Seventeen-Mile Drive; and this touch, coupled with his passionate kisses, had almost made her forget her resolution.

When these memories overwhelmed her, Laura would repeat over and over to herself her plan to get him to marry her. Such repetitions soothed her mind but did little to calm the hot yearnings of her body. If he did not propose, if he left her in this condition, she did not know what would become of her. She had heard whispers of certain houses where women sold their bodies for the pleasure of men, and in the past she had wondered how any woman could so degrade herself; but now she thought that such degradation might be preferable to the painful yearnings she was experiencing. Tossing sleeplessly on the narrow cot, she realized that a woman's body was meant to be loved, to be fulfilled, to bear children. She was twenty-four years old, a woman grown, and her body was demanding its rightful due.

However, she found her worries to be needless. The very next day her problem was solved. An emergency occurred at her father's store in Sacramento, a matter that his employees could not handle; and in a dark and angry mood, Samuel Purcell had to return to his business to put things in order.

Before he left, Laura had to bear the brunt of a lengthy harangue, spiced with threats and strictures, on how she should behave while he was away. She was to stay with her mother, close to the tent, while the pernicious Chautauqua was present in the Grove; and she was not to converse with any of the Chautauqua people or even to discuss the programs with friends who were godless enough to attend.

Laura, smiling inside at the thought of how upset he would be if he knew what she had been doing, willed herself to appear docile and obedient during this unpleasant scene, even though she well knew that such apparent humility would not satisfy him, for it never did.

Even when she did not talk back to him, even when she appeared to bow to his will with good grace, he was never satisfied. It often seemed to her that nothing she ever did, or could do, would pacify him. He seemed to *want* her to fight back so that he could rail against her.

Her face burned at the memory of so many humiliating punishments: of switchings when she was young; of having to raise her skirts to expose her bloomers to the willow rod, and her father's gaze.

But she was too old to spank now. Instead, her father's tirades had become more ferocious. Instead of the whip, he now used words to beat her. But, she reasoned, she could ignore words, blot them out; and this was what she did now, thinking of Nick and of the Chautauqua, dreaming of the words she so desperately longed to hear from Nick's lips, until her father finally turned away from her and retired to his bed.

The Chautauqua! Laura, wearing her dark gray dress brightened by a small corsage of field flowers and a white lace collar borrowed from her friend Molly Harding, was filled with excitement and anticipation. She walked with Molly toward Chautauqua Hall, the rambling building that had been constructed that year to replace the huge tent they usually erected at the junction of Forest and Seventeenth streets.

Moving along with the crowd, Laura could see the belfry of the building up ahead, and her excitement mounted to a high pitch. She turned to Molly with a smile. "Is it going to be as exciting as I think it is?"

Molly returned her smile and said, from her knowledge as a veteran Chautauqua goer, "Oh, you'll enjoy it, Laura, I'm sure. It's always different every year, but it's always interesting and educational. It's too bad that your folks can't attend."

"Yes, I'm sure they'll be sorry they missed it, but I'll tell them all about it," Laura lied, amazed at how accomplished at the art she was becoming.

The new building smelled richly of new lumber and was already half-filled when Laura and Molly got inside and found seats. Clutching her program, Laura settled into the folding wooden chair with a secret feeling of delight.

Nick was scheduled to lecture this morning, and she could hardly wait. She was certain that he would be excellent, and the added thrill of their secret relationship made her tense with anticipation.

Her mind was so full of thoughts of Nick that she scarcely listened to the first speaker. When Nick finally stood at the podium, she sat forward excitedly, causing Molly to stare at her and laugh.

"He *is* handsome, isn't he?" Molly said. "I wonder if he's married."

Laura, abruptly conscious of her unseemly behavior, leaned back in her chair and tried to appear nonchalant. "Yes, he is good-looking," she said calmly, "but I wasn't really looking at him. I thought I saw my mother down in front, and I thought perhaps she might be feeling better and decided to come. But I was wrong—it was just someone who looked a little like her."

The lies come easier and easier, she thought. *I'm turning into a shameless hussy, and all because of Nick Orlando*.

And then Nick raised his hand, the audience quieted, and he introduced himself and began to speak. "Our subject today, ladies and gentlemen, is Abraham Lincoln. . . ."

Laura sighed. She had been right. He was very good. During the first lecture, the audience had rustled, coughed, and shifted about in their chairs. During most of Nick's lecture there was dead quiet, as the audience listened with full attention.

He has a real talent, Laura thought proudly as she listened to the mellifluous flow of his voice. He knew how to use his voice, his hands, and his eyes in a most dramatic way.

Suddenly she realized that he had paused, and then she saw that he was looking directly at her. Could he make her out in the crowd? He smiled slightly, and as he began to speak again, Laura had the strange feeling that he was talking for her ears alone.

"My friends, I have talked to you about Abraham Lincoln as a youth, as a surveyor, as a lawyer, as a politician, and so forth. Just now, another anecdote about this great man came to me, one in which he was not in any of those roles, but one that reveals his great wit, his rare ability to make sport of himself.

"At one time, the American Hotel in Springfield, Illinois, was a gathering place for Lincoln and some of his friends and acquaintances, men such as Stephen Douglas, John Calhoun, General Shields, and other men of public renown. They would gather to imbibe and to yarn away the evening.

"On one particular evening an unusual event occurred. One of the chambermaids rushed into the barroom in great agitation and told the landlord that while she and another chambermaid were undressing in their room, they discovered a man under the bed. The landlord asked for volunteers to capture the villain, and all the men present volunteered. They found the man still in the chambermaids' room, and captured him, taking him down to the barroom. The question was, what to do with him?

"It was decided to try him immediately, setting up an impromptu court, as it were, something that happened all too frequently in that time and place. But since the man's transgression wasn't all that serious, most of them looked upon it as an occasion of sport, although it may be assumed that the poor culprit did not view it as such. Judge Thomas Brown was present and was selected to preside. Josiah Lamborn, the Illinois state attorney, was chosen as prosecutor, and Abraham Lincoln and Stephen Douglas were given the chore of defending the prisoner, while the others served as jurors in the mock trial. It might be noted in passing that the prisoner was a singularly ugly man.

"Lamborn chose to imitate the high-flown style of oratory much in vogue at the time, and began his prosecution thus: 'May it please Your Honor, and you, gentlemen of the jury: the legislature of Illinois, though it has legislated upon every subject it could think of, has omitted to pass any act against a man being born as ugly as he pleases. If such an idea ever occurred to my friend Lincoln here, when in the legislature, I know he would at once dismiss it, not only as too personal but as repugnant

to his honest heart. As for myself, I like ugly men. An
ugly man stands on his own merits. Nature has done
nothing for him, and he feels that he must labor to make
up the deficit by amiability and good conduct generally.
There is not an ugly man in this room but has felt this. . . .

" 'No, gentlemen, ugliness is nothing. It is manners
that are everything. The ugliest man who ever lived never
intentionally frightened a woman—nay, never was so unfortunate as to do so. But *this* creature, this mendacious
wretch, would doubtless enter for a prize of beauty at a
vanity fair! And how has he failed his duty to society?
Why, gentlemen, by crawling under the bed upon which
two fair damsels were about to expose their loveliness. . . .' "

Nick coughed behind his hand, then continued, "Mr.
Lamborn spoke at length in this vein. When he finally
finished, Mr. Lincoln rose and said with a perfectly grave
countenance: 'Gentlemen of the jury, the remarks of my
friend Lamborn about ugly men come home to my bosom
like the sweet odors of a rose to its neighboring great
sister, the cabbage. It was a grateful, a just tribute to that
neglected class of the community—ugly men. I thank him
for his kind remarks.

" 'I wish to say something for my client, although it
must in candor be admitted that he had "gone to pot." I
don't see why we should throw the kettle after him; he
may be the victim of circumstances; he looks very bashful
now, and it may be that the girls scared him; who knows?
At least I claim for him the benefit of a doubt.

" 'Why, gentlemen, many us have, or might have, suffered from a concatenation of circumstances as strong as
that under which my client labors. Let me relate to you a
little personal anecdote in illustration. When I was making a secret canvass of this country, with my friend Cartwright, the Pioneer Preacher, we chanced to stop at the
house of one of our old Kentucky farmers, whose log-
cabin parlor, kitchen, and hall were blended in one, and
only separated at night by sundry blankets hung up between the beds. As we were candidates for the august
National Congress, our host treated us with the privacy of
a blanket room. During the night I was awakened by

someone throwing their leg over me with some force. I thought it was neighbor Cartwright, and took hold of it to give it a toss back; but it didn't feel like one of his white-oak legs, and while I was feeling it to ascertain the correctness of my half-awake doubts, a stifled scream thoroughly awakened me, and the leg was withdrawn. Why, gentlemen, would you believe me? It was the leg of our host's daughter! Imagine my position if you can! What an apparent breach of hospitality! While I was imagining an excuse for my conduct, the old folks struck a light, and the blanket between our bed and that of the buxom damsel was discovered to have been pulled down! More damning proof, thought I. I feigned sleep, but kept one corner of my left eye open for observation. The blanket was soon fixed up, and I was greatly relieved to hear the damsel explain to her mother that she herself had invaded our bed while dreaming, caused by some undigestible vegetables she had eaten at supper. Our host was serene and affable in the morning, and I had no need to apologize; but, gentlemen, imagine what an escape I had, and have mercy on my client.' "

Nick paused again, looking out over the audience. He was quite a distance away, but Laura was sure that she detected a mischievous glint in his eyes. There had been gasps during his story, at the slightly risqué parts. Laura was a little shocked herself, and she wondered if Nick had told the story for her benefit. And then she thought of her father. If he had been there and heard Nick's tale, his judgment would have been confirmed—this was indeed the "devil's show"!

"Oh, yes, I almost forgot," Nick said. "The jury returned a verdict of 'scaring the girls,' and the judge sentenced the culprit to be whipped in the yard behind the hotel, by the girls he had frightened so."

Another gasp passed through the audience, and then here and there bursts of laughter were heard, and applause began, scattered at first, then becoming general and heavy.

When it was time for the noon recess, Laura had again to resort to lying. Nick had told her that after his morning lecture he would be free for the rest of the day, and that she should meet him at the wagon gate during the noon break.

She had already conceived a plan; and as she and Molly left the building at noon, she told the other girl that she had to return to the family tent to check on her mother and to prepare their lunch.

Molly, who planned to have lunch at one of the tent restaurants, accepted Laura's story readily enough. They said goodbye, and Laura hurried off through the thinning crowd to her rendezvous with Nick.

For the next few days, Laura felt as if she were in heaven. Every day she attended at least some of the Chautauqua events—she particularly enjoyed the musical programs and Nick's lectures—and the rest of the time she and Nick spent together.

The only problem on her immediate horizon was the fact that it was growing increasingly difficult for her to stop Nick when he attempted to go too far in their love-making, and her anxiety that he would not ask her to marry him. She did not even attempt to think about what would happen when her father returned from Sacramento. Her mother seemed to have become resigned to her absences; and although she complained bitterly when Laura was home, Laura was certain that she would not tell Samuel, for fear of the scene that would surely follow.

And then, after four blissful days, disaster struck. Her father, who was supposed to be in Sacramento until the following Monday, returned unexpectedly on Friday and found his wife home alone.

When Laura returned home, quite late in the evening, she walked into the tent to find her father sitting in the main room on a straight-backed chair, his face hard, his eyes cold and unyielding.

The heady joy that had been with her all afternoon drained away with dizzying speed when she opened the door and saw him there, to be replaced first with fear and then with an anger to match his own.

Why had he come back early? Couldn't she have even a

few days of happiness? And what did his premature return mean to her plans?

She stopped before him, but held her head erect and gazed defiantly at him.

Samuel Purcell stood slowly until he towered over her, his height and breadth shadowing her, letting her feel his power and his anger.

"Well, daughter?" His voice was low, but tense with his barely controlled feelings. "Mary tells me you've been out. In fact, she has admitted to me that you have been home hardly at all for the past few days. What do you have to say for yourself?"

Her heart thrumming wildly, Laura took a deep breath and attempted to keep her voice steady. "I have been attending the Chautauqua, Father. I am a woman grown, not a child, and I think I have a right to go where I please and do as I wish, so long as I do not do anything wrong."

Samuel Purcell's face became a dark and ugly red. "How dare you talk to me like that? You are my daughter, and as long as you live beneath my roof and eat the food I provide, you will do as I say!"

Laura raised her trembling chin and kept her gaze locked on his. "No, Father, I won't. Not any longer. Can't you see that it's impossible for me to live this way? I'm no better than a prisoner. I must have some freedom, or I'll die!"

Her father clenched his fists, as if to keep himself from striking her. Despite her resolve, Laura felt herself quailing inside. She had seen him almost insane with rage before, but never like this; yet, she could not and would not back down.

"You dare say this to me?" he said in a choked voice. "To the father who has raised you and cared for you? You dare to talk to me like this, like a common strumpet? Oh, the devil has gotten into you, girl! I knew it! I sensed it over there in Sacramento, and I knew that I had to come back at once. You've been seduced by that sacrilegious devil's show, and you've been seeing some man, I'm sure." His eyes flashed with satisfaction as Laura flinched. "You see, I knew it! I was right."

He wheeled on his wife, who sat huddled in the rocker that she had pulled into the sleeping quarters behind the curtain. "Mary, fetch me my whip. I'm going to have to beat the devil out of this girl. Do you hear me, woman! Fetch me my whip!"

Laura could hear her mother moving slowly from the chair, and her fear and anger almost overwhelmed her. "I won't let you whip me, Father. It was bad enough when I was younger, but I am a woman now, and it's not seemly. . . ."

His contemptuous snort struck her like a slap in the face. "Not seemly? Not seemly for a father to discipline his own child, no matter what the age? You shall feel the whip, my girl, and you shall feel it harder than you ever have before, for your sins are greater this time. Take off your dress!"

Folding her arms over her breasts, she glared at him defiantly.

"No, Father."

"I said take off your dress!" he thundered. "You will receive your due punishment in your drawers so that you get the full benefit of the lash."

She began to back slowly toward the door. "I will not. I will not subject myself to this indignity again."

"And I say that you will!"

With a single stride he was upon her, and in the next instant Laura felt his rough hand at the throat of her bodice as he grasped the material and gave a mighty yank downward. She almost fell to her knees as the fabric gave way, and he stepped back, holding one complete side of the garment in his hand.

Stunned, Laura looked down at herself, then looked up to see his gaze fixed on the flesh of her shoulders and breasts, his eyes wild and staring with an expression that filled her with horror. Now, at long last, she could recognize that expression.

Behind him, she saw her mother standing in the parting of the curtains, her face pale, her eyes vacant as windows into nothingness. Her mother knew, too! That was what she had been hiding from all this time with her feigned illnesses and vapors.

Whirling, Laura snatched up her mother's shawl from where it was draped over the rocking chair and wrapped it around her. "You're the one who is evil, Father. Instead of punishing me, you should look into your own heart. Ask yourself why a man would want his grown daughter to take off her clothes for him, why he would enjoy beating her. Ask yourself that, Father. It's not natural, can't you see that?"

Backing toward the door, she watched his face and saw his gaze falter. Taking advantage of his indecision, she turned and fled through the open door into the night, not knowing where she was going or what she would do; she was simply seeking escape from an impossible situation.

She ran blindly for several minutes, then found herself at the point, looking out at the white foam and dark waves illuminated by a gibbous moon that struggled in and out of passing clouds.

The wind was cold on her fevered face, and she realized that she was breathing with great shuddering breaths that hurt her chest. She had not backed down this time, and her father had not been able to punish her. She had won a victory, of sorts, but now what was she going to do?

She could not possibly stay with her parents any longer. She would have to leave. She must find Nick!

Nick Orlando lay on his narrow camp bed, his head propped up by a fat, goosedown pillow, and a thin, dark cigar in his hand, a pencil-thin stream of smoke curling up from it.

Idly he watched the smoke drift toward the roof of the large tent that served as a dormitory for the Chautauqua's male performers. His thoughts were of Laura Purcell.

She was a most unusual young woman, and she was driving him to distraction. He had seen her a half-dozen times now, and he was no nearer his goal than he had been on that first day. Or perhaps he was nearer the goal, but he could not make it past her final defenses, despite the fact that he was sure she wanted him as badly as he wanted her. He could not understand such determination. If you wanted something that badly, why refuse it? Was she afraid that he would get her with child? He had assured her that he knew how to prevent such a thing from happening. From what Laura had told him, it was simply a matter of ideals, or morals: nice women did not let men make love to them before the marriage vows were spoken. Was such an ideal worth the deprivation that she was putting them both through? Nick thought not.

Each time he touched her, he burned with lust and a desire stronger than anything he had ever known. Each time he touched her, she blazed like a torch—he could actually feel the heat coming off her body—and yet she would not allow him any more than passionate kisses and a bit of fondling! Why, he thought dourly, didn't he just give up on her?

Yes, that was the question, and he had no ready answer. During the past few days, he had even considered the unthinkable—marriage! A man could do much worse, for she fit most of his criteria, save for the fact that she had no money. Of course, her father did, but from what Laura had told him of the man there seemed little likelihood of his sharing it with a son-in-law. Still, if it was a fait accompli, if the deed was done, might he not come around in time? Wouldn't he want to see his daughter comfortable? On the other hand, from what she had told him about the old bastard, perhaps not.

He was aroused from his reverie as someone dropped down heavily on the end of his cot. He looked up and saw Lester Owens, one of the Chautauqua musicians.

"Well, Lester old man, how are things going?"

Lester, a short, pudgy man with a fringe of ginger-colored hair, sighed heavily. "Could be better, Nick. Genevieve is down with some kind of chest ailment and the doctor says she won't be able to play, maybe not for days. Do you have another one of those cigars?"

Nick fished one out of his pocket and gave it to the other man. Genevieve, he knew, was the pianist for the musical aggregation that performed in the afternoons and during the evening slide presentations. "I'm sorry. That is bad luck."

Lester lit the cigar and drew on it deeply. "I'll say, since we don't have anyone to fill in for her, because of Bob Hooper's wife having her baby last week."

"There must be *someone* you can get."

Lester exhaled cigar smoke. "Probably. But first we have to find that someone, and then make sure they're up to doing our numbers. Oh, by the way . . ." He paused, with a sidelong look at Nick. "There was someone outside asking for you a bit ago. A young woman. She says she has a message for you, and she won't give it to anyone else."

Nick sat up, his mind beginning to race. "A young woman? Why didn't you say so at once?"

"Oh, I didn't think it was terribly important," Lester said with a sly look. "Anyway, she's waiting just outside for you."

It must be Laura. But why would she come here, to the men's tent, after curfew? Something must have happened.

Grabbing his jacket, Nick hurried to the entrance and stepped out into the darkness. He could see no one. "Who is it?" he called softly. "Are you there?"

"Here!"

He could barely hear the soft voice, and then a pale figure stepped around the side of the tent.

He hurried forward. "Laura, is that you?"

"Yes, it's me," she said in a faint voice.

He was close now, and enough light came through the tent wall to show him that she was disheveled and was clutching a shawl closely around her upper body.

"Come," he said, taking her arm gently. "Let's go around the corner here."

Back in the shadows under the trees, the scent of pine sharp in his nostrils, he pulled her into his arms and felt her tremble. She was breathing raggedly, as if she had been sobbing, and he was overcome with a sudden tenderness. By God, he did care for her! He could not deny it.

"Laura, what's troubling you? What's happened?"

Silently she spread her arms, holding the shawl out

from her body, and he caught a glimpse of a white under-
vest, pale flesh, and the remains of her bodice.

"He did this. He was going to beat me!"

A righteous anger blazed through him and his fists
clenched. "Who? *Who* did this to you?"

She wrapped the shawl tightly around herself again.
"My father. He came home early from Sacramento. It was
. . . it was . . ."

Her words ended in a sob, and Nick was consumed
with rage at the man who had done this to his own
daughter. He pulled Laura close against his chest and
spoke into her hair. "He should be horsewhipped. I'd like
to do it myself."

Laura leaned back a bit to look into his face. "That
wouldn't help. It wouldn't change what has happened. I
can't stay in Pacific Grove, Nick. I have to leave, but I
don't know what to do. I have only a little money. I'm
ashamed to ask you, but I have no one else to turn to.
Could you take me with you when the Chautauqua leaves?
I'll find some kind of work—I'll wait tables if necessary—
but I must get away from him. Will you take me?"

The moon, coming out from behind some clouds, cast
its pale light into her upturned eyes, and Nick felt his
heart begin to pound. He had never wanted her so much.
His mind was working with lightning rapidity. "You told
me that you play the piano and that you play well, is that
right?"

She looked at him in confusion. "That's right, but I
don't . . ."

He grinned broadly and kissed her full on the mouth.
"Then I believe that I may have a solution to your problem, and it will be much better than waiting tables."

"A solution?" she said eagerly. "What do you mean?"

He kissed her again before answering. "I learned just a
while ago that the Chautauqua orchestra is in dire need of
a pianist. What do you think of that?"

She smiled in hope. "And you think they might employ me?"

"I don't see why not. I'll go in and tell Lester right
away, so he won't go looking for someone else, and then

I'll take you to the women's dormitory and have them find a bed for you there. In the morning you can play for Professor Lawton, the conductor, and after you're hired you can go to your tent and get your clothes and things."

Her eyes widened, and he patted her back in reassurance. "You can wait until your father is out. He must go out sometime during the day, doesn't he?"

She nodded slowly.

"Then it's all settled. You'll come with us as part of the Chautauqua, and we can be together whenever we wish. You see, it'll all work out just fine."

She managed a wan smile. "The conductor has to hire me first."

He laughed. "If you can play at all decently, I'm certain he will. How could he resist both your beauty and your talent? I know I can't."

He swept her into his arms, immensely pleased that he had been able to help her. Overcome with tenderness, he held her gently, stroking her hair. In that moment, he felt that he would have done anything for her, anything at all.

Suddenly he heard the rattle of hurried footsteps coming through the leaves, and a rough hand seized his shoulder and spun him around, causing him to release Laura, who shrank back into the trees with a soft moan. Nick looked up into the glaring eyes of a heavy-shouldered, bearded man almost as tall as himself. Nick knew at once that he was looking at Laura's father.

"Whelp of the devil!" a deep voice said harshly. "Seducer of helpless young women!"

Nick jerked out of the man's grasp and tugged his vest straight, glaring back at him. He recognized Purcell as a formidable opponent and had no wish to face him down, particularly at this moment; but it seemed he had little choice. The man appeared prepared to force the issue. From what Laura had said, the man was a bully, and Nick knew from experience that if he did not stand up to him right now, the battle would be lost.

He said, "If you are referring to me, sir, I will thank you to keep your libelous remarks to yourself."

Samuel Purcell narrowed his eyes but did not move to

touch Nick again. Still, Nick could feel the heat of the older man's anger.

"Do you know who I am, young man?"

"I presume you are Laura's father. She has told me of you." Nick let his face show his contempt, and Purcell's face tightened.

"And yet you can stand there and look me in the eye, when I have just seen you holding my daughter in your arms out of sight here in the dark? Have you no shame?"

Nick drew himself up as straight as he could. Truthfully, this big, burly man frightened him a little; but his fear of appearing a coward in Laura's eyes was greater than his fear of her father. Also, the man's colossal arrogance angered him.

"I feel shame when I deserve to feel it, but in this instance, no, I feel none, for I have done nothing to be ashamed of."

"You consider it nothing to seduce an innocent girl from her loving family? What kind of a man are you?"

Nick looked at the older man without flinching. "A better man than one who rips his daughter's clothing off, one who threatens to beat her for nothing more than attending an innocent and educational event."

Purcell took a step toward him, and Nick's every instinct urged him to step back; but he stood fast, setting himself for an attack.

"I have a right to treat her any way I like. I am her father, sir! I am responsible for her."

Afterward, Nick was never certain why he said what he did. He was so caught up in the drama of the situation, of the role he was playing, that the words just seemed to spill out of their own accord. "Not any longer, sir. From now on that privilege will belong to me!"

Samuel Purcell gave a grunt of surprise and stepped back as if he had been struck. His gaze darted to Laura, who was huddled against the trunk of a large pine. "What madness is this?"

Nick took a deep breath. "No madness, sir, I assure you. Your daughter and I are going to be married just as soon as I can arrange it. Perhaps tomorrow. And when I am her husband, I will make it my duty to see that you and your brutal ways will no longer plague her!"

Laura gave a muted, glad cry, and then for a moment there was complete silence, except for the sound of the condensed fog dripping from the pines. Samuel Purcell was the first to break the silence. "Is this true, daughter?"

Laura's voice was shaky, yet she spoke the words loud and clear; and Nick could hear the delight and relief in her voice. "Yes! Yes, it's true!"

"Then you are no daughter of mine," Samuel Purcell trumpeted. "I renounce you. From now on you are dead to me and your mother!"

The quaver in Laura's voice was gone as she said, "If you think to hurt me by saying that, you are wrong, Father. Being your daughter has brought me nothing but unhappiness and abuse. I *long* to be free of you!"

Nick, surprised by her vehemence, was proud of her for having the nerve to speak out. She had spirit!

And then the import of what he had said echoed in his mind. He had just declared his intention of marrying, and in front of witnesses!

Chapter Five

"LAURA, my darling, my own true love. You smell lovely. Like violets."

Laura stretched like a cat under her husband's touch, enjoying the feeling of his hands stroking her bare back and buttocks, and the warmth of his body pressed tightly against hers.

They were lying nude, face to face, on a large four-poster bed in their hotel room; the window was open, letting in a soft breeze that also caressed her back.

Laura raised her mouth to his and received his kiss, hot and ardent. As his tongue darted between her lips, she felt a jolt of pleasure that started in her mouth and ran the length of her body, causing her pelvis to arch against his.

Nick pulled his mouth away from hers and buried his face in her hair, laughing. "Oh, I was right about you, my love. Dead on. I knew that beneath all that proper exterior there lurked a volcano of passion just waiting to be unleashed."

Not really displeased by his comment, she made a token protest. "Nick, really! You do say the most awful things. You embarrass me."

"Do I?" He laughed again, and rubbed his lower body against hers, causing her to react in kind.

"There's nothing awful about it, my pet. Love is one of the best things that was ever created, and there is nothing more exciting or wonderful than the feeling of a man and a

woman together, their bodies pressed together in pleasure. Tell me, if you can, that you don't agree."

She nuzzled his throat, feeling cherished and very happy.
"Well, I can't say that I disagree. It *is* rather nice."

"Rather nice? *Rather?*"

Rolling her onto her back, he lowered his head and
began teasing her nipples with his tongue until she writhed
with excitement; and then with his lips he traced a flaming path down her stomach to the secret heart of her sex,
where his mouth inflicted on her an exquisite torment
that soon had her tossing and moaning with rapture.

"Enough! Please! Come into me, darling. Now!"

"It's more than rather nice, isn't it? *Isn't* it?"

"Yes! Oh, yes! It's marvelous. It's wonderful, Nick, and
you're wonderful!"

With a triumphant sound of pleasure he entered her,
and she wrapped her legs around him, pulling him close
and into her, and they moved in unison then.

It *was* a glorious feeling, making love. It made her
whole body come alive in a way that she had never
known, and she was grateful to Nick for making that
possible for her.

He had gotten her so aroused that it took only a few
moments for her to attain that peak of pleasure that she
had come to desire and expect; and then they lay sweetly
together, cuddled like a pair of children.

As she lay there, relaxed and contented, Laura's thoughts
drifted back. Could it have been only one month ago that
she was so miserable and unhappy? It seemed much,
much longer. The life she had known with her parents
seemed as if it had occurred in another world, another
time. She thought of the life she was living now as her
"new life," and it had begun on that night, just one month
ago, outside the men's dormitory in Pacific Grove. In a
way, it was almost like having been born again.

Laura smiled to herself as she recalled the moment
when Nick told her father that they were going to be
married. The declaration had shaken her father, and it
had surprised her, but she had been quick enough to

voice her agreement, afraid that Nick might change his mind.

But he had not, and they had been married, the very next day, in fact. Later that same day she had played for Professor Lawton, and he had liked her playing and had offered her a job with the orchestra; and she and Nick had moved into their own tent for the last few days of the Chautauqua in Pacific Grove. Samuel Purcell had not bothered them again.

And now they were on tour with the Chautauqua, going from place to place, bringing education, culture, and a measure of entertainment to small towns where such things were in short supply, and she was loving it. For the first time in her life she was living as an adult, a mature woman, and doing work that she enjoyed.

But the thing she enjoyed most, her own dark secret, was the pleasure she had discovered in the physical side of marriage.

Of course, the only marriage she had ever witnessed firsthand was that of her parents, and that had certainly given her no hint that pleasure was any part of the bargain. As far as she had been able to ascertain, there had been little if any affection. Her mother, when she discussed the physical side of matrimony at all, had given Laura to understand that such things were a painful duty that a wife must perform strictly for her husband's benefit. How sad that she had never learned different.

However, it had not been pleasurable for Laura at first. On their wedding night, she had been overexcited and afraid, as well as totally ignorant; and although Nick had been gentle and patient, she had suffered some pain, and the act had provided no real enjoyment for her.

But they had made love again in the morning, and that time it was much nicer; and each night and day after that it had grown nicer still, until now she felt completely at ease and entirely enthralled with the exquisite sensations that Nick aroused in her. Now she felt that she was complete, a real woman, and her feelings showed in her appearance, she thought; for she could see that she had grown quite sleek and glossy, as if all the love and petting she was receiving had given her skin a glow and added a sparkle to her eyes.

Only one small cloud loomed on her horizon—the fact that the Chautauqua season would soon come to an end. She had attempted to get Nick to discuss the matter with her, but he seemed reluctant to think about their future, simply saying that something would turn up. Laura found his vague attitude worrisome. She was a planner by nature and training; and although she would have liked simply to forget about their future and leave it in Nick's hands, she was unable to do so.

She had already learned that if Nick did not want to discuss something, there was no use in trying to get him to do so, as he became testy if she insisted; and the last thing she wanted to do was make him angry. She would just have to trust his judgment. After all, he was a man, and he had been taking care of himself for some time. Surely he knew what he was doing.

Now, yawning, Nick rolled away from her to sit up on the edge of the bed.

"That was wonderful, pet." He gave her a pat on the shoulder, then went over to the washstand and proceeded to wash away the evidence of their lovemaking.

Laura watched him adoringly, looking with pride and love at his lean, muscular body, admiring the way he carried himself.

It was only when he started putting on his clothes that she asked, "Nick, why are you getting dressed?"

He turned and smiled at her. "I have some friends in this town. I promised them that when I next came through I would drop in to see them. Since we're free this evening, I thought I'd keep my promise."

This was the first time she had heard of this! She sat up, frowning in dismay. "Then I'd better hurry and get dressed! Why didn't you tell me earlier? What kind of people are they? What shall I wear?"

"Whoa there, my girl. You don't understand." He held up a hand, laughing. "I'm afraid these friends are gentlemen, and what we have in mind is a friendly game of cards. No ladies allowed, you see."

Experiencing an inexplicable hurt somewhere within her breast, Laura sank back down on the pillows. "Oh! A card game?"

Nick finished tying his cravat, gave himself an admiring glance in the mirror, and turned to her. "Now, don't sound so shocked, my dear. I know the Chautauqua members frown upon such worldly pursuits, but I haven't always been a member of the Chautauqua, and I'm afraid that now and then my minor vices get the better of me. I'll tell you what I'll do. If I win this evening, I'll get you that dress you so admired in the shop on Main Street. Now what do you say to that?"

His expression and voice were cajoling, and Laura tried to hide her hurt. But how could he possibly leave her so soon after they had just made love? A moment ago they had been as close to being one person as it was possible to be, and now he was deserting her for the evening, to enjoy himself with his male friends.

As he bent over her, she swallowed her disappointment and gave him a dutiful kiss.

"Don't wait up for me, I may be late. I'll be having supper with my friends, also."

Supper! She would have to go to supper by herself, and everyone would know that Nick had left her alone for the evening. She stared at the closed door after he had gone, feeling bereft and lonely, thinking of the long, dreary evening ahead of her.

Then she thought of Constance Dowes, another female member of the orchestra, with whom she had struck up an acquaintance. Constance was a rather plain young woman who seemed older than her years. She had a sharp tongue and what Laura considered a cynical attitude toward life, yet she was extremely bright and was good company.

Constance had often told Laura that if she was free some evening, the two of them should get together so that Constance could show Laura photographs of the trip to Europe she had taken last year with her aunt.

Until now, Laura had been too wrapped up in the happiness of her new marriage even to consider the other woman's offer.

Perhaps they could even dine together.

Feeling cheered by the thought, Laura proceeded to wash and dress in a simple, cool outfit of blue-green linen, which she had purchased with her first month's pay. The summer weather was still quite warm, so she needed no wrap. With a sorrowful look at the rumpled bed—she did not have the heart to straighten it—she left the room and walked up one flight to Constance's floor.

Feeling rather nervous, she rapped lightly on the door. There was no immediate answer. She was about to turn away, then decided to knock again, and this time she did so more firmly. Within a few seconds she heard footsteps inside, and she was a bit surprised at how relieved she felt.

The door opened, and Constance's tousled head poked out. "Oh, it's you, Laura! I couldn't think who it might be. Come in. Excuse my dishabille. I was just getting dressed to go out to supper, but I'm not in that much of a rush."

Gratefully, Laura entered the small room, which was rather untidy—strewn with clothes, books, and sheet music. Constance was attired only in her bloomers, vest, corset, and stockings, and Laura was a little surprised to see that she had quite a nice figure, which her usual rather careless manner of dressing helped to conceal.

Reaching into her clothes closet, Constance turned about, smiling. "What brings you to my door, Laura? I do hope it's not word of an extra rehearsal."

Laura shook her head. "No, not that. It's just that I have an unexpectedly free evening, and I remembered your mentioning once that I might like to see the photographs of your trip. I know it's very short notice, and I'll understand if you're too busy."

Constance laughed. "No, I'm not all that busy. At least, not really. So tonight would be fine. But where's Nick?"

Laura glanced away. "Oh, he has a meeting in town tonight with someone he knows. Something to do with some business he's interested in."

She looked around to see Constance staring at her shrewdly. Laura realized that her expression must have shown something of her unhappiness over Nick's absence, for the other woman came to her and put a comforting arm around her shoulders, hugging her briefly.

"Men!" she said with a scornful laugh. "They have their little meetings and their nights out. Don't let it worry you, dear. It's a common male phenomenon. I suppose this is the first night he's left you alone since the wedding?"

Laura nodded shamefacedly. Constance had seen right through her.

Constance gave her shoulder another squeeze, then returned to her dressing. "It's something you'll have to get used to, dear. It's a part of the male nature. It seems that they were never meant to sit on the nest all of the time. They need to stretch their wings now and then. At least they *think* they do. You'll get used to it. We all do."

Laura was surprised at Constance's worldly knowledge and suddenly looked at her in a different light. "You mean you've been married?"

Constance, buttoning up the front of a plain brown basque, gave her a rueful grin. "Don't sound so astounded, Laura. I may not be a beauty like you, but I've had my share of admirers, including, for a brief spell, a husband."

Laura flushed in embarrassment. "I didn't mean it that way, Constance. It's just that you never spoke of a husband, and you don't call yourself Mrs."

"It's not a part of my life I'm particularly proud of." She examined herself in the pier glass and tugged her bustle straight. "I simply never think of myself as a Mrs. We weren't married more than a few weeks when he left me for a kootch dancer. He always did have a weakness for sideshows, did Bertie."

Laura gasped, but Constance's wry grimace warned her against any expression of pity.

"He was a trumpet player and a member of the orchestra in which I first began playing professionally. He was what they call a real fiddlefoot, always on the move, and I should have known better. Today I like to think I *would* know better, but I was very young and he was very handsome, what they call a ladies' man." Constance shrugged lightly. "It was one of the follies of my youth, and one that I would just as soon forget, so let's not speak of it anymore. Have you had your supper?"

"Not yet."

"Then let's eat together. I'm sure we'll both be glad of the company. Let's try that little place around the corner from the hotel. I had dinner there last night and the food was very good. The prices are reasonable."

The restaurant proved to be clean and comfortable, and a friendly waiter showed them to a nice table by the window. Laura picked up the menu and, feeling hungry, ordered the fried-chicken dinner, which came complete with beverage and dessert.

As she laid down her menu, Constance smiled at her. "You're still a bit shocked, aren't you? About my having been married. I can tell."

Laura flushed again. "I'm not shocked, Constance, not really. Certainly there's nothing wrong in your having been married. It's just that I think it was awful of your husband to leave you like that. You must have been terribly hurt."

Constance looked down at the table. "Yes, I'll admit I was badly hurt at the time, but I eventually recovered." She looked up again. "Despite what it says in the songs, you do not die from a broken heart, Laura. Believe me. I recovered, and met other men, who were kinder."

"But you never married again?"

Constance shook her head. "Legally, I'm still married to the scoundrel. Bertie has never surfaced again. I've never been able to find him so I can get a divorce."

Laura, fascinated by this glimpse into what seemed to her the seamier side of life, could only shake her head. "Does that kind of thing happen often, men leaving their wives like that?"

Constance sighed heavily. "Often enough. Or I should say, all too often. The truth of the matter is, men are not monogamous by nature, while women are. It makes for a very unequal arrangement; but here, I shouldn't be talking to you like this. You're a new bride, with the dew still on the rose. Don't mind what I say, Laura, you know how

I go on. Many marriages are very happy, and many men
are faithful and loyal. You can't judge them all by a few
bad apples. Now let's change the subject to something
more cheerful."

Laura was just as happy to talk about something else. In
a strange way, she found Constance's disclosure exciting,
yet in another way disquieting. It made her think of how
attractive Nick was, and how the other women of the
Chautauqua hovered around him constantly, smiling co-
quettishly and making up to him.

At that moment the waiter arrived with their food, and
it looked and smelled marvelous.

Laura very much enjoyed eating in restaurants. After so
many years of preparing and eating the dull, bland food
that her father demanded, it was pleasant to be able to
choose from so many items, and the fact that she did not
have to do the cooking gave the food an added appeal.

After a few moments Constance glanced up from the
rare steak she had ordered. "What about you and Nick?
What are you going to do when the Chautauqua closes for
the season?"

Laura frowned. "I don't really know. Whenever I question Nick about it, he shrugs it off, telling me that there's
no rush, that something will come up."

"Yes, that sounds like Nick," Constance said with a
smile. "From what I know of him, he's not the kind of
person who gives much thought to the future; but don't
worry, I've often heard him say that he was born under a
lucky star, and I must admit that things always seem to
work out for him. In my opinion, one of the luckiest
things that has happened to him is finding you."

Laura blushed furiously, both at the compliment and
because Constance seemed to know more about Nick than
she did herself. It was humiliating to her to know so little
about her own husband.

"Do you know much about Nick?" she asked slowly.
"We've known each other for such a short time, and he
hardly ever talks about his past."

Constance took a sip of her coffee before answering,

and Laura noticed that her expression became somewhat guarded.

"No, I don't know Nick very well," Constance said. "Just casually. We both came to work for the Chautauqua at the same time—this is the second season for us both. I know that he's well liked and that everyone admires his speaking skills. He really knows how to hold and work an audience."

Laura looked down at her hands, which were locked together in her lap. "Did he . . . Do you know if he had many women friends, before me?"

Constance's eyes were shrewd, appraising. "Laura, I could tell you that I had never seen him with another woman, but you're far too bright to believe that. Besides, it would be unnatural. After all, Nick's an attractive man, and before he met you he was unattached."

She leaned forward. "Let me give you a few words of unasked-for advice. Never worry about the women your man knew in the past, just as he shouldn't worry about the men *you* knew. What happened before two people met and fell in love is unimportant. I have seen so many people make themselves needlessly sick with jealousy over something that happened years ago." She sat back. "Just remember one thing. It was *you* he chose to marry, not some other woman. It's you he loves now. That's all that matters."

Laura smiled quickly. "That sounds sensible."

"I'm very good at giving advice," Constance said dryly. "I only wish I were as good at taking it." She pushed back her chair. "Well, shall we go back to the hotel and look at the photographs?"

Comfortably seated on the sofa in Constance's untidy room, Laura held the large photograph album in her lap and sighed at the pictures of Paris and London. "I envy you," she said wistfully. "Do you know that this town is the farthest I've ever been from Sacramento, California?"

Constance turned another page. "I certainly wouldn't have been able to go myself if it hadn't been for Aunt Mildred. She not only has a great deal of money, but a great deal of time as well, and she doesn't like to travel alone. It was sheer luck that made her decide on me as a traveling companion. It was a wonderful experience for me."

Raising her gaze from the album, Laura stole a surreptitious glance at the small clock on the dresser. It was ten o'clock. Perhaps Nick was back by now.

"It's been a lovely evening, Constance. Thanks for putting up with me. I'd better get back now, in case Nick has returned."

Constance gave her an amused look. "I doubt you can expect him back this soon, Laura. When men are playing cards, they forget the time. I wouldn't worry if he doesn't get in until quite late."

Laura made a rueful face. "I'm so inexperienced, Constance. How long does it take before you can really begin to feel comfortable with being married?"

"I'm a poor one to ask," Constance said with a laugh. "I was only married a very short time, remember? However, from what I've observed, I would say that it must take at least a year, maybe two."

"Still, even if it's too early to expect him back, I'd better get to bed. We have an early rehearsal tomorrow, or have you forgotten?"

Constance grimaced. "How could I forget?"

Laura gave the other woman her hand. "Thanks for your company, Constance. I enjoyed myself."

Constance leaned over and kissed her cheek. "I did, too. We must do it again sometime. The next time Nick has business in the evening."

It was not until Laura had reached her room that it dawned on her that Constance had referred to the fact that Nick was playing cards, when all Laura had told her was that Nick had business to attend to that evening.

Chapter Six

*I*T was after midnight and still Laura could not sleep. She tossed and turned, trying to get comfortable, but there seemed to be no position that could soothe her anxiety. Where was Nick? Why didn't he come home?

Every time she heard a footstep in the hallway she sat up expectantly; and every time the footsteps passed on by, she sank back down, feeling unhappy and growing more concerned. Had something happened to him?

At last, at one-thirty, just when she had finally dozed off, she heard the door open and close. Feeling a flood of relief, she called out, "Nick, is that you?"

A slurred chuckle came at her out of the darkness. "Who else would it be, my love?"

She heard stumbling footsteps coming toward her, then she felt the weight of his body as he sat down on the bed. He fumbled for her face with his hand. "Did you miss me? Did the little wifey miss me?"

Leaning down, he kissed her. His lips were wet, and the smell of alcohol was sickeningly strong on his breath. She shrank away.

"Nick, you've been drinking!"

Nick chuckled again, foolishly. "Give the little lady a silver dollar!"

The bed shook again as he fell back on it, and in the faint light from the open window Laura looked down at him in dismay, for he was already asleep and snoring.

Furious, she sat looking at him; he was still completely dressed and was snoring like a pig! Well, she was not going to undress him, not even remove his shoes. Let him awaken and find himself like that in the morning!

Angrily she retreated to the far side of the bed and cried herself to sleep.

Nick awoke slowly as a beam of sunlight brightened the darkness behind his eyes. Where was he? Then awareness came to him—he had made it back to the hotel room.

Opening his eyes, he looked down at himself. *Just* made it, by the look of things. He was still fully dressed, and he smelled abominably of stale whiskey. He turned his head and saw that the other side of the bed was empty. Then he saw Laura busy at the wash basin.

He watched her for a few moments. She was a pretty sight, standing there in her drawers and vest. Even without her corset her waist was small, and her bottom was nicely rounded. He could tell from the stiffness of her back that she was angry at him. But that did not bother him particularly. He was confident that he could jolly her out of it, particularly when he told her that he had won heavily last night and could buy her that dress she had admired.

Sitting up, he swung his feet to the floor and scrubbed a hand down across his face. Luckily, no matter how much he drank he never suffered a hangover, another facet of his usual good fortune.

He stood and tiptoed up behind Laura. Reaching around her, he cupped her breasts in his hands. He felt her body go tense, and he began to nuzzle her ear.

"Are you angry with me, sweetheart? I guess I can't blame you too much. I know I came in late, and I must have been in deplorable condition. But I couldn't leave the game earlier, you see. I was winning, and it's not considered good form to leave when you're a big winner. I did it for you, too, you know. Now you can buy that dress you've been wanting. Please don't be angry with me."

Her body began to soften under his hands, and he smiled into her hair. It was going to be all right.

Marriage, Nick was finding out, was both better and worse than he had anticipated. He enjoyed having a lovely woman available for loving whenever he wanted it, and he knew that he was envied for having such a beautiful and intelligent wife. On the other hand, it was difficult getting accustomed to less freedom. Never before had it been necessary to think about anyone other than himself; and he was not particularly happy about having to account to another person for his actions. Still, it was not working out too badly. Laura kept his clothes clean and mended, their rooms clean, and she could cobble up a good meal when required. She would soon adjust to the fact that she could not keep too tight a rein on him. He had observed other new brides and knew that they had to be broken in, like good horses. She would soon get used to the idea that he could not be with her all the time; that men had things they liked to do that did not include women. One way to pacify her, he realized, would be to decide what they would do when the Chautauqua closed for the season. He had been a little delinquent about that—it was almost the end of the season; but he had a line on something now, working for an old friend, and it sounded like just the ticket.

Everything considered, it was not a bad life, being married, and things were going pretty well; but then they almost always did for him.

During the next few weeks, Laura grudgingly got used to the fact that at least once or twice a week Nick went out by himself. She did not like it, and she told him so; but he ignored her complaints, until she resignedly accepted that this was the way things were.

Part of his excuse was that she was usually busy a good part of the evening anyway; and this of course was true, for the orchestra always played during the slide presentations in the evening, and this kept her busy until about nine o'clock most nights.

The thing she hated most, however, was when Nick came home under the influence of alcohol. She hated the smell—sour and stale, like that of whiskey mixed with vomit—and she hated the foolish way he talked and acted.

Attempting to talk with a drunken man, she discovered, was much like trying to talk with an idiot: they both made very little sense.

Some nights when he came home he would simply fall into bed, asleep before his head hit the pillow. Other nights, unfortunately, he would be amorous.

She could not decide which nights she disliked most. Making love with Nick when he was drunk was nothing like their lovemaking when he was sober. Gone was the considerate, gentle man; in his place was a rough lout who took his pleasure, then rolled off her to fall into a stupor, caring nothing for her satisfaction. Still, this was only one or two nights a week, and the rest of the time he was his usual charming and considerate self. Perhaps she should not ask for too much, she thought.

It was only a few days before the end of the season when he finally told her that he had found a winter job—in fact, two jobs, for there was to be employment for her as well.

Excited and grateful, she kissed and hugged him. She had been wrong to doubt him, after all. Something *had* come up, just as he had promised.

"What is it?" she asked excitedly. "Is it a good job?"

He grinned and gave her waist a squeeze. They were in their hotel room resting before her evening stint with the orchestra. "It can be as good as we make it, my love. It's a position with real opportunity."

Relieved and happy, she echoed his laugh. "Well, don't keep me waiting! Tell me what it is."

"Well, there's this man I know, Alfred Hayes, who owns a small string of theaters. Once he tried to hire me to manage one of them, but at the time I had something better to do. At any rate, I contacted him recently, told him that I was married now, and asked if he had anything for me, and he said that he did. He's opening a new vaudeville theater in a small town across the Hudson River from New York, and he has been looking for someone to manage it. How's that for a stroke of luck?"

Laura tried not to let her disappointment show. When

Nick had first mentioned the theater she had thought he meant a legitimate theater. But vaudeville!

"It sounds like a good job, dear, but you said jobs for us both. What would *I* do?"

Nick grinned and squeezed her waist again. "That's the beauty of the whole thing. This is just a small theater, and they won't be using a full orchestra, just a piano and a drummer. You'll play the piano, of course. That way we keep the money in the family. The only others we'll have to pay will be the girl in the ticket office, the drummer, and a stagehand or two.

"Also, I seem to remember that you once told me you were good at figures. Do you think you could handle the bookkeeping? If so, that'll save us even more money."

Nick's enthusiasm was infectious, but Laura was still concerned about the fact that it was a vaudeville theater. "There's just one thing, darling. Isn't vaudeville, well, risqué? And vulgar? I don't know if I want . . ."

Nick laughed heartily. "Have you ever seen a vaudeville show, love?"

"Well, no. Father would never have permitted it."

Nick kissed her forehead. "My innocent little puritan. Vaudeville can have its naughty moments, true, but the kind of acts that Alfred wants us to book are family acts. He believes that what they call 'refined' vaudeville is the coming thing. You've heard of the singer Tony Pastor? Well, he just opened a new theater in New York City with this kind of show. Presenting shows for a family audience is where the money is. So you needn't worry. Your morals will not be corrupted."

Laura blushed. "I didn't mean to sound like a prig."

Nick cupped her breast with his hand. "That's quite all right, my love. After all, you're definitely not a prig where it counts. Have you heard the old saying that a wife should be three things? A lady in the parlor, a cook in the kitchen, and a wanton in the bedroom, and that she should never confuse the roles. Well, you are the perfect wife—you fit all three requirements."

Laura could not help but laugh, while pretending to be shocked. "Nickolas Orlando! How can you say such things?"

"With my tongue," he said, drawing the mentioned member across her lips, causing her to shiver.

The Melodeon, as Nick had warned Laura, was a small theater. It was also very old and appeared badly in need of repair. Laura eyed it with misgiving. This was supposed to be the basis of their new careers, their fortunes?

After a tiring train journey across the continent, they had arrived in New Jersey today, and Nick, full of enthusiasm, had insisted they go to the theater at once.

Now he jumped down from their rented carriage and turned to help her down. Noting her dubious look, he said, "I know it doesn't look like much right now, but Alfred has promised to send over a crew of workmen to get it into shape. In a week or so you won't know the place."

Laura managed a wan smile. He was so pleased and excited, and she wished she could feel the same. She let him lead her to the entrance doors, which were coated with dirt and soot.

As they entered, she lifted her skirts to keep them off the floor, which was thick with an accumulation of what appeared to be years of grime. Of course she was wearing a dust ruffle, but there was no need to get it so filthy that it could never be cleaned. The inside of the theater was dark and smelled of mildew and dust. Nick moved away from her and she heard him fumbling along the wall.

"Ah, yes, there it is! Alfred was supposed to have arranged for the gas to be turned on. Let's see if it works."

Laura heard the sound of a match striking, and the hiss of gas, and then the warm glow of the gaslight came on, illuminating a very dusty but quite attractive brass sconce on the wall of the lobby.

"Wait a minute, Laura, I'll light another lamp. I don't want you tripping over your skirts."

Another light soon glowed on the other side of the lobby, and Laura looked around. The lobby was small and in bad repair, and she dreaded to see the interior of the theater itself. It appeared that it would take a tremendous amount of work to get the theater in condition to be used.

Nick was back by her side. "Now, I want you to wait here for a minute while I go inside and light some lamps. The inside of the theater is dirty, too, but it's in much better shape than the outside and the lobby. I'd like you to see it all at once, so just wait until I call you."

Sighing, Laura stood where she was, as Nick disappeared in the dimness. She had strong misgivings about this venture, but it was too late to turn back. They were committed. Perhaps she would have felt better about things if she had been more rested. It had been a long train trip, Laura's first; and although she had found it exciting it had also been taxing, since they had not been able to afford sleeping compartments. She was eager to see their new quarters and to take a long, hot bath and have a cup of tea, but Nick would not hear of it—she had to see the theater first thing.

"All right, love! Come in!"

Nick's exuberant voice rang out hollowly from the empty theater, and a pale glow of light seeped out from under the dusty drapes that covered all aisle entrances.

Laura chose the center aisle, gingerly pushed aside the heavy drape, and entered the theater.

All along the side walls, gaslights glowed from quite attractive fixtures. Their warm light illuminated the rows of red velvet-covered seats, which seemed, under their coatings of dust, to be in good condition.

The stage, larger than she had anticipated, was shielded from sight by curtains in the same shade of red velvet, which also seemed to be in good repair.

Along the walls and the lower portion of the boxes were some very nice ornamentations framing well-executed paintings of what Laura took to be famous scenes from theater history. The whole interior was, as Nick had said, in far better condition than one would expect after seeing the outside. All that was really needed here was a good cleaning, and the place would be quite charming.

Smiling, this time sincerely, Laura walked down to where Nick was standing and put her arms around him.

"You're right, Nick, my first impression was wrong. It will be beautiful. I can't wait until we get it cleaned up and in operation."

He hugged her tightly. "That's my brave girl. I knew you would be able to see what it could be."

"When will the workmen be coming?"

"Alfred said this coming Monday. That will give us almost a week to get settled into our new quarters and get some linens and other things we'll need."

Laura raised her head from his shoulder, where she had rested it when he took her into his arms. "Speaking of our quarters, shouldn't we see them now? I'm tired, and I badly need a bath."

He kissed her forehead. "Of course, love, they're right upstairs."

She gave him a rueful look. "I do hope they're not in the same condition as the theater."

Nick laughed and took her arm. "I'm sure not. The apartment has been in regular use, and Alfred assured me that it is clean and quite livable. An elderly couple lived there until just recently, and Alfred says they kept the place spotless. The only reason they left was that the old man became ill, so they decided to move in with their son and his family. The place is completely furnished, except for linens and kitchen utensils. I do hope you'll like it, but even if it's less than perfect, we're getting it rent free, remember, and it will be our very own."

Laura echoed his words softly: " 'Our very own.' That does have a nice sound, and it will be wonderful to be able to stay in one place for a while. And we'll have so much more privacy."

Nick grinned wolfishly. "Ah, yes, privacy. Privacy so that I can have my way with you to my heart's content." He patted her bustle hard enough to make the frame squeak, and shook his head. "You know, it's a damned shame to cover up something so delectable with that awful cage."

Laura laughed. "Well, it's the style, as you very well know, and it must have been invented to protect us women from the heavy-handed attentions of cads such as yourself."

"Cad, is it?" he said with mock outrage. "Just wait until we get upstairs, my love, and I'll show you what a cad really is."

Laughing together, they mounted the stairs to the second floor, where there was a good-sized landing. The landing was in good repair and looked as if it had recently been painted. The walls were a pale yellow, which made the landing look bright and cheerful, and Laura hoped that this was a good omen for the rooms, the door to which Nick was just unlocking.

When he threw open the door, she gave an exclamation of surprise and delight. Here all was not darkness, as in the theater below; here the windows let in ample afternoon sunlight, revealing a small entryway with two built-in box benches, with latched tops, and a nice-sized parlor, both papered in a very pretty paisley design in a soft rose color. The rug, which bore a pattern of roses, was only slightly worn, and the furniture, although a bit old-fashioned, looked serviceable.

As Nick had said, it was completely furnished. Taking up most of the room was a horsehair sofa, an armchair with a tapestry-covered cushion and a matching footstool, a small walnut rocking chair, a walnut end table, and a lamp with a red velvet shade and crystal pendants.

At the other end of the room was a small walnut dining-room table with carved legs and four matching chairs.

"Of course the people who lived here took their personal things," Nick was saying, "their ornaments and all, but we'll be able to get our own, in time."

"Oh, it's nice!" Laura exclaimed, clapping her hands. "It's much nicer than I had hoped for." She threw her arms around his neck. "Oh, Nick, this will be our first real home!"

"Then let's give it a proper housewarming." His hands cupped her breasts, and his mouth found hers.

For just a moment she returned his kiss, then she tried to pull out of his arms. "Not here, Nick. I need to get to our hotel and have a bath."

"Yes, here," he muttered. "You realize how long it's been? We had absolutely no privacy on that blasted train."

"But where? There isn't any linen on the beds."

Again she tried to pull away, but he would not let her go. "We'll find a way," he said, a wicked glint in his eyes. "There's always the floor. I promised to show you what a cad really is, didn't I?"

His hands were worming their way under her clothes as he unsnapped and unbuttoned; and despite herself she went soft and pliable under his touch. He was right—it had been several days since they had made love; and she was reminded anew just how much his touch could arouse her.

"You're shameless, absolutely shameless," she muttered, as he began to pull her down onto the rug.

By the end of the week, Laura had made the flat her own. It had been great fun buying the kitchen utensils, dishes, and linens for her own home, and even though the expenditure had made inroads into their remaining funds, it had been well worth it.

On Monday, as Alfred Hayes had promised, the workmen arrived. The first thing Nick had them do was to clean and fix up the main body of the theater, so that they could begin to audition talent. As Laura had thought, the interior of the theater was not in bad repair. Once the dust and grime had been removed, a few touches of fresh paint made it quite attractive.

As soon as the interior was in order, Nick placed an advertisement in the newspaper: "Wanted for new vaudeville house: refined vaudeville acts; singers, both serious and comedy; knockabout comedy acts; acrobats. Willing to interview any act suitable for a family audience. See Mr. Orlando at the Melodeon Theater, from 9:00 A.M. until noon, and from 2:00 until 5:00 P.M. weekdays."

Laura studied the advertisement with satisfaction and pride. She had written it herself, and it was a symbol of the fact that she and Nick were building a life and a profession of their own; as such, it meant a great deal to her.

She was looking forward to the auditions, for she planned to do her housework early and late, so that she would be available to accompany the auditioning acts on the piano. It was all tremendously exciting, and she was happier than she had ever been in her life.

"Next act, please."

Nick's voice echoed in the chill of the nearly empty theater, and Laura, seated at the upright piano, looked up at the stage to see two young boys swagger out from the wings.

They looked to be about the same age, perhaps thirteen or fourteen, and they were attired similarly in green knickerbockers, white waists, black stockings, dancing clogs, and derby hats. Despite their obvious youth, they appeared fairly sure of themselves, and Laura was amused by their cocky manner.

"What's the name of your act?" Nick called from his seat in the fifth row.

"Fields and Weber," said the shorter of the two.

"What kind of an act?"

"Song and dance."

"What are you going to do for us?"

"An Irish song and clog dance. 'The Land of the Shamrock Green.' "

"All right, just give the music to the piano player there, and we'll get on with it."

The taller youth looked embarrassed. "Well, I'm afraid we don't exactly have the sheet music," he said, looking down at Laura with a pleading look. "But the tune is an old one, and I can hum it to her."

Laura peered over at Nick. They had been viewing acts since nine that morning; it was now nearly four in the afternoon. She could tell from his expression that he was tired and about to refuse to listen to this pair.

She said quickly, "I'm sure I'll be able to manage, Mr. Orlando. Just give me a few minutes with these young men."

Nick said grudgingly, "Well, all right, Laura, if you want to do it."

The two youngsters' faces broke into wide grins, and they scurried down the steps of the stage and over to

Laura at the piano. The tune they hummed was familiar to her, and it took only a few minutes for her to master it.

Soon the youths were back on the stage, and after a few bars of introduction they commenced singing. By the time they had reached the chorus, Laura was trying hard not to smile as they sang:

> "Here we are, an Irish pair,
> Without any troubles or care;
> We're here once more to make people roar
> Before we go to the ball."

When they finished, she flashed Nick a warning look. She was afraid that he would say something to hurt their feelings; despite their cocky manner, she sensed beneath their facades a vulnerability.

Nick caught her glance, nodded, and cleared his throat before speaking to them, as they stood on the lip of the stage and stared down at him expectantly. "It wasn't at all bad, lads, but I'm afraid you're not quite what we're looking for."

Laura saw discouragement cloud their faces, and she felt sorry for them.

"Come back in a few years," said Nick, as the boys clumped down the stage steps, "when you've had a little more experience."

The smaller boy glared at him defiantly. "In a few years, sir, you won't be able to afford us," he said, his aplomb restored.

"Maybe not, but I'll just have to take that chance." As the boys stormed out of the theater, Nick walked over to Laura. "Impudent young pups! If cockiness were talent, they would already be a roaring success."

She laughed. "They weren't all that bad, darling. They really danced very well, although I must admit that the words to that song were dreadful."

Nick stretched and reached around to rub the small of his back. "Well, one thing I know, with those faces and those voices, they sure weren't Irish, and that's a fact. But they do have the brass that it takes to succeed in show business. In a few years they just might make it."

Chapter Seven

*T*HE Melodeon opened on October 15, 1881, with seven acts: the Parson Sisters, a vocal duet; Leland and Price, knockabout comics; Danny O'Neil, comedy songs; Alfred Morrison, romantic ballads; Millicent Peal, male impersonator; the McQuires, a dance team; and Fisk and Company, a trained-dog act.

None of the performers was well known, for Alfred Hayes had supplied Nick with a limited budget; however, Nick thought they were all talented, the best of the dozens of acts that had auditioned for him.

Another advertisement had been placed in the paper, this one trumpeting the grand opening of the Melodeon, a vaudeville theater showing entertainment appropriate for the entire family; and handbills had been posted all over town.

Laura, wrapped in a heavy cape against a chill autumn wind, stood in front of the theater looking up at the marquee. The theater now looked much different from the way it had the first time she had seen it. It was amazing what a little elbow grease, carpentry, and paint could do, she thought. Everything was ready for the opening tonight, and Laura, in a fine state of excitement, was as nervous as a cat.

The repairs and refurbishing of the theater and the hiring of the acts had gone well; the only remaining hurdle to be overcome was the opening night. Would they attract a good crowd?

Laura shivered in the cold afternoon breeze. Living all her life in California had not prepared her for eastern weather; still, she found the change of seasons interesting, if not entirely comfortable.

As she turned back to the entrance of the theater, the only cloud over her happiness came into view, Harriet Hayes, coming out of the lobby. Harriet was Alfred Hayes's niece, whom he had suggested for the position of ticket seller and general helper at the Melodeon.

Harriet was a ripely pretty girl, with thick auburn hair that she wore pulled back into a mass of natural ringlets, dark, rebellious eyes, and red, pouting lips. She was, in Laura's opinion, lazy, arrogant, and uncooperative, especially where Laura was concerned. When Nick was around she was all provocative glances and coy posturings.

When Laura had complained about her, Nick had only shrugged. "What can I do? She's Alfred's niece, and he's paying the bills. It's his theater, Laura. Just try to get along with her the best you can."

Laura realized the logic of his statement but nonetheless was angry. It was not fair that they should have to put up with this useless girl and pay her out of the profits of their labor. Laura did not want to admit, even to herself, that the girl's obvious interest in Nick worried her. Things between her and Nick were so good now. He was too busy to have his "nights out with the boys," but was with her every night. Of course, at the end of the day they were both usually so tired that they wanted only to eat a simple meal and fall into bed; but at least she knew where he was, and he did not come home staggering drunk.

As Laura passed Harriet, who was going into the ticket booth, she acknowledged her with a slight nod.

Harriet stared back at her with an odd look of triumph, tossed her head, and entered the ticket booth with her cashbox. Laura noted that the girl's cheeks were very flushed and her hair was disarranged. But Laura had more important things to do than worry about Harriet's appearance.

Inside the theater, Laura had to look around a bit to

find Nick, finally locating him backstage in one of the dressing rooms. He seemed extraordinarily glad to see her, grabbing her by the waist and spinning her around, then gathering her into his arms and kissing her soundly.

She returned his kiss, then pushed him away, laughing. "What on earth has gotten into you, darling? And what are you doing back here?"

"Oh, opening night has gotten to me, I guess. And I was fixing a mirror in here. Molly Parson complained that it was falling out of the frame every time she used it."

Laura kept her smile, although she had a strong intuition that Nick was hiding something. She had learned by now that when Nick was dissembling, he became overactive and boisterous.

The feeling persisted, and she looked nervously around the room. As she did so, she noticed a lace handkerchief on the old chaise at the end of the room. She recognized the handkerchief as Harriet's, and a dull knot of suspicion began to form in her stomach.

She walked over to the chaise and picked up the handkerchief. "It looks as if Harriet has been in here," she said tightly, holding it up in front of Nick's eyes. "I don't recall sending her in here to do anything."

Nick grinned engagingly and shrugged. "You're right about her. She's never around when you need her to do some chore, and I've been suspecting that she sneaks off someplace and has herself a snooze. This must be where she's been hiding out. I wish we weren't stuck with her, but what can we do?"

Laura searched his face carefully but could detect no sign of guilt or guile. She desperately wanted to believe him.

That evening, the Melodeon came alive. The globes of the gas lamps sparkled, and the polished brass gleamed. In the warm light, the faded spots on the stage curtain and the worn spots on the seats did not show.

Backstage, the performers dressed, made up, and then gathered to chat as they waited for the curtain to rise. At the piano, Laura, in a new, royal-blue mohair ensemble, played popular selections as the audience filed into the theater. She noticed with pleasure that the advertising had been successful; they were going to have a good house.

First on the bill were the Parson Sisters, two blond, buxom young women in their mid-twenties, with sweet clear voices; they were well received by the audience.

Laura was nervous in the beginning, but when she heard the hearty applause for the first act, she relaxed a bit and began to enjoy herself. To work with her, Nick had employed an elderly but excellent musician, Ted Lawrey, who played several different instruments, depending on the type of material being performed. Laura liked Ted, who was a genial, kindly man, and she enjoyed playing with him; so, once she had relaxed, the program went smoothly and more quickly than she would have imagined possible.

When the program was over and the audience had gone, Laura and Nick went into the small office off the lobby to count the receipts. When the money was counted, she turned to Nick with a wide smile. "Just look," she said happily, showing him the figures. "And we still have another performance. Why, if we do that good a business every day, we'll be rich in no time at all!"

Nick laughed and leaned over to kiss her on the nose. "I hate to tell you this, my love, but we won't do this well every day. This is Saturday, don't forget, and of course the weekends draw bigger crowds. But even if we do half or two-thirds as well on the weekdays, we should come out all right. Why don't you deduct our expenses now, and see what we have left over?"

Laura bent over her ledger. "Let's see, we're paying the Parsons forty dollars a week. Leland and Price, forty dollars as well. O'Neil, twenty-five dollars. Morrison, thirty dollars. Millicent Peal, thirty dollars. The McQuires, forty dollars. And Fisk, thirty dollars. That comes to a total of two hundred and thirty-five dollars a week for the performers, and then there are Harriet's and Ted's salaries, the general expenses, and our salaries. Let's see . . ."

For a moment she scribbled furiously. "That should still give us a decent profit, of which we get our percentage. Oh, Nick! It's all going so well!"

It continued to go well for the next year, except for a few minor problems, one of which was the continued, annoying presence of Harriet Hayes, who seemed to grow lazier and more insolent as the months went by.

As far as Laura was concerned, Harriet was useless as a general helper, never to be found when there was cleaning to be done, careless in making change—the receipts seldom matched the ticket count—and she was still putting on what Laura thought of as a "show" whenever Nick was around.

The eastern winter was again in full possession of the city; and although Laura bundled herself up in a heavy coat, mittens, and a wool scarf whenever she went out, she was always cold. Nick scoffed at her, telling her that she was dressed like an Eskimo, even in the flat; and she replied by retorting that they might as well be in the far reaches of the North.

Despite the weather, the Melodeon continued to draw good crowds, and as they became better known, even larger audiences. The strange thing was that as the Melodeon grew more successful, Nick seemed to become more restless.

Laura had tried to find out what was troubling him, but he always brushed her questions aside with a joke or some other bit of foolishness. He had also started going out "with the boys" again, often leaving her to close up the theater and count the cash, saying that there was really no need for both of them to be there every night; which might have been a fine piece of logic except for the fact that it was always he who went out, and she who stayed.

Another thing that bothered Laura was the fact that she had not gotten pregnant. From what she knew of the matter, pregnancy was usually so easily accomplished that a young woman had to fear even one sexual encounter; but she and Nick made love constantly and took no precautions, yet her monthly continued to arrive regularly.

She wanted very much to have a child by Nick, and thought that now, since they were settled down in one place, was the perfect time to conceive. She took good care of herself, ate well, got enough rest, but so far there were no results. She had not discussed the matter with Nick, for she assumed that he would be as happy as she to have a child to bless their union.

The one person she had confided in was Constance, with whom she corresponded regularly. She valued Constance's opinion and knew that nothing she could write or say would shock her, so she was able to be completely honest with her.

Constance answered her letters promptly and seemed pleased to keep up their friendship. Laura suspected that the other woman enjoyed the role of mentor on love and life; but since she always found Constance's advice practical and helpful, Laura was quite willing to play the role of disciple. She had even written to Constance concerning the problem of Harriet, and Constance had suggested that if Laura was friendly with Alfred Hayes, she should be frank with him and tell him how his niece was behaving.

"After all," she had written, "if you never tell him that you are unhappy with the girl's work, he is bound to assume that she is doing her job well and that you are satisfied with her. No need to be forceful about it, just tell him politely and calmly that you are not pleased by the girl's work habits. Use your feminine wiles on him, if need be. Play the poor, overworked, delicate woman who is not receiving the help she bargained for and is paying for. Laura, you're going to have to learn that in this world, which is a man's world, a woman must sometimes use guile to achieve her purpose."

Laura had been amused and yet somewhat annoyed by this advice. She was certain that Constance knew of what she spoke, but the idea of consciously playing a role with Alfred Hayes made her feel guilty and dishonest. It was not her nature to dissemble. Even when she had been attempting to get Nick to marry her, she had never pretended to be anything she was not, and she had used no trickery.

Why was it not possible for a woman to speak directly to a man, to lay her cards on the table, so to speak, as would another man? It seemed unnecessarily complicated that she must think out ahead of time what she would say, and how she would act, so that Mr. Hayes would take pity on her and listen to her. Still, if that was what it would take to clear up the situation with Harriet, she would swallow her disinclination and do as Constance suggested.

However, things never got to that point, for before she could arrange a talk with Alfred Hayes, she had a very disturbing conversation with Harriet. The confrontation occurred on a dark, cold Saturday afternoon in mid-December.

Laura had just counted the afternoon's receipts and found, again, that the total did not match the ticket stubs. Laura was not in a good mood anyway—Nick was out, despite the heavy snow, and she was feeling lonely and cranky.

Leaving the paperwork on the table, she went in search of Harriet, who was supposed to be helping to clean up the theater for the next performance.

It took her twenty minutes to find the girl, during which time her annoyance mounted. She finally located Harriet backstage, all but hidden behind a stack of props, where it seemed she had built a cozy little nest, complete with kerosene lantern, a comfortable chair, and a stack of dime novels. Since Laura had been calling Harriet's name all over the theater, it was impossible that Harriet had not heard her.

Glaring down at the younger woman, Laura stood with her hands on her hips. "Didn't you hear me calling you?"

Harriet looked up at her sullenly.

"I'm speaking to you, Harriet, and I would appreciate the courtesy of an answer, even though courtesy is something that you evidently know little about!"

Harriet's expression did not change, but she did finally speak: "I guess I didn't hear you."

"Why aren't you helping with the cleaning, as you were supposed to?"

The girl shrugged and finally put down her book. "I wasn't feeling too well," she said sullenly.

Laura sighed in exasperation. "If you weren't feeling well, why didn't you come to me and tell me, instead of hiding out back here where no one could find you?"

"I wasn't hiding. You found me, didn't you?"

Laura's face grew hot with the anger she was attempting to control. "Harriet, you are the rudest young woman it has ever been my misfortune to meet, and I am sick and tired of putting up with your bad manners, your laziness, and the fact that your cashbox never balances. I'm going to speak to my husband, and then to your uncle, and demand that they let you go!"

When the words were out, Laura felt an enormous relief. She should have done this weeks ago!

To her surprise, Harriet seemed not at all disturbed. With a slow, self-satisfied smile she said, "I wouldn't do that if I were you, Mrs. Orlando. If you do, you might be in for an unpleasant surprise."

Laura stared at the girl, nonplussed. Harriet seemed very sure of herself. A flutter of unease disturbed Laura's mind. "I'll thank you to explain that remark, Harriet."

"Do I need to do that, Mrs. Orlando?" Now her smile was arrogant. "Don't you really know what I mean?"

Laura, growing more uneasy by the moment, felt herself losing ground, but tried to conceal it. "I have no earthly idea what you're talking about. I think you're out of your mind, Harriet!"

Harriet's smile widened. "Well, you just talk to Nick . . . to your husband, Mrs. Orlando, and see if he wants to fire me. I think you'll soon find that he doesn't. In fact, I think you'll find that he's quite satisfied with me. And I wouldn't suggest that you go to Uncle Alfred, either—not without talking to your husband first. If you do, it could cause you all sorts of difficulties."

Harriet's words, and her attitude, were making Laura furious. There were implications here—unpleasant implications. How could she have the audacity to speak up like this?

Her fists so tightly clenched that her nails dug into her

palms, Laura stared at the girl in icy anger. "Well, we shall see about that when I talk to my husband. But you will be leaving, have no fear on that score!"

As Laura whirled away, she heard Harriet laugh softly.

Nick was back before the evening performance, smelling of whiskey and in an expansive mood.

Laura knew from experience that when he had been drinking it was difficult to speak with him on serious matters, but her anger and indignation were so strong that she had to have the matter of Harriet Hayes settled immediately. She felt that her position and self-esteem were at stake.

She led him into the small office and seated him behind the worn desk. "Nick, we must have a serious talk about Harriet."

He evaded her glance. "Harriet? Right now? Can't it wait? I have things to do."

She shook her head firmly. "No! It's waited far too long already."

Nick sighed, leaned back in the chair, and put his feet up on the desk top. "Well, fire away. What has she done this time?"

He had an air of long-suffering patience, the manner of a man who had to listen to such complaints regularly, and this infuriated Laura. "What kind of an attitude is that? You *know* how she is. I've told you a dozen times that her cashbox never balances, that she will not do the work assigned her, and that she is rude to me, yet you never do anything about it. I've asked you to talk to Alfred about her, but you always put me off. Why is that, Nick? What kind of a hold does the girl have over you?"

"Hold? What do you mean by that, for hell's sake?" His feet thumped to the floor and he reached for her hand. "Sweetheart, I've explained to you that Alfred is fond of her. She's the daughter of his only sister, and the family is very close. If I go to him and complain about Harriet, he's going to be upset. Now, you know that Alfred has given us a fair deal here. He's been very generous—much more so than most men in his position would have been. Do you want to jeopardize our good relationship?"

Laura stared into his face. He was smiling and his eyes were twinkling; it was the expression he usually wore when he was trying to cozen her into or out of something. All at once she wanted to hit him, to jolt him into awareness of the seriousness of what she was saying, to make him, for once, discuss the problem openly and honestly.

She tore her hand from his grasp. "I think it's more than that, Nick. A lot more. I can see it in Harriet's face, in her eyes. She looks at me as if she's hiding something from me, something that gives her the power to be rude and hateful to me, and at the same time realizing that I can do nothing about it. Have you any idea how difficult that makes things for me?"

Nick stood up, stretching, still smiling. "You're upset, Laura. I know that the girl is lazy, but she *is* very young, after all. If you could just remember that, and not expect too much of her. And now, it's getting near time for the evening curtain. We'll talk about this later, when you're calmer. All right, my love?"

Without waiting for her reply, he planted a kiss on the top of her head and strode blithely out of the room, leaving her staring after him in disbelief.

How could he be so insensitive, so uncaring of her feelings, so willfully blind?

She well knew that when he did not want to discuss a subject, he was as evasive as an eel; and it was clear that he had no intention of discussing the subject of Harriet. It was also crystal clear that he had no intention of discharging her or of going to Alfred Hayes about her. In short, Harriet had been right in every particular. Laura felt as if she and the girl were locked in combat, and that Harriet, with Nick's help, had just dealt her a mortal blow.

Stiffly, she turned and strode from the small room, heading toward the dressing rooms, trying to switch her thoughts from personal to business affairs.

Tonight was a rather special night, as the Melodeon was offering, for the first time, a very unusual act: the Magnificent Montinis, a group of talented acrobats from Europe, who were just getting started in the United States. Laura had by now seen many such troupes, but none who could do what the Montinis did. There were six of them, all family members; and during the climax of their act, when they were all flying through the air at once, it seemed as if gravity exerted no pull upon them. They built human structures of great complexity and daring; in addition, they were attractive and pleasant people. In all ways they were amazing, and Laura wanted to be certain that they had everything they needed before the performance.

Usually when she was working she could put aside whatever was bothering her. She was conscientious about her duties and felt that personal matters should be excluded during business hours; but tonight she was too upset to make her usual adjustment.

The questions kept hammering at her: Why wouldn't Nick discuss Harriet's behavior? Why did he always brush aside Laura's complaints, as if they had no weight or meaning? Why did he always defend the girl?

Lurking underneath the conscious questions were the questions she was not ready to face: Was Nick having an affair with Harriet? Was that the reason the girl was so sure of herself? Or did Harriet know something about Nick, something that was to his discredit, something that gave her leverage over him? Of these two alternatives, Laura would much have preferred the second.

Chapter Eight

*T*HE sound of the train whistle was soporific, and Will Adams felt completely relaxed as he sat looking out the club-car window at the panorama of the snow-covered countryside.

On the table beside his comfortable chair was a glass of excellent bourbon, and in his hand was a good cigar. The club car was cozy and warm. *Mrs. Adams's son is doing all right*, Will thought contentedly as he inhaled the fragrant smoke.

Across from Will were two drummers discussing their products and their territory and complaining about all the traveling they had to do. Will smiled to himself. He enjoyed traveling. In fact, he considered it one of the best features of his line of employment.

When he was a small boy, back in eastern Texas, he used to lie awake in his bedroom at night, listening to the cry of the train whistle in the distance, dreaming of far-away places and adventurous deeds. He had never fully understood how a sound so mournful could evoke such exotic images; he knew only that the whistle called to him, making him feel restless and edgy, making him want to be somewhere else, anywhere else.

And he was still much the same. If he stayed in any place too long, the old restlessness came over him, the old feeling that everything exciting was happening somewhere else.

It was fortunate for him that his job fit so well with his

tastes and character. And it was a good job, one that many men would envy, offering travel in style, excellent accommodations, and close contact with talented and interesting people. In return for these benefits, all Will had to do was to discover these talented and interesting people and get them to sign with Barnum, Bailey, and Hutchinson. Since the mammoth Barnum and London Circus was the greatest and most famous show in the world, this usually was not difficult to do.

Reaching out for his glass, Will took a pull of the mellow bourbon. He was on his way now to look at a troupe of Italian acrobats whom Phineas T. Barnum had heard about from a friend in New York.

The troupe, the Montinis, were new to this country, and were going to perform at a small vaudeville house outside New York City. The friend had warned Barnum that Adam Forepaugh, Barnum's greatest business rival, was also interested in the group of acrobats; and that if Barnum wished to sign them, he had better get someone to contact them quickly and get their names on a contract. And so that was why at this moment Will Adams was on the train speeding toward the small town on the Hudson across from New York. He was in Chicago when Barnum's telegram had reached him.

Far ahead of the club car, the whistle blew, and Will, looking out the window, saw an old farmhouse frosted with white and flanked by the winter skeleton of a huge tree. It looked so much like the house where he had been born and raised that for an instant Will experienced a pang of homesickness.

Despite hard times and poverty, he had been happy as a child. The youngest of four children, he had been gladly welcomed into a warm and friendly family where what you were counted far more than what you had, and where each member was encouraged to be an individual.

His mother, Matty Pierson Adams, was an intelligent and talented woman who could sing, play the piano, sew a dress, or concoct a filling meal out of almost nothing, and all with equal skill.

His father, Harry Adams, was a hardworking farmer, a

man who loved the land, even when it did not return his attention and devotion in full measure.

Although the family did not have much in the way of material possessions, the children never thought of themselves as deprived. There was so much love, so much warmth, that it was impossible for them to consider themselves poor.

Will, as the youngest child, was somewhat spoiled by his elder brother and his two sisters; still, he was required to do his share of the chores. Since his father could not afford to hire help, all the family members had to be utilized as a labor force.

Will's brother, Edward, had inherited his father's love of the land, and the two girls, Mercy and Helen, had wanted nothing more from life than to settle down as wives and mothers. They were all still back there in eastern Texas. Edward was working the old family farm, and the two girls were married to neighboring farmers and had children of their own. All very settled and content, they could never understand their younger brother's fascination with traveling, and looked upon his wanderlust as an abberation, or a passing illness, from which he would eventually recover. Whenever Will went home for a visit, they would parade all the neighborhood spinsters and widows before him in an orgy of matchmaking; for they were certain that if he only had the love of a good woman, he would settle down, hopefully in Texas.

Now Will turned away from the train window. Well, in his thirty-three years he had loved a number of women, both good and bad, and one of them he had loved enough to wed.

He had met her in Paris when he had gone there at Barnum's behest to look at a reported oddity—the so-called Lion Man, Lionel Germaine. The Lion Man had proved to be genuine—a young man of eighteen whose body and face were completely covered with long, wavy golden hair. Tall and well built, he was an excellent specimen of abnormal hair growth, an oddity much desired by all sideshows, and Will had signed him at once. In fact, the Lion Man was still with Barnum and was considered a great drawing card.

But the act of signing Lionel paled in comparison with something else that happened at the Germaine's modest home, for it was there that Will met Lily; and the moment he saw her, his whole life changed.

As soon as Will saw the exotic, dark-haired girl with the exquisite, delicate features, he realized that he had never really been in love before. The feeling that swept over him was indescribable and deliciously painful. He had always scoffed at those who spoke of love at first sight, but now he realized that it was not only possible but that it was happening to him.

Lily was at the Germaines' with her mother, an attractive, middle-aged woman, a longtime friend of the Germaine family. Will learned that first evening that Lily's father was dead, and that the family had once possessed great wealth but had recently fallen on hard times. Now, although there was sufficient money to support Lily and her mother comfortably, they had severed connections with their illustrious past and lived simply. Still, to Will Adams, the glamour of the past hovered over Lily like a perfumed cloud, lending her an aura of mystery and fragility; and despite the difference in their backgrounds and cultures, he knew that he was deeply in love with the slender girl.

Fortunately for him, Lily was as taken with Will as he was with her. They saw each other daily, and it was the happiest time of Will's life. He cabled Barnum that he had signed Germaine and that he was staying in Paris for another month.

At the end of that month, he proposed to Lily, and she accepted gladly, on the condition that her mother must first approve of the match.

Will had been terribly afraid that the older woman would not give her approval; after all, her family had noble blood in their veins, and Will was every inch a commoner, and unashamed of it. However, his fears were groundless. Lily's mother willingly gave her consent, telling Will that he was a good and a strong man and that she would be proud to have him as a son-in-law.

The wedding was small but beautifully done. The only guests were the Germaines and a few friends of the bride's family. Outsiders, he thought, might not approve. Nor had Will notified his own family. He had wanted to be married quickly and knew that his family would have wanted a huge wedding, with all the usual confusion and fuss. Also, knowing them as he did, he knew that they would not like the idea of his taking a foreign bride. Texas was good enough for them, and they expected it to be good enough for him as well. Thinking of Lily in Texas, among his family, made Will smile ruefully. He would inform them later, when the marriage was a fait accompli.

After the wedding, Will extended his stay in Paris for another month, a month of such happiness that he lived in constant fear that such bliss could not last.

Lily was such a wonderful woman, as sweet and as gentle in spirit as she was in face and body. In his wildest dreams Will could not have imagined such a perfect wife, and every day he thanked God that he had discovered her.

After their month-long honeymoon, Barnum asked Will to return to the United States, where, besides acting as a talent scout for circus attractions, Will helped Barnum manage some of his various enterprises.

However, when Will mentioned his employer's wishes to his wife, Lily confided that she would rather not leave France. She told him that she was with child and was not feeling well enough to travel.

Will, overwhelmed by the knowledge that he was going to be a father, assured her that they would stay in Paris at least until the baby was born. He made an arrangement with Barnum that allowed him to act as his scout in Europe, so that he would not have to be away from Lily during her pregnancy. They rented a small house on the outskirts of Paris and settled down to await the arrival of the baby.

The pregnancy proved difficult for Lily, who was not strong, and Will worried over her health. Still, he loved seeing her body swell with the growth of their child, and the glow that emanated from her delicate face. He could not decide whether he wanted a son or a daughter. It would be fine to have a son to carry on the family name, but it would also be delightful to have a miniature of Lily.

Lily teased him, saying, "Ah, my sweet, but what if we have a girl who looks like you, so large and ruddy? Or a boy like me, all delicate and pale? What would you say then?" And he would laugh and hold her lovingly in his arms and say that nature would never let such a thing happen.

Lily gave birth to their child on a stormy night in December. The doctor had difficulty making his way through the storm and was late in arriving. Will knew that he would never forget the sound of his wife's screams as their son struggled to make his way into the world, nor would he forget the look on Lily's pale face as she looked at him for the last time as her life's blood ran out while the doctor tried vainly to stanch it.

The last thing she said to him was, "Take care of our son for me. I love you, darling Will."

For months it seemed to Will that he had died with her. Nothing moved him. Nothing interested him. Sunk in despair, he sat in the house where they had lived so happily, drinking and staring at the portrait of Lily that had been painted by a famous French painter before Will had met her.

It was his mother-in-law who finally brought him back to life. In no uncertain terms she reminded him that although Lily was gone, his son still lived and needed his care and love.

Slowly, Will emerged from his apathy; and although at first the sight of the child caused him more pain than pleasure, in time he could not resist the appeal of the tiny fingers clutching his, the toothless mouth widened in a winning smile. Will named the child Justin and transferred to him much of his love for Justin's mother.

When Will's strength and will to live returned, he knew it was also time to return to his homeland. Realizing that he could not take the child away from his mother-in-law and that he could not care for the boy himself, he asked her to go to New York with him. Since her whole life was now wrapped up in her grandson, she agreed willingly.

Will settled his small family in New York City, where he purchased a small brownstone that was to be his anchor and Justin's home. It was where Will stayed when he was not traveling. As soon as he had scouted this new act, he would go home to visit with his son, now six years old, a tall, well-built lad, already stamped with the size and strength of his father, and with his mother's fine features and dark hair and eyes. Will always thought it kind of the fates to have given him a son with something of both parents.

Will's family back in Texas still did not know of his marriage or of his son's existence. Will could not bring himself to tell them. It was as if in keeping his son a secret he was protecting him. Will's family were kind and generous people, yet they had the prejudices of their time and class; and he knew that he could not expose Justin to their disapproval. And by now so much time had passed that an explanation would be extremely awkward. It was too late.

Will sighed, shook himself mentally, and reached for the last of his drink. He should not have let his thoughts travel so far in that direction; it only depressed him and sapped his energy.

He noticed that the train was slowing and heard the conductor call out the name of his stop. Will began to feel better immediately as the familiar excitement seized him. In each town, new or familiar, the same thing happened to him: there was always the feeling of excitement, of something or someone waiting to be discovered—the most amazing act or the most unusual human oddity.

It was a crisp, cold night. Will, who had already purchased his ticket from the bold-eyed redhead in the ticket booth, stood outside the theater, smoking his cigar and watching the crowd, which seemed in very good spirits.

He noticed many women and a few children in their teens. At the matinees, he surmised, there would be even more children.

It was certainly true that vaudeville was becoming an

entertainment for the whole family, and as such was growing increasingly popular. Indirectly, this was good for the
circus business, for as vaudeville became more popular it
needed more acts, and naturally the need for more acts
produced more performers, and many of those were suitable for the circus.

The crowd was almost all inside now and Will's cigar
was smoked down. Putting it out, he entered the theater,
which was quite nice inside, he noticed, and took his seat
in the fifth row, where he was close enough to get a good
view of the performers and yet back far enough that he
did not have to look up at the stage. As he settled into his
seat, Will heard music over the chatter of the audience.

To his left and down in front he saw a piano facing the
stage, and a tall, well-shaped woman—if the back view
was a true indication—wearing a deep blue dress, seated
at the piano. Next to her stood a short, elderly man with a
fringe of gray hair, playing a violin.

The music was a cut above what was usually provided in
such small theaters, and for some reason Will was in-
trigued by the figure of the woman at the piano. Perhaps
it was the way she held herself, so straight and proud, yet
not rigid or stiff; in fact, as she played she moved with a
supple grace that was quite delightful to watch.

Then the program started and he focused his attention
on the stage. Will had always loved theater of almost
every kind; and despite his long years of viewing talent,
he had never tired of it or lost his willingness to be
surprised and entertained. Each performance he attended,
whether it was a play, an opera, a variety show, or a
circus, he viewed with an open mind, always hoping for
the best, eager to be entertained. To this day, he still
enjoyed the circus, as many times as he had seen it.

Of course, in theaters such as this one, sometimes the
acts were dreadful, sometimes pitiful, and other times
mediocre; yet, often what he saw was good, and sometimes very good indeed, and it was those times that made
all the other experiences worthwhile.

This night, the act that Will was interested in was listed
on the bill as next to closing, the choice spot on any bill,

but he was in no particular hurry. He was quite content to watch the early acts, rating them in his mind; and while he had some criticisms, for the most part they were fairly good, certainly better than usual for a small house such as this.

First on the bill was a mouth balancer, billed as the Iron-Mouthed Man, who, with the aid of special apparatus and obviously very strong teeth, performed a variety of gymnastics while supporting himself only by the grip of his teeth on the apparatus. He was not bad, although Will thought that he needed a few more tricks in his repertoire before he could move up into the big time.

Next came a male singer of character songs, who specialized in lightning changes. Will thought his material good and his changes excellent, but the man's voice left something to be desired. After the male singer came a trained-pig act, which was quite out of the ordinary for an animal act, and then a mediocre male and female song and dance team.

During the intermission Will took the opportunity to walk down front, hoping to get a better look at the woman playing the piano.

He approached just as she rose from the bench and turned toward him. He was pleasantly surprised to see that she was even more attractive from the front than from the back, and he smiled at her and gave a slight nod.

Prompted by the desire to hear her voice, and not wanting her to escape his presence so quickly, Will said, "I've been enjoying your music, ma'am. You play very well."

The woman's cheeks turned pink, and she gave him another quick glance from her blue eyes before lowering her gaze to her hands. "Thank you, sir," she said in a rather low but very feminine voice. "Now you must excuse me."

Will spoke hurriedly again, to forestall her leaving. "I would like to introduce myself. I am Will Adams, a talent scout for the Barnum and London Circus. I'm here to scout one of your acts. Can you tell me where I might find the manager of this establishment?"

Her face broke into a sudden smile, and he caught his breath. When she smiled her face lit up and she projected a luminous beauty that transcended mere physical appearance.

"I'm pleased to meet you, Mr. Adams, even though your purpose here appears to be to deprive us of one of our acts. But then I suppose we should be flattered by that, since it must show that we have an eye for talent. I am Mrs. Orlando. My husband and I manage the theater."

Will gave an inward sigh of relief, while at the same time feeling a stab of disappointment. Since she was the wife of the manager, and Will was a scout for talent, they *were* in the same business, and thus there was nothing untoward in his being so bold as to speak to her without an introduction. The disappointment was due to the fact that she was married. He had noticed the ring on the third finger of her left hand, but he knew that single women often wore such rings to discourage unwanted male attention, especially when they were in vulnerable positions.

"I should like to meet your husband, Mrs. Orlando, if that's possible," Will said, not altogether truthfully. He really had nothing to discuss with the theater manager; however, such a meeting might be construed as a friendly gesture between professionals in the same field, and it might give Will the opportunity to talk further with this lovely woman.

"I think that might be arranged," Mrs. Orlando said. "There won't be time during the intermission, but if you'd care to stay after the performance . . ."

"That will be fine. If the Montinis are as good as the word we had about them, I'll want to speak with them after the show anyway."

The Montinis *were* as good as reported; and when the last act was over and the audience began to leave the theater, Will made his way backstage to meet them.

After a good bit of confusion—only the youngest Montini had more than a few words of English—the elder Montini, who was the leader of the troupe, finally understood what

Will was offering. With a great many smiles and gestures, the Montinis agreed to join the Barnum and London Circus in the spring, and Will was given the name of the Montinis' manager so that a contract could be drawn up.

As Will was concluding his conversation with the acrobats, he noticed Mrs. Orlando with a tall, good-looking man, whom he assumed was her husband.

When Will was finished with the Montinis, Mrs. Orlando led the man over. "Mr. Adams, this is my husband, Nickolas Orlando. Nick, this is Mr. Will Adams."

Nick Orlando held out his hand, and Will took it. "How do you do, Mr. Adams. I'm pleased to meet you. My wife tells me that you're a talent scout for the Barnum and London Circus and are here to look at the Montinis."

Will nodded. "Yes, that's right. We had a report that they were extraordinary, and I'm happy to say that I heartily agree. I've just offered them a contract for the coming season."

Orlando smiled, showing square, white teeth. "Well, I guess we'll have to make the most of them this winter, then."

Will returned the smile. "It's kind of you to meet with me, considering that I'm here to steal one of your acts."

Orlando shrugged. "Well, there are always the winters, when the circus is shut down, and I wouldn't stand in the way of any group who has a chance to better themselves. Besides, we have to keep the acts turning over, to satisfy our customers. We're not like the circus, moving to a new town every few days. And being a small house, we can't expect to attract the really big acts. All we can hope for is to get the good acts on the way up."

Will nodded. "Or on the way down. How long have you been managing this theater?"

"Just a little over a year. It was in terrible shape when we took it over, but now we're doing pretty well, everything considered."

Orlando was smiling again. He smiled a bit too easily, and too often, Will thought.

"I say, Adams, would you like to stay and have a bite of supper with us as soon as Laura totes up the receipts?" Orlando asked. "Laura always arranges a cold collation for us after the show, and I would enjoy talking with someone who is in the business, so to speak. I've worked with circuses and carnivals in the past, and I'm sure that both Laura and I would enjoy hearing about what's going on in the circus world."

Will hesitated for a long moment before answering. He very much wanted to see more of Laura Orlando, and the husband seemed a pleasant enough chap, even if there was something about the man that bothered him. Besides smiling too readily, it seemed to Will that Orlando was a bit too friendly and was somewhat facile with words.

Of course, it could simply be that Will was jealous because the man had such an attractive wife. But, whatever the reasons for his reservations about Orlando, it would not do any harm to have supper and some conversation with the attractive couple.

"I would enjoy that," he said. "It's not often I get a home-cooked meal."

"Well, it's just a light repast, as I said, but there is some nice cold roast beef, some of Laura's good bread, and a fair bottle of wine."

"And I made a lovely trifle just this afternoon," Laura added.

Will made what he hoped was a gallant bow. "That certainly settles it, if I had any doubts."

"Capital, capital!" Orlando said effusively. "Now, why don't you and I have a drink while Laura balances the receipts. It won't take her long. She's very quick with figures."

"Thank you. That would go down very well. It's a cold night." As Laura left them, Will added, "So your wife does your books, does she?"

Orlando nodded. "Yes. Luckily, she has a good head for figures. I usually help her with the counting, but I'll be the first to admit that mathematics is not my strong suit. Her talent at figures serves us well, saving the amount that a bookkeeper would cost."

"She seems an ideal woman, your wife," Will said, watching Orlando's face closely for his reaction.

"Oh, she is that," Orlando said, grinning. "She's absolutely the perfect woman. Or close to it. That's why I married her."

Will gave a mental shrug. That seemed to end his vague hope that there was trouble in the marriage.

And what would you do, Will asked himself, *if there was? Were you really entertaining the thought of attempting to seduce a married woman? You should be ashamed of yourself!*

And yet he was not. Chastise himself as he might, he could not erase the mental image of Laura Orlando in his arms. A most disturbing image indeed!

The Orlando apartment, which was above the theater, was clean, neat, and attractive; and the cold collation was delicious and pleasantly served.

During the meal, despite his remark that he wanted to hear about the world of the circus, Orlando did most of the talking. Will had to exert a very conscious effort to keep from looking continually at Laura; and when he did risk a glance, he found her strangely reluctant to meet his eyes. Was it possible that she was fighting the same attraction that he felt? Surely it was not simply the fact that he was a stranger that made her flush so, when their glances did cross.

Will thought that he had Orlando categorized now—he was one of those charming, glib people, all good humor and winning ways, but with little substance underneath. Will had met many of his type in the world of entertainment, and many of them had been con men and drifters. He suddenly found himself wondering just how long the Orlandos had been married. Usually, Orlando's type of man was not the sort to cling to home and hearth. If they had been married only a short time, it was likely that Laura was in for a cruel surprise when the novelty of matrimony wore off for her husband.

Of course, Will thought, it was none of his business; yet

he hated to think of this lovely, radiant young woman left bereft and disillusioned.

He smiled over at her. "You certainly have fixed this flat up nicely. Have you two been married long?"

Laura looked a bit flustered; it was Orlando who replied, "Just a little over a year."

Will experienced a feeling of sadness. He hoped that he was wrong about Orlando, but, as a practiced student of human nature, he was afraid he was not.

Just before he left their quarters he excused himself to use the commode; and while he was in the small room set apart for this function, he gave way to a sudden impulse. Taking out one of his business cards, he wrote on the back of it: "If you should ever need me, you may contact me at the address on the reverse side of this card."

He was not certain why he did it or what he really meant by it; he knew only that he felt a compulsion to forge a link of some sort between himself and Laura.

As he left, he presented one of his cards to each of the Orlandos, making sure that Laura received the one with the message on the back.

It was no doubt a foolish thing to have done, and Will had no idea of what he had hoped to accomplish by doing it, yet he felt in some way the better for it. As he walked down the narrow staircase and opened the street door to the snow and the cold, he thought, *You're a strange piece of work, Will Adams. A strange piece of work!*

He strode along the street, oblivious to the cold, whistling softly to himself.

Chapter Nine

*T*HERE was a sparrow sitting on the windowsill, looking in through the open window at the small kitchen table where Laura liked to have her breakfast.

Smiling, Laura broke off a bit of her breakfast roll and slowly dropped the crumbs in front of the bold little bird, who gobbled them up greedily.

Spring had not quite arrived; but a less than frigid breeze stirred the curtains and caressed Laura's face. It was still fairly cool outside; and after living cooped up most of the winter in the tightly closed rooms, she felt the need of fresh air and sunlight, however pale it might still be. It had been a hard winter for Laura, because of both the severity of the weather and her growing disenchantment with Nick.

It had all started, of course, when she had tried to get him to fire Harriet, and from there it had gotten steadily worse.

More and more often Nick left her alone to manage the theater while he attended to what he referred to as "important other business"; and refused to tell her just what this other business was. Whatever it was, he returned home late almost every night, always showing the effects of liquor. On more than one occasion, angry and hurt, she had put extra blankets on the sofa in the parlor and locked the bedroom door against him.

She had expected that he would be furious at this, but,

queerly enough, on those nights when he found the bedroom door latched against him he would go quietly to sleep on the sofa.

Somehow, this behavior, this acceptance, disturbed her far more than his anger would have. It seemed such an unnatural attitude. Why didn't he complain?

As the winter wore on he made love to her less and less often, and she became more certain that he was having an affair with Harriet.

But what was she to do about it?

All her beautiful dreams and plans for their future seemed as barren as the winter landscape outside. Where was the cheerful, sensitive man she had married? More often than not, he was withdrawn and moody. Could she have misjudged him that much? Or had he changed?

Despite their personal problems, the theater continued to do very well. They had built a reputation for family entertainment, and since there was not much else in the way of entertainment in the immediate area, they continued to prosper. The only problem with that was the added work for her. Nick barely helped her at all now. In the beginning he had seemed so interested, so full of energy, and he had worked very hard. But now that they were well established, he seemed to be losing interest. Laura could not understand it.

Sighing, she gave the sparrow the last few crumbs of her roll, then left the kitchen. Nick, contrary to his usual habit, had risen early to attend to some business—again this mysterious "business"—and had gone out, saying that he would be back before the matinee.

Laura was feeling restless and uneasy, as if she wanted something but did not know what. It was a feeling she disliked, because she had no idea what she could do to stop it.

Finally, she decided to straighten out the small writing desk that Nick had given her last Christmas. She stored her personal bills and letters there, and the drawers and pigeonholes were getting crowded.

Starting with the top pigeonholes, she began making two piles of the contents—one to keep and one to discard.

The last item from the pigeonhole gave her pause. It was a business card that read, Will Adams: Representative for the Barnum and London Circus. Idly, she turned the card over, and for the first time she noticed the handwritten message on the back: "If you should ever need me, you may contact me at the address on the reverse side of this card."

She remembered him giving her the card, but she had stored it away without noticing the message. Staring at the card now, she felt a strange mixture of feelings. She had met Will Adams only once, but she remembered him very well. Perhaps too well. He was not an easy man to forget.

The card conjured up his image in her mind's eye—a tall, strongly built figure, with crisp, curly, light brown hair, and sharp gray eyes in a craggy, rather imposing face. He projected a feeling of strength and power. She remembered noticing at the time that those gray eyes missed very little. Had he sensed something about her that night that told him she might need his services in the future? But how could that possibly be?

When he had come up to her that night in the theater, he had startled her. There was something about his personality so powerful that it had almost intimidated her.

Laura knew herself to be the kind of person who did not like to assume things; and yet she was certain that he had been attracted to her, and that was partially what had frightened her at the meeting. In that first instant, when their eyes had met, she had felt something between them as strong as a magnetic current and dizzying in its implications. Which was utterly ridiculous, for he was a complete stranger, and she was a married woman!

This attraction, which she was certain he had felt, too, was the reason why she had tried to avoid his gaze all evening. It had all been so strange, so new. Her only real experience with men had been with Nick, and what she had felt for Will Adams was different.

She had been attracted to Nick from the very beginning and had fallen in love with him quickly; but she had never before felt that strange surge of electricity that she had felt when she first looked into Will Adams's eyes. All she had been sure of was that she was feeling something dangerous and exciting and that she must not allow herself to be swayed by it. She was a married woman, and she should not be feeling such an attraction for another man.

Again she read the message on the back of the card; and as she did so she experienced that peculiar, tingly feeling she had felt in Will Adams's presence.

And what a strange message! Why on earth should he think she would ever need his help? It was rather presumptuous of him!

Nonetheless, reading the words brought a musing smile to her lips and a lifting of her spirits. Even if she never saw Will Adams again, it was nice to know that he felt protective of her, that he had offered his help if she should ever need it. It was quite romantic in a way; and God knew she had little enough romance in her life at the present.

It was odd, too, that she felt convinced that his offer of help was genuine. He had the sort of strength that made him seem a natural protector. Carefully she put the card in the "save" pile and filed it back in the pigeonhole.

Despite his promise, Nick had not returned to the theater by matinee time.

Feeling misused and angry, Laura had to open the theater herself, preparing the cashbox and supervising the stagehands. To make matters worse, it took her twenty minutes to locate Harriet, who should have been seeing to the refreshment stand; and when she finally did find her, the girl looked terrible.

Staring at her, Laura realized with some surprise that Harriet's appearance had deteriorated to an alarming degree. Her hair needed a good combing, her eyes had dark circles, like bruises, under them, and she was putting on an unbecoming amount of weight. It was bad enough that the girl was sullen, uncooperative, and mean-spirited; now she was unpleasant in appearance as well. Again resentment gnawed at Laura as she thought how unfair it was that Nick would not discipline the girl.

When Nick still had not returned by the time the matinee was over, Laura began to worry. Had something happened to him? She did not know whether to be concerned or angry; and, feeling a mixture of both emotions, she went into the office and balanced the receipts, finding, as usual, that the cashbox was off.

She was edgy and out of sorts as she left the office to go upstairs. Should she prepare the usual cold supper, or would it be too late by the time Nick deigned to come home?

She was sick and tired of having to do most of the work. It simply was not fair! It was like being back at home with her parents, where she had felt like an unpaid housekeeper. She was supposed to have a great deal more freedom now, and yet, in effect, because of all the work she had to do she had no free time at all.

Angrily she opened the door to the flat and slammed it behind her. Maybe a nice wash would calm her down and make her feel better. Unbuttoning her blouse, she entered the bedroom and stopped short.

The room, which she had left neat and uncluttered, was a shambles. The drawers to the chest were open, the contents spilling out onto the floor; the door to the clothes cupboard stood open, and the lid of the large chest at the foot of the bed was raised.

Feeling her heart begin to pound with apprehension, Laura slowly approached the clothes cupboard. Looking in, she gasped. Nick's clothes were gone!

She whirled about and hurried to the chest of drawers. All of Nick's drawers had been emptied. Further examination revealed that the large theatrical trunk, and a good portion of the other luggage, was gone.

Backing up to the bed, Laura slowly sank down upon it, as the meaning of what she was seeing dawned on her. It was very clear that Nick had gone, and not just for a short trip. He had taken all his things—every last one. Abruptly she jumped up and ran across the room to the little jar on her dresser where she kept the household money.

It was empty.

Then another horrible possibility occurred to her. The bank! Had he emptied their bank account as well?

She glanced across the room to the small ornamental clock beside the bed. It was too late to find out today; she would have to wait until tomorrow morning.

Laura spent a sleepless night, tossing and turning in the double bed, her mind a melange of images and memories, all going around in circles, one thought leading to another, and then back to the beginning. And of course Nick did not come home; she no longer expected him.

In the morning, pale and tired, she had only coffee for breakfast and waited anxiously for the time when the bank would open. She was first in line at the teller's window; and when she asked to see the balance of the Orlando account, which was in both their names, the young man in the teller's cage went cheerfully to check the records for her.

But when he looked at the records, his expression showed sudden surprise, and she realized that her worst fears were true.

He looked up soberly. "I'm sorry, Mrs. Orlando, but it seems that Mr. Orlando closed out this account yesterday." His look asked the question that he was too polite to voice.

Laura sagged against the counter. Nick had taken all of their money, except for what she had in her purse!

And then another thought struck her. "What about our commercial account, the one for the Melodeon?"

Looking worried now, the teller went to check the account; when he returned his face was expressionless. "I'm afraid that he closed that account, also. Is there anything else, Mrs. Orlando?"

Laura shook her head and said dully, "No, thank you. Nothing else."

As she left the bank, trying to hold her head up as if nothing were the matter, as if the world had not just collapsed around her, Laura felt a tide of despair sweeping over her.

The theater account had held all the receipts for the

past week. Out of it, all the theater expenses were supposed to be paid, including the wages of the staff and
the performers and the percentage that was paid weekly
to Alfred Hayes. The only money left now was what she
had taken in yesterday afternoon and last night, not nearly
enough to keep the theater open for the next week. What
was she going to do?

When she got back to the theater, feeling shaken and
disoriented, the first person she saw was Harriet Hayes,
waiting for her just inside the lobby.

She had no desire to speak to Harriet and tried to
pretend that she did not see her, but Harriet walked up to
her and plucked at her sleeve.

Laura still refused to meet the girl's gaze. "Yes, Harriet, what do you want?"

"I want to see Nick. Where is he?" The girl's voice was
strident with some deep emotion that Laura could not
identify.

"Mr. Orlando is away on business," Laura said immediately. She could not bear the thought of this arrogant girl
knowing that her husband had left her.

She tried to pull away, but Harriet obstinately maintained a firm hold on her sleeve. "He didn't say anything
to me about going away!"

The girl's remark pierced through Laura's cocoon of
weariness and despair. She spun about angrily. "And why
should he have told *you*? You're just one of the hired
help. Hardly important enough to be let in on his plans."

Harriet's pale face flared with ugly spots of red. "I'm
important to him. Important enough to have his baby!"

"What?" Laura said stupidly. Surely she had not heard
correctly! "What did you say?"

Harriet's voice rose in shrill triumph. "I said that I'm
important enough to him that I'm carrying his child! What
do you think this is?" She patted her rounded belly. "Did
you think that I was just getting fat?"

Laura stared at her in horror. "You're going to have
Nick's baby?"

"That's what I said. And that's why I have to talk
to him. I can't wait any longer. My family is beginning

to get suspicious. Nick promised me that he would leave you and marry me, and it has to be *now*. I told him that if he didn't do something soon, I was going to tell you myself. So now you know, and *I* want to know where he is!"

For a moment Laura feared that she would faint. She had thought she had taken all she could, that she had hit the bottom of despair, and now this. This awful child, this girl, was going to have Nick's baby—the baby that she, Laura, had so desperately wanted! And now Nick was gone. He had left Harriet, too. In fact, she thought suddenly, that must be the reason he had left, or certainly the main one.

If Laura had not hated Harriet so much, she would have felt pity for her; but at this moment she was too stunned to feel anything other than a dull pain. "Mr. Orlando is gone," she said slowly. "He left sometime yesterday."

"Well, you just said that," Harriet said tartly. "I want to know when he's coming back."

Laura said dully, "There's something you might as well know, Harriet. He's not coming back. He took all of his things."

Harriet's face blanched, and she clenched her fists. "I don't believe you! You're lying! But it won't do you any good. It's me he loves, and you might as well face that fact."

Laura shook her head wearily. "I'm not lying. He's gone, and not only that, he took all of our money, the theater money as well."

She turned away and started toward the stairs, her footsteps dragging, leaving Harriet staring after her.

Halfway up the stairs, she heard the sound of pounding feet as Harriet charged up behind her. "I don't believe you! I want to see your flat."

Drearily, Laura nodded. She no longer cared. All she wanted now was for the other woman to leave her alone so that she could have a good cry, a cup of tea, and then perhaps she could sleep, and forget for a while what had happened. Later, when she was rested, and after some of the pain had dulled, she would think of what she was going to do.

When she opened the door to the flat, Harriet rushed in past her, heading directly for the bedroom.

It seemed a sacrilege for Harriet to invade their bedroom, hers and Nick's. Yet it hardly mattered now.

Moving like an automaton, Laura went into the kitchen and put on the kettle. Only then did she follow Harriet into the bedroom, where she found the girl standing immobile in the center of the room, looking dazed and disbelieving.

"It's true, isn't it?" Harriet whispered, looking at Laura with wild eyes. "He's gone, Nick's gone! What am I going to do?"

Laura shook her head with a weary sigh. "I can't help you, Harriet, and even if I could, I wouldn't. You're going to have to solve your own problem, just as I'm going to have to solve mine."

"I'm sorry," Alfred Hayes said. He looked embarrassed but resolved. "After all that has happened, I'm afraid that I'll have to put someone else in charge of the theater."

Laura, her hands clasped tensely in her lap, leaned forward. "But *I* can manage the theater, Mr. Hayes. Lately Nick has been interested in other things anyway, and I have been doing most of the work. I've always done the books, and I'm certain that I could hire the performers. It would only take me a short time to pay back what Nick took."

Hayes cleared his throat and fingered his cravat. "You're probably right, Mrs. Orlando, and I know this places you in an awkward position, but I don't really think it suitable for a woman to manage the theater. And truthfully, you would always be an unpleasant reminder of Nick's perfidy, and of, er, the unfortunate matter of my niece.

"You can stay on until the end of the month. That will give you three weeks to make other arrangements. That's the best I can do. By the way, I'll be sending you another ticket seller, another niece of mine. Now that Nick is gone, I assume that it's safe to do so. And if it's any consolation, I am sorry, really I am. You're a fine, hardworking woman, and you deserve better, but I have to think of my own interests. Goodbye, Mrs. Orlando."

He doffed his hat, gave a stiff little bow, and left quickly. Laura watched him go, feeling that her last hope was disappearing with him.

Feeling suddenly much older than her years, she got up from behind the battered office desk and went upstairs to the flat. It was after the evening show, and the building was empty.

She knew that she must pull herself together, that she must fight off this terrible lethargy that was sapping her will and her strength. She would need all her intelligence, all her will, to reorganize her life; but somehow she could not throw off the feeling of despair that pulled at her body like quicksand. All she wanted to do was sleep. . . . No, what she *really* wanted was to sleep and then awaken to find that the last two days had been only a bad dream.

As she lit the gaslights in the flat, Laura looked around her. The silence seemed almost a physical presence. It was eerie. She had been alone in the building often enough before; but before, she had always known that Nick was coming back, eventually. The fact that he was not, this time, made the loneliness frightening.

Sighing, she walked to her desk. She might as well see what the total of her household bills was. She would still be receiving her salary for the next three weeks, but out of it she would have to pay the gas and water bills and buy food. Of course, she would no longer receive a percentage of the take, as that would be going to Alfred Hayes to help pay back what Nick had stolen.

Stolen! What an ugly word. How *could* he have done it?

Opening the desk, her gaze was immediately drawn to the top left pigeonhole, and she thought of Will Adams's card.

When she had last looked at it she had been certain that he meant what he had written on the back. Now she wondered if she was right about that. Did he really expect her to call upon him if she needed someone?

Riffling through the pigeonhole, she found the card and

again read the bold handwriting on the back: "If you should ever need me, you may contact me at the address on the reverse side of this card."

She turned the card over. Under William Adams, Representative for the Barnum and London Circus, was a post-office-box number in New York City.

Staring at the address, she felt a wave of indecision. Should she? *Could* she? She felt that it would be very forward, very bold; yet, perhaps that was what was needed at this crucial moment. *If I were a man*, she thought, *I wouldn't hesitate for an instant*. Well, she would sleep on it. To the devil with the bills; she would work on them in the morning. Now she needed the blessed oblivion of sleep.

When Laura first awakened, still drowsy with sleep, she reached across the bed for Nick. When her hand encountered the empty bed, she awakened fully and lay there waiting for the now-familiar feeling of despair to wash over her.

She lay there for some time, her eyes closed, feeling bleak and unhappy but not experiencing the complete depression she had felt for the past two days. Her mind was clear, and she realized that some of her energy had returned. *I'm going to live*, she thought wryly; *and so I'd better set about the business of how I'm going to take care of myself*.

Getting out of bed, she put on a robe and prepared herself a hearty breakfast. There was no sense in starving herself as she had been doing. She was going to need all her strength in the weeks to come.

She took a pad and pencil to the table with her, and as she ate she made a list of the possibilities that were open to her. Next to each possibility she penciled in the pros and cons. She could look for a position as pianist with another vaudeville or variety house, or with an orchestra; but such positions seldom paid much, and there was no chance of advancement. In such a position she could never better herself.

She could advertise for piano students and teach, but

getting enough students to support herself would take
time, and she did not have enough money to take care of
herself until such time as she was established.

She looked at what she had written. Such a terribly
short list! Were those the *only* things she could do?

No, there was her accounting ability. At the Melodeon
she had handled all the bookkeeping. Perhaps she could
find a job somewhere keeping books. In such a position
she would perhaps have a chance, however small, of bet-
tering herself. There was the matter of her sex, of course.
No doubt many employers would react as had Alfred
Hayes: they would prefer a man.

Again she thought of Will Adams. Could he help her in
this respect? He knew many theater operators, not to
mention circus and carnival operators. He might know of
someone who needed a good bookkeeper, someone already familiar with the entertainment business. Perhaps it
was even possible that there was an opening with the
Barnum and London Circus; they must employ several
people to handle their accounting chores, including the
payroll. Of course, working for a traveling show would
mean being on the road again, as she had been with the
Chautauqua; but after what happened here, perhaps that
would not be such a bad thing. Also, since all her experience
had been in the theatrical field, such an enterprise should
be more likely to look upon her with favor, despite the
fact that she was a woman.

A sudden thrill of hope surged through her. It was only
a chance, of course, but now was the time to take chances.
What did she have to lose? What was the worst thing that
could happen if she wrote to Will Adams? He might not
answer. He might answer and refuse to help her. Or he
might answer and offer to help her, but with an ulterior
motive in mind. Well, she believed she could handle all
three possibilities. This was no time to stand on her pride.
Will had made an offer of help, and she would proceed as
if it was genuine. If it was not, she would deal with that
when the time came.

Another alternative suddenly occurred to her—she could
write to her father, begging his forgiveness and pleading

to be allowed to come back home. She dismissed that solution without further consideration. No matter what happened, she would not return home. Whatever happened, it could not be worse than the humiliation she would suffer at his hands.

Returning to her desk, she took out a sheet of her best notepaper and her good pen and began to write to Will Adams.

Chapter Ten

WILL Adams sighed as he looked at the stack of mail he had just removed from his post-office box.

He had been on the road for the past three weeks, and it was amazing how much mail could accumulate in that short space of time. He would put it into his case and take it to his hotel room, where he could go over it at his leisure. He knew from experience what he could expect— several letters from people who had acts that they thought he should see; a number of bills; and a few letters from friends and family.

But once in his hotel room, a cigar in one hand, a glass of bourbon in the other, the top envelope in the stack of mail caught his eye at once. Picking it up, he read the return address: Mrs. Nickolas Orlando. Tense with sudden excitement, he ripped open the envelope.

When he had given Laura Orlando his card, with the message on it, Will had hoped that she might contact him, but he had no real expectation that she would. Now the sight of her name on the envelope caused him to remember how he had felt as a young boy suffering the pangs of first love.

Somewhat embarrassed by his feelings, he nonetheless could not stop himself from unseemly haste as he pulled the folded sheet of notepaper from the envelope and spread it out on the hotel bed to read:

Dear Mr. Adams:

When last we met, you were kind enough to offer me your help if ever I should need it.

At the time of our meeting, I did not believe that I should ever avail myself of your generous offer, but at present I find myself in a difficult and uncomfortable situation, and there is no one else to whom I can turn for help.

Due to unusual circumstances, I must leave the Melodeon by March 31. Before that date, I must find a position, preferrably one in the field of bookkeeping.

My hope is that since you know many people who run theatrical enterprises, you might know of someone who has need of such services. I have kept all the books for the Melodeon for the past year. In addition, for the past several months I have performed many of the duties of theater manager.

If you should know of anyone who could use my services, I would greatly appreciate your letting me know as soon as possible, as time is of the essence.

I will be very grateful for any help you can give me.

Sincerely,
Mrs. Nickolas Orlando (Laura)

Perusing the letter again, Will tried to read between the lines. The only personal touch in it was her given name, in brackets, after her formal signature, but it was odd how that one word warmed his heart.

"Due to unusual circumstances." That could mean any number of things: that her husband was ill; that he had died; that he had been fired by the owner of the theater; or that he had left her—which would not be out of character for the kind of man that Will believed Orlando to be. At any rate, something unusual had happened, and the fact that she had said, *"I* have to leave," and not *"we,"*

seemed to indicate that Nick Orlando was no longer a part of her life.

Will was surprised at how delighted he felt at this possibility. If something had indeed happened to Orlando, or if he had deserted Laura, she must be in desperate circumstances. It was not something to rejoice over!

Lord, but she was an amazing woman! She was not asking for money. She was not asking for charity, but for a job. It was not the kind of help that he imagined giving her. His daydream had been more on the order of her fleeing her husband to find comfort, solace, and shelter in his, Will's, arms. The details had never been filled in. When he had given her the card, his intentions had been sincere but very vague. Yet, he really had wanted to help her, to do something for her. Like a knight of old, he had wanted to slay a dragon for her.

Smiling at his own fancy, Will shook his head. And what did she ask him for? A job! Strangely enough, he might be able to help her in that regard. The Barnum and London Circus just happened to be looking for additional help in their accounting office, and Will, who had known P. T. Barnum for a number of years, was fairly confident that the old man would honor his recommendation, even though Laura was a woman. Barnum, despite his flamboyance and the fact that he often appeared to be opinionated, was amazingly open-minded about many things.

And what do you expect Laura to do in repayment for the favor, he asked himself, *throw herself into your arms?*

Well, hardly that, but it would be nice. He laughed at himself. First things first.

He looked at the date on the letter. Today was March 29, and the letter was dated the 8th. What must she be thinking? That he was not going to answer? That his offer had not been sincere? He must go to her at once.

After all, she was only across the Hudson. *If* she was still there!

During the three weeks since Alfred Hayes had issued his ultimatum, Laura had been frantically busy. Not only did she have to manage the business of the theater, she had to seek a position for herself. She could not just wait, hoping that Will Adams would solve her problem.

Although she examined each day's post anxiously, there was no reply to her letter to him. And although she kept telling herself that it was very possible that he was traveling and would not receive her letter in time to reply to it, she could not suppress a feeling of disappointment, which was foolish, of course. The chances of his answering her letter had always been poor; Laura was fully aware of that.

So, each morning, she purchased a newspaper from the boy on the corner and read the advertisements as she ate her breakfast. So far there had been few positions offered for women for which she felt qualified to apply; and when she answered those ads she felt were in her purview, she found dozens of other young women waiting for interviews, or she found the position already filled.

If there were too many other applicants waiting, she had to leave, since she had to be back at the theater by one o'clock to get things ready for the matinee.

As her deadline for leaving the Melodeon approached, Laura began to feel the specter of panic nipping at her heels. It was only with the greatest effort that she retained her emotional balance, knowing that if she ever succumbed to panic she would be out of control and unable to help herself.

And then, just three days before she was to leave, she answered an advertisement for a pianist to play practice music at a ballet school. It was not what she had wanted or hoped for, and it would not pay much, but at least it would keep body and soul together until she could find a position that offered something better.

Laura had felt so discouraged that morning that she had almost not gone to apply for the job. What was the use? she thought. There would be many other applicants, or the position would be filled. Yet, she had dressed herself carefully and gone to the address in the advertisement, and found, to her surprise, that there were only four other women there before her. Listening to each of them as they played for the ballet mistress, Laura realized that none of them played as well as she did. To her further surprise and relief, she was offered the job, and she accepted. She was to start the following Monday.

Sunday was March 31, the day she had to be out of the flat.

On Wednesday morning she went looking for a room, and on Thursday she found one—small, and sparsely furnished, but inexpensive and not too uncomfortable. By Friday she was packed and ready to leave. She intended to move out after the post came on Saturday.

In a strange way, she now felt quite calm. She had lost her husband, her living quarters, and a position that she had enjoyed; and yet she received a certain satisfaction from knowing that she had coped with the situation and had not been defeated by circumstances not of her own making. She had achieved, by her own efforts, a place to live and a job. It was not much, but, by heaven, she had done it herself, and that fact gave her renewed confidence.

When the post came on Saturday there was still no letter from Will Adams, and she was surprised at the disappointment she felt. Annoyed with herself, she picked up the one piece of mail that the postman had brought her, a letter from Constance Dowes.

As she settled down to read the letter, Laura looked around the sparkling clean flat. All the personal traces of her and Nick's habitation had either been removed or packed, and the rooms were now much as she and Nick had found them on that first day when they had arrived at the Melodeon.

Thinking back to that day and of how happy she had been, Laura felt tears begin to burn behind her closed eyelids. How she had been looking forward to her new life! How certain she had been that things were finally going well for them, that nothing but hard work stood between her and Nick, and success and happiness. Now, only a year and a few months later, it was all shattered, all gone. Nick, whom she had thought a kind, loving, charming man, whom she had believed loved her, had betrayed her. She knew now that Nick's charm and personality were a facade only, hiding his fatal weakness. She should have seen him for what he was; but she had been so eager to believe what he seemed to be, and so desperate to get away from her family, that she had been a willing victim. She had learned a valuable but painful lesson, and she supposed she should be grateful for that. If nothing else, it would make her wary of trusting a man again so readily.

This caused her to think of Constance, who had gone through much the same thing, and she felt suddenly close to the other woman. Constance had tried, obliquely, to warn her, but Laura had been too enamored and too naïve to notice. She would never be that naïve again. *I've eaten of the apple,* she thought rather melodramatically, and tried to smile through the tears that began to fill her eyes. Then suddenly, for the first time since Nick had left, she was crying uncontrollably, in great, racking sobs that shook her whole body. She could feel her eyes and the membranes in her nose and throat swelling, and still she wept, until the tears were gone and all she could do was gasp and shudder.

When the storm subsided, despite her swollen and tear-stained face, she felt better. Some awful pressure was now gone. Perhaps she had needed to weep, to let out all the anger, all the feelings she had been keeping bottled up inside.

Feeling much calmer, she went into the bedroom and bathed her face in water from the pitcher, drying her skin with her handkerchief and tidying up behind herself. It was important to her that the apartment be left in even better condition than that in which she had found it.

She was back in the parlor and was reading Constance's newsy letter when she heard the bell ring.

Putting down the letter, she started for the door, wondering who her caller could be. Not Alfred Hayes, she felt certain. He had told her that he would be arriving on Sunday with the new manager. Perhaps it was Maude, his other niece, who was the new ticket seller. She was a thin, plain girl—just the opposite of Harriet—who worked hard but was not very bright; she had been pestering Laura with stupid questions ever since her arrival.

Straightening her hair and hoping that her face was halfway presentable after the spell of weeping, Laura opened the door. There stood a tall figure; and she looked up into the face of the man she had only seen once but had never forgotten—Will Adams, with his hat in his hand.

His unexpected appearance so startled her that for a moment all she could do was stare up at him; then, realizing that she was gaping like a fool, she found her voice. "Mr. Adams! I'm sorry, you caught me unawares."

He smiled apologetically. "Yes, I can imagine that I did." His eyes seemed to be searching her face, and she wondered if it still bore the ravages of her storm of tears. Self-consciously, she turned half-away, and then was stopped by his voice: "May I come in?"

She stepped back from the door, feeling gauche and awkward. "Of course. I didn't mean to keep you standing out there."

He followed her into the parlor, seeming not to notice her embarrassment. "I just received your letter yesterday. I've been out of town, you see. And since it stated that you would be leaving on the thirty-first, I thought it best to come around in person. I hope you don't mind."

She turned and motioned to the couch. "Of course I don't mind. Please, Mr. Adams, have a seat. I'm sorry that I cannot offer you any refreshment, but everything has been packed."

"No refreshments are necessary," he said, looking at her closely, as he seated himself on the divan while she took the armchair opposite.

"Mrs. Orlando, I'll come right to the point of my visit. As I said, I just received your letter when I returned from my travels, and I did not want you to think that I hadn't answered out of any lack of desire to do so."

Laura shrugged. Now that he was here, in person, in reply to her request, she felt extremely awkward about having sent the letter.

"I realized that you might not get it right away," she said as steadily as she could. She felt nervous and ill-at-ease under his direct gaze. "And in the meantime, since I wrote it, I have managed to find employment, but I do want to thank you for coming. It was most kind of you."

He leaned forward, putting his hands upon his knees;

and even though he was still several feet away from her, Laura felt almost as if he were touching her.

"Would you think it bold of me if I asked you of the circumstances that led you to the necessity of leaving your home and your work here? Has something happened to your husband?"

Suddenly feeling cold, Laura dropped her gaze to her lap. His request was couched in polite terms, and his voice was kind, yet she simply could not bring herself to confide in him the fact of Nick's abandonment. Tears were again coming to her eyes, and she shook her head almost angrily. "I'm sorry, Mr. Adams, truly I am. Under the circumstances, you have every right to ask, and I would tell you, except that it is very personal, and quite painful. Perhaps at a later time . . ."

She managed to look up and meet his eyes, and saw his sympathy there. For a mad moment she almost wished that he would pull her into his arms and kiss away her pain. She could imagine how it would be to cuddle against his broad chest, to feel his lips on hers and his strong arms around her, to surrender, to let him take care of her. But the moment finally passed, and she managed to get herself under control.

He reached out toward her, as if to touch her, then quickly pulled back his hand. "I apologize. My question distressed you, I can see that. But may I ask this: What kind of a position have you secured?"

Coloring slightly, she said, "I have taken a position as pianist for the Koschinsky School of Ballet. I start on Monday next. It's not precisely what I had hoped for, but it will do until I can find something better suited."

At least, she thought, *he will know that I have not been just sitting around waiting for his reply; he will realize that I am capable of taking care of myself.*

He leaned toward her again. "It would appear that you have taken care of things quite well without my help. However, I must tell you that I have come here today with an offer that perhaps will be more to your advantage. It is quite a coincidence really, but just the day before I returned to New York and found your letter, P. T. Barnum had apprised me of the fact that he was looking for a bookkeeper to be added to the office staff that travels with the circus. When I read your letter, it was as if fate had come knocking at my door."

Laura, attempting to suppress her sudden excitement, stared down at her clasped hands. What should she do? A job with the Barnum and London Circus would be a wonderful opportunity, but she had already committed herself to Madame Koschinsky. Also, there was no guarantee that she could obtain the position with Mr. Barnum. Perhaps he, like Alfred Hayes, was prejudiced against working women.

"But would he employ me?" she asked slowly. "Would I really have a chance at the job?"

Will smiled reassuringly. "Yes, I think I can safely promise you that he would. P.T. and I have known each other for some time, and we are on good terms. He has always valued my opinions, my recommendations, and I would be happy to put in a good word for you. When I was here last, I was told how well you kept the books for the theater. I know you are fully capable."

"But I have already committed myself to the position with Madame Koschinsky," she said with a sigh. "If I should apply for this one with Mr. Barnum, and if I should *not* get it, I would be without either position."

"But that's the beauty of it. I told you it was a great coincidence. P.T. is going to be in New York for several days preceding the Easter weekend, arranging for the reception for Jumbo, the huge elephant that he has purchased from the London Zoological Gardens. Perhaps you've been reading about it in the newspapers?"

Laura shook her head. "I'm afraid not. For the past few weeks my reading has been mostly confined to studying the positions-offered columns."

"Well, P.T. has arranged for a huge parade on Easter Sunday to welcome the animal; but, as I said, he will come in several days before to take care of the final arrangements. He will be staying at the Fifth Avenue Hotel, and I can arrange for you to meet with him at your convenience. If he offers you the job, and I'm convinced that he will, you won't have to go to work for several weeks, which means that you can go ahead and report for duty to the Koschinsky

School of Ballet on Monday. If you get the job with the
circus, you will have plenty of time to give your notice.
If you don't get it, you will still have your job with the
ballet." He gave a shrug. "What do you have to lose?"

Laura felt a rising excitement. Was it possible? Might
she really hope? He had said that she had nothing to lose,
and that seemed to be true. Should she miss such a
chance simply because she was hesitant and unsure? It
would be ridiculous to do so!

Slowly she looked up into Will Adams's eyes. His gaze
was remarkably straightforward; but so had Nick's been,
and look what he had done to her. Was Will Adams the
same kind of man as Nick? They seemed to have some
characteristics in common, such as a love of travel and an
unwillingness to settle down. Could she trust this man? She
knew that he desired her—she had recognized that the first
time they met. Was this just a ploy to put her in his debt?

She found herself shaking her head to clear away the
confusing thoughts, and saw his expression change to one
of dismay and disappointment.

For some reason, this reassured her more than any words
could have, and for the first time since he had arrived,
she smiled. "No, Mr. Adams, I wasn't shaking my head in
the negative. It was just to clear my thoughts. As you say,
I have nothing to lose, and perhaps a great deal to gain. I
should be very pleased to accept your generous offer."

Will Adams got quickly to his feet—he moved very
lightly for such a large man—and reached his hand toward
her, to help her up from the chair.

At his touch, a current, as hot as scalding water, ran
through her hand, her arm, and down her body, causing
her to tremble. She had agreed that she had nothing to
lose, but now she wondered, belatedly, if she was right.

She felt something dangerous in this strong, self-assured
man. Yet, to be honest, perhaps what she was afraid of
was in herself. No matter, she *must* seize this chance. It
was as if for the past few weeks she had been living in a
small, dark room, then a narrow door had opened, offering a cheerless vista, through which she had been about to
go. Now a large door was swung wide, opening into an
attractive if unfamiliar world. She must go through it!

Chapter Eleven

IT was Easter Sunday, and Broadway was packed with humanity. It looked as if every man, woman, and child in New York had come out to see Jumbo on his triumphant journey from the ship to Madison Square Garden, where the circus was performing.

Laura, feeling lighthearted and eager as a child, stood next to Will Adams and attempted to peer around the hat of the large lady standing in front of her.

She had seen the huge elephant earlier, when Will had taken her to the dock to see the great beast unloaded from the British freighter *Assyrian Monarch;* but Will had insisted that she should also see the parade.

"You've got to see how P.T. does things," he said, laughing. "He really knows how to put on a show."

And what a show it was! The parade that accompanied Jumbo on his ride from the ship to Madison Square Garden was like nothing Laura had ever seen or expected to see.

There were chariots that looked as if they were made of solid gold; ornate, glass-walled serpent dens; and tableau cars, some drawn by teams of deer and zebras. Lions and tigers, in barred cages, roared their accompaniment to the music of several brass bands.

Marching in review were hundreds of horses, more than a dozen elephants, and hundreds of costumed circus performers. And over all the other sounds rang the clarion call of the wondrous Orchestmelochor, an ornate steam calliope, the sound of which, Will told her, was reputed to carry for more than five miles. Placing her hands over her ears as the beautifully ornamented contrivance rolled by, Laura could well believe it was true.

The noise and the spectacle reassured her that there was still wonder in the world and made her feel like a child again. In fact, she was filled with such energy and joy that there was no room left for regret or unhappy feelings.

And then a roar went up from the spectators as the huge, iron-banded crate bearing Jumbo came into view. Drawn by sixteen sturdy horses and pushed by two smaller elephants, the great crate moved slowly and majestically down the avenue, as the people murmured in awe and cheered lustily. On the sides of the crate, in bold letters, were the words: MONSTER ELEPHANT, JUMBO!

The crate was solid on three sides, and opened only at the top of one side, so all that could be seen of the great pachyderm was the top of his head and his huge trunk, which waved over the heads of the drivers like a gigantic, thick-bodied reptile, causing great "oohs," and "aahs" to rise from the crowd.

Laughing, Will leaned down to Laura. "You see, P.T. is just letting the crowd see enough of the animal to titillate them. If they want to see the rest of Jumbo, they'll have to pay to do so, and most of them will, of course. P.T.'s a consummate showman."

Laura nodded happily. Right now, she thought, she felt so good that she would agree to almost anything, but in this case agreement was easy.

Her meeting with Barnum, which had taken place two days earlier in his luxurious suite at the Fifth Avenue Hotel, had been one of the most exciting things that had ever happened to her. Even she, with her sheltered upbringing, had heard of Phineas T. Barnum and his wonderful shows. She had read about him in newspapers and magazines, and she had always longed to see the strange and wondrous people and things that he exhibited. In particular, she had always wanted to see the little man,

Tom Thumb, and his tiny bride, Lavinia. When Laura was just a child of ten, she had seen, in a borrowed magazine, an article on the tiny couple and had been fascinated. The article had included a picture of the couple on their wedding day, and Laura had never forgotten how charming the miniature pair looked, just like little dolls standing in front of the preacher—the bride, sweet-faced and graceful in her beautiful white gown and veil; and the groom, plump and cherub-faced, holding her tiny hand in his. Beside them stood an even smaller couple, their attendants, Commodore Nutt, and the bride's sister, Miss Minnie Warren Bump.

Tom Thumb, whose real name was Charles S. Stratton, had been only twenty-five inches tall when Barnum had discovered him; at the time of his wedding he was thirty-five inches tall, and because of easy, rich living, he had swelled up to a plump fifty-two pounds. His pretty bride, Mercy Lavinia Warren Bump, was thirty-two inches tall and weighed twenty-nine pounds.

It had seemed impossible to Laura that human beings could be so small, and she had longed to see them for herself. Of course, Samuel Purcell would have been horrified at the very thought of his daughter attending such a sinful show!

Through the following years Laura had seen other articles about the many wonders Barnum had presented in the past—Jenny Lind, the incomparable singer, called the Swedish Nightingale; Chang and Eng, the bizarre, so-called Siamese Twins; and many, many more. She had never dreamed back then that she would someday meet the famous man who had made so many wonders available to the world. Now, not only had she met him, but she had taken tea with him, sat in his presence, talked with him, and had, finally, been hired by him at a respectable salary, to work for his great circus. She could scarcely bring herself to believe her good fortune.

She was terribly nervous when Will had picked her up at her humble lodgings. He had arranged the meeting for the evening, after her day was finished at Madame

Koschinsky's, so that she would not have to take time off from her work.

Laura had agonized long over what she should wear, and had finally decided that she could only be what she was, and that Mr. Barnum was looking for a bookkeeper, not a fashion doll.

Still, she dressed carefully, in the blue dress she had worn on that first night she had met Will, and took extra pains with her toilette. There would be no harm in being as attractive a bookkeeper as possible; and since she had met Nick, Laura had learned that an attractive and charming woman had a much better chance of getting what she wanted from a man than did a plain woman. She disliked the fact that this was so, for it did not seem fair; however, she had also learned that life was often unfair, and that, since there were certain things that were impossible for her to change, she should take advantage of them, if possible, rather than fight them.

Looking at her reflection in the mirror, she wondered if she was compromising her beliefs in thinking this way; but then she decided that she was only being practical. At any rate, looking as attractive as she could would surely not work *against* her.

Will came to fetch her in a handsome carriage, and she felt both ill-at-ease and excited by his company. He looked very elegant in his dark evening clothes, and his top hat made him appear even taller and more imposing. The look in his eyes when she opened the door to her rooms made her glad that she had taken care with her appearance and gave her a feeling of pride in herself. She took his arm and walked with him to the carriage, tingling with anticipation and pleasure.

When they reached the Fifth Avenue Hotel and Will helped her down onto the sidewalk in front of it, she was terribly impressed and at the same time anxious not to appear ill-at-ease or gauche.

She let him escort her up the steps to the entry doors, holding her head erect and her back straight, and trying not to stare at the doorman in his splendid uniform and the well-dressed men and women coming into and out of the hotel.

Inside, she attempted, simultaneously, to look as if she belonged here while trying to see everything that she could. The lobby was magnificent! How marvelous it must be to be able to stay at a place like this and to feel at home here, she thought.

As she had on that day when Nick had taken her to the Del Monte Hotel in Monterey, she vowed that someday she too would feel perfectly at home in such a place.

When they reached Mr. Barnum's suite she was even more impressed. It was unbelievably large and beautifully appointed, with every kind of luxury and convenience.

The door was answered by a small, slender, youngish man wearing spectacles; his neatly trimmed goatee gave him a professorial air. When he saw Will he smiled somewhat nervously and bobbed his head.

"Mr. Adams. We've been expecting you. Do come in."

Will extended his arm, and Laura took it and stepped self-consciously into the beautiful suite.

When the door was closed behind them, Will turned to the small man. "Mr. Bailey, may I present Mrs. Nickolas Orlando. Mrs. Orlando, this is Mr. James Anthony Bailey, Mr. Barnum's business partner."

Laura made a small curtsy, acutely embarrassed that she had automatically assumed Bailey to be some sort of butler or other servant. On the way over to the hotel, Will had given her a brief rundown on the history of the Barnum and London Circus, making her aware that James Bailey was quite famous in his own right, perhaps the greatest managerial genius and organizer the circus world had ever known. Before joining up with Barnum, Bailey had, with his partner, James F. Cooper, operated Cooper, Bailey and Company's Great International Allied Shows, which had taken over the Great London Circus, and Sanger's Royal British Menagerie, to form the huge circus that had been a close competitor to Barnum's before they had joined forces and become the combined Barnum and London Circus.

"Phineas is still dressing. He asked me to see that you had tea while you waited." Bailey gestured to a large silver tea tray that covered most of the low table in front of the velvet-covered sofa. On the tray were a lovely silver teapot, a water pot, a sugar bowl and creamer, several delicate china cups and saucers, and a lavish assortment of sandwiches and cakes on china plates. To Laura, who had eaten only a light meal in the morning, it looked delicious.

Bailey observed her with a slight smile. "Would you care to pour, Mrs. Orlando?"

Laura, with both men's eyes on her, felt nervous and awkward, but she nodded. "Of course."

Self-consciously she seated herself on the sofa and, praying that she would not drop or spill anything, reached for the huge silver teapot. She had just finished pouring without mishap when a booming voice rang out, "Will! Will Adams! Good to see you."

Laura glanced up to see a large figure in evening clothes. As Phineas Taylor Barnum came toward them, she could not help staring, for, despite his obvious age, he presented an imposing figure.

He was well over six feet tall and was heavily built. When he reached the sofa, Laura gazed up into a pleasant, wrinkled face with shrewd blue eyes and a large, puttylike nose. This rather imposing head was crowned by a fringe of curly gray hair. Her first impression was that he had great personality and power; and when he smiled down at her, she was overwhelmed.

"Ah, this must be Mrs. Orlando, the young woman you told me about, Will. Well, she is certainly the prettiest bookkeeper I've ever seen." His booming laugh echoed in the room, and Laura smiled nervously, flushing under his gaze.

He continued, "Mrs. Orlando, Will here tells me that you're very capable in your field, and he also tells me that I should hire you. What do you think?"

Such a direct question threw Laura off balance, but it seemed to her that Mr. Barnum was the kind of man who appreciated frankness, so she ignored her fears and spoke out. "I agree," she said quietly. "I am very good with figures, and I am accurate and dependable. Since Mr. Adams tells me that you're in need of such services, I think it would be to your advantage to employ me."

Barnum's booming laughter again rang out. "Well, that is certainly direct enough. You have spirit, Mrs. Orlando. And since I have been trusting Will's judgment for some years now, I will do so again.

"Now, where is my tea? I'm famished."

Sitting next to Laura on the sofa, Barnum reached for one of the filled tea cups, then helped himself to a large slice of plum cake. Laura watched in fascination as he ate the cake in a few bites and washed it down with tea.

He then turned toward her, smiling. "You know, I never touch strong drink, not even wine. Haven't for many years. Oh, I used to love my bottle of champagne, or port with my meals, but I finally decided that it was ruining my health and my life. In one afternoon I poured out seventy bottles of excellent champagne onto my lawn."

He chuckled, the sound rumbling up from his not-inconsiderable paunch. "That was certainly the most expensive watering that lawn ever had. It didn't do the grass much good, either. I haven't touched a drop since. Gave up my cigars, too, some years later. I'll be seventy-two come July of this year, and I don't expect I would have made it if I had kept on the way I was going."

His quizzical look seemed to demand some sort of answer, so Laura nodded and smiled. An old quotation of her father's came to mind, which seemed appropriate. "The body is the temple of the soul," she said, sounding rather pompous, but Barnum bobbed his head, grinning.

"That's very true, Mrs. Orlando, very true. And we must keep that temple clean and strong." He glanced over at Will, who was at that very moment lighting a cigar, and said disapprovingly, "That's sound advice that other people could well heed to their advantage."

Will grinned lazily. "Everybody doesn't have your willpower, P.T."

"Humph!" Barnum snorted, then turned back to Laura. "Now, about the position. There are some things you should know before you accept it."

Laura, suddenly nervous again, swallowed. Did he mean he was going to give her the job? "And what are they, sir?"

Barnum held up one meaty hand, with the forefinger extended. "First of all, it will not be an easy job. We run a large and very complicated operation, and we often work under conditions of vast confusion." He looked over at Bailey. "Isn't that true, James?"

The younger man grimaced nervously, pulled a silver dollar from his pocket, and began to twirl it between his fingers. "Phineas is correct, Mrs. Orlando. Usually, an accounting office is a place of calm and quiet, but in our business, particularly when we're on the road, it is more often than not a place of chaos. There are always emergencies, you see. Items to be purchased, unexpected moneys to be paid out for one thing or another. You won't find it well ordered like the offices of a normal business."

"We have a large number of employees," said Barnum, helping himself to another slice of cake. "Besides the performers, there are the roustabouts, the animal keepers, costume people, and so forth. That means we have quite a large payroll, and that means a great many records to be kept."

Laura, not wanting him to think that he was discouraging her, leaned forward to pour him another cup of tea. "It all sounds very exciting. Most bookkeeping positions are fairly dull."

"Yes, it is exciting," Barnum said dryly. "But it is also hard work, very taxing of the energies, and there can often be an awful amount of pressure. Do you think you can work under those circumstances?"

Laura nodded firmly. "I do."

"You will be on the road a good portion of the year, you know, and although we try to make the accommodations as comfortable as possible, you will be sharing sleeping quarters with the other single women. Many of the amenities you're used to may be missing, I'm sorry to say."

Laura looked directly into his eyes. "I have been on the road before, Mr. Barnum. With the Chautauqua. I can manage, never fear."

Barnum set down his cup and saucer with a clatter. "Very well then. I see no further objections. James, do you agree?"

Bailey gave a birdlike bob of his head. "Will vouches for her, and she seems a capable and sensible young woman. As far as I'm concerned, the position is hers."

Barnum turned to Laura with a broad smile and took her hand in his. "Well, young woman! Welcome to the Barnum and London Circus, the Greatest Show on Earth!"

And now she was watching this exciting panoply and knowing that she was a part of it. She realized that in joining the circus, even in a business capacity, she was taking an extraordinary step. She was leaving behind the conventional life she was used to, moving into a strange, colorful, magical world that would, no doubt, offer many surprises, perhaps not all of them pleasant; and yet, strangely, it seemed to her, she had no real fears for her future. She felt that she had made the right decision, that this was what had been meant for her.

Looking up, she caught Will's glance, and he grinned down at her, apparently as caught up with the colors and sounds of the parade as she was. "I've seen it dozens of times," he shouted down to her, "and yet it always thrills me to my soul."

Laura laughed with delight. "I've never seen anything like it. Can the circus itself be any more wonderful than this?"

He reached down and took her hand in his, and the warm strength of his hand sent that current racing through her body again. "Tomorrow night you can find out for yourself, my dear Laura. It will be Jumbo's first performance in this country, and you should see it. Would you like to go with me?"

Laura wanted nothing more than to say yes, yet she hesitated. If she let Will take her to the circus tomorrow night, that would be the third time she had been in his company within four days. She very much enjoyed being with him, too much in fact; after all, she was still a married woman. And then there was the physical attraction that she felt for him, an attraction that was so strong it frightened her, and was growing stronger every day.

Should she see so much of him? Was it proper? Was it *safe*?

His eyes were still fixed on hers, and Laura realized that she had not answered. And then another of the brass bands boomed past, playing a rousing march, and the music seemed to touch off something reckless in her, something a bit wild and rebellious that she had not known was in her. *Why shouldn't I go?* she thought, as the drums boomed and the cymbals crashed. *Why should I worry about my duty as a married woman, when my husband has betrayed me and run off and left me? Who do I know here that I should worry about what people might think? I'm being offered another chance at another kind of life, a life that seems to hold pleasure and excitement, something that I have never really known. Why should I let my fears keep me from experiencing it?*

She smiled up at Will. "I would love to go. I've never seen a circus."

She felt his hand squeeze hers, and the pressure was as intimate as if he had touched her breasts under her clothing. Suffused with a warm glow, she watched the rest of the parade go past, wondering what Nick would think if he could see her now, and thinking that her present happiness was, in a way, a kind of revenge against his betrayal of her.

Laura had thought that the great circus parade was the most amazing thing she had ever seen; but she found the circus itself even more astounding.

The following night, when she arrived at Madison Square Garden with Will, she found the huge building packed with thousands of people seated in the rows of seats that circled the perimeter of the enormous oval arena. The sheer volume of humanity was staggering.

Tall pillars, sporting flags and pennants, supported the lofty ceiling, which to Laura seemed fantastically high. The arena of the great building was sectioned off by a low fence, and inside this fence were three large rings.

The outer area was a huge track, or hippodrome, as Will called it. "That's where the chariot races take place," he told her, as she looked wide-eyed at everything.

"This has to be the most enormous room I've ever seen," she whispered in awe.

Will laughed. "Well, P.T. always does things in a large way. Wait until we get on the road. The main tent seats even more people than the Garden does."

Laura shook her head. "That's hard to believe."

Her words were cut short by a deafening trumpet fanfare, as the four brass bands struck up at once, and a muted roar rose from the crowd as the introductory pageant began to circle the tent, glistening and glittering under the electric lights. Unaccustomed as she was to electric lights, Laura was fascinated. It would have been much less spectacular under gas lamps, she was sure.

When the opening parade was over, the performers came into the rings—giants and jugglers; bareback riders and acrobats; wire walkers; lion tamers and snake charmers. Laura found her head constantly turning back and forth. Whenever she focused on one thing, she was afraid she was missing something exciting in another ring.

She loved it all, or almost all; the beauty and grace of the performers in their spangled clothing, the daring of the performers who risked their lives so that the audience might be entertained. The only things she was not certain she cared for were the oddities, or freaks, those strange offshoots of humanity with their bizarre bodies and strange faces, who were exhibited so that normal people might goggle at them. The dwarfs, of course, were cute, and so not threatening; and the giants, although frighteningly large, still looked like people. However, the Lion Man, with his covering of long, golden hair, did not look at all human, and the two-headed girl—who was really two young black women, grown together at the back—Laura found particularly disturbing.

Still, they fascinated her, for however misformed they were, they *were* people, after all, and she could not help but wonder how they felt about being stared at constantly.

But Laura's mind was soon diverted from the problems of the freaks, for there was so much else to see: the Roman Hippodrome, with its golden chariots, magnificent horses, and daring drivers; and then, at last, the magnificent Jumbo, unveiled to the waiting crowd in the company of a baby elephant named Tom Thumb, whose size made the giant pachyderm seem even more enormous.

And then finally it was over, and in a confusion of pleasure, with her mind still full of colors, sounds, and lights, Will took her to the performers' tent to see Phineas Barnum, so that she might tell him what she thought of his "Greatest Show on Earth."

Barnum appeared larger and more flamboyant here, in this setting, as the performers hurried past them to their dressing cubicles. Laura knew that she was babbling in her enthusiasm, but the old showman seemed not to mind.

He informed her that there was someone he wished her to meet. As he moved aside, Laura saw the tiny couple who had been standing behind him—a very small, very fat little man, and a tiny woman.

Barnum waved a hand theatrically over their heads. "General and Mrs. Tom Thumb, may I present to you Mrs. Orlando, who will be joining the show this season as a bookkeeper."

The little man bowed rather stiffly, and Laura had difficulty suppressing a gasp of surprise. Although his wife seemed as diminutive as she had appeared in the wedding picture that Laura had seen as a child, the General was larger both in height and in girth, although it was the girth that was most noticeable. The plump, cupid-faced young man now looked like a pompous, miniature, mustachioed businessman, complete with receding hairline and drooping jowls. Still, it was a thrill to meet him; and when they took their leave of Barnum and went out into the cool evening air, Laura felt dizzy with the effects of the evening.

Will, escorting her through the still-considerable crowd, gazed down at her and smiled. "Well, did you enjoy it, Laura?"

She looked up at him, her face aglow. "Did I enjoy it? How can you ask? It was marvelous! The most wonderful thing I've ever seen! The only problem was that there was so much that I couldn't see it all. I imagine you could see it again and again and still find new things to marvel at."

He grinned at her enthusiasm. "Ah ha, I knew it! We have you caught now. So you think you'll like working for the circus?"

She nodded quickly. "I can truthfully say that I cannot imagine any job more exciting."

Maneuvering between two very large gentlemen, Will led her toward the curb. "I made a reservation for us at Delmonico's for a late supper."

He looked at her intently, and his words seemed more a question than a statement.

She nodded, suddenly realizing that she was ravenous. She had had only a light meal at noon; she had been too excited to eat much, and now her stomach was complaining. "That was very thoughtful of you, Will, but you may be sorry. I feel as if I could eat enough for two."

He laughed. "Good! So do I. Have you ever been to Delmonico's?"

She shook her head. "No. Nick . . . We never seemed to have time to come into New York City. We were always too busy with the theater."

He tucked her arm under his. "Well, then it's time that you did. It's a wonderful city, exciting, full of life. Come on, there's an empty cab."

Delmonico's proved to be an elegant eatery, and Laura could tell, by the headwaiter's attitude, that Will Adams was a familiar and valued customer.

It was the kind of place that normally would have awed her and made her feel awkward and out-of-place, but tonight, because of her high spirits engendered by the spectacle of the circus, Laura felt almost at ease. After all, she told herself judiciously, none of these people in their expensive clothes and jewels were any better than she was, they had just been more fortunate. When you came right down to it, it was money and money alone that allowed them to patronize such a place, and money could be earned. Certainly, some of the money came from families of old wealth and prestige; but at some time in that family's past, *someone* had to make the original fortune, and that someone probably came from a background no more illustrious than hers! This notion gave her considerable comfort; and when the headwaiter deferentially seated them, she walked to the table with her head held as high as any queen, and more than one pair of male eyes followed her progress.

Taking the chair the headwaiter pulled out for her, Laura suddenly realized that what mattered was how you felt about yourself. If *you* thought you were special, and acted as if you were, other people would believe you. It seemed such a simple truth, and yet so important, that she wondered why it had not occurred to her before.

Will ordered a wonderful meal, with three different wines, and Laura helped herself to it all with no restraint.

The sound of genteel conversation, the clink of good silver and crystal, the rich decor—all seemed to form a perfect climax to a wonderful evening. Laura felt grateful to Will for giving her such pleasure, and found it difficult to keep her gaze off his face. He was such an attractive man physically that he was a constant delight to look at, and yet the attraction he held for her was not merely physical. There was a quiet strength in him, a solidness, that drew her, and a sheer animal magnetism that made her quiver whenever he happened to touch her. Although she tried not to think of it, her mind kept coming back to the possibility that he might attempt to make love to her this night, and the thought both frightened her and filled her with a fevered yearning. In her present mood, she felt both vulnerable and daring, and considerably confused.

After dinner they rode to her lodgings in a hansom cab, and Laura found herself trembling at his proximity. He took her hand and held it gently, and as the cab moved through the soft darkness, they sat quietly listening to muffled clip-clop of the horse's hooves.

At that moment she longed for him to take her into his arms. She wanted to feel his lips on hers, his hands stroking her body; it would assuage the hunger that was running through her veins like fire, and it would also pay back Nick for what he had done to her. And yet another part of her, the sensible part—which was barely managing to keep the upper hand—knew that it would be a mistake at this time. What was she going to do?

When they reached her building, the decision was made for her. As the cab rolled slowly to a stop, Will leaned toward her, cupped her face with one large, warm hand, and kissed her tenderly, full on the lips. Laura felt that all her bones had turned to liquid.

And then he drew his mouth away, albeit reluctantly, and opened the cab door, got out, and reached up to help her down.

Laura's head was swimming and her knees felt weak. She was too dazed to know if she was disappointed or relieved.

He walked her to the door, kissed her hand, and looked deeply into her eyes. "It was a lovely evening, Laura. I can't tell you how much I enjoyed your company. I hope you will let me call upon you again soon."

Laura, trying to gather her wine-muddled senses, looked up at him with what she hoped was a grateful smile. "It was the most wonderful evening I've ever spent. Thank you, Will, for arranging it. It was very kind of you."

He gave her an odd, lopsided smile. "Kindness, my dear, had nothing to do with it. But at any rate, we have some time left before the circus goes on the road, and I would love to show you something more of New York. I'm going to be busy for the next few days, but if you're free Saturday night, perhaps you would like to see a show and have dinner?"

She hesitated, then nodded slowly. Despite the strictures of her upbringing, the words echoing in her head that told her that nice women, married women, even those whose husbands had deserted them, did not make social engagements with other men, the practical side of her could see no sense or fairness in these rules, which were no doubt made by men she thought.

"I would like to go," she said firmly, and was rewarded with a gleaming smile.

He bowed over her hand. "Until Saturday night, then. I'll pick you up at six, and we'll dine after the show."

Fumbling in her purse, Laura found her key and inserted it into the lock. As the door swung open, she turned and looked back at him, wishing that she had the audacity, or the courage, to let him know in some way that she wanted him to kiss her again; but he made no further move toward her, except another half-bow, and with that she turned and opened the door. She glanced back once, to see him watching her with an intense look on his face.

She had no way of knowing that after she had closed the door, he stood for several moments on the doorstep, staring at the door, before turning away to the hansom cab.

Chapter Twelve

IN the hansom cab, Will ordered the driver to wait for a few minutes, and sat staring at Laura's door, reluctant to leave and thus officially end their evening together. It had been a wonderful evening, one of the pleasantest he had spent in many years, and he hated for it to be over.

To view the circus through Laura's eyes had been to see it as if for the first time. Her pleasure and excitement had also been his, and the expressions of awe and wonder on her lovely face had aroused in him a powerful tenderness. God, how he wanted to make love to her!

Perhaps he had been a fool not to press the advantage that her mood had offered him. In the cab, he had felt her yearn toward him as much as he yearned toward her, and he had sensed her vulnerability; and yet, somehow, he had restrained himself, knowing that her feeling was inspired partially by the wine they had drunk at dinner, the evening's exciting entertainment, and her anger at her husband. If he had made an advance, he might very well have been able to seduce her; but what effect might that have had on their future relationship? Although he had not known Laura Orlando for very long, he did know that he wanted more from her than a casual, one night's bedding. If he had made love to her, it was entirely possible that on the morrow she would have awakened ashamed and angry at herself for yielding, and her anger would be directed at him as the instrument of her shame. Also, when he *did* make love to her, Will wanted it to be because she wanted *him*, not because she was avenging a betrayed love; for Will was now certain that Nick Orlando had abandoned Laura—there was simply no other plausible explanation for her situation.

At last he turned away with a sigh and directed the driver to take him home.

The matter of where he was lodging in New York had not come up during any of his meetings with Laura. He supposed that she assumed he was staying in one of the better hotels, which he sometimes did, and he had been careful to say nothing that would disabuse her of that notion. It made him feel dishonest to some degree, yet he felt that it was necessary. It was far too early in their relationship to tell her of his marriage and of his son. When and if the time came to make these things known, Will hoped that she would be able to accept the somewhat unusual situation.

The house was quiet when he let himself in with his latch key, for Justin went to bed early, which befitted a small boy, and Will's mother-in-law was also in the habit of retiring early.

It was not a very large house, but it was pleasant and well suited to his needs, and was located on the East Side. His mother-in-law had brought her own furniture from Paris, and so the house had a grace and elegance that Will knew he would never have managed on his own, and Justin was being raised in an atmosphere of gentility and with a certain amount of privilege.

Will and his elderly mother-in-law shared a mutual respect and affection. Will always called her by her first name, Pearl, and he enjoyed her company. Pearl was an intelligent woman, with a quick wit and an inquiring mind. Although tiny in stature, Pearl was relatively active for her age—a requisite for the raising of a small, very nimble boy. Still, she was getting on in age, and Will often wondered what he would do if she were to fall ill, or to die. She and Justin were very close—she was the only mother the boy had ever known—and if anything were to happen to her, Justin would be inconsolable.

There was an oil lamp burning in the entryway for his return. Picking it up from the lacquer table, Will walked through the exquisite rooms, looking at them with deep pleasure as he passed through each one. Pearl had decorated the house in an Oriental manner; and although at first the style had seemed strange to him, Will now found its simplicity soothing and beautiful.

He paused before the fireplace in the small sitting room; it was his favorite room in the house, a place where he could read and study in quiet. Over the mantel, in a delicate ormolu frame, hung a portrait of Lily.

He studied the gentle countenance; the large, dark eyes; the delicately boned face; the tender lips curving in just the barest hint of a smile. Lily, dear Lily! As lovely and exotic as the flower whose name she bore. Even after all these years, the love Will had for her still burned bright when he looked at her portrait. Never in all the years since her death had he felt a love as strong as that which he had felt for her. Not until now, not until he had met Laura.

Would Lily understand? Would she mind that he had now, at long last, found someone for whom he could feel the same deep passion as he had felt for her? Or would she be happy for him? Would she be pleased that he had at last come fully back to life? He rather thought that Lily would be glad for him, knowing that his feeling for Laura in no way diminished what he had felt for her. She had been a very understanding woman.

Finally turning away from the portrait, Will made his way upstairs to his son's room.

He tiptoed to the side of the small bed where Justin slept; and holding the shielded lamp high in his hand, he leaned over the sleeping boy.

Justin lay curled on his side, one hand over his head, the other curled against his chest. His thick, dark hair tumbled down over his forehead, and in sleep his face looked very young, showing traces of both the baby he had been and the boy he was becoming.

Will's heart swelled with tenderness and love as he leaned down to brush his lips across his son's forehead.

Would Laura, when she learned of Justin, be able to feel toward him something of what Will felt? Or would she . . . ? That was a problem for the future, if there was a future for them. *All I can do at the moment,* he thought, *is hope that there will be.*

The rain had started early in the morning, and by afternoon, when the circus train pulled onto the siding where it would unload, it had increased to a steady downpour.

Laura, standing on the observation platform, pulled her waterproof cape tightly around her and leaned out to peer into the rain, attempting to see back to the rear of the train, where the animals and the wagons were being unloaded.

She was getting rather wet, despite the cape, but she did not really mind. This was something that she had never seen before, and, caught up in the excitement of the unloading, she meant to see all that she could despite the weather.

Milly Andrews, one of the wardrobe girls, stood beside her, her small, pale face alight.

"It's really something to see, isn't it?" she said in her sweet, high voice. "But it's rather frightening in all this rain. Don't you agree?"

Laura turned to the smaller girl and smiled; they had met only two days earlier. Milly, too, was new to the circus, and, like Laura, she was fascinated by all the details of running the huge show.

Laura thought she knew quite well what Milly meant. Under the darkening sky and the heavy beat of the rain, the scene unfolding before them looked like something out of another, wilder world.

There was a desperate scurry of activity and much noise—the roaring of the animals; the shouts of the men; the clatter of the wagons. Laura imagined that the unloading of the sixty or so specially constructed railroad cars must be a tremendous undertaking even in the best of weather, and with the added hazard of the heavy rain, it must be a much more difficult and even a dangerous task.

"You're right," she replied. "It is rather frightening. I'm glad that we don't have to be out there wading through all that mud."

Milly bobbed her head. "So am I! Sometimes I've wished that I could be a man, but at times like this, it's not so bad being a woman."

The two young women exchanged smiles, knowing that most of the men with the circus, whatever their job, would be expected to help with the unloading and the erecting of the huge tents.

Laura wondered if Will was out there with them, getting his fine suit all muddy, and she smiled at the image; but she somehow doubted that he was.

"Oh, look!" Milly cried. "They're unloading Jumbo and the other elephants."

Laura leaned forward to see, just as Jumbo trumpeted his displeasure at being driven from his nice dry car into the cold rain. The sound was loud and wild, and was soon echoed by the other elephants, most of them old-timers. The great strength of the elephants would be used to raise the huge main tent.

One by one the great creatures lumbered down the ramps leading from the boxcar doors, then they plodded out onto the muddy ground and were led toward the area where the tents were to be erected.

Earlier this week, Will and a helper had gone ahead to the first town on their route, where they had checked out the field where the circus was to be held and staked out the locations for the main tent and the subsidiary tents. They had also hired people to put up signs and distribute handbills to towns and cities as far as seventy-five miles away. People journeyed from remote farms and villages to see the wonders of the Barnum and London Circus.

When she had asked Will why they distributed their advertising in areas so far away, Will had told her of the special discount excursions offered by the railroad. "This way," he had said, "we only have to set up in the largest towns. It's much less expensive for us, and allows people from the surrounding smaller towns to see the show. We have an arrangement with all the railroads for these special excursion rates."

At the thought that she would soon see Will again, Laura felt her face grow warm, despite the cold rain that ran down her cheeks. During the train ride she had thought of him far more often than she should have. Although the thought of him still made her nervous and edgy with what she admitted to herself was physical desire for him, she was now quite certain that she could trust him.

After that night when he had taken her to the circus, Laura realized that his interest in her was much more than carnal. Thinking now of how vulnerable she had been that night, she experienced a mixture of embarrassment and chagrin. If she was honest with herself—as she always tried to be—she had to admit that if he had tried to seduce her that night, she would not have put up much resistance. But he had not; he had been a perfect gentleman. What confused and embarrassed her was not knowing whether she was glad of this or sorry.

Feeling a tug on her arm, she glanced around to see Milly staring worriedly down the line of cars. "Are they having trouble back there? I can't see very well."

Laura peered out into the rain and saw one of the large tableau wagons listing to one side of the ramp that had been placed against one of the flatcars. As she and Milly watched, the wagon broke loose, wobbled dangerously, then careened down the ramp into the mud, as the men waiting at the base of the ramp scattered in all directions, shouting and cursing. In the distance now Laura could hear the ring of hammers on metal as the heavy stakes for the tents were hammered into the muddy ground.

"Oh, I wish we were closer to the tent ground," she said suddenly. "I want to see it all."

"I wish we were, too," Milly said. "If only it weren't raining, we might have gone out and watched, but I don't think they want us in the way right now."

As a particularly vile curse echoed up from where a group of men were attempting to unload the animal cages,

Laura had to smile. "I imagine you're right," she said, clapping her hands over her ears.

Chilled and wet, Laura and Milly remained on the observation platform while the main tent was being erected. They were too far away to get a close look, but Madame Costa, the wardrobe mistress, took note of their interest and loaned them a pair of opera glasses.

By the time the roustabouts were ready to hoist the main tent, the rain had slacked off to a drizzle; and so they were able, with the aid of the glasses, to see the elephants and the men working together to raise the incredible weight of the canvas, which until then had been lying spread out on the ground like the discarded skin of some gigantic beast.

Laura, whose turn it was to have the glasses, gave a soft gasp as the canvas structure began slowly to rise like a living organism.

Handing the glasses to Milly, Laura shook her head in wonder. "It's incredible that they do it so fast. It's so much *work!*"

"They've had lots of practice, I guess," said Milly, quickly raising the glasses to her eyes. "Oh, look, Laura! It's up. It looks enormous!"

"Mr. Adams told me that it's the largest tent in the world, or at least Mr. Barnum claims it is. They say it can seat twenty thousand people. And there are three other tents as well, one for the museum, and *two* menageries. Actually there are four, including the cook tent."

Milly sighed and lowered the glasses. "At least you know someone who can tell you about these things. I suppose it's always difficult for a newcomer. The old-timers know everything and the newcomers know nothing. I guess newcomers are naïve, and naïveté is always a little funny. Sometimes I feel so new to everything, so . . . so dumb! I'm always asking stupid questions that cause the other girls to laugh at me."

Laura patted the younger girl's shoulder. "You'll learn in time, Milly. I have a lot to learn, too. And I've been told that circus people are a particularly close-knit, clannish group, and they don't accept outsiders readily."

Milly nodded. "I've heard that, too. In fact, Madame Costa warned me about that when I came to work for the circus. She said that I would be accepted in time, after I had 'proved' myself. Whatever that means."

Laura leaned her elbows on the observation-car railing. The sky was clearing rapidly now, the clouds moving away to let in shafts of sunlight. "I think she means that we have to prove we can do our share, hold up our end, take whatever comes along, and stand up to it."

"I can do that," Milly said, her head back, determination in her voice. "I already love the circus, and I want to be a part of it."

Milly's sudden smile was contagious, and Laura found herself answering it. "I feel the same. The way I see it, if we do our jobs well, are friendly and polite to the others, and don't complain when things get uncomfortable or unpleasant, then we'll eventually be accepted into the circus world."

The last words were barely out of Laura's mouth when the last of the rain clouds parted to reveal a glorious rainbow, one end of which vanished into a low bank of white clouds. The other end of the brilliant arch of color came to rest directly on the center of the main tent. Both girls stood staring at it with shining eyes.

By evening all the tents had been raised and the equipment and animals had been unloaded. The bleachers still had to be erected in the main tent, and the finishing touches taken care of, but the hard work was completed.

Marvelous smells were issuing from the cook tent, and Laura heard her stomach rumble in a decidedly unlady-like manner. After putting on her oldest and stoutest boots and her most worn skirt, she and Milly left the women's sleeping car and made their way through the mud toward the cook tent.

Now that the rain had stopped, it was a beautiful night, the stars bright and shimmering against a black-velvet sky. Laura took a deep breath of the moist air, which was redolent of crushed grass and growing things. She felt full of energy and expectation. She had not, she realized suddenly, thought about Nick for days. It seemed that the pain of his leaving was fading, and that her life with him was in the far distant past.

And then her thoughts swung to Will. Would she see him tonight? She realized that he must have been terribly busy all day, but would he look for her this evening?

Her thoughts were interrupted by Milly's light voice. "You won't leave me alone, will you, Laura? I mean, inside the cook tent. Even if your friend should come along, you won't leave me to eat alone, will you?"

Laura, looking at the other girl, felt a sudden surge of tenderness. Milly was such a sweet little thing, so tiny and delicate-looking that she might be mistaken for a child; and yet Laura knew that she had a kind of tough strength in her that had enabled her to get this job, and to declare her intention of keeping it despite the sometimes rough teasing of the more experienced women she worked with. Also, she could share Milly's apprehension. She too felt nervous about eating with a large group of people, most of whom knew one another fairly well, none of whom knew her at all, except for Will; and for all she knew he might be dining with James Bailey or other important people with the show.

Laura, although only a few years older, felt like a mother to Milly. She put her arm around Milly's waist. "Don't worry, we'll eat together. I'm feeling just as shaky as you are. As long as there's at least two of us, we'll have our own company. Come on, let's hurry. I'm starving."

The cook tent was crowded with wooden trestle tables at which weary and muddy men and women were seriously attending to the contents of their plates and mugs.

Serving tables were set up at one side, and a long line of people stood waiting to be served. Milly and Laura took their places at the end of the line. The odors of the hot food made Laura's mouth water; to keep her mind off her hunger, she looked around the tent, taking stock of her fellow travelers.

They were a very mixed group, ranging from well to

poorly dressed, representing, she supposed, the circus hierarchy.

At a nearby table, a tall, good-looking man with a long, black mustache, dressed in a well-cut cloth coat with a fur collar, was holding forth before his apparently approving table mates.

Next to him were seated a small, very pretty blond woman wrapped in a blue cloak, and a blond man who was good-looking enough to be a matinee idol.

Milly, seeing the direction of Laura's glance, leaned near her to whisper, "The man with the mustache is Mr. Turnbull, the ringmaster, and the man on his left is Gunther Helsing, the lion tamer. Isn't he the handsomest thing?"

Laura nodded. "He is very good-looking."

Milly sighed. "But he's already taken. That pretty little woman on the other side of Mr. Turnbull is his lady friend. Her name is Betinna Brouder, and she's a bareback rider."

Laura looked at the pair with renewed interest. "Their names sound German," she said.

"They are. Most of the performers come from European circuses. Madame Costa says that they have had circuses there much longer than we have."

Milly laughed. "But then I guess they've had everything longer than we have, haven't they? Anyway, you'll find that performers tend to group together with their countrymen, and that certain *types* of performers stay together too. For instance, clowns tend to eat with other clowns, roustabouts with roustabouts."

Laura made a face. "Does that mean I'll have to eat only with others of the office staff?"

Milly giggled. "Well, no, but tonight we'll be lucky to find a place to sit at all. Because it's the first night on the road, and raining, everyone is eating in the tent. Usually some of the top performers eat in their own caravans. Look around and see if you see any vacant spots."

Laura shook her head. "Milly, for someone who was just complaining that she had no one to tell her things, you've certainly learned a great deal!"

Milly grinned, "Well, Madam Costa *does* love to talk, and I've always been a good listener."

Laura again scanned the tent. Along one wall were the tables where the freaks or prodigies were congregated. They were talking and laughing among themselves, and Laura found herself staring at them with fascination. As she had when she visited the circus with Will, she found herself both attracted and repelled. It was as if she could not make up her mind just how she felt about them.

Milly, noting the direction of her gaze, spoke up. "Aren't they fascinating? Isn't it odd what nature can do? I always wonder how they feel about being like they are. I should think it would be horrible to be stared at by people as if you weren't even human, but most of them don't seem to mind it. If they do, they certainly don't show it. They must be awfully brave."

She paused, then added, "You know, most people call them *freaks* and that's such an ugly word. Mr. Barnum refers to them as *prodigies*. It has more dignity, don't you think?"

Laura, who found that Milly's words echoed her own sentiments, nodded thoughtfully. "But I have to say that I'm a bit afraid of them," she admitted shamefacedly.

Milly made a clucking sound. "Oh, you shouldn't be, Laura. After all, no matter how they *look*, they're still people. Inside, I imagine, they're just like you and me. It's just their outside, the way they look physically, that is different, and they can't help that. After all, God made them that way, didn't He?"

Laura had to smile. Milly really was an amazing little thing; and despite her childlike appearance, she had an uncanny mature ability to cut through all pretension and nonsense and put her finger on what was important.

"You're absolutely right, Milly," she said.

When it was their turn to be served, Laura eagerly picked up a tray and plate and extended them to the sweating, red-faced cooks. By the time she had reached the end of the line, her tray was embarrassingly full, and she hoped that her eyes were not bigger than her stomach.

At least, she was happy to see, Milly's tray was almost as full as hers.

Now that they had their food, they had to find a place to sit and eat. The tent seemed quite full; and although they looked around carefully, they could find no empty seats.

Finally, Milly spotted a few empty places at one of the tables where the prodigies were seated and nodded in that direction. "There are some empty places over there. Do you think they would mind if we joined them?"

Laura felt a sudden nervousness seize her. The table was where the Lion Man was seated, and the Lion Man was one of the human oddities that had made Laura most uneasy.

"Well," said Milly, striding purposefully forward, "they seem to be the only seats available, so I guess we'd better take them before our suppers get cold."

Ill-at-ease, Laura followed along in her friend's wake, wondering what had happened to the confidence she had felt earlier.

Stopping at one of the empty seats, Milly smiled brightly. "I hope you won't mind if we join you?"

Laura, her heavy tray no longer supportable, placed it on the table in front of an empty seat and noticed unhappily that all eyes at the table had shifted to her and Milly. It was an unnerving experience, for there was no way of knowing whether their attitude was friendly or otherwise; their eyes were guarded, their odd faces expressionless.

Milly, blithely ignoring the sudden silence that had fallen at the table, sat down on the bench next to a slender, dark-haired woman who wore a full beard. "I don't know about you all," Milly said, giving them another glowing smile, "but I'm just about hungry enough to eat Jumbo himself!"

Laura saw the bearded woman's teeth gleam between the wings of dark hair as she smiled, and she felt a warm glow of relief as the others at the table seemed to relax a bit.

The bearded woman gazed up at Laura. "Please be seated, my dear. We would be happy to have you join us. You are both new to the circus, are you not?"

Laura sat down between Milly and a skeletally thin man who was attacking his food with apparent relish, and tried not to stare at the Lion Man, who was sitting directly across the table from her.

Milly answered, "Yes, ma'am, we are. I work with Madame Costa in wardrobe, and my friend here will be working in the business wagon."

The woman nodded graciously. She was, Laura noticed, very feminine in all respects other than the lustrous black beard that covered the lower half of her face. The hair on her head was luxuriant and dressed in the latest fashion, and her clothing was well cut and became her slender but well-rounded figure. Her voice was cultured, and Laura noticed that she spoke with a slight accent.

"But I am forgetting my manners," the woman said, gesturing gracefully with one hand. "I am Madame Zenobia, and you can plainly see my specialty. No?"

Laura felt herself flush at this reference to the beard, but Milly looked at Madame Zenobia admiringly. "It's a beautiful beard," she said. "Very unusual."

Madame Zenobia threw back her head and gave a clear, bell-like laugh. "I am going to like you, little one. You see with a clear eye, and you speak with an honest tongue. It is unusual indeed, and of course that is why I am here, why we are all here, because of our unusualness."

She looked at Laura. "And now what is your name, little one, and that of your friend?"

"Oh, I'm sorry. I'm Milly Andrews, and my friend is Laura Orlando, and we are delighted to make your acquaintance."

Madame Zenobia patted Milly's hand. "Such a polite little one! Well, I am delighted to make your acquaintance, also. And now to introduce the others at our table. The young woman across from me is Belle Taylor, who is billed as the Four-Legged Girl."

The young woman to whom she referred looked to be about twenty, and was short, with soft brown hair and a pretty face. With her legs concealed by the table, she appeared completely normal. Laura nodded in greeting and answered the girl's shy smile.

"And the gentleman seated next to her is Herman Dawes, the Half Man."

Herman Dawes, a middle-aged man with a pleasant face and a receding hairline, his lower body also hidden by the table, appeared in no way unusual.

"Across from you, Laura, is Lionel Germaine, better known as the Lion Man."

Laura reluctantly lifted her gaze and looked directly into two of the kindest and bluest eyes she had ever seen. At close quarters and fully clothed, the Lion Man presented a somewhat incongruous picture: he looked like a friendly animal attired in human clothing.

Above his suit jacket and shirt, his head and face were entirely covered with long, wavy, golden hair. Only the eyes, intelligent and human, proclaimed him a man. Even his hands were covered with long golden hair.

Laura stared at him for a tongue-tied moment, and then suddenly he smiled at her, showing perfect white teeth; and as he did so, her nervousness and fear of him abruptly vanished. The hair on his face, which looked soft and silky, was combed from his cheeks and nostrils in a graceful pattern; and although he did not look quite human, he was, in his own way, quite strangely beautiful. Milly, Laura now noticed, was staring at him openly with what appeared to be frank pleasure.

"Your hair," Milly said, "it looks so soft!"

Lionel laughed heartily. "You may touch it if you like," he said in a warm voice.

Milly, with a nervous little giggle, stood up and leaned across the table to stroke his golden cheek. "Oh, it is!" she said to Laura, her eyes shining. "It's quite as soft as silk. Just feel."

Feeling everyone's eyes on her, Laura hesitantly leaned forward and gently touched the hair on the side of the Lion Man's face. It was indeed soft and silky. Embarrassed, she drew back her hand.

Evidently sensing her discomfort, Lionel smiled reassuringly. "It's quite all right," he said. "I don't mind at all, you know. I am an oddity, I fully realize that fact, and people are naturally curious, and sometimes even frightened of me. If they touch me, then they realize they have nothing to fear from me."

Madame Zenobia said, "And now to the gentleman seated next to you, Laura. His name is Luther Goodwin, and, as you can see, he is the Human Skeleton. In some ways Luther is luckier than the rest of us, for he can eat all he wants and never get fat."

Goodwin, still chewing, looked up and nodded cheerfully. Swallowing his food, he announced in a surprisingly deep voice, "I'm five-foot-eight and weigh seventy pounds. Never gain an ounce no matter how much I eat." After making the pronouncement, he returned his attention to his food.

"On the other side of Luther is Alwyn Crest, who is known as Samson, the strongest man in the world, and his wife, Lettita, who is a snake charmer."

Laura and Milly leaned forward to see the tall, broad-shouldered man with the shaved head and his voluptuous, red-haired wife.

"Of course there are many more of us." Madame Zenobia waved a hand around at the other tables. "But I will not attempt now to point them out to you. You will meet them all in good time. And now, enjoy your dinners, young ladies."

Laura and Milly, who had been eating slowly during the introductions, now attacked the contents of their trays hungrily, letting the conversation of the others ebb and flow around them.

Laura found the food surprisingly tasty, but her appreciation of it did not keep her from listening attentively.

Halfway through the meal, she noticed a group of people leaving a nearby table. It appeared that they were all related, for they shared the same thick, dark hair, smooth, olive skin, aristocratic noses, and lustrous dark eyes. They also carried themselves with identical arrogance.

Laura took particular note of one man who was a bit taller and slimmer than the others, and a haughtily beautiful woman wearing an expensive black-velvet cape.

As they left, the tall man turned and stared at the table where the freaks were seated. His eyes, dark and hooded, met Laura's for a long moment, but she could not read his gaze.

Herman Dawes, the Half Man, said something to Belle Taylor that Laura could not hear; and then Laura was astonished to hear the sweet-faced, four-legged girl speak loudly in a rather common accent: "Well, I think she's a proper bitch! I know some think 'er beautiful, but she 'asn't a kind bone in 'er body, and she thinks she's bloody well the Queen of the May! The way she treats poor Benjy, and 'im so gone on 'er, too. And Lionel as well. All you men fairly fawn on 'er, and think you're bloody well in 'eaven if she gives you so much as a kind word. It's enough to make a sensible person sick, that it is!"

Laura could not restrain a quick glance at the Lion Man, who was staring after the passing group. She could not see his face, for his head was turned; but when the group had left the tent and he turned back to face her, Laura saw that his keen blue eyes held an expression of pain and sorrow.

Noting that Laura was looking at him, he smiled wryly and shrugged. It was obvious that this strange-looking man had romantic yearnings toward the beautiful woman in the cape, and a great feeling of sympathy washed over Laura. How sad to have a hopeless love; for surely, if ever a love was unlikely to be returned, it must be Lionel's. The lovely, haughty woman clearly had many admirers, including the unfortunate Benjy, whoever he was.

Trying not to let her compassion show, for she did not wish to embarrass him, Laura asked casually, "That group of people who just left . . . who are they?"

"The Salieri family," Lionel said softly. "They are one of the star attractions, a trapeze act."

Laura nodded thoughtfully. She was already getting some idea of the hierarchy of the performers and knew that such acts were the aristocrats of the circus. She said tactfully, "They seem very . . . sure of themselves."

Milly, who had been silently eating during this exchange, gave a slight snort. "I don't think 'sure of themselves' quite describes it. I thought they were downright rude and arrogant. They just swept out of here like they were royalty or something!"

Lionel smiled gently. "Well, they are royalty, you know, at least as far as the circus goes."

Milly snorted again. "Oh, I know. I heard you say they're a top act, but that doesn't make them any better than you or me, just luckier. It really makes me cross to see people tilt their noses in the air like that. It gets my dander up!"

Madame Zenobia turned to Milly with a smile. "Ah, I see that the little one has struck straight to the truth of the matter. The truly great do not have to proclaim their greatness, and should retain humility in the face of success. It is true that the Salieri family is a great act, that they have much talent, but it is also true that they have a great arrogance, and little generosity or love toward their fellow man. Perhaps, particularly in their line of work, they should remember the old adage, 'Pride goeth before a fall.'

"And now, young ladies, I am very fatigued, and tomorrow will be a long day. I must retire to my caravan. I wish you both a good night's sleep and pleasant dreams."

The others at the table soon made their farewells, and soon Laura and Milly were left seated alone with their now-empty plates.

"Well!" Milly said, looking at Laura with shining eyes. "Was that interesting, or was it not? I think they're fabulous people! I can hardly wait to get to know the rest of the performers. How about you?"

Amused by the girl's enthusiasm, Laura nodded. "Yes. They were very nice, and it was quite exciting. And you were right about them: they're just regular people. I'm glad you decided we should sit with them."

Milly flashed her gamine grin. "Did you get a good look at Lionel Germaine? Isn't he the most beautiful thing you've ever seen?"

Laura stared at Milly in astonishment. She *had* thought the Lion Man rather attractive, in his strange way, but from Milly's manner it sounded as if she was speaking of a possible male conquest.

"Yes, I did find him pleasant to look at, in an odd way," she said cautiously.

Milly continued to beam. "I thought he was simply gorgeous, like a magnificent lion who has been magicked into human form, or a prince who has been turned into a lion. He has the kindest eyes," she added dreamily, "and he seems awfully intelligent."

All at once, Laura was exhausted. The energy and excitement that had carried her through the long day had drained away, and the combination of the warmth of the tent and the hot food had done their work on her.

"Milly, we'd better get back to the sleeping car. I'm dead tired, and, as Madame Zenobia pointed out, tomorrow will be a busy day."

Milly nodded and picked up her tray. "You're right. But personally, I'm still so excited that I don't know if I'll be able to sleep."

Laura sighed and shook her head. Where did Milly get such energy?

Laura suddenly realized that she had not seen Will all evening. Perhaps he had dined with Mr. Bailey or some of the other important men with the circus.

Phineas Barnum, she knew, was not with them at the present. Will had explained that he did not travel often with the circus these days, but spent much of his time with his second wife at their estate, Waldemere, at Seaside Park in Bridgeport. However, Barnum still took an active part in securing talent for the show.

Laura found herself feeling a little dejected; she had not seen Will all day. She should not, of course. Will Adams was simply a friend, nothing more. Actually, she scarcely knew him. It was foolish of her to think, with all the business he had to attend to, that he could have found time for her.

Yet, in spite of this sensible reasoning, she found that when she finally retired to her narrow bunk in the women's sleeping car and closed her eyes, among the jumble of images in her head—the unloading of the cars, the dinner with the human oddities—was the image of Will Adams. Her last thoughts before she drifted off to sleep were of how it would feel to lie naked and open in his arms.

Chapter Thirteen

THE Geek, clad only in a dirty loincloth, gazed up at the audience from the bottom of the pit as he slowly waved the squawking chicken back and forth before their fascinated eyes.

Nick suppressed a shudder of revulsion as he stared down into the foul pit. Dirty enough to begin with, the Geek's scrawny body had been further disguised with handfuls of wet earth, and his dark, bushy hair had been teased and brushed so that it stood up on the top of his head, adding to his frightening appearance. The dirt, the mad glares, and the grunts were to convince the rubes that they were seeing some species of wild man, and the pit was to make them think that such measures were necessary for their protection.

Nick, wondering how circumstances could bring any man so low as to become a carnival geek, backed out of the crowd around the pit and headed to his own show tent. As he left, he heard the Geek give a shrill cry, the chicken emit a choked-off squawk, and the crowd—all of them men—give a collective sigh.

Nick shook his head in disgust. Of all the carnival acts, the Geek was the most despised by all the carnies, and yet it always drew large audiences. The act required no talent. All that was needed was a drunkard with a strong stomach who had sunk so low that he would do anything to keep himself in whiskey, and a live chicken. The entire

157

act consisted of the Geek making fierce, growling noises and threatening gestures to the audience; and then, when he had stretched their patience and curiosity to the maximum, he bit the head off the live chicken. He was paid off in whiskey and scraps of food from the cook tent.

Most of the larger, classier carnivals would not even use a geek act, but the Maridan Magic Carnival was neither large nor classy, and the owner, Madame Lola Maridan, would book anything that would bring in the marks and make a few dollars.

She also had her games rigged, Nick knew, and the ticket takers were schooled in the art of shortchanging the customers. No, Nick thought, you couldn't say that the Maridan was one of the better carnivals traveling the country; but then, it wasn't one of the worst, either, and it had provided him with a haven when he needed it.

This thought, unfortunately, led him to think of Laura. Quickly he tried to turn his thoughts away from this uncomfortable subject, for thinking of Laura and the shabby way he had treated her made him feel guilt and anger, two emotions he was not at all comfortable with.

Nick had an image of himself as an intelligent, charming man who was blessed with good luck. Most of the time his life had proved out this belief. But, after months or even a year or so of good fortune and success, he always seemed to be driven to do something foolish, something that brought destruction down on his head.

Although Nick was not given to introspection, occasionally he could not help but wonder why he did these things.

It had all started out so well for them. The theater had been flourishing, and he had been happy with Laura; and then, when the initial struggle was over, when things were running smoothly, he had started to get restless. It was a familiar itch, or rather two itches—the gaming tables and women.

Perhaps if he had not let Alfred Hayes persuade him to hire Harriet, the whole thing might have been kept under control. If it had been any other girl, Alfred would not really have cared; in fact, he might even have helped Nick to get the girl to an abortionist. But no, it had to be Alfred's niece, and Nick had to be foolish enough to foul his own nest. And the crazy thing was, Harriet wasn't even half as good in bed as Laura, for whom he had genuinely cared; so why had he done it?

Of course, it had not all been his fault: the girl had thrown herself at him, had virtually begged to be taken. How could any red-blooded man spurn an attractive woman when she spread her legs and invited him into her embrace?

Well, he might as well stop thinking about it, for it was over, finished. Nick did feel badly about taking all the money and leaving Laura without a cent, but at the time, in a panic over Harriet's threats to tattle to her uncle and Laura, he had needed to get away in a hurry, and he had needed the money to support himself until he could find something else. At any rate, Laura was a bright woman and would find some way to take care of herself. Perhaps Alfred would let her continue managing the theater. If so, she would be all right. At least he had been instrumental in getting Laura away from her father; she should be grateful to him for that.

His spirits began to lift as he walked toward his own show tent. He had fled in disgrace and he had been forced to take the first job he could find, but to some extent his usual luck had held. His mentalist act with the carnival did not pay him a great deal, but he had been exerting his charms on Madame Maridan, the widow who owned the carnival; and he had reason to believe that she was not adverse to his attentions. It had taken him several weeks to soften her up, but tonight he had finally been invited to her wagon to dine, and he was looking forward to it with considerable optimism.

Lola Maridan was a buxom woman of perhaps forty-five, or a well-preserved fifty, with sharp, dark eyes from which all innocence had long ago disappeared, an arrogant nose, a dusky complexion, and a mass of black hair that appeared to Nick to owe much of its color to the dye bottle.

She was a good-looking woman, in a hard way, and she was nobody's fool. Nick had sized her up right away as a formidable opponent; but then he enjoyed a challenge, particularly one that might pay other than amatory dividends.

Despite the fact that Lola paid the lowest possible wages and was given to poor-mouthing, Nick suspected that she had plenty of money stashed away. From what he had heard, she lived very well. Those who had been inside her wagon said that it was richly appointed and that she dined on the best food and drank the best liquor. She certainly wore expensive clothing, and it was apparent to Nick that she had a temperament that was given to self-indulgence.

It was also plain to him, from the way she had looked him over when they first met, that she had an eye for men. There was a certain type of woman, strongly sexed, who looked at a man's trouser front before looking at his face, and that was the kind of woman Lola Maridan was. Evidently Nick had passed muster, for she had hired him, and he had expected her to make an advance to him soon afterward. But she hadn't and this had piqued his curiosity.

After a few days of subtle maneuvering, Nick realized that Lola *was* interested, but she was also cautious. Evidently she was not the type to plunge into an affair without considerable forethought. There was also the matter of Bruno.

Bruno was a hulk of a man, over six feet tall with tremendous, knotty shoulders and hands like hams; apparently he was Lola's bodyguard. His shaved head and battered features defied an accurate estimate of his age. Nick had yet to see the man smile, and his small, rather piglike eyes seemed to convey only two emotions—distrust and truculence. As far as Nick could ascertain, Bruno served only one function with the carnival, and that was to watch over Lola. Wherever she went on the grounds, Bruno was always behind her, his suspicious gaze darting this way and that, as if longing for someone to make a threatening gesture toward Lola so that he might tear them limb from limb.

At first Nick had assumed the man was either Lola's husband or her lover, but he never saw her do or say anything to him that gave much support to this theory. Whenever Lola was in her wagon, the man stood outside her door, his beefy arms crossed over his muscular chest; and at night, Nick discovered as he was prowling about one evening, Bruno slept under Lola's wagon.

Why Lola needed a bodyguard was an interesting question, and one to which the other carnies did not have an answer. At any rate, to get to Lola, one first had to get past Bruno, which had proved to be a slight deterrent to Nick's plans, but not an insurmountable one, for although Bruno was as fierce and devoted as a trained watchdog, he had just about the same intellect.

Nick made sure that he found ways to make himself noticed by Madame Maridan; and now she had, at last, evidently decided that she could trust him, at least to the point of inviting him to dine with her.

Nick was outside his own tent now. He stood looking up at the painted canvas sign that proclaimed: "Nicolo the Great! Mentalist Without Peer! Knows All! Sees All!" In the center of the canvas was a badly painted semilikeness of Nick, dressed in evening attire, with a handkerchief tied over his eyes and his right hand raised.

Nick had learned the tricks of the mentalist trade while working with Lady Elizabeth Beedle. Lady Elizabeth had been billed as "Mentalist Extraordinaire—Adviser to the Royal Family."

Actually, the closest she had ever come to a real English lady was to shine one's shoes, for she had been a maid in London before hooking up with a stage performer, one Cyrus Chamberlin, from whom she had learned the secret codes and tricks of the mentalist.

As her assistant, Nick had learned the codes from her; and since he had a natural flair for showmanship and a strong stage presence, he had branched out with an act of his own, with which he had done rather well for a time.

When he had fled from Harriet and her pregnancy and had run across Madame Maridan's carnival, he had been looking for a way to keep out of sight and a means to support himself until he got back on his feet. The old mentalist act seemed a natural. He rather enjoyed fooling the public; and, unlike many of the acts that toured with the carnivals, there was a certain cachet attached to being a mentalist, for one got to perform in a dress suit and, as far as performing acts went, to present a gentlemanly image.

Of course, he had to have an assistant, someone to go out into the audience and take the rings, watches, and other personal articles from various people and hold them up. Then Nick, blindfolded on the stage, would call out, with apparent arcane knowledge, what the items were and to whom they belonged, a man or a woman, taking his clues from his assistant's words as she held up the articles.

He had incorporated a certain refinement of his own into the act, adding to the code words so that when the owner of the item was a woman, he could say she was "young and lovely," or "mature and stately," along with the color of her hair or eyes. This addition seemed to please the women more than his seemingly uncanny ability to identify, although firmly blindfolded, the items his assistant held in her hand. Before beginning his performance he always selected a member of the audience to place the blindfold on him.

The assistant he had found at the carnival, a young girl named Melanie Phalen, was the daughter of the owner and operator of the ring-toss booth. She was very young, about fifteen, and since both her mother and her father worked the booth, Melanie was not needed to help them. Her father was glad enough to have her earning a bit of money, and it had worked out well for all concerned.

She was a pretty girl with long, pale hair and large, pale blue eyes fringed with dark lashes. However, she was very underdeveloped for her age, and looked much younger—a fact that Nick had considered in selecting her. Despite his appetite for women, he had no taste for children, so Melanie, with her flat chest and narrow hips, was no temptation to him. At this point he certainly needed no additional irate male relatives baying after him.

Her childlike appearance was a plus in another way. Nick, always quick to know what impressed an audience, had her dress in simple, childish frocks that accentuated her youth and apparent freshness. The women adored her and felt her no threat, and the male audience—many of whom did not share Nick's disinclination for very young girls—found her charming in another fashion. Melanie was also intelligent and, having been a carnie all her life, not quite as innocent or naïve as her appearance indicated. She quickly learned the codes and instinctively knew how to play up to the audience. She was proving to be a great asset to Nick's act.

The act that evening went well, and afterward Nick had trouble getting away, for he found himself surrounded by fluttering townswomen and their reluctant husbands and escorts, as they asked him countless questions about his act and how he had learned such feats of mental legerdemain. He knew that most of the questions merely provided an excuse to see him close up; and one bold-eyed woman even managed to slip a note into his hand, asking him to meet her later at an address in town.

Nick smiled and nodded at them all and answered their questions readily enough, but he was eager to be off to keep his appointment with Lola Maridan. He had a feeling that tonight she was going to let down her guard, and he anticipated an evening that should offer him at least a good dinner and drink, and at most a pleasant tumble in Lola's bed, which was rumored to be made up with red silk sheets. Once he had taken her to bed, Nick was confident that she would open up to him—he smiled to himself at the pun—and that he might eventually be able to find out what her assets were and if there was any way in which their relationship might prove advantageous to him.

At last he was able to escape from his admirers and make his way to his quarters for the bottle of wine he had purchased in the last large town they had played. It was a rather good port, and he hoped that Lola would be impressed. He decided to leave on his evening clothes, in which he knew he looked quite dashing, as a reinforcement to his image as a gentleman. Then he walked across to Lola's wagon, which was parked off by itself a bit away from the other wagons.

As he had expected, Nick found Bruno standing at the wagon steps, arms crossed over his chest, looking rather like a sideshow strong man, which Nick suspected he had been at one time. Bruno, upon seeing Nick approach, gave him a baleful glare, but did not try to stop him.

Nick, amused by the man's surly resentment of him, nodded to him coolly as he mounted the steps. Still, a nervous little tingle twinged at the back of his neck as he knocked on the door and waited for Lola to answer. Nick had often thought of Bruno as little more than a watchdog, but he knew that there were some dogs that would attack a man simply for the sheer joy of it, and he was not at all certain that Bruno was not that sort.

However, the big man made no move toward him, and in a few moments the door was opened by Lola. Nick was delighted to see that she was dressed informally in a red velvet robe and a white feather boa.

"Come in," she said in her rather rough voice, which was unusually low for a woman, and which Nick found intriguingly sexual.

As he stepped into the wagon, he saw at once that the stories were true. Large and luxuriously furnished with red plush furniture, the interior had been divided into two rooms—a sitting room and bedroom.

The bedroom area was curtained off by heavy, red velvet drapes, which were now tied back with rich gold-tasseled cords, revealing a large bed with a red satin coverlet and masses of red velvet pillows. Nick hoped that the fact that the bedroom section of the wagon was exposed was a good omen for the evening.

Smiling, he held out the bottle of wine and made a small bow. "I thought this might be nice for after dinner."

Reaching out a hand gleaming with jewels, Lola took the bottle and looked at it appraisingly. The label must have pleased her, for she gave him a thin smile, and placed the bottle on an ornately carved table that stood against a wall covered with red and gold flocked wallpaper.

"Thank you, Nick. Would you like a whiskey before dinner?"

Nick saw that the table also held a sturdy crystal carafe and two heavy glasses. "Yes, thank you, I believe I would."

Lola turned to the table and poured two hefty drinks into the glasses, then handed one to Nick.

"Well, here's to crime," she said, tossing off half the drink in one swallow.

Nick felt like wincing, but he carefully kept his expression bland. Despite Lola's bold good looks and potential wealth, she had a vulgar streak in her, and Nick, who was a snob of sorts, did not care for very common women. He could tolerate a lack of education, and a few common mannerisms, but he seldom found a vulgar woman attractive. Still, there were other considerations here, and it had been more than a week since he had had a woman, so he decided he could overlook Lola's lack of refinement.

He took a sip of his drink and looked around the room with a show of appreciation. "You have beautiful quarters, Madame Maridan," he said politely, looking rather pointedly at the red velvet bed. "Did you decorate it yourself?"

Lola tossed off the other half of her drink and reached for the carafe. "Yes, I did. I know what I like, and I wanted to be comfortable above all else. And why don't you call me Lola? 'Madame Maridan' always makes me feel like I'm running a whorehouse." She laughed coarsely. "More whiskey?" She gestured toward his glass.

Nick shook his head. He knew that this woman was no fool, and he wanted to keep his wits about him while dealing with her.

"Sit?" Lola gestured to the red plush settee.

Nick nodded and took a seat. "You know, when I came to your door, I found Bruno outside. For a moment I thought he wasn't going to let me in."

There, that left her a good opening to explain her surly bodyguard; but Lola only shrugged and said, "Oh, Bruno takes his job seriously. I guess he'd kill for me if I asked him to."

A pointed look accompanied this remark, and Nick, taking note, looked down into his glass. This one was not going to be easy to sweet talk. However, she was drinking heavily. Perhaps after a few more drinks . . .

Trying to keep the conversation going, he looked at the beautifully set small table in the center of the sitting area. "Do you cook in your wagon?"

Lola shook her head, grimacing. "Can't abide cooking. Never could. Cookie prepares my meals in the cook tent. Of course, I don't eat what the rest of you eat."

"Of course not," he said, giving her his best smile. Good Lord, he thought, the woman was difficult to converse with! He had to do all the talking. How on earth could he get her to open up? "Have you had the carnival long?" he said rather desperately.

She nodded. "Ten years. Ever since Mr. Maridan died."

Nick lowered his head. "Oh, I am sorry. I didn't mean to resurrect sad memories for you."

She shrugged her plump, white shoulders. "Doesn't matter. He was an old bastard, if you want to know the truth. Tight as the skin on a grape. I wasn't sorry to see him go."

Nick took a swallow of his drink, wondering how best to reply to this. "Well, it looks to me as if you've done all right on your own."

She gave him a sharp look. "Not too badly, although there have been some who thought they could take advantage of a woman on her own. They soon learned better."

Another warning, thought Nick. *She's letting me know that she's in charge of things here, that she's nobody's fool, and that if I think I can move in on the money action, I'd better think again.* She was a tough woman, a real challenge.

"I believe I'll take that refill now," he said, holding out his glass.

She gave him a broad smile as she filled the glass almost to the brim. "Good! Can't abide a man who don't drink. Can't trust 'im. Here's mud in your eye, Orlando."

This time Nick matched her drinking style, and felt a flood of heat spread outward from his belly as the strong liquor warmed his body and his blood.

Lola did not show the effects of the liquor, except that

the shoulder of her robe had slipped down, exposing the top of one massive white breast. Nick, staring at it, felt a stirring in his loins. Remembering her appraising glance at that portion of his anatomy when they had first met, he made no attempt to conceal his condition; and sure enough, her gaze soon wandered to the juncture of his thighs, where the growing protuberance was making itself increasingly evident.

Her hard, dark eyes began to glisten, and her expression appeared to soften.

Well, Nick thought with some amusement, *at last I've found something she is interested in!*

Keeping her gaze fastened on the bulge in his trousers, which grew apace with the length of her stare, she reached blindly for the carafe. "One more drink," she said with emphasis. Nick wondered whether she meant that this was the last drink of the evening or the last drink before dinner.

He did not have to wait long to find out.

As Lola drained this last drink in a gulp, Nick followed suit, not wanting her to think him less able to handle his liquor than she. After emptying the glass, Lola set it down on the low table in front of her with a thump. Nick was just reaching out to place his glass beside hers, when her arm darted out and she grasped his swollen organ with her plump hand.

The effect on Nick was galvanic. Surprised and somewhat pained—her grasp was none too gentle—he could not keep himself from jumping. Gazing into her heavily madeup face, which was now only inches from his own, he faced her wide smile with trepidation.

"Well, I'll say one thing for you, Orlando. You're fine in that department. I never could abide a man with a tiny pecker. They may have the best will in the world, but they can't give a real woman the satisfaction she craves. Now, let's see if you know what to do with your equipment."

Lola stood, pulling him up by his erect member, and began leading him toward the bed.

Befuddled by the whiskey, which he had drunk too

quickly, and thrown off balance by her aggressiveness, Nick suddenly found himself on the bed, on his back, as her eager and efficient fingers unbuttoned his fly and found his flesh.

He heard Lola give a pleased grunt as she freed his "equipment," as she had called it, and gave it a squeeze.

Still rattled, he tried to regain the initiative by turning her onto her back; but with her considerable heft and strength she resisted all his efforts. Before he quite knew how it happened, she had his trousers off, as well as her velvet robe; and she was astride him, enveloping him with her strong white thighs and soft belly, her huge breasts pressing and bouncing against his chest as she rode him as if he were a bucking horse. He attempted to move beneath her, to take some part in the sexual congress, but it was soon clear that this was not necessary. She was doing it all by herself.

Feeling very definitely that she had put him at a disadvantage, the only thing Nick could retain pride in was the fact that he remained capable; under the circumstances, a lesser man might have failed.

Lola attained her climax with considerable speed and enthusiastic noise, before Nick had even recovered from his initial shock.

She climaxed at least twice more before he found his own release, which was somewhat delayed by the novelty of the situation, but this seemed to please her, for when she finally dismounted and sank, panting, beside him, she gave his now-limp member a friendly but none too gentle pat.

"You lasted real good, Orlando. A lot of men don't have the staying power."

Nick received the compliment in stunned silence. Although Lola seemed quite happy with his performance, his own pleasure had been less than satisfactory. As a man, he was used to making the advances. He enjoyed using his skill to seduce a woman, to bring her and himself to pleasure. Certainly he had known women who appeared to enjoy lovemaking as much as men did, who made it known that they were available; even some who would initiate the first advance, but usually in a subtle way. Never before had he met a woman who was completely the aggressor, who made all the advances and took control of the act itself. Why, the damned woman had practically raped him! It was demeaning!

Sighing lustily, Lola rose from the bed and moved over to the washstand, where a pitcher of water and a bowl awaited.

Nick turned his head away as she performed her ablutions noisily. If conversation had been difficult before, what on earth was he going to say to her now?

Lola turned away from the washstand and pulled on her robe. "Up and at 'em, Orlando. Supper's in the warmer, and I'm hungry as a horse. I'll have it on the table in a jiffy."

Feeling both chafed and ill used, Nick got up from the bed and cleaned himself before putting on the rest of his clothes. His shirt was soiled from Lola's makeup and would have to be washed, and his jacket was creased and wrinkled. Hell's bells! She could at least have had the decency to wait until he got undressed.

He was in a surly mood when he sat down at the small table, but Lola seemed not to notice.

As promised, the food was far above what was served in the cook tent, and Lola devoted her total attention to its consumption. Nick, despite his grumpy mood, was hungry too, and the meal was eaten in silence.

When it was over, Lola rose from the table and gave him a hard smile. "Well, I still have some work to do on the books tonight, Orlando, so I guess you'd better be off."

She did not offer him any of the port he had brought for after dinner. She walked to the wagon door and opened it. "I'll let you know when I want you again."

This was obviously a dismissal, and Nick got up from the table with as much dignity as he could muster under the circumstances. Without a word, he crossed to the door, then hesitated for a moment—habit was hard to break, and he would normally have given her a warm kiss in farewell—but he was damned if he was going to thank her for making a fool of him.

A moment later he was outside, walking toward his quarters, feeling Bruno's cold gaze on his back as he walked away. Nick had to wonder just how much the man had heard as he stood outside the wagon door.

Despite the recent physical release, Nick was tense and angry. Things had gone not at all as he had planned. He had learned nothing of Lola's finances, and he had certainly not made any impression on her emotionally.

Suddenly, the ridiculous nature of the situation struck him, and he gave a wry smile. Well, he had always maintained that he enjoyed a challenge, and here was certainly one of the greatest he had ever faced! He would not give up yet, and perhaps tomorrow he would be able to laugh at what had occurred tonight; but, thinking of Lola's curt words of dismissal, he grew angry again.

She had said that she would tell him when she wanted him again. Just what the devil did she mean by that? Would she now expect him to answer her beck and call, to be ready to service her at *her* convenience? Why, that was outrageous! Just what did she think he was?

He was no dog, to come running when Lola Maridan whistled!

Chapter Fourteen

LAURA, seated at her desk in the office car, was finding it very difficult to keep her mind on the heavy ledger that lay open before her.

In the distance, she could hear the sounds of the circus: the cries of the animals, the brassy music of the calliope, even the raucous shouts of the barkers.

She longed to be out there where the excitement was— there was still so much she wanted to see—but she had been asked to report to the office car early so that she might familiarize herself with office procedures and be given her instructions.

The rolling offices of the circus were considerably more comfortable and modern than Laura had expected. A large black safe dominated one end of the car, which was filled with counting tables and desks for the staff.

There was even a Remington typewriting machine, operated by a rather dignified woman, a Miss Gladys Orms, who seemed in complete control of its intricacies. The machine, one of the new models that printed in both upper and lower case, fascinated Laura; and she vowed that when she was better acquainted with its operator, she would ask the woman to teach her how to use it, for it seemed to Laura that the use of these machines was a coming thing, and that being able to operate one would be a useful skill.

Amos Potter, who was in charge of the office and the

staff, was a portly, bewhiskered gentleman who appeared to be in his early fifties, with a rather brusque exterior that Laura suspected hid a kindly heart. He gave Laura her work instructions in a clear and concise manner, and seemed pleased when she understood them easily.

Besides Amos Potter, she had met Miss Orms, Mr. Grey, and Mr. Clyde, who handled the accounting of the money, and a young man named Oliver Wayne, who, like herself, would be working on the books.

It had been a busy and confusing morning, and she was looking forward to her dinner break, when she intended to grab something portable from the cook tent and use her dinnertime to wander around the circus grounds.

But at present she had best stop daydreaming and attend to her work, as she could easily be discharged before she had really begun. Lowering her head, she focused her attention on the books, making her entries in the neat, clear hand of which she was proud.

Immersed in her work, she was startled to feel a touch on her shoulder. She glanced up and saw Will smiling down at her; he was holding a small, cobalt-blue vase that held one perfect, yellow daisy and a sprig of fern.

Meeting his gaze, she felt a wave of warmth and pleasure roll over her. "Will! What are you doing here?"

His smile gave his face a boyish look. "I've just come by to wish you well in your new job, and to bring you the flower for your desk. I'm sorry that it isn't a rose, but the daisy comes from the field behind the tents, and I thought it was somehow symbolic."

He held it out to her, and Laura took it, inadvertently touching his hand as she did so, and feeling that thrill that his touch always evoked in her.

"Thank you, Will. It's beautiful."

"I can't stay but a minute. Potter runs a tight ship here, but he gave me permission to interrupt you just this once, since it's your first day."

Laura glanced at Potter, who was standing nearby. He harumphed, and pointedly looked away, but Laura could see that he was not displeased.

Will said, "Would you like to go into town tonight for

dinner? There is an excellent restaurant in my hotel, and I can show you a bit of the town. It's really quite nice."

Laura did not have to consider her answer. She had been planning on seeing the circus tonight, for she had never seen the show on the road, but the circus would be there tomorrow night and the next; and she knew that Will might have to leave at any time, if Barnum needed him to check out a new act or to conduct some other business.

Still, she did not want to appear unbecomingly eager, so she hesitated for a moment, as if thinking over his invitation, before replying, "Why, yes, that might be nice."

His answering smile held back nothing. "Marvelous! I'll pick you up at your sleeping car when you've finished work."

Although their working hours were very long, the day had passed quickly, under the pressure of learning the rituals of the new job and the prospect of the evening ahead.

By the time Will arrived at the women's sleeping car, Laura had changed into a new outfit that she had purchased just before leaving New York—a fashionable green summer silk with a deeply gathered back. Although she had purchased it ready-made, the dress fit her well. When she had put it on over her underthings and bustle, it accentuated her small waist and high bust, giving her an elegant line. With this she wore a small straw hat decorated with flowers and a bit of green veiling, worn to the back of the head so that her fringe of curls would show in front.

A full-length mirror had been attached to the door of the sleeping coach, and as she looked in it Laura found herself radiant and pretty. She hoped that Will's eyes would reflect the same image.

When she came down the car steps to meet him, she found that Will was as well turned out as she. His fitted coat, fawn trousers, and sparkling linen showed his tall, well-built body to good effect. They would make a very handsome couple, she thought. She took his arm, and he led her to the rented carriage he had waiting.

*   *   *

As Will had promised, the restaurant was excellent. They were given a good table in a secluded corner, and Laura, relaxing with the wine and the good food, felt that she had never been happier.

Still, there was one nagging little voice that now and then penetrated her euphoria. She tried not to listen to it, but her practical side could not ignore it. What the small voice whispered was that she had had this same conviction of happiness once before, during the early days with Nick.

As she raised her glass for another sip of wine, Laura commanded the voice to be still. Life was made up of both happiness and unhappiness, and neither one could negate the other. She would not let the realization that she might be unhappy again, in the future, spoil the moment.

When their meal was over, Will took her walking through the town. It was, as he had said, a pleasant place, prosperous-looking and neat, and she admired the shop windows in the glow of the gas lamps. When they turned back toward the hotel, she was sorry that the evening was ending.

Holding Will's arm, she felt the energy radiating from it into her body, making her blood feel heated and as bubbly as the champagne they had drunk at dinner.

Unable to help herself, she pressed more closely against him, feeling the firmness of his arm against the side of her breast. As she did so, she felt his arm begin to tremble and was overcome by a confusion of feelings—shame at her wanton gesture, and joy that she could affect him like this. Oh, she wanted him so! There was no use denying it. She wanted to be in his arms, in his bed.

Will's steps slowed; and as they approached a dark patch of trees on the hotel grounds, he suddenly pulled her into the shadows. In an instant his lips were upon hers, as he pulled her hard against him.

The feeling of his mouth on hers was pure pleasure, pouring heat into her, heat that moved thickly and sweetly from her mouth to her breasts, causing them to swell and tingle, to her belly, which grew taut with excitement; and then down, down, until she thought she could not bear the painful pleasure of her want.

Briefly, he removed his mouth from hers and pressed his face to her cheek. His voice was a groan, a plea. "Laura! Oh, Laura! I swore to myself that I wouldn't touch you again until you gave me a sign, but . . ."

Eagerly she moved her face so that his lips were again on hers, and then pulled back so that she might speak. "There! I give you a sign, Will. My darling Will! I feel the same as you do. It may be shameful, but I can't help it."

For a moment he stood as if frozen, his arms locked around her; and then he tilted her face up with one hand, as if to search for the truth in her eyes. His voice dropped to a hoarse whisper, and the sound of it excited her still more. "Do you mean it, Laura? Tell me that you mean what you say!"

"Oh, I mean it, my darling! I mean it with all my heart. I want to be with you."

Will let his breath go with a ragged sigh. "We can go to my room in the hotel. It's room three twenty-five. Follow me in about ten minutes."

He squeezed her fiercely, until she feared her ribs would break, until she protested laughingly, "We will be close enough in a few moments, my love."

His breath was hot against her ear. "I feel that I'll never be able to get close enough to you, that I'll never get *enough* of you." He drew away reluctantly. "I'll go in now. You wait a few minutes, but not too long, or I'll die of frustration. Remember, room three twenty-five."

"I'll remember. It's engraved on my memory."

With one last, lingering kiss he left her, then turned to wave when he was again in the light.

Laura heard her ragged breathing and felt her heart hammering with excitement and fear, for despite her bold words she was frightened. She had known no other man than Nick. Now she was going to bed with another man—a man who, however much she wanted him, however kind and generous he might be, was a stranger. What was she starting? To what was she committing herself? The questions danced in her mind, making her feel jumpy and nervous, yet her desire and affection for Will were much stronger than her doubts.

After a few moments of nervous pacing in the shadows, she resolutely walked toward the hotel, her heart rate increasing with every step.

As she entered the lobby, Laura attempted to calm herself. The hotel had electricity, and the lobby was brilliantly lit. She felt that everyone in the room was looking at her, that they all knew just what she was doing, what she was going to do.

Filled with guilt and apprehension, she rang for the elevator, trying to will down the blush that she knew was staining her cheeks. When the metal cage arrived, she gave a sigh of gratitude for the fact that no one else was waiting to take it.

She faced the operator with grim determination and said as coolly as she could, "Third floor, please."

The elevator operator, a gnomish man in a red and black uniform, nodded soberly and turned his gaze toward his lever.

Does he suspect? she wondered. *A woman alone. Does he know that I'm not a guest?*

The elevator jerked to a stop. Holding herself regally erect, Laura exited and looked to the right and the left to see in which direction the room numbers ran.

It took her a few minutes to find the room; when she did, she was torn between wanting to rush inside, out of the sight of guests wandering the corridor, and a trembling reluctance.

At last the fear of being seen won out, and she rapped softly on the door. It was opened immediately, and she was pulled inside by Will's eager hands.

He said hoarsely, "I wasn't sure you'd come."

Laura could not speak, not trusting her voice. She had time to notice only that he was wearing a dressing gown and that the room was very attractive. Then she was on the bed, and he was beside her. After that, time lost all meaning. Through a glorious haze of passion, she let him undress her, slowly, tenderly; item by item he removed her clothing. After the removal of each item he rained kisses on her, leaving her dizzy and breathless; and when she finally lay naked and exposed before him, Will began to explore her body, with his hands, lips, and tongue, bringing her to such a pitch of wanting that she moaned and writhed beneath his ministrations, longing for him to enter her.

Reaching for the tie of his robe, she fumbled it loose with unsteady fingers; and then her hands felt the smooth flesh of his muscular belly. As she touched him, he murmured her name in a voice so filled with passion that it shook her like a touch upon the most intimate part of her.

And then he was on her, against her, and she felt the size and the power of him.

With a whimper she opened herself to him and then felt him move to enter her. He was still repeating her name, softly but joyously, like a chant; and then she felt him take her, fill her until the pleasure was so unbearable that she felt her body contract with the ultimate spasm, and she reveled in the explosive contractions inside her as he moved rapidly within her.

But no sooner had she experienced the pleasure of release than the tension began to build again, as intense as ever, and she began to move with him, taking delight in his obvious excitement, her passion fueled by the force of his, until she again felt the surging joy of climax; and it was still not enough. It was as if her body, deprived for so long, could not get enough loving. Her final surge came just before his, and at last they lay sated and panting, coiled in each other's arms, enjoying the tender aftermath of their fierce and tender lovemaking.

The ringing of the alarm clock jarred Laura to wakefulness, shattering her pleasant dream of being in Will's arms.

Reluctantly releasing the dream, she stretched and opened her eyes. She felt wonderful. Her body was tender and swollen with lovemaking, and it was marvelous!

Looking at the clock's reproving face, she yawned and slipped out of her berth. It was going to be difficult getting into the mood for work today. She longed to lie abed and savor the sensations she had experienced with Will last night. Nick had awakened her to passion, and their lovemaking had been wonderful, but with Will it was something more, something greater than the sum of its parts. She could not wait to see him today, or, more important, tonight; when he had returned her to the circus train they had agreed that the following night they would repeat their wonderful first time together. Although temporarily sated, they had both been aroused again by their good-night kiss in the shadows of the train. It was as though an insatiable and wonderful hunger consumed them, a hunger that years and years of lovemaking could never slake.

Fully awake, dressed, and replete with a hearty breakfast, Laura found herself with a few extra minutes before she was due at the office car.

There was already considerable activity on the circus grounds, and on an impulse she turned her steps toward the main tent, where pennants and banners were snapping in a brisk breeze.

Just outside the tent a group of clowns, looking very ordinary in practice clothing, were rehearsing a routine that featured several of the midget clowns and a very small wagon. Laura found herself smiling, for even without their bright costumes and makeup the routine was funny. The men knew how to use their bodies and faces to greatest advantage.

Laura heard voices from inside the tent, and lifting her skirt to avoid some horse droppings, made her way inside the dim cavern.

In the center ring, attired in plain tights and a short skirt, Betinna Brouder was practicing her routine, with the help of an older man.

Laura watched with wonder as the tiny woman, apparently frail and delicate, ran and leaped onto the back of a white horse so large it made her look even tinier. There she stood, as the horse galloped its circuit of the ring, and then she flipped into the air and landed again on the back of the moving horse. The physical feats that these people could do were amazing. The human body was a wonderful contrivance when properly trained, she thought.

At that moment she felt a tug on her sleeve and looked around to see young Dooley Waters looking up at her, his small, freckled face creased with earnestness. He was holding an envelope toward her with his other hand.

Dooley was one of the messengers employed to relay messages on the huge circus grounds, and Laura wondered what message he could possibly have for her. Perhaps it was for Amos Potter, and Dooley wanted her to take it to him to save time.

Surprised, and a little fearful, she took the envelope, which had her name scrawled across the front in a hurried script.

Opening the envelope, she removed a sheet of paper and read: "My Very Dearest: I am devastated that I must cancel our plans for this evening, but an emergency has arisen, and I must return to New York on the early train. I hope to be not more than a few days. Forgive my abrupt departure and think of me while I am gone. Love, Will."

Laura swallowed and read the words again. Dooley was still standing there watching her, but she scarcely noticed him. Will gone? What on earth could be the emergency that had called him away so abruptly? Into her mind came the memory of awakening one day to discover Nick gone, without any warning whatsoever.

Giving her head a sharp shake, she frowned at Dooley. "Do you know why Mr. Adams had to leave so quickly? Did Mr. Barnum send him on a trip?"

Dooley, his innocent eyes bright, shrugged. "I don't think so, Miss Laura. It may be because of the telegram."

Laura's gaze sharpened. "The telegram?"

Dooley nodded. "Yep. This morning, real early, a telegram came for Mr. Adams. I saw the boy deliver it. It was after Mr. Adams read the telegram that he wrote this out and asked me to take it to you first thing."

"And you don't know if the telegram was from Mr. Barnum?"

Dooley looked doubtful. "I don't think so. I heard the messenger say that it was from New York City, and I happen to know that Mr. Barnum is up at his home in Waldemere, 'cause he just sent a message from there yesterday."

"Well, thank you, Dooley." Laura's voice was tightly controlled. "I guess I'd better get on to the office now."

Dooley tipped his hat. "Just doing my job. See you later, Miss Laura!"

He left at his usual trot, and Laura turned and started walking slowly toward the office car. A telegram from New York—an emergency. What could it be? Despite her efforts to keep them at bay, suspicions began to nibble at the edges of her mind. She had been told, by her mother and by many articles in women's magazines, that men looked down on "easy women"; that often, when they had had their way with them, they had no further use for them. But surely that was not the case with Will! Will cared for her; he had said so both with actions and words. They cared for each other. It was different with them.

But that small, nagging voice, that agitator in her mind, would not be still. "Are you sure?" it whispered. "Are you absolutely certain?"

As the train thundered toward New York, Will Adams stared morosely at the less than ample breakfast before him at his table in the dining car.

He really had no appetite, but eating would give him something to do, and he did need the strong hot coffee that accompanied the food. He felt tense with repressed anger and apprehension, wishing that the train could move faster, wishing that there were some way he could be instantly at his son's side.

Pearl's telegram had said that the boy was gravely ill. Since she was not given to exaggeration, and since she would not have wired him unless the situation was serious, Will knew that he had every reason to be concerned.

At the thought of anything happening to Justin, he felt the familiar sick pain that always accompanied such thoughts. Life had robbed him of his son's mother; surely, if there was any justice, it would not take his son from him as well. Yet, Will knew, there was little justice in the world.

And now, of all times, just when he had found happiness again . . . It was as if someone or something could not bear to see him too content.

Will did not know what effect his abrupt departure would have on Laura; he could only assume that she would be upset. He had not had time even to write a proper note. Since he could not very well explain to her the reason for the hurried trip, she would very likely feel abandoned. He could only hope that she would trust in his feeling for her.

He drank a cup of the aromatic coffee and managed to eat a slice of toast with jam.

It seemed an eternity before the train reached New York. When at last it arrived, it was in the middle of the afternoon rush hour, and Will's frustration grew as he attempted to hail a hansom cab.

When he finally arrived at the house it was early evening, and a strange, melancholy light, heavy and golden like that in a Turner painting, hung over the city. His heart pounding, Will paid off the cab and ran up the stairs.

As his key rattled in the lock, the door swung open, and Mrs. Anderson, the housekeeper, stood there, her usually jolly face pale, her eyes red from weeping.

Will looked at her in dismay as her face crumpled at the sight of him. "Chloe! I'm not too late? He's not. . . ?"

Chloe put out a sturdy hand, as if to comfort him. "Oh, no, Mr. Will. It's not that. But he's awful bad off. Dr. Thompson and Miss Pearl are with him. I'm so glad you're here. Miss Pearl has been awfully worried."

Will breathed a deep sigh of relief. His son was still alive, and he would see to it that he remained that way, no matter what.

Chapter Fifteen

"CLUMSY girl! Watch what you're doing!"

Diana Salieri's dark eyes glared at Milly with contempt, and Milly felt her face grow hot. She was fitting Diana for a new costume, and it was an almost impossible task.

First of all, the woman complained about everything—the material, the design—and she fidgeted so much that it was very difficult to pin the fabric without sticking her somewhere. Milly longed to give her a good jab, so that she really would have some reason to complain.

Looking up, Milly caught Madame Costa's warning glance. Madame understood quite well what was going on, Milly was sure, but her look was a warning that the Salieri arrogance must be endured.

Milly sighed, longing for the fitting to be over and done. Most of the performers were easy to get along with. Some of them were a little fussy about their costumes, a little temperamental perhaps, but Milly didn't mind that. Even the other Salieris, while arrogant enough, heaven knew, were not *too* unreasonable. Only Diana Salieri, who evidently thought she was a princess.

Milly muttered under her breath as Diana moved again, this time leaning down to her small poodle, Pucci, who reclined close by on a blue silk pillow. "Is Pucci getting bored? Well, Mama is, too, but hopefully we'll soon be finished." Her deep sigh carried the implication that she was surrounded by incompetents and grossly lesser beings, and that she could hardly wait to be away from the fitting room.

Well, Milly thought crossly, *the feeling is mutual, Miss High and Mighty!*

Milly could not understand how Lionel, Benjy, and the others could be taken in by such patent artificiality. True, Diana was very beautiful on the outside, but her disposition and temperament certainly were not. Men were *such* fools! They never seemed to look beyond the superficials when it came to women. A pretty face, a seductive figure, that was all they ever saw. Blinded by sexual attraction, they would marry some pretty, empty-headed young thing, and then after the honeymoon was over they would find out, to their dismay, that they had tied themselves to a shrew. They paid with the rest of their lives for their bad judgment. Milly had seen it happen often enough.

Women, now, were more sensible. Women usually looked a little deeper. They seemed to know that you could not choose a husband and future father of your children solely on the basis of a handsome face. There were exceptions, of course; but in general, women looked beyond exteriors. Most women, that was.

Diana Salieri, of course, was one of those exceptions. A shallow woman, she was obviously incapable of recognizing Lionel for what he really was—a cultured, intelligent, kindly man, with much love and affection to give. Diana saw only a freak. She could not even see his unusual beauty.

Milly, putting another pin into Diana's costume, wished that Lionel would look at her the way he looked at Diana. If he would, *she* would not treat him like dirt.

At that moment, little Benjy, the dwarf, came trotting into the dressing tent on his short, bowed legs, bearing a tray on which were a pitcher and a tall glass.

His earnest face, attractive despite the large forehead and the slightly recessed features, was apprehensive. "I'm sorry to be so slow, Miss Diana, but cookie was busy and I couldn't hurry him up any."

He held the tray toward Diana apologetically, and Milly had to turn her gaze away. Did he realize how pitiful he looked and acted around Diana? Like a little dog begging for a kind word; when in truth he was more apt to receive a kick.

Diana gave Milly a sharp glance. "Stop for a moment, girl. I must have something to drink. I'm perishing of thirst."

This last was directed to Benjy, clearly a rebuke so that he would know that he had not performed quickly enough for her satisfaction. "Pour me a glass, Benjy."

Eagerly the little man set the tray on the work table and jumped up on a stool so that he would be able to reach and pour from the pitcher.

Diana watched him with an amused smile on her haughty face.

As she might watch a performing monkey, Milly thought bitterly. Why couldn't Benjy see it? About other things he was not stupid in the least.

Smiling hopefully, Benjy climbed down from the stool with the glass and carefully handed it to Diana, who delicately tasted it while Benjy watched anxiously.

When she finally smiled, his face lit up from within, as if she had given him a precious gift. "It's good?"

Diana hesitated for a moment, then nodded. "It's quite refreshing, Benjy dear. Thank you so much."

Benjy jumped up and down. "Is there anything else you want? Anything else I can do for you, Miss Diana?"

Diana emptied the glass and returned it to the little man. "You may walk Pucci. The poor, dear creature needs the exercise, and then you may bring her back to my wagon."

Benjy looked as pleased as if she had just knighted him. "Of course, Miss Diana. At once. I'll have her back to you in half an hour."

All of them watched as Benjy attached the narrow leash to Pucci's jeweled collar, as the dog looked on apathetically, and then Benjy led the reluctant animal out of the tent and into the sunlight.

"Such a helpful little man," Diana said condescendingly. "And now let us see if you can be as helpful, Milly, and extricate me from this viper's nest of pins. It is time for my practice."

Silently, Milly helped her out of the fitted costume, then watched out of the corner of her eye as Diana slipped into a red silk wrapper.

As Diana turned to go—without even a word of goodbye or a thank-you to the wardrobe women—her elder brother, Santiago, and her younger brother, Davalo, came into the tent. Santiago's darkly handsome face was set in a frown. He immediately addressed his sister in Italian, and she answered in kind.

Evidently they had never been taught that it was impolite to speak a language in front of others who did not understand it, Milly thought; and then she smiled rather smugly, for she *did* understand Italian, since her mother had come from Italy.

Santiago was saying that it was time for their daily practice session and Diana was late. Diana was blaming her tardiness on Madame Costa and Milly.

Milly felt her face grow hot with anger. She and the other wardrobe girls worked long and hard, and here was this arrogant, well, bitch—there was just no other word for it—treating them like dirt under her feet.

Milly set her lips and glanced around to see how Santiago was reacting to his sister's statement, and her gaze met that of Davalo, the younger brother. Davalo, evidently recognizing her anger, flushed slightly and looked away.

As Santiago and Diana started out of the tent, Milly heard Santiago remark that he had seen Diana's little "monkey" coming out with Pucci, and then he made a facetious comment about Diana's little circle of admirers. With a laugh Diana retorted in English that Santiago might scoff, but the lesser orders did have their uses.

Through the open tent flap, Milly could see Benjy. He had certainly overheard the cutting remark.

Milly could almost taste her anger. If there was any justice in the world, someday Miss Marvelous would get her comeuppance. The world could not be so unfair as to allow her to ride roughshod over everyone, to have her own willful way forever. No, one day she would push someone too far, and he would take his revenge on her. It was only a matter of time.

Davalo, who had remained behind, made a tentative gesture. He looked embarrassed and upset. "I am sorry," he said in his heavy Italian accent. "You understand Italian, do you not?"

Milly, still angry, nodded. "I understand enough."

Davalo gave an expressive shrug. "Then I must apologize for my sister. She often speaks without thought. She is very tense just now, and when she is tense she is often apt to be thoughtless and even unkind."

Milly gave an unladylike snort. "Well, we all get tense now and again, but we don't usually use that as an excuse to insult people."

Davalo flushed, and his set expression mirrored an anger of his own. He said somewhat stiffly, "Yes, everyone gets tense, but in most cases their tension is not a matter of life and death. In our case it often is, you see."

Realizing that he was speaking of the dangers of their profession, Milly felt her anger weaken. "I realize that," she said softly. "I can understand if Diana is nervous about a new routine, or something of that nature, but it's still no excuse to be nasty. Benjy is a good and true friend to her. He deserves to be treated better."

Davalo nodded. "You are right, but Diana is . . . Diana. Even I, as her brother, must admit that her disposition is not always the best, but her flying—ah, *that* is perfection. She is an artist!"

Milly shook her head in exasperation. "You mean that because she is good at what she does, people must put up with her . . ." She wanted to say "cruelty" but did not dare. "With her bad temper?"

"Yes, I suppose that is what I am saying. Sometimes genius, specialness, has to be forgiven things that would be objected to in ordinary people."

Milly snorted again. "Well, I don't mean to argue with you, but I happen to think that's a pile of nonsense!"

The aerialist shook his head. "It may seem so to you, but it is a fact of life, nonetheless." He took on an intense look. "You know what we do. You have seen us perform. We use no net, and we perform feats of great complexity and danger. Every time we go up, every time we fly, we risk death. Does that not give us some privileges?"

"Of course, and you have those. You have beautiful quarters, you are paid very well, and you are the stars of the circus. I think that should be sufficient. I shouldn't think it would be necessary to treat other people as if they were not quite human. But thank you for your apology, Davalo. I know it's from the heart, and I know you're not responsible for the actions of your sister. It was kind of you."

Davalo bowed slightly. "Your gratitude is not necessary, Milly. I simply wished you to understand. I bid you good afternoon."

She had mixed feelings as she watched him walk away. He was a very attractive young man and the nicest and most approachable of the Salieri family. It *was* kind of him to apologize, she thought; yet, he was still tarred with the same brush of arrogance. To say that Diana should be forgiven any rudeness she chose to inflict on other people just because she was good at what she did was both unfair and illogical.

Sighing, Milly turned back to her work.

"And then, as they walked out, I heard her say, 'the lesser orders have their uses,' as if she were talking about slaves or something! Can you believe her arrogance?"

Laura and Milly had just finished supper in the cook tent and were strolling around the grounds.

Milly's gamine face was pink with emotion, and Laura felt a surge of affection for her. Little Mother of All the World, Milly seemed to feel insults to others as much as she would have had they been directed at herself.

"She really does sound awful," Laura said. "I can't imagine what a man sees in a woman with such a dreadful disposition. You would think they would see past her outer appearance."

"That's just what I was thinking while I was fitting her. Sometimes I really don't understand men. Do you?"

Laura shook her head, thinking about Will. Three weeks had passed since he had left for New York, and she had not heard one word from him. Why had he been called away, and what was he doing? He could at least have written!

During the one night they had spent together, Will had seemed to feel for her what she felt for him. All his actions and words had told her that he cared for her, had strong feelings for her. And now this . . . this abandonment!

What did it mean? Was he, like Nick, simply an exploiter of women? From what she knew of Will, it was difficult to believe, and yet he and Nick did have some things in common. A wanderlust, for instance. Had she been taken in again? Now that Will had had her, did he no longer want her? The more she thought about it, the more hurt and confused she became.

"Don't you agree? Laura, aren't you listening to me?"

With a start Laura dragged her thoughts back to the present and smiled down into Milly's eager little face. "I am sorry, Milly. I was wool-gathering. What did you say?"

Milly laughed. "I didn't mean for my question about understanding men to throw you into a dark mood. In fact, what I was just saying was that now that I've aired my grievances, I thought we should just forget about Miss High and Mighty and the injustices of the world, and talk about something more cheerful. Do you want to see the show tonight?"

Laura nodded. During the past weeks she had been able to see the evening show several times and to familiarize herself with the grounds—which were always laid out in the same pattern—and with the routine of the traveling circus. Each town was different, and yet in many ways they were so much the same that often it was difficult to tell one town from another, for despite the differences in the towns, the ritual—and Laura thought of it as just that—was always the same.

First, the circus parade, all color and sound, made its way through the town, announcing the presence of the show and collecting a second parade of townspeople who followed it back to the circus grounds. Leading the parade

was the circus band, resplendent in their colorful uni-
forms, their polished instruments shining in the sun; then
came the elephants, slowly swaying in their embroidered
and tasseled headpieces and blankets, each ridden by a
beautiful girl in spangled tights and feathers; the animal
wagons, brightly painted in red and gold, the animals
pacing back and forth in their cages as the wagons rolled
behind the draft horses; beautifully caparisoned horses
and riders; clowns tumbling, falling, bouncing, stopping
to tickle a child's chin or to offer a woman a flower; and
then the calliope, rending the air with its brassy music,
the very essence of the circus itself.

The shows, with very minor variations, were always the
same: the crowded seats, the laughing children, the smells of
food and crushed tanbark—they were all engraved in Laura's memory.

As the weeks had passed she had overcome her shyness
around the prodigies—which was how she thought of them
now—and had grown quite fond of Madame Zenobia,
Lionel Germaine, and little Benjy, and she was getting to
know many of the others, as well as the big-tent performers, such as Harold von Haupt, the daring German highwire
artist, who walked the thin wire as casually as he might
have strolled a sidewalk, performing feats of daring and
skill that took Laura's breath away; Lucinda Banks, a
cheerful, sturdy young woman billed as the Human Pro-
jectile, who allowed herself to be lowered into the mouth
of a huge cannon and fired through the air into a waiting
net; Rodney J. Landers, leader of the equestrian team,
which included his petite wife and daughter, who, despite
their tiny size, handled the horses with assurance and
supple grace; and so many more, many of whom risked
their lives daily to amuse and entertain the crowds.

And then there were the clowns. Laura was particularly
fond of the clowns, for with their brightly painted faces
and outlandish clothes they seemed to have a touch of
magic about them, bringing laughter to children and adults
alike with their outrageous antics.

Of course, she did not become friendly with all the
performers, for the circus world was, in many ways, much

like the outside world. You met all kinds of people. Some you liked very much, some became mere acquaintances, and others you disliked.

Milly had become her closest friend, and the more Laura saw of the younger girl the more she admired her. Milly was a genuinely good person, caring, open-natured, and generous, almost too much so. It was her inner toughness that saved her, that and her practicality. Everyone seemed to like Milly, except perhaps Diana Salieri; but then, as far as Laura could see, Diana cared for no one except Diana Salieri.

Often during those weeks, Laura wished that she could discuss the matter of Will with Milly. Perhaps Milly's common sense could help her sort out her feelings; and yet Laura found herself unable to talk about Will, even with her best friend. But it had never been her nature to unburden herself to anyone. Perhaps it was her family background; she certainly could never talk to her father, and her mother was not the type to invite confidences. Also, it was pride, she supposed. She did not want anyone's pity, and she felt that exposing her weaknesses and doubts to another person would lessen her in their eyes. She would just have to work it out herself.

At any rate, there was one thing she was certain of—she would not let any other man do to her what Nick had done, make her ill with unhappiness and worry, and almost break her spirit. Nick had hurt her deeply, yet she had pulled herself up by her bootstraps and had gone on. No matter what she felt for Will, or for any other man, she would not be put through that again. She must put Will out of her mind. She had her job, she had friends, and she had her freedom. It would have to be enough.

"Let's walk through the museum tent before we go to the big tent," Milly was saying. "I'd like to see how Madame Zenobia's new gown looks on the platform."

Laura smiled. She knew very well what Milly's real reason was for wanting to visit the museum tent, where the prodigies were exhibited along with other wonders and inventions, and it had nothing to do with Madame Zenobia's gown.

"If you like, Milly. But first let's stop by the cook tent; I want to get an apple for Jumbo."

"Fair enough, although I do think you've chosen a rather large pet, Laura. To tell you the truth, he frightens me a little. He's so *big*! I think I prefer the little midget elephant, Tom Thumb. He looks like a baby, and babies are always appealing."

"Well, I certainly agree that Jumbo is no baby, but I think he's magnificent. I've been told that he's a tremendous drawing card, and that they're selling Jumbo cigars, Jumbo hats, and Jumbo fans. He's bringing in a lot of money." Actually, it was Will who had told her this, but Laura did not want to bring his name into the conversation.

Milly shook her head. "I suppose that's a good thing. I imagine it must cost a small fortune to feed an animal that size."

Laura nodded. "His trainer told me that on an average day Jumbo consumes two hundred pounds of hay, two bushels of oats, one of biscuits, fifteen loaves of bread, three quarts of onions, five buckets of water, plus apples, oranges, figs, nuts, cakes, candles, and . . ." she leaned over to whisper in Milly's ear, "an occasional bottle of whiskey. The trainer says that he can gulp down a whole quart at once."

"Whiskey! I didn't know that. What would happen if he ever got drunk, do you suppose?"

"That's not likely to happen, with all the food he consumes."

"And the food the circus provides him doesn't include all the peanuts the crowds feed him. I'm just glad I don't have to pay his food bill!"

The animal tent was hot and filled with strong, but not unpleasant, smells.

Jumbo, in his enclosure, stood swaying ponderously back and forth, his huge trunk swinging from side to side, while his trainer talked to the crowd circled around him.

"Yes, folks, Jumbo is the largest elephant in the world. He stands eleven feet six inches high at the shoulders, and he's fifteen feet across the head from ear tip to ear tip.

His trunk is seven feet long, and he weighs six and one-half tons. Still, for all his size, he is a gentle beast, and intelligent. Just look at his eyes."

Laura and Milly managed to squirm through to the front of the crowd, and Jumbo raised his trunk and fixed his small, intelligent eyes, set in their nest of wrinkles, on Laura.

"Why, he recognizes you, Laura!" Milly said in wonder, and Laura felt a surge of pleasure. She did not know why, but she felt drawn to this magnificent animal. Perhaps it was because he looked so old and so wise, and, as his trainer had said, so gentle, despite his great size and strength.

Holding out her hand, palm up, she presented him with a large red apple.

"Here is one of Jumbo's friends now," the trainer told the crowd. "She's going to give our Jumbo a little treat. Now watch how delicately he takes the fruit."

Laura heard a collective sigh from the crowd as Jumbo reached out with his flexible trunk and gently, gracefully, took the apple from Laura's hand, moving it slowly to his mouth, all the time looking at her with what she saw as appreciation and gratitude. She often wondered what was going on in Jumbo's great head. What kind of thoughts did an elephant have? His eyes looked so human, and faintly sad.

After saying goodbye to Jumbo, the two young women proceeded to the museum tent. Waving to the ticket taker, who recognized them, they entered and made their way toward the platform where the prodigies were exhibited.

It was strange, Laura thought, how different the freaks seemed when on stage. Perhaps it was the costumes, or just the fact that they were on public view, showing their uniqueness, making their differences visible.

For instance, Belle Taylor, the Four-Legged Girl, looked just as normal as anyone when she was dressed in regular clothing with her long skirt covering the two extra, smaller limbs that grew between her legs. Except for a somewhat awkward gait, caused, Laura supposed, by the interference of the two small, dangling appendages with her normal legs, she in no way appeared unusual.

But when, as now, Belle was on exhibition, she was attired in a short skirt and was seated so that all four legs were shown from the knees down, all attired in identical shoes and stockings. The two center legs looked like a child's, as if Belle had a small girl hidden beneath her skirts.

Despite the fact that Laura had, to a great extent, gotten over her squeamishness concerning the prodigies, seeing Belle like this always gave her an odd feeling. She had been told that Belle, besides having the extra legs, had two sets of sexual organs below the waist. Laura supposed that nature had intended Belle to be twins but that something had gone wrong within the womb, causing her to be born as somewhat more than one, and yet less than two. Laura could not help wondering about the rest of the missing twin. Was it somewhere inside Belle's body? It was an eerie, unsettling thought.

Besides the people whom Laura had met that first night at dinner, many of whom were now her friends, there were dozens of others whom she now knew casually—the Elephant Boy, a young man of perhaps seventeen, with legs so huge and even-sized from thigh to foot that they looked like those of an elephant; the Turtle Woman, a black woman who had only short stumps for arms and legs; the Tattooed Man, who had pictures tattooed over every single exposed inch of his body; the Living Half-Man, who was only a torso, with nothing below his waist, who had trained himself to walk on his hands, using them as he would have used legs.

And then there were the famous Wild Men of Borneo, Plutano and Waino, reportedly captured by a ship's crew after a dreadful struggle when the crew landed on a jungle island in search of water. In reality, Laura knew, the pair were brothers, born Hiram W. and Barney Davis. Not much larger than dwarfs, they were good-natured and quite gentle little fellows. They were, however, unusually strong, and could pick up a six-foot man with ease.

Laura and Milly walked alongside the platform to where

Madame Zenobia was standing. The Madame's new gown, an elaborate, off-the-shoulder affair in pink satin with a jeweled neckline, was pronounced beautiful; and then at last they arrived at the destination Milly had been heading toward all along, the end of the platform where Lionel Germaine was pacing back and forth, showing his white teeth in a parody of fierceness, his cape whirling dramatically as he turned.

He did look beautiful, Laura thought, and, like his namesake, the lion, there was something noble and majestic about him. The tent was lighted by electricity, and the light shone on his golden hair, making it gleam.

She sneaked a quick glance at Milly and saw the look on her friend's face. Yes, there was no doubt about it: Milly was smitten.

Laura felt a soft wave of sadness. Men! Was loving them always such a problem? The problem between Lionel and Milly was not that Lionel was a freak, for Milly loved circus life and wanted to stay with it—and within the charmed circle of the show, their life could probably be very pleasant; but Lionel was obviously obsessed with Diana Salieri, who cared not a snap of her fingers for him. It was like a dreadful round-robin that could only make all of them unhappy. Laura's heart wept for her friend. It seemed to her as if both her own and Milly's love affairs were doomed.

"Look!"

Milly's sudden nudge jarred Laura out of her reverie.

Laura's gaze followed Milly's pointing finger to see Diana Salieri, on the arm of her elder brother, Santiago, strolling down the long tent. They were in their show tights, with capes thrown over their shoulders. Now and then Diana would point to one of the prodigies on the platform and speak to Santiago in a low voice.

"Now what do you suppose they're doing in here associating with the 'lower orders'?" Milly asked in a tight voice.

Laura said, "Maybe we'd better leave."

"No! Darned if I'm going to let them drive me away."

Diana and her brother had reached them now. Diana's

glance passed over them disdainfully and then moved on to Lionel, who had stopped and was staring at Diana with a hopeful expression.

In a carrying voice Diana said something in Italian, and Santiago laughed, throwing back his head.

Milly tensed, and Laura whispered, "Did you understand what she said?"

"I certainly did!" Milly said angrily. "She said that Lionel looks like a big lapdog. She said that he has more hair than Pucci. I'll tear that bitch's own hair out for her!"

"No!" Laura's anger blazed. She seized Milly's arm and felt it actually vibrating in fury. "She could get you fired, but I doubt she could do much to me. Let me handle this."

She took two steps forward. "Miss Salieri?"

Diana looked at her haughtily. "Yes?"

"I heard what you just said about Lionel. It was nasty and insulting. I think you should apologize."

"Apologize?" Diana seemed amused. "A Salieri never apologizes."

Laura felt her anger rising. "Then perhaps it's time you started. This isn't the first time you've been overheard making rude remarks about these people."

"These *people?*" Diana's lip curled. "They're not people, they're . . ."

"That's enough!" Laura said angrily.

Diana recoiled slightly, her eyes widening. "Who are you to talk to me like this?"

"Who I am is not important," Laura said steadily. "But if you do not apologize, I shall go to Mr. Bailey and report what you've been saying. You know Mr. Bailey does not like trouble between the employees."

"Oh, yes, I recognize you now. You're a . . . a bookkeeper, I believe." Diana tossed her head. "Well, you may do as you please. It will not matter. I am a Salieri, and a Salieri is not subject to your Mr. Bailey, nor anyone else. Come along, Santiago, we shall go now."

Santiago, who had remained aloof during the conversation, extended his arm, and Diana took it. They swept out of the tent, heads held high.

Milly, beside Laura now, gave a gasp of indignation. "That woman is absolutely impossible! She actually believes that she can get away with anything, that she can do as she pleases!"

"She probably can," Laura muttered. "I might as well have saved my breath."

Remembering, she darted a glance at Lionel. He was staring after Diana with a strange look. Little Benjy stood beside him, his hand touching Lionel's thigh, as though in sympathy.

In a low voice Laura said, "Do you think Lionel heard what she said? Does he understand Italian?"

"I don't know. But if he does, he certainly understood what that woman said. She spoke loud enough for everyone to hear her." Milly's eyes were moist as she stared at the Lion Man.

"We'd better go, Milly. If he did understand her, he's probably embarrassed about us overhearing."

Milly nodded, and they started out of the tent. "I know he's enamored of Diana, but I think he likes me, a little," Milly said wistfully. "Don't you think so, Laura?"

"Of course," Laura said quickly. "That's quite obvious."

Milly smiled suddenly. "That's what I thought. Well, as you can no doubt tell, I like him, too."

Laura sighed inside. She had spoken the truth—it was clear that Lionel liked Milly—but as far as Laura could see, it was nothing more than the affection of a brother for a little sister. Laura was very much afraid that if Milly was romantically interested in Lionel Germaine, she was going to end up being hurt.

As they exited the museum tent, Milly looked down at the watch pinned to her bodice. "Good heavens, I'm late! I've got to run, Laura. Are you going in to watch the show, or are you going back to the car?"

Laura shrugged. "I think I'll watch the show. I hear the Montinis have added a new trick to their routine. Besides, I never get tired of seeing the show—it's always different in some way."

Milly nodded. "I'll see you afterward, then. I'd better get to the dressing room before Madame Costa fires me."

Laura watched Milly hurry away, her pale hair flying, for she still often wore her hair like a young girl, tied back and flowing.

Slowly Laura turned and walked toward the entrance of the main tent. Mentioning the Montinis had made her think of the months they had played at the Melodeon, and of her first meeting with Will. *Oh, Will,* she thought. *Where are you, and why haven't you written to me? I can get along without you. I will get along without you, if I have to; but I would much rather get along with you. Please come back to me!*

The huge tent was crowded, full of bustle, color, action, and noise. The introductory pageant had already started by the time Laura had purchased a candy apple and had found a seat.

Usually the blare and the brightness of the spectacle put Laura into a good mood, but tonight something seemed wrong. It was probably just her own dark mood; but tonight everything seemed a bit off-center; too loud, too garish, and, oddly, a little frightening. Watching the now-familiar parade, she felt a little like Alice in Mr. Carroll's book. It was odd how your perceptions of things could change from one day to another.

Carefully she took a bite of the stickily coated apple, savoring the contrast of flavors and textures, watching as the pageant concluded, and the acts came into each of the three rings. Soon, caught up in the performances and feeling some of the crowd's enthusiasm and excitement—for its emotion was contagious—Laura managed to forget her odd mood.

The Montinis' new addition was spectacular, and there was a new act where a man rode a velocipide at great speed down a narrow, circular, looped slide. It looked extremely dangerous, and the crowd seemed to love it.

And then, with a brassy fanfare, the Salieris entered the center ring. A handsome group in their spangled capes, headdresses, and tights, they strutted like peacocks into the ring, waving as they went.

Laura made a moue. Such an arrogant lot; and yet the

crowds loved them, and she did have to admit that as performers they were exceptional.

As the band played, the Salieris regally removed their headdresses and capes, then began to climb the ladders to the platforms near the top of the tent. The eldest brother, Santiago, a muscular man with heavy arms and shoulders, was the catcher; he took his place on the trapeze at the far end of the rigging, lowering himself into catching position, head down, hanging by his knees. The others climbed to the platform opposite him and posed and gestured to the upturned faces of the crowd.

And then the act began. First, the handsome Sergio reached out and grasped the flying bar, swinging out smoothly in a long arc. When he reached the top of his swing, he jackknifed neatly, rolled into a single somersault, then straightened his body before interlocking his hands with those of his brother.

Meanwhile, the younger brother, Davalo, had caught the returning trapeze as it swung back, gripped it, and swung out. At the moment when Sergio let go of Santiago's wrists, Davalo let go of his trapeze bar, and the two flyers somersaulted past each other, Davalo grasping Santiago's hands as Sergio seized the trapeze vacated by Davalo.

Laura let out a relieved sigh that mingled with the sighs of the crowd. No matter how often she saw them, she was still awed by the grace, precision, and control of the aerialists.

The two young men performed several more tricks, then it was Diana's turn. Like a queen, she stood there far above the crowd, her head held regally erect, her body gleaming in spangled tights; she looked magnificent.

Laura shook her head ruefully. Diana *was* beautiful. Was there no justice?

Then Diana grasped the bar and swung out toward Santiago, who was swinging down to meet her. In her shimmering costume, Diana appeared to float in the air like a bird, her body twisting, turning like a great, leaping fish before reaching for her brother's hands. The crowd gave a startled gasp. For a moment there had been a hesitation, a hitch in the perfect rhythm. It had been a less than perfect catch. Laura frowned. She had watched the show many times now, and she had never seen any of the Salieris in anything other than perfect form. Yet, when Diana made her return swing to the empty bar, there was no hesitation, and the crowd relaxed.

Whatever else Diana Salieri was, she *was* brave, for the Salieris worked without a net. Laura could no more imagine doing something so dangerous than she could imagine flying. In fact, Laura grew nervous merely watching the performers undertaking the dangerous stunts. Despite all the exaggeration of the publicity men, they did put their lives at risk at every performance.

Now Diana was preparing to take the bar for her second trick. Laura, peering up to the top of the huge tent, thought that the aerialist hesitated longer than usual before leaving the platform, but that was probably only her imagination.

Suddenly Diana was making her swing, strong and graceful as ever, and then she was in the air, tumbling, once, twice, perfectly executed, and now she was reaching out for her brother's hands. . . .

For an instant, Laura could not believe what was happening. It was the concerted gasp from the crowd, a huge, frightening exhalation, that convinced her that what she was seeing was real.

The sight of Diana's plummeting body was seared upon Laura's brain; she knew she would never forget it. Despite her apparent lightness in the air, Diana did not fall like a wounded bird. She fell straight down like a stone to the hard, packed earth of the circus floor.

Chapter Sixteen

*F*OR a long moment it seemed as if time had stopped, frozen at the instant when Diana Salieri's body crashed to the sawdust that covered the earth floor of the tent.

And then bedlam broke loose. In the audience, women screamed, men shouted; in the center ring, a dozen people raced to Diana's body, a body crumpled like a broken doll.

The crowd had surged to its feet, and Laura, although her legs were weak, stood as well, unable to tear her gaze away from the terrible fascination of the tragedy. She could see that one of the people in the center ring was the circus physician, and she also recognized little Benjy, in his distinctive clown makeup, crouched beside the body. And then two men carrying a stretcher came hurrying into the ring.

In the next instant, both bands struck up, and a tumble of clowns poured into the far ring, while the bareback riding team galloped into the near ring.

In a few minutes Captain Turnbull stood before the center ring, megaphone at his mouth. The bands stopped playing so that he could get the attention of the crowd. "Please take your seats, ladies and gentlemen. The show will go on. Miss Salieri's accident is unfortunate, but she is not fatally injured. She is being rushed to the nearest hospital, so do not worry, she is in good hands. Just sit back and enjoy the remainder of the show."

The bands struck up again, and Laura watched as Diana's limp form was taken out of the center ring on the canvas stretcher. Slowly, all around her, people were taking their seats, their voices buzzing. Laura heard the man in front of her say to his wife, "Certainly it's a terrible thing, but you heard what the man said. She's not fatally hurt. I'm sure she'll be all right."

The talking died down when the Montinis took the center ring; and within what seemed a very short time it was as if the accident had never occurred.

Laura, feeling sick to her stomach, stared at the spectacle below her in disbelief. A woman had just died—she was certain that it was not possible to fall that far and survive—and the circus was going on as if nothing had happened. She had heard the saying, "The show must go on," but it had always been a meaningless phrase to her. Now she was seeing it in action.

In an attempt to regain her calm, Laura took several deep breaths. In a few moments she was breathing normally again, and her pounding heart had slowed its beat. The audience was sitting quietly, intent on the show.

Despite her horror at what had happened, Laura knew that this was a more acceptable alternative than what would have occurred if Captain Turnbull had stopped the show and told the crowd that Diana was fatally injured. Only panic would have resulted from such an announcement. It could not have helped Diana in the least, and possibly could have resulted in a mass exodus, and possibly injuries or deaths. It was better this way. The audience was calm; they would go home excited by the thrill of the accident but unaware of the horror.

Yet, it must be difficult, she thought, to keep performing, knowing that one of your own lay broken and bleeding, or dead. What about the other performers who did dangerous stunts? How could they go on now, knowing that the same thing might happen to them? They were made of strong stuff, these circus people.

Slowly she made her way down to the backstage area where the performers gathered before and after their appearances in the main tent.

There she was hit by the reality of the tragedy—pale-faced performers speaking in hushed voices. She saw Milly and Madame Costa standing off to one side, and she hurried over to them. Milly looked subdued and shaken, the sprinkle of freckles across her nose and cheeks standing out against the pallor of her face.

"Oh, Laura! Were you in the audience? Did you see what happened?"

Laura nodded, unable to speak.

"Oh, it's so awful! I know I was complaining about her only this afternoon, and I can't pretend that she was a nice person, but to have this happen . . ."

Laura nodded. "I know. I couldn't believe it even when I saw it happening. I still can't believe it. Do you know if she's dead?"

Madame Costa said sadly, "Yes. The ringmaster told the audience otherwise, of course, for nothing would have been helped by telling the truth then. It is the usual procedure. The truth they will all read about later, in their daily newspaper, and they will feel very important for having been there when it happened."

"Does anyone know what caused her to fall?"

Madame Costa shrugged. "Sergio says that when they waited on the platform she appeared a bit unsteady. He asked her if she wanted to go on, but she told him she was all right.

"And Santiago said that when she embarked from the platform for her second swing, he could see that her timing was fractionally off, but it was too late to do anything except pray. He says that she did not reach his hands—that it was only an error of an inch or so that caused her to fall to her death. They are all devastated."

"I can well imagine," Laura said somberly.

Glancing up, she saw Lionel standing nearby. It was not easy to read his facial expression, but the slumped position of his body and his hanging head revealed his despair. Little Benjy sat on an overturned keg, weeping like a child, his face smeared with the remnants of his clown makeup. He was being comforted by Madame Zenobia.

The feeling of strangeness came over Laura again in full force. She had just seen the dark side of circus life, the side that could bring danger and death instead of joy and pleasure; and she was not certain that she would ever again be able to watch the show with the same feeling of pleasure.

The shows went on as usual, but it changed the circus and its people.

The usual banter between the performers was gone; everyone was subdued and, Laura was sure, thinking of their own mortality. Little Benjy, who had been such a happy man, had sunk into melancholy and would seldom speak to anyone, although he performed nightly in front of the audience as if nothing had happened.

Lionel was less obvious about his feelings, but he too seemed to have lost his good humor and usual zest for life, and his emotional condition had its effect on Milly, who spent a great deal of her free time with him now, although she complained to Laura that Lionel seemed not really to know that she was there.

Strangely enough—or perhaps not so strangely, given the nature of the human animal—the crowds were bigger than ever. Amos Potter said that it was *because* of the accident, that many people came hoping to see something of the sort happen again. Laura found it difficult to believe that people could be so callous.

Although she could not say that she missed Diana in a personal way, seeing the young woman die before her very eyes had a profound effect on Laura. She found herself dreaming of the incident again and again—waking in the darkness to find her heart pounding wildly. She also missed Milly's company, now that her friend spent so much time with Lionel. When she was with Milly, Milly kept her from thinking quite so much of Will and his mysterious absence.

Diana Salieri's death had far-reaching repercussions.

First, there was the matter of the police investigation. The local police had arrived with the ambulance and had asked a great many questions concerning the circumstances of Diana's death. It was clear that the officer in charge was not particularly fond of circus people; it was also clear that he suspected foul play. Yet there was no solid evidence. When the verdict finally arrived, it was death from accidental causes.

However, the suspicion of foul play led to all sorts of rumors and speculations, which raced through the circus like wildfire. This, in turn, ignited arguments and fears, until the prevailing mood of the circus people was one of suspicion and dissension.

If it had not been for her job, Laura would not have known what to do with herself. Potter, having seen what she could do, had been giving her more and more responsibility; and the pleasure she took in this proving of her ability helped in small measure to assuage her loneliness and unhappiness.

It had been more than a month since Will had left, and there still was no word of him or his whereabouts. Laura fairly ached with the need to know what had happened to him. She even thought of going to Mr. Bailey and asking if he knew where Will was, but her pride stopped her. What on earth would he think? He must know that she and Will were—had been—friends. If she asked him such a question, he would know that Will had not communicated with her since his departure, and she knew that she could not face the pity that she was certain she would see in his eyes.

She tried not to think of Will, to keep her mind on other things, but her last thought at night, before she finally managed to sleep, always was of him. Where was he, and why hadn't she heard from him?

Will Adams gazed down at his son's pale, drawn features. The boy was sleeping, but the sleep seemed to bring him no rest. His fever had not broken; and although the doctor was giving him laudanum, Justin still was in constant pain. Even now, in his shallow sleep, he moaned and turned restlessly.

Pearl had told Will that Justin's illness had begun with a

fever and headache, stiff neck and back, and muscle pain and tenderness. By the time Will had arrived at his side, the boy's fever was dangerously high, and he had lost the ability to move his right leg.

When Will had asked the doctor what disease could do this to his son, the doctor had been unable to give him a satisfactory answer, saying that he had treated only one or two cases of infantile paralysis before, and that at the present time the origin and the possible cure of the ailment were unknown. "We can only treat his fever and give him laudanum for the pain," the doctor had stated. "And pray, Mr. Adams."

"You say you have seen this before? What usually is the outcome?" Will had demanded. "And don't give me any candy-coated answers. I want the truth!"

The doctor had sighed. "The truth? I'm afraid that there is no definitive truth where this ailment is concerned, Mr. Adams. From my experience, which I must admit is very limited, and from the experiences of my peers, it would seem that the outcome of this disease can range from death, evidently brought on by paralysis of the breathing apparatus, through permanent paralysis of the limbs, to complete recovery, with no residual paralysis. We can only pray for the latter."

Now, feeling the start of tears of fatigue and anger, Will rolled his hand into a fist and struck his leg—his strong, healthy leg—wishing it could be he who was suffering instead of Justin. Will had not prayed in a long time, but he was doing so now, hoping that there was someone up there to hear him, someone or something that could help his son.

Occasionally, when he could tear his thoughts away from Justin, Will thought of Laura. Only a few weeks had passed, but the memory of their night together now seemed like a dream to him. He should have kept his word to himself. He should not have made love to her; it was not fair to her. He knew that he should write to her, explain his absence, but that would mean having to tell her about Justin and explain why he had not done so before now.

His own happiness did not matter. All that could move

him now was the thought of the survival of his son; but
Laura deserved better than a man who had made love to
her and then disappeared, a man she could not count on.
She had already had that kind of a man. Will thought that
he probably loved her; but in his present state, drained
emotionally and physically by Justin's illness, he could
think of nothing else. In his weary and confused state, he
thought that perhaps he should strike a bargain with God.
Offer up his own happiness in return for the life of his
son.

And so, sitting there in the dim room, looking at his
son's frail, tortured body, Will offered up a prayer, a plea.
He would not see Laura again—at least not in a personal
way—if God would let his son live. It seemed a reasonable thing to do. He would write Laura tomorrow and tell
her that he was forced to be away for some time, on
personal business, and that under the circumstances he
would not, and could not, make any claim on her affec-
tions. The tone of the letter would be cool, and she would
be hurt, he knew; but it was for the best, the best thing
for both of them. She could then forget him, and find
someone else, someone who had no secrets, no other
loyalties. The idea of Laura with another man caused him
anguish, but that did not matter if Justin would only live.

Tenderly he reached for the damp cloth with which to
wipe the boy's forehead, willing into his touch all his
strength and health, and all his love, willing that it should
flow into the small body before him. For right now, Justin
was the only thing in his life that mattered.

Part Two

1885

Chapter Seventeen

New York World:
January 23, 1885

WOMAN IN BUSINESS

Here is one who has been more than successful.

That woman's work is no longer confined to the four walls of the home, that she is capable of leading the strenuous life of the nineteenth century, is fully illustrated in the life of Mrs. Nickolas Orlando, the subject of this sketch, whose picture appears herewith.

Mrs. Orlando is employed by the circus belonging to P.T. Barnum and James Bailey, where she fills a position that would ordinarily be filled by a man.

In her capacity as manager of advertising for the circus, she is responsible for creating posters and billboards, as well as newspaper and magazine advertisements. In such a position, she must supervise a large number of employees.

Mrs. Orlando was previously employed by Barnum and Bailey as a bookkeeper in their accounting office. She rose to her present position through diligence, and the exercise of her fertile imagination. According to P.T. Barnum, "Laura

*Orlando is not afraid to think big, to try some-
thing new. I value her and her capabilities most
highly, most highly indeed."*

*To say that Mrs. Orlando has made a success
in a profession almost exclusively male does not
do her justice. Not content with past methods,
she has introduced into her work many innova-
tions that are decidedly clever and has proved
beyond doubt that conspicuous advertisement is
the very life of trade.*

Sitting in her rooms in New York, Laura read the
article with both pride and some embarrassment; pride
because she had worked so hard to achieve her new
position and was finally being recognized for it; embarrassment because she thought that the picture accompa-
nying the article made her look rather hard, and this
likeness, along with the words of praise in the newspaper
article, was being distributed for all the world to see,
making her feel, in a way, exposed.

Looking out her window, she could see the little tree in
the backyard. It was showing touches of green, and here
and there a crocus was pushing up through the still-cold
soil.

Another spring. Soon it would be time for the circus to
take to the rails again, and she could hardly wait. During
the winter, although she kept busy planning new advertising campaigns and designing new posters for the coming
season, she felt only half-alive. In just a few weeks it
would be three years since she had gone to work for
Barnum and Bailey, and she was still fascinated by circus
life.

Three years. Three years of traveling, of learning, of
working; three years during which she had worked and
thought her way into her present, enviable position. The
time had passed so quickly; mostly, anyway. And she had
no regrets. No, not one, not even about Will Adams.

Of course, if she was honest with herself she would
have to admit that this was not quite true. She still thought
of Will; still remembered what it had been like to lie in

his arms; still remembered the pain and anger she had felt upon reading his cool, unemotional letter, which stated that personal affairs required that he remain in New York for an unknown period of time, and that he would not feel right about asking her to wait for him. The letter which told her that since he found himself unable to make any kind of commitment at this time, perhaps it would be better for both of them if she put him out of her mind and her life, and that he would always remember her with fondness. Fondness!

She smiled to herself now, bitterly. Yes, the letter had hurt terribly. It had provided no real explanation for his behavior. It seemed, as she had feared, that after she had so foolishly given herself to him he no longer wanted her.

Well, perhaps it was all for the best. Without that letter she might not be where she was today. After the letter, all her thoughts and energy had gone into her work. She had become very familiar with all aspects of circus operation, and she had seen things that could be vastly improved upon. She had, hesitantly at first, made suggestions. Some of these suggestions were acted upon, with favorable results. This led to more of her suggestions and ideas being used.

She had become interested in the advertising function and had devised several rather daring and unusual ideas, one of which had come to Barnum's attention. He had liked it, tried it, and was very pleased with the results. A short time after that, he had transferred her to the advertising department; and just six months ago, with the retirement of the manager of advertising, Barnum had promoted her to that position.

It was not an easy job. At first there had been problems, chiefly with the male employees whom Laura had to supervise, for some of them objected to working for a woman; but that was mainly in the past now, although it had taken her some time to prove herself to them, much longer than it had taken to prove herself to P. T. Barnum and James Bailey.

And then there was the matter of their competition. There were a number of other large circuses touring the country, including Barnum's bitterest rival, The Great Forepaugh Show. Adam Forepaugh was a tough and aggressive competitor and was not above using every means at his disposal to diminish Barnum while enhancing himself; and one of those means was advertising through posters and "rat sheets."

Rat sheets were posters used to insult or discredit the competition. There was usually an element of humor and exaggeration in them, so that the general feeling was of a more or less friendly battle.

One of Laura's favorites—from before her time with the circus—was one in which Barnum used one of Aesop's Fables to sneer at his arch rival. The poster showed Barnum as an ox towering over Forepaugh, who was depicted as a frog. The legend at the bottom of the poster stated: "This old four-clawed frog always was too full of wind and 'busted' in the vain attempt to puff himself up to the proportions of the gigantic BARNUM OX."

Forepaugh's answering rat sheet depicted Forepaugh as a giant looming above his tiny rivals Barnum and Bailey. It was captioned: "A Giant Among the Pygmies."

However, another of Forepaugh's rat sheets, issued when Barnum and Bailey launched their first three-ring circus in Madison Square Garden, had been less humorous. At that time, The Great Forepaugh Circus had only two rings, and Barnum and Bailey's three rings had evidently put Forepaugh out of sorts. He accused Barnum of "Fraud, Falsehood, and Downright Deceit!" maintaining that Barnum's advertisement for the precircus parade in New York had claimed more cages, elephants, and costumed people than had really appeared. "Note the Discrepancy! A Gross Exaggeration Without a Single Word of Truth!" The rat sheets appeared everywhere, blaring the words like a shout.

Although Forepaugh decried Barnum's honesty, his own was just as suspect. In 1883, during the height of Jumbo's popularity, Forepaugh had advertised that *his* elephant, Bolivar, was really the largest elephant in existence, which was not true. Jumbo was, without dispute, the world's largest elephant. However, Forepaugh's statement was never accepted by the public, and Jumbo's claim to fame remained intact.

And the battle continued. At the moment, Laura was designing a courier, a type of publicity pamphlet, glorifying Barnum, for Forepaugh had only recently had a new one printed for himself.

James Bailey was never mentioned in any of the publicity material, for he was a very shy and retiring man and discouraged any mention of his name. Still, he was a master at publicizing his circus, and he and Laura often worked closely together. She had grown to respect and admire this quiet man who stayed in the background, allowing Barnum to stand as the figurehead of their great circus. Hutchinson, the third partner, had withdrawn from the partnership at about the time Laura had joined the show, and she had never known him.

Sighing, she put aside her artwork for the courier and stretched, thinking ahead to tomorrow.

P. T. Barnum had invited her to spend a few days at Waldemere, to which she was looking forward. She had been at Barnum's home on several occasions during the past three years and had grown quite close to Barnum's wife, Nancy.

Despite the vast difference in their ages, the Barnum marriage seemed a very happy one. Laura had watched the two together, and it was obvious that the showman adored his beautiful, charming wife. His round face fairly beamed whenever he was near her, and his pride in her, especially when she played the piano for their guests, was obvious. Nancy, in turn, always listened attentively to her husband and laughed heartily at the jokes and conundrums he was so fond of telling. Watching them, Laura sometimes found herself overcome by longings that she had difficulty in exorcising.

Her marriage to Nick had been so different. She could think back on it now without pain, but it still clouded her thoughts like a rather shameful secret. To avoid embarrassing questions, she told people that she was widowed. It seemed preferable to admitting that her husband had abandoned her.

Laura would have liked to know where he was, so that she might sue for a divorce, for all she wanted from him now was to be free of him. The thought that she was still legally married to Nick Orlando almost made her sick.

But there was no use in thinking about that now. She had better get her things packed for the trip tomorrow.

Will Adams studied the note in his hand. It was an invitation from Nancy and P.T. to spend the weekend at Waldemere.

Pensively, he placed it on the desk before him and, leaning back in his chair, clasped his hands behind his head as he stared out the study window at the pale March sky.

He would like to accept. He had not been to Waldemere in a long time, and he could use a bit of a holiday; but along with the note was a list of other guests being invited, and Laura's name was on that list.

Laura. He wanted desperately to see her. He missed her terribly, even though it had been three years since he had seen her.

Three years. He thought back to the night when he had bartered his happiness for his son's recovery. He must have been half-mad with worry to have done such a thing. And yet, Justin *had* recovered, almost completely. Now, three years later, the only reminder of his terrible illness was a slight limp in his right leg.

If he went to Laura, if he apologized . . .

But it was too late now. The damage was done, her trust in him destroyed. If he went to her now, she would, understandably enough, demand explanations. He would have to tell her about Justin, about his marriage, and then attempt to explain why he had not told her the truth from the very beginning. It was simply too complicated. And, despite the fact that he was certain that his bizarre bargain with God was not the reason that Justin had recovered, he felt a degree of superstition about breaking that compact.

Laura was successful now. She had an important position, and, according to all reports, she appeared to enjoy it. She did not need him.

Pushing aside the note from the Barnums, Will picked up the other letter he had received that day. It was from James Bailey, and it stated that Bailey's assistant had been forced to resign his position because of his wife's illness. Bailey wanted to know if Will could possibly see his way clear to accept the job.

Will reread the last paragraph: "Will, I know that you enjoy doing the talent scouting, and I realize that personal problems have kept you away from the circus proper much of the time for the past three years, but I presume that by now these matters have been resolved. I cannot think of a better man for the job. I really do need your experience and expertise. Please say that you will accept. I know Phineas would be very pleased."

There was nothing Will wanted more than to accept; but if he did, it would mean being in constant contact with Laura, and under the circumstances he did not think he could endure that.

To see her and pretend indifference. To be near her and yet not be able to touch her, make love to her. It would be more than he could bear! That was the reason he had refused invitations to Waldemere when he knew that Laura would be there; that was why he had asked Barnum to be relieved of those of his duties that required his being with the circus when it traveled.

Of course, during that first, awful year, it had been necessary for him to stay with Justin most of the time. But later, when Justin was recovering and Will had gone back to work, he had returned only to his scouting duties, avoiding the circus and the possibility of encountering Laura.

Lowering his head into his hands, Will let his shoulders sag as despair, cold as an Atlantic wave, swept over him.

This was how Pearl found him when she entered the room. He did not know she was there until he felt her light touch on his shoulder. Startled, he looked up and saw his mother-in-law's sensitive, dark eyes fixed on him with concern.

When she spoke, her voice was gentle. "What is it, Will?"

Will straightened his shoulders and tried to bring a brighter look to his eyes. "Why, nothing, Pearl. Just a bit tired, I suppose."

Smiling slightly, she shook her head. "It will do no good to try to fool me, Will. I have been watching you. Why don't you tell me what's been bothering you for so long now."

He patted her hand. "Really, Pearl. It's nothing at all for you to worry about."

"Hmph!" Her ladylike sound of scorn let him know that he had not convinced her. Seating herself in the chair next to his desk, she folded her small, delicately shaped hands in her lap and gazed at him severely. "You might as well tell me what is troubling you, Will, for I intend to give you no peace until you do. As I said, I have been watching you, and what I have observed is not at all to my liking. You've been depressed and unhappy, and it pains me deeply to see you this way. I know it's not about Justin, since he is doing fine. So, it must be something else. Now tell me."

Will, gazing into his mother-in-law's dark eyes, so like Lily's had been, suddenly and without volition found himself talking. Haltingly, it all spilled out—his feeling for Laura, the progress of their relationship, the fact that he had not told Laura about Justin, his bargain with God, and the fact that he could not forget Laura. Then he told her about Bailey's letter and the job offer.

At last the words dried up and Will slumped in his chair, drained yet somehow feeling relieved and cleansed, as if a great burden had been lifted from him.

Pearl took a deep breath, shook her head in reproof, and then smiled at him sympathetically. "My poor boy. Holding all that inside you all this time. Why didn't you talk to me sooner?"

Will sighed heavily. "I didn't wish to burden you with my problems, particularly when you were so worried about Justin."

Pearl motioned irritably. "You men! You think that you must always be so brave, so strong, that you must bear everything and never, never reveal any weakness. It seems you have never learned, as women have, that there are times when it is necessary to rely on others, to seek support and help. There are times when our own particular blindness keeps us from seeing solutions, times when someone else, not so emotionally involved, can see and tell you what is the best course."

Lightly, she tapped his hand with her fingers. "And that is just what I intend to do, give you my advice, and I suggest very strongly that you take it.

"Now, first the matter of the young woman herself. It has been a long time since Lily's death, and you are still a young man, a normal man, and it is perfectly natural for you to love again. You should feel no guilt. I knew my daughter well, and she was not the kind of woman who would demand that you remain faithful to a memory. She would have wanted you to be happy.

"As to your not telling Mrs. Orlando about your marriage and Justin, I presume that was because you feared she might find it difficult to accept us. You were afraid that she would be shocked, because . . . because of Lily's background. Is that not correct?"

Feeling like a small boy called up in front of a kindly schoolmaster, Will nodded sheepishly.

"I also presume that by now you have realized that this was wrong of you, Will. Of course, it does no good to tell you this now, except to help you realize your error, but you should have allowed the young woman to make this decision for herself."

"But I was afraid I would lose her. I was going to tell her, in time, after we knew each other better."

Pearl nodded, her dark eyes knowing. "But that time never seemed to come, did it? At any rate, that is in the past. What we must do is to try and set right the present.

"Now, as to your bargain with God. You must admit that the promise was made when you were distraught and confused. Well, I believe that God is kind, and it is very difficult for me to believe that He would demand such a price from you for allowing your son to live. I believe that the bargain was entirely on your part, and that God will not hold you to it. I love Justin as much as you do, Will, and I would not put him at risk for the world, but I believe that what I say is true.

"If I were you, I would thank God for your son's recovery, and then get busy reestablishing your own life. I would accept Mr. Barnum's kind invitation to his beautiful home. I would then use that opportunity to talk to Mrs. Orlando, to explain as best you could why you did what you did, telling her, of course, about Lily and Justin. Then I would beg her understanding and forgiveness. Even if she cannot forgive you, you will be no worse off than you are now, and you will at least know that you have done the decent thing."

Gazing into his mother-in-law's understanding eyes, Will experienced a surge of hope. Pearl was right. He must do something. If he was very fortunate, Laura would forgive him; and if she did, and if she could also accept the fact of his previous marriage, and his son, then he would ask her to marry him.

If she could not forgive him, at least he would have made some atonement for his treatment of her, and he could pick up his life again, knowing he had tried.

"It won't be easy," he said slowly. "It will be difficult to face her, and perhaps even more difficult to get her to listen to me. Laura is a spirited woman, and I treated her badly."

Pearl nodded. "I did not say that it would be easy. Things worth doing are often difficult, but you feel better already, do you not, for having made the decision?"

Will smiled for the first time in what seemed like days, and it felt good. "You're right, Pearl, as always. I only wish I had talked to you sooner. I'll leave for Waldemere in the morning, after I've had breakfast with Justin."

Chapter Eighteen

LAURA always received a great deal of pleasure from her visits to Waldemere. As soon as her carriage entered the outer gate, where the statue of a peaceful Indian greeted visitors, she felt she was in P.T. Barnum's world, a very pleasant world, luxurious and larger than life.

Waldemere, which meant Woods-by-the-Sea, was a product of love. Past the Indian guardian at the gate there were splashing fountains, groves of hickory trees, and gardens; beyond them was the mansion itself, a sprawling, ornate, gingerbread castle, as large as a hotel.

The huge house had been built in a mélange of styles, Gothic, Italian, and French, which, strangely enough, worked together in a very pleasant manner. It was rather like Barnum himself, Laura often thought: larger than life and full of warmth.

The interior of the house was decorated by many wonderful, beautiful objects that Barnum had accumulated in his travels—paintings, statues, vases. A marble bust of Jenny Lind stood on a pedestal in a place of honor, and there were marble models of Tom Thumb's dimpled hand and foot.

Altogether it was an extremely pleasant and luxurious place in which to be a visitor. There were countless guest rooms, and almost all of them had their own bathrooms and lavatories. Barnum, who was quick to adopt every modern convenience, also had telephone service, both for general use and a direct line to the police department, as well as magnetic burglar alarms.

As the carriage drew up before the main house, Laura could see the white silk flag, bearing the initials P.T.B., fluttering from the flagpole above the high, glass cupola, signaling that Phineas was in residence. Laura smiled to herself. It was a gesture that a king might make, but then Phineas was a king in his own particular way.

When Laura stepped down from the carriage, Nancy Barnum was there to meet her.

"I'm so glad you could come, my dear. I think it's going to be a wonderful weekend. We have some very interesting guests coming, and the weather promises to be perfect. I'm putting you in your usual room, of course."

Laura smiled and returned Nancy's kiss. Nancy had a way of making you always feel welcomed and special, as if you were the most important guest present.

"I'm really glad you asked me," she said as Nancy escorted her into the house. "You know I love Waldemere. I've always thought that you must feel like a queen living here. It's so beautiful."

In her bedroom, Laura removed her hat and cape and stepped over to the large window that looked out over the lawns and the water. The sun was low in the western sky and gave a soft, golden glow to the scene.

Gazing out, Laura experienced a yearning sadness. Perhaps what brought it on was the beauty of the scene and the knowledge that everything, no matter how one wished to cling to it, changed.

Even Waldemere would not always remain the same. Even now it was becoming obsolete. She wondered if the great house, somewhere deep in its wooden heart, knew this. But it would do no good to make herself gloomy with such fanciful thoughts. She was here now, and so was Waldemere, and she would enjoy it to the best of her ability.

Turning away from the window, she wondered who the other guests were. Nancy had not told her. Sometimes Barnum had very famous people here, and that was always interesting; but the times when the guests were basically ordinary people were sometimes the most pleasant.

On her first visit, Laura had hoped, and feared, that Will Adams might be one of the guests, and she had spent hours planning just how she would act when she saw him: she would be cool and aloof, showing no sign of how much he had hurt her. She would be beautiful and charming, and all the men would notice her, so that Will would realize just what he had given up.

But in all the times she had been to Waldemere, Will had never been present. She knew that he and Barnum were good friends, and she was curious as to why Will had never been a guest here. She could have asked Phineas, but it would have been embarrassing, and she was not certain that she wanted to know the answer. Perhaps Will came only at those times when she was not invited. If that was true, his absences were intentional.

A knock sounded on the door, and she called, "Come in."

It was a young man with her baggage, followed by a fresh-faced young maid named Megan, whom Laura knew from previous visits.

Laura smiled at them both, then seated herself in the comfortable, oak rocking chair as they went about their business. It *was* a grand feeling to be waited on.

The young man soon left, and the maid began unpacking Laura's things with care and efficiency. "What dress do you wish to wear to dinner, ma'am?"

"I think the blue-green watered silk with the matching bag, and the black slippers."

Megan took the chosen garment from the traveling trunk and held it up to the light. "It's very beautiful, ma'am, if I may say so, and is no doubt very becoming to you."

Laura laughed. "You certainly may, and thank you."

"Do you wish me to draw your bath now?"

"Yes, please, and do put in some of those violet salts."

Megan smiled. "They do smell lovely, don't they? Just like a garden. Will you want me to come back later to help dress your hair?"

Laura shook her head. "After you draw the bath I won't need you. I'll do my own hair."

"Very good, ma'am." Megan went into the adjoining

bathroom, and soon Laura heard the rumble of the plumbing and the rush of water.

Laura, rocking gently in the golden glow of the lowering sun, felt both relaxed and expectant, as if something nice, a pleasant surprise, was coming. Smiling to herself, she enjoyed the feeling, while wondering idly what it meant.

Of course, being at Waldemere was always a pleasant experience; and often, due to Barnum's penchant for the unexpected, her visits were full of surprises, but somehow Laura felt that tonight would be something special.

Feeling fresh and rested and knowing that she looked attractive in the blue-green silk, Laura left her room and turned to close the door behind her.

As she turned about again, she saw a man standing opposite her. He obviously had just emerged from his room, directly across the hall from hers.

For a frozen moment, she could not believe her eyes; but when she did, she felt a hot flush rise from her chest to her face, and an almost overwhelming mixture of emotions caused her to stand rigid in near panic. It was Will Adams!

Through her confusion she noticed that he was as handsome as ever, although he seemed much thinner, and his expression was unusually sober.

He was staring at her as intently as she was at him, but his face showed no surprise at her presence. Her first coherent thought was that he must have known that she would be here, or else he cared so little that her being there did not even upset him.

Well, if that was the way it was to be, she could be as nonchalant as he was. Gathering her forces, she nodded politely without speaking, managed to move her legs—which felt as weak as water—and started toward the stairway. The sound of her name, spoken with a passionate intensity, drew her to a halt, and she stood, weaving slightly, her heart hammering.

"Laura. Please wait. I *must* talk to you."

Slowly she turned and faced him, still attempting to regain control of her runaway emotions. "It's been a long time, Will," she said as steadily as she could. "Three years!"

He nodded, his eyes darkening. "I know, Laura, I know all too well. And although you may not believe this, I've missed you every minute of that time."

A slow rise of anger began to burn away the confusion that the sight of him had caused. "If that's true, you have a peculiar way of demonstrating it!"

He winced. "I deserve that, I know, but that's what I wish to talk with you about. I have an explanation and an apology to give you, if you feel it in you to listen."

Laura clung to her anger like a life raft. "Well, I'm not certain that I care to hear any explanation at this late date, although I certainly could have used one a bit sooner."

Will reached out a hand as if to touch her, then let it fall. "You're angry. I expected that, and, as I said, I deserve it; but, Laura, please hear me out, for old times' sake, if for nothing else."

Laura hesitated. She did owe him a debt of gratitude for getting her a job with the circus, but certainly his behavior had canceled any such debt.

"Please, Laura. It's against my nature to beg, but I'm begging you to listen to me. Afterward, if you wish never to see me again, I'll leave you alone. You have my word on that."

Laura lowered her gaze to her hands, which she found were clutching her bag in a crushing grip. However angry and hurt she was, however much she longed to lash out at him, she knew that she still cared for this man.

She raised her eyes to his. "All right, Will. My curiosity is aroused. I can't imagine what kind of excuse you might offer for what you did, but I'll listen to you. That, however, is all I can promise. And it will have to wait until after dinner, for it's time we went downstairs and joined the others."

A look of relief passed over his face. "Thank you, Laura. You are being most generous." He made a small bow, smiling. "May I escort you downstairs, Mrs. Orlando?"

He offered his arm, and hesitantly she took it. As she did so, she felt the familiar thrill course through her body.

No matter what he had done to her, her treacherous body still responded to him like a blind and seeking organism, incapable of thought or logic, wanting only to be near him. It was not fair that he should still stir her after all this time! She hoped that her agitation and confusion would not be visible to the other guests as she and Will descended the stairs together and went into the dining room.

Usually, Laura looked forward to mealtimes at Waldemere, for Barnum had an excellent cook, and to eat in the lovely dining room, surrounded by interesting company, was always a pleasure.

However, this evening she could not have given an accurate account of what she had eaten or who had been present. She evidently had made conversation with the guests on either side and across from her, and otherwise behaved in a normal manner, for no one seemed to notice anything unusual about her behavior; but she had done it all as if moving through a dream. She had no idea of what she was going to say to Will when she was alone with him, and certainly no idea of what explanation he would offer her for his silence.

After dinner, the company adjourned to the music room, where Nancy entertained them with selections on the piano. Laura was too distracted to enjoy the performance. After the music, Barnum, who seemed in an especially jovial mood, regaled them with stories and conundrums. Laura joined in the laughter and banter rather desperately, trying to focus on the moment so that she would not have to think of what was coming later.

Finally, Barnum made a show of taking out his pocket watch. "Well, it's about time for an old man to be in bed, but the rest of you needn't feel that you have to follow suit. I have new slides for the stereopticon, for those of you who are interested. I will see you all at breakfast."

As Phineas Barnum made his stately way toward the staircase, Laura shot a quick glance at Will, who was getting up from his chair. She had relaxed during Barnum's stories, but now her heart began to pound anew.

She both wanted and dreaded to be alone with Will; but she had agreed to hear him out, and so it must be done.

Then Will was standing over her. "I thought I'd take a short walk around the grounds for a bit of fresh air. Would you care to join me?"

Laura kept her voice low. "Why, that would be very pleasant, Mr. Adams. Thank you."

Will extended his hand to help her up, and she took it, knowing that his touch would start the same old fire within her.

As Laura rose, Nancy, who was sitting nearby, looked up. "Are you going to bed, Laura? I was just going to set up the projector."

Laura said quickly, "No, I was just about to take a turn about the grounds with Mr. Adams."

Nancy gave her a quizzical glance, and Laura had to wonder how much the woman knew or had guessed.

Smiling slightly, Nancy said, "It's clear out tonight, but quite chilly. You'd best take a wrap, Laura."

Nancy had been right—the night was quite chilly; but there was a nearly full moon, and the sky was clear save for a few pale clouds that reflected the moonlight.

As they slowly walked along one of the many paths that transversed the grounds of Waldemere, Will was silent. In the distance Laura heard a cow lowing, and then the neigh of a horse.

Laura felt somehow unreal walking with Will, at last, along the graveled pathway with the shapes and shadows of flowers, plants, and trees around them, half-seen in the moonlight. It was, she thought, like being inside one of those glass balls that held its own small world within it, as if she and Will were separated from the rest of the world, alone inside their own bubble of time.

In a lovely patch of moonlight, there was a wooden bench, surrounded by plants that filled the cold night air with the scent of growing things.

Will gestured at the bench. "Shall we sit here, or will it be too cool for you?"

Laura shook her head mutely and seated herself. Will sat down beside her, and she could feel the warmth of his body next to hers; and she shivered so that he asked again if she was warm enough.

And then he began to speak. Slowly at first, haltingly; and then with more assurance, he told her about his marriage to Lily, and about Justin, and Justin's sudden, dangerous illness. When he came to the part about his bargain, he spoke awkwardly, attempting to explain his mental state after those weeks and months of vigil by his son's bedside.

As the words spilled out, Laura felt her hurt and anger melting away like ice under a warm spring sun. He had not left because he did not care for her! He had had a reason, no matter if it was misguided, for his actions.

When at last he fell silent, she reached out and gripped his hand fervently. "Oh, Will! I don't know what to say. But it was all so unnecessary, can't you see that? You should have told me of your marriage and your son. I would have been surprised—naturally I would have been— but having been married and having a child is certainly nothing to be ashamed of.

"As for your promise to God, I can see how you might have felt at the time. In the same circumstances I might have done the same thing. But oh, I'm so glad that your mother-in-law is a sensible woman, and that she talked to you! Otherwise, I would have gone on thinking that you had simply used me and thrown me aside. Whatever else happens now, at least I can look back on our relationship and not be ashamed of it. Oh, Will! I am so glad you told me!"

Will's face looked pale in the moonlight. "Laura, there is something else, something I should have told you."

She felt his hand tighten on hers. "Yes, Will?"

His grip loosened. "Never mind. I guess it's not really important. Then you will forgive me? I never meant to hurt you. I thought I was doing what was best for both of us."

Laura felt tears in her eyes. "Of course I forgive you!"

And then she found herself in his arms, not knowing who had made the first move; and his mouth was on hers, filling her with a warmth that pulsed into every part of her body, until she felt that she was aglow with desire.

Between kisses Will repeated her name over and over, as if he could not believe that she was in his arms; and soon his hands were on her breasts, and she was wishing that her lovely gown would magically dissolve so that nothing would be between his searching hands and her hungry flesh.

In the past three years there had been no other man, and her body, now fully aroused, demanded its due. When he lifted her from the bench to hold her against him, she pressed her mouth to his ear and murmured, "Oh, Will! I've missed you so. There's been no one else. No one but you."

He began to tremble, and the tremor passed from his body to hers until they were both shaking.

"Will you come with me, Will?" she asked huskily. "My room is just across the hall from yours. I can't bear to let you go, now that I've found you again. I can't!" The last words were like a cry, and Laura found herself sobbing with an overpowering physical desire.

Hurriedly and unsteadily they made their way back to the house and, sneaking past the music room, up the stairs.

The upstairs hallway was mercifully empty, and in a moment they were in Laura's room where a fire had been laid, and Laura's nightdress was arranged on the bed, above her slippers. A small table lamp dimly illuminated the room with the glow from its pink shade. In the rosy glow, Laura and Will stood looking at each other wordlessly for a long moment, then came together like two halves of the same being, and then moved apart.

Frantically, they stripped; their hunger was too great for a leisurely undressing.

When at last they were naked and Will's body was against hers, Laura felt her own body shudder mightily. She had been in such a state of sexual excitement that just the feel of him against her had brought her to climax.

Pulling him with her, she moved to the bed and let herself fall beneath him. Already she was aroused again, wanting him inside her, wanting to be possessed by him.

"Now," she whispered harshly as she opened herself to him. "Come into me now, Will. Oh, my darling!"

Will raised his body and plunged himself into her, as if seeking the very center of her being. Laura moaned with a pleasure almost too great to bear as Will filled her and began thrusting furiously. He climaxed with a tremendous shudder of his body, and for a moment they lay quiescent, the only sound that of their ragged breathing, as she lay there with him still inside her.

Raising his head, Will kissed her cheek tenderly. "My lovely Laura! How I've dreamed of you, thought of you, but nothing I imagined was as wonderful as this."

Laura sighed against his cheek. "Yes, my darling, I know. I know."

Her own passion, still unsated, caused her to tighten herself around him; and to her pleased surprise she felt him begin to grow again within her.

Slowly and sensuously she started to move beneath him, reveling in the touch of him against her sensitive parts, experiencing the welling of emotion and passion, loving the marvelous sensations that coursed from their joining throughout her whole body; and then he rolled with her, lifting her so that she was on top of him, all the while moving beneath her, holding her by the hips. At first the novelty of the position startled her, but she soon found that in this position she could feel him all the better; and that she was able to direct the pressure to the areas where she received the most pleasure and satisfaction.

Wild with abandon, she rotated her hips, then leaned forward so that she was better able to draw him deeper into her and move her body more rapidly upon that lovely staff that brought her so much rapture.

This time they achieved their satisfaction together, and Laura felt as if she had been shaken by some great upheaval, as she trembled and gasped, clinging to him fiercely.

Her last thought, before sleep claimed her, was that she had never, never in her life known such physical and emotional pleasure. She felt as if the act they had just completed had melded her to Will so that they were now one person forever, and she knew that she wanted never to be without him again.

Chapter Nineteen

SULLENLY, Nick Orlando stared at the empty whiskey bottle, then hurled it across the room with a curse.

It struck the flimsy wall, knocking loose another piece of dirty wallpaper, but the shabby bedroom was in such a sorry state that another piece of loose wallpaper made little difference.

Throwing himself back on the rumpled bed, Nick stared at the ceiling, his gaze following the stains and spots that spread like some loathsome disease across the faded paint.

How had he come to this? What kind of bad luck was dogging him? In the past, he had had his troubles, but he had always managed to rise above them, to find something new and better to do. He had prided himself that he had always gotten by, that no matter what misfortune plagued him, he would eventually overcome it.

But now nothing went right for him. He had no luck with cards, and even his luck with women seemed to be failing, although he thought he knew the reason for that. It was that damned bitch, Lola Maridan; she had placed some kind of a jinx on him.

He cursed violently under his breath. He needed something to drink, but he had no money, and Peggy would not be home until late afternoon. The bitch could have left him a few dollars. Just his luck to hook up with a miserly woman; yet, she was the only one willing to take him in after that trouble with the owner of the vaudeville house where he had last worked. Who would have thought that the old bastard would still be possessive of his wife after all those years? Nick had approached her only because she kept casting longing eyes at him. He had been doing it as a favor, really; also, he figured that if he kept her satisfied, she would put in a good word for him with her husband. In addition, she had been very generous with her liquor, and would slip him a few dollars now and then—not like Peggy, who doled out her money with an eye dropper.

But then the vaudeville-house owner had caught Nick in bed with his wife, and that had ended that!

Flinging one arm across his face, Nick felt tears burn his eyes. Once, he could have gotten any woman—any woman he wanted—and could have kept her in thrall to him by his lovemaking. Now he had fallen so low as to find it necessary to sponge off an overage actress, whom he had difficulty in satisfying.

Damn Lola! She was not a woman, she was a monster. He had been a fool to think that he would ever get anything out of her. She had used him, drained him, and in some way managed to steal his manhood. Whenever he had sex with her—"making love" was far too gentle a phrase to express what they did—he felt as if he had been violated, and yet he found himself unable to say no to her. It was not just that she was his employer; there was also a contest involved, a contest for superiority, which Nick felt that he would inevitably win, in view of his past experience with women.

But Lola had beaten him in the end, the bitch. A new man had joined the carnival, a strongman, bigger and younger than Bruno and far better-looking.

Shortly after the new man's arrival Lola had dropped Nick, with no explanation whatsoever. Despite the fact that he had longed to be free of her incessant demands, he was shaken; women did not leave him, he left them. What made it even worse, he was left feeling diminished and defeated, for he still had not been able to dominate her.

During his affair with Lola, if it could be called that, he

had taken to gambling heavily, attempting to win in another arena than the bed, but his luck seemed to have deserted him there as well. He hated the way these losses made him feel, and so he began to drink more and more. He knew that it was not good for him physically, and it certainly did nothing to raise his estimation of himself, but he could not seem to stop. And it was all Lola's fault.

After the show every night he would lie on his bunk thinking of ways to get back at her; but it was Bruno who finally did what Nick had been unable to do.

When Lola had taken up with the young strongman, she had also dispensed with Bruno's services as a bodyguard. Bruno, a man of simple and elemental emotions, had not taken it well. He had gone to Lola's wagon one night while her new lover was working the show, and had beaten Lola badly, then fled.

Nick, hearing about it, had felt a fierce joy, and in an effort to restore his flagging self-esteem he had attempted to bed his young assistant, Melanie. Melanie, however, hadn't proven susceptible to Nick's charms, and had set up such a hue and cry that it had been necessary for him to flee once again.

Since then his path had been downward, ever downward, and somehow Nick found himself powerless to stop the slide, until here he was in this rattrap of a room, living on Peggy's charity, without enough gumption left even to try to set his life right.

If he had stayed with Laura, they might own their own theater by now.

Rising from the soiled sheets, Nick walked over to the battered desk that functioned as a support for a gas ring and as a storage place for food.

Rummaging about in the contents of the desk, he found half a loaf of bread, reasonably fresh, and a pot of jam. The bread had been wrapped in a piece of newspaper, and as he pushed the paper aside a picture caught his eye. It could not possibly be, of course, and yet curiosity made him smooth out the paper so that he could see the picture more clearly. His pulse began to pound. It was Laura, looking far more sophisticated and mature, to be sure, but Laura nonetheless!

He glanced at the headline, then read the article through quickly, and once more, slowly this time. Little Laura, a success, famous, even! Well, *she* had landed on her feet, hadn't she? It looked as if his leaving her had not caused her much harm. He shook his head, finding it difficult to think of the Laura he remembered in such a position. She must have changed a good deal from the inexperienced girl he had married.

Married! By God, he *was* still her husband. Maybe that was his way out of this quagmire.

Taking the paper, he moved over to the rump-sprung chair and sank down into it, staring at Laura's picture all the while. She did look beautiful, although a trifle stern. Maybe it *was* time to try to patch things up with her. He could get himself cleaned up, raise a little money some-where—enough at least for a decent suit, and railway fare. . . .

Yes, it was time to pay a little visit to his beloved wife. She might not welcome him with open arms, but he had won her once. He could do it again!

When Laura arrived at the depot to board Barnum's private train, the first person she saw was Milly.

"Oh, Laura, I'm so glad to see you!"

Milly ran to her and gave her a hug, then stepped back the better to see her. "Oh, you look gorgeous! That's a new outfit, isn't it? The winter certainly hasn't harmed you. I saw the article in the *World*. I was so proud of you. Oh, I have so much to tell you!"

Laura laughed. Milly was as excited and exuberant as a puppy, and as endearing. "You're looking pretty good yourself, Miss Andrews, and I see you have a new outfit, too. It's very becoming."

Milly's pale cheeks turned rosy. "Thank you. I made it myself. I finally decided that I should stop dressing like a schoolgirl or someone's maiden aunt." She spun around slowly. "It's very fashionable, don't you think?"

Laura pretended to study the gown with a critical eye.

It *was* very handsome; the color, coral, flattered Milly's delicate skin and brightened her eyes, and the fitted bodice accentuated Milly's tiny waist and made the most of her modest bosom.

"Very modish indeed," Laura said with a smile. "You are a veritable fashion plate."

Milly flushed again. "I wore it today hoping that Lionel would like it," she said frankly.

Laura shook her head despairingly. "Oh, Milly!"

Milly shrugged. "I know you think I'm foolish to spend all my affection on him when he only thinks of me as a little sister, but someday he's going to realize that I'm a woman." She grinned. "And I thought this might help."

Laura put her arm around the shoulders of the younger girl. "Well, if he doesn't notice you in that, he's hopeless. You haven't seen him all winter?"

Milly shook her head. "No. I went back home to spend some time with my family. I enjoyed it. It was nice being there for Christmas, but when spring started to come in, I began to get itchy. I guess the circus is in my blood now. If I could only have Lionel *and* the circus, I'd be in heaven. You've got to help me, Laura. I've let it drift on too long. This year I've decided to make a concerted effort."

Laura gave Milly's shoulder a squeeze. "Well, in that case, I don't think Lionel has a chance. Come on, we'd better board; we can talk on the train. Come on back to my compartment and we'll have a nice visit."

"If I weren't your best friend, I'd be envious," Milly said with her gamine grin. "You've really come up in the world. Your own compartment! How pleasant are the benefits of success!"

Laura grinned back. "You're quite right, and since you *are* my best friend, you may share them with me."

The two women went back to Laura's roomy compartment, which occupied a third of one of the private cars, and which would be Laura's home while the circus was on the road.

"Why, it's just like a little apartment," Milly said, looking around admiringly.

"More like a bed-sitting-room," Laura said, removing her hat. "Would you like some tea?"

"I'd love some."

Milly walked slowly around the pleasantly furnished room. "Who are your neighbors? No one noisy, I hope."

Laura smiled. "No; Mr. Bailey believes in the proprieties, so my neighbors are Betinna Brouder, the bareback rider, and that new young woman, the one who does the act with the lions and the snakes—what do they call her, Madame Mystic, isn't it?"

Milly shivered. "You'd better hope that she doesn't keep her snakes in her room. They give me the shivers, but I've heard that she has a very good act and that they're paying her a lot of money."

"Well, I guess I should be honored. They've put me with performers from the top acts."

Drawing aside a red curtain that hid one corner of the room, Laura revealed a small cupboard upon which rested a small spirit stove.

"Isn't it convenient?" she said, lighting the flame. "I can heat water for coffee, tea, or cocoa, and toast bread and cake, and perhaps cook sausages. In addition, there's room to store some tins and the like. I won't always have to rely on the porter or the cook tent when we're in towns." She glanced around at Milly. "Now, tell me all about your winter."

"Oh, there's not much more that I can tell you. I had a nice visit at home, but now I'm anxious to get back to work. But I haven't heard about you yet, Laura. You know, you look radiant. Something nice must have happened to you this winter. Did you meet someone interesting?"

Laura smiled a Cheshire cat smile. "You might say that, although it's not anyone new."

Excitement turned Milly's face pink. "Oh, do tell me about it! Who is it?"

Laura took a deep breath, then let it out. "Will Adams."

Milly clapped her hands. "Oh, Laura, how wonderful! I know you haven't talked about it much, but I knew how unhappy you were when he just up and left. Is everything all right between you two again?"

Laura nodded. "He explained everything to me. I'll tell you all about it after tea."

"And so he's going to be traveling with the circus as Mr. Bailey's assistant," Laura said happily, as she ate the last cookie on the plate and sipped the last bit of tea in her cup. "We'll be together all season, and when the season's over, I'm going to meet his son and mother-in-law."

Milly sighed, leaning back against her seat. "Oh, Laura, it's all so romantic I can hardly stand it. Do you think you'll marry him?"

Laura said musingly, "He hasn't said anything about marriage yet, but I think he means to ask me."

"And will you say yes?"

Slowly, Laura nodded. "You know, I feel as if I'd been frozen for these past three years, and I'm just now thawing out. Now I realize that we all need somebody. These past years I was trying to deny it, because I'd been hurt twice and didn't want to risk being hurt again. Now I think I was wrong. You have to take risks if you want happiness. If you don't, you're not really living!"

"I agree," Milly said, leaning forward eagerly. "That's why I keep on trying to make Lionel really aware of me as a woman; and like I said, this year I'm going to really make an effort to get through to him."

"You know, maybe he's afraid, too," Laura said thoughtfully.

Milly's expression turned melancholy. "He wasn't afraid to love Diana, and she certainly wouldn't have brought him anything but unhappiness, even if she *had* loved him back!"

"But Diana didn't love him back, you see, and she never would. Perhaps that was her real attraction for Lionel. It was safe loving her, for there was really no chance that she would ever return his love. With you, now, it's a different matter. You're a warm woman, with love to give in return. Perhaps that's more than he can face."

"You know, you just may be right." Milly looked at Laura with rising excitement. "But if that is true, what can I do about it?"

Laura smiled. "We'll think of something. You said this is the year to make it happen, and I want you to be as happy as I am."

"Oh, Laura. You *are* a good friend!"

Milly jumped to her feet, and the two young women embraced as the engine whistled its warning that the train was starting.

Another season, Lionel thought, looking out the club-car window as the train began to move. The thought made him inexplicably sad.

The last three years had slipped by, leaving no mark on his life, and making him feel directionless, as if he had been marking time, and he did not care for the feeling.

At the same time, he felt too lethargic to do anything constructive about the way he had been living. It was all because of Diana's death, of course. He knew that his feelings were unhealthy, but he could not prevent himself from clinging to Diana's memory.

Although he had known that his love for the beautiful aerialist was unrequited and impossible, still she had been the focus of his devotion; and her sudden and tragic demise had seemed to take something out of him, something important, without which he could live only a kind of half-life.

It was clear, he thought, 'hat he was never meant to know the joys of reciprocated love. The only two women he had really cared for had not cared for him, at least not romantically, and even the meager satisfaction of loving them from afar had been taken from him. He might as well resign himself to a loveless life.

Of course, he was not the only one marked by Diana Salieri's death. The whole circus had been changed by it. First, there had been the police investigation, set in motion by her family, who had believed that Diana's death had not been an accident. They had claimed that she was never dizzy on the wire, and that she had felt exceptionally well that afternoon. They whispered darkly of drugs or poison—something that would not kill her outright, but would make her dizzy enough to lose her important timing. The Salieris had demanded an autopsy, and one had been performed, but no traces of poison or drugs had been found.

But the Salieris had not been convinced and had made a number of accusations against other performers, whom they had claimed were jealous of Diana. The only thing that the police had discovered was that there were indeed many people who disliked Diana, but since there was no evidence of wrongdoing, they had told the Salieris they were sorry and had closed the case.

Even after three years, the bad feelings lingered, and many of the performers and the Salieris were still not on speaking terms.

The most damaged by the incident, however, was little Benjy, the dwarf clown, for his devotion to Diana had been the most excessive. She had been Benjy's goddess; and when she died, it was almost as if he had died with her. The little man managed to continue performing, but sometimes Lionel thought that behind the paint and the funny clothing there was nothing but an empty shell. Lionel had considered himself and Benjy good friends, but now they scarcely spoke; and when they did, Lionel felt that they never really communicated.

Still, there had been some good things in Lionel's life the past three years, two of which were Milly and Laura, whom he now considered his close friends.

Milly was now assistant to Madame Costa, and she designed many of the costumes worn by the performers. Milly, of course, was not ambitious in the same way as Laura was, but in some ways she seemed the happier for it. Nothing ever seemed to quench her good spirits for very long, and it was a trait that Lionel envied.

He smiled bemusedly as he thought of Milly, and something stirred within him, but he immediately pushed it down. He knew very well that Milly had a crush on him, for she made no effort to keep her feelings a secret, but he felt that it was just that—a girlish infatuation that would not last.

Thinking about this made him very uncomfortable. He knew that if he allowed himself to take Milly and her infatuation seriously, if he let himself believe that she could really love him, he would be hurt. He was certain that as soon as he let himself care for her, and let her *know* that he cared, she would lose interest in him. He also feared her pity, for he knew how tenderhearted she was, a regular little mother to everyone. No, he must save her, and himself, from being hurt. It was better to have her friendship forever than to believe in her love and lose it *and* her friendship.

Looking away from the window, Lionel saw Benjy entering the club car, in the company of Alwyn Crest, the strongman, and Luther Goodwin, the human skeleton. Seeing Lionel, the three men came over to join him.

"Lionel, good to see you!" Alwyn's deep voice boomed out.

"And you, Benjy," Lionel said gently. "What have you been doing during the off season?"

Benjy looked at him apologetically. "Didn't have a very good year, Lionel," he said in his high, thin voice. "Was sick mostly. You know, the lung thing."

Lionel nodded. He knew that dwarfs were susceptible to a type of lung ailment peculiar to their kind, and that many of them died young because of it.

"I'm sorry, Benjy. That's an awful way to have to spend the winter. Are you feeling better now?"

The little man shrugged. He seemed disinclined to say anything further.

The waiter brought their drinks then and set them on the table.

"What you need, Benjy," Luther said, clapping Benjy on the shoulder, "is some of Dr. Goodwin's tonic. A good tumble in the hay with a willing woman. Now, I understand there's a new act with us this year, Rosie's Trained Ponies. I've met Rosie, and she's not much bigger than you are, but she's a real woman for all that, and nicely shaped. If you like, I'll introduce you, and you can—"

Luther stopped short, halted by the cold, almost hostile look on the dwarf's face.

Looking at Lionel and Alwyn, Luther raised his eyebrows. "What is it? Did I say something wrong?"

Without a word Benjy hopped down from his chair; and with a curious and touching dignity, he waddled away from the other men and out the club-car door.

Luther shook his head in puzzlement. "Now what has gotten into him, do you suppose? Since when is it an insult to offer a man an introduction to a beautiful woman?"

Alwyn shook his head. "Luther, you know very well that Benjy's not been the same since Diana Salieri died."

Luther puffed out his cheeks and reached for his drink. "But it's been three years, dammit. Besides, the woman was a bitch, we all knew that. She treated Benjy like a trained dog."

Lionel leaned forward. "We know that, Luther, but that doesn't make any difference to Benjy. The little fellow worshipped her, and he'll never forget her."

Alwyn, who was not insensitive, gave Lionel a quizzical look, and Lionel felt his color rise. He did not like to consider himself in the same category as Benjy, a pathetic victim of an obsession. *But do the others see me in that light?* he suddenly wondered.

"What you said insulted him, Luther," Alwyn said. "And insulted Diana's memory. Try to remember not to mention love, sex, or romance around Benjy. It always sets him off."

"Well," Luther said finally, "I'll try to remember that. I didn't mean to hurt the little fellow. But now let's talk about something more cheerful. From what I hear, it looks like it's going to be a good season. Will Adams is coming back as Bailey's assistant, we have several new acts, and the weather is wonderful. Let's drink a toast to the show and the new season! May it be successful, and may nothing go wrong."

"I'll certainly drink to that," said Alwyn.

The three men raised their glasses in a toast. But Lionel had a sudden and cold premonition—there was trouble ahead.

Chapter Twenty

BUYING a large bag of peanuts from Old Laupin, the peanut vendor, Laura gave him a sunny smile, which he answered in kind.

To Laura, Old Laupin represented the essence of the circus, the indefatigable spirit and courage that kept the show going. Not really old—the appellation seemed to be something of an honorary title—Edourd Laupin had once been one of the greats of the high wire.

His act, so those who had witnessed it said, had been one of extreme daring and grace, and despite the great risks he took, he had seemed to be charmed.

For many years he had been a top act, playing both in Europe and in America to packed and enthusiastic audiences, and then one day his luck had failed. The resulting accident had left his beautiful and athletic body badly broken. His career on the high wire was over.

Despite his mental and physical pain, he had not left the circus, although from all accounts he could well have afforded to do so. Instead he had stayed, filling lowly but necessary jobs. Always ready with a smile and a word of encouragement, he was much loved by all the circus staff.

Leaving Old Laupin, Laura walked toward the animal tent, intending to visit her old friend, Jumbo. The first few days on the road had been hectic, and this was the first free time she had had.

It was a beautiful day, warm and clear, and Laura breathed long and deeply of the circus smell. There was nothing else on earth like it, she thought; and suddenly a great happiness welled up in her. She was so fortunate! Her world was so wonderful just now. She was successful, she was doing work she enjoyed, and she loved and was loved in return. What more could any woman ask?

Although she and Will had been terribly busy during the days, there had been the nights. . . . Laura felt herself go warm and soft inside just thinking of those nights.

Considering how little sleep she had been getting, and the amount of work she was doing, she should have felt worn out, but instead she felt wonderful, exceptionally alive and strong. It was as if their lovemaking were a miraculous tonic that made her more than human.

Smiling softly to herself, Laura entered the animal tent, which was already filling up with the afternoon crowd, and made her way through the throng to Jumbo's enclosure.

No matter how often she saw the huge elephant, she was impressed by his great size, and it always pleased her in some obscure way to watch the crowd's reaction to him. Some stood far back in awe and fear, while others crowded in close, trying to feed him or just touch him.

Jumbo recognized her immediately and raised his trunk in greeting. It always thrilled Laura when he did this, for she felt that a great spirit and an active intelligence existed within this great creature, and it was a privilege to be recognized by such an entity.

One by one, she offered the peanuts, and he took them delicately from her hand, as the crowd watched.

Concentrating on the elephant, she barely noticed that one of the onlookers had crowded very close to her. Instinctively she moved away, but the person crowded her again; it annoyed her, and she finally took her attention from Jumbo and turned to the interloper.

She found herself staring into the face of her husband, Nick Orlando.

She was stunned. The remaining peanuts in her hand

fell unnoticed to the ground as she stared unbelievingly into his smugly smiling face.

It could not have been more than a few seconds that they stood staring at each other, but to Laura it seemed an eternity, as her thoughts ran rampant. It couldn't be! Where had he come from? And, more important, *why* had he come? The one thought that emerged clearly was that his sudden appearance could bring her no good. Despite the fact that she had wanted to find him in order to obtain a divorce, Laura knew in her bones and her gut that he was going to cause her trouble.

Finally, after what seemed an embarrassingly long time, she managed to speak. She was pleased to hear that her voice was steady and calm. "Nick! This is certainly a surprise."

Nick's smile widened. "I thought it would be."

Then his expression turned earnest and sincere, and Laura felt herself harden inside. She knew that expression all too well—it was the one he always wore when he wanted to convince you that he was being honest and open.

"Laura, I've been looking everywhere for you, you know. I had no idea where you had gone, and I didn't have the funds to hire a detective. You can't imagine how glad I am to have found you at last."

Again the boyish, charming smile; and Laura's heart sank. The fact that he was "working" on her only confirmed her suspicions.

He said, "Can we go somewhere and talk?"

She nodded reluctantly. It was best to face up to this now and find out what he was after. At least she could now approach him about a divorce.

As they walked away from the animal tent, she looked him over critically. His clothes were neat enough, but cheap and flashy, and he had aged much more than three years would have warranted.

He was thinner, his color was bad, and he had the beginning of a small belly, despite his overall thinness. Small veins made faint traceries of red on his cheeks and across his nose. *He's been drinking heavily,* she thought;

*and obviously he hasn't been doing very well for himself.
He's probably going to ask me for money.*

Strangely, this thought lightened her spirits. If money
was all he wanted, she would give it to him with the
understanding that he would cause no problem about the
divorce. All he would have to do would be to give her an
address where the papers could be sent for his signature.

She thought of something else: Will!

She wanted Nick away from the circus before the two
men met. There was also the fact that she had told everyone that she was a widow. If Nick went around telling
people who he was, it would be embarrassing for her.

She took him to her compartment aboard the circus
train. Once inside, he glanced around appreciatively.

"Now this is very nice, I must say. You've apparently
done very well for yourself, my dear, but then I always
knew that you were a smart girl." Despite his approving
words, his tone was faintly accusing.

Laura, trying to maintain her calm, removed her hat
and placed it carefully on the rack, then turned to face
him with a level gaze. "I was forced to be, since you left
me penniless when you ran away."

Nick flushed and for a moment lowered his gaze. "I
know you have every right to be angry with me, but I
mean it when I say that I never meant to hurt you. I don't
know why I got involved with Harriet, although it was as
much her fault as mine. It certainly wasn't that I didn't
love you, Laura. I did, and still do."

He was staring at her intently now, his eyes moist and
pleading. The hurt, sensitive boy, she thought, remembering the many times he had used this ploy on her in the
past, and how naïve she had been to let him get away with
it. Well, she was no longer naïve, and his charm no longer
had any power over her. She shook her head firmly.

"It won't do you any good to take that tack, Nick. I'm
going to be perfectly honest with you." She began to
pace, choosing her words carefully; she felt surprisingly
little anger, only a cold determination that Nick should
not interfere with the new life she had built so carefully
for herself.

"When you left me I was desolate." She paused to look directly into his eyes and was pleased to see him wince. "You left me with nothing. You took my self-respect, my hope, and all of *our* money. I had nowhere to go, and I was inexperienced. The only thing I had was a bit of luck, and my own enterprise. Fortunately, it was enough, but that is certainly no thanks to you!

"Now I have finally managed to make a new life for myself, and you have no place in it, Nick, no place at all. I don't know why you have finally came back, but if you think there's any chance of our being man and wife again, you had better disabuse yourself of that notion at once!"

Breast heaving with emotion, she stopped pacing and looked at him, forcing him to meet her gaze. His eyes were unreadable.

"Just how *did* you find me?" she demanded.

"I saw your picture and the story in the newspaper."

Laura sighed. She should have guessed. The article had said that she was successful. If it had been an article saying that she had been found destitute and ill, would that have brought him? She thought not.

"So why have you come, after all this time?"

Nick reached out for her hands, but she drew back before he could grasp them, and he turned his hands palms upward, as if that were what he had been intending to do.

"I told you, Laura. I've never stopped loving you, and these past years have been hell for me, knowing that I failed you, knowing that I had hurt you badly. I've been wretched. You can't know how much I've wanted to find you, to make amends to you."

Laura resumed pacing. So he was going to stick with his story! Did he really think that she would believe him? And how could she convince him that she was no longer vulnerable to his manipulations?

She took a deep breath. "Nick, I simply don't believe you. I believe that you have looked me up because you read that article about my success. I believe that you want *something*. Money, perhaps. If that is so, please be honest with me. You owe me at least that much!"

Nick again raised his hands. His expression was woebegone. "You wrong me, Laura, although after what I've done to you, I suppose that's to be expected. I'll admit that I've had some difficulties, that I am not, at the moment, doing well, but I didn't come to you to ask anything of you other than your forgiveness. I'm really hurt that you think so little of me that you can imagine that I came here to cause you harm in any way. By the way . . ." He looked at her ingenuously. "Do you happen to have something to drink, and perhaps a bite to eat? I've had a long trip."

Laura, with a sigh of exasperation, went to the food cupboard and began to arrange a tray. As she laid out the cheese, crackers, fruit, and a bottle of brandy, her mind felt numb. Nick was not going to admit why he had looked her up; he was going to take his own good time about it, and she had the awful feeling that he was not going to be easy to get rid of.

When she had placed the tray on the small table before him, she noticed that, despite his claim of hunger, he drank a great deal more than he ate.

Although she seldom drank alcohol, Laura poured herself a glass of brandy. Perhaps it would help ease the apprehension that gripped her.

"When are you planning to leave?" she asked bluntly, as he finished his third glass of brandy.

He looked at her innocently. "Well, I hadn't really thought about that," he said thoughtfully. "You see, I had hoped that you might forgive me, that you might . . ." He looked down humbly. "I had hoped that you might forgive me and take me back."

He looked up again, his eyes pleading. "Nothing like what happened before will ever happen again. I would devote my life to making it up to you, I swear it! Remember how happy we once were? Remember how it was between us in the beginning? It could be that way again, if you would only . . ."

Laura wearily shook her head, which was beginning to ache. "Haven't you been listening to me at all, Nick? It's all over between us. It has been since the day you left me.

I don't love you, and I could never love you again. If you need money, I will give you some, but I want something in return. I want a divorce. I certainly have the grounds for it."

Nick placed his hand over his eyes in a dramatic gesture. When he spoke, his voice was muffled. "I can't ever agree to that, Laura. I love you too much to give you up that easily. Just give me a little time, time to convince you that I've changed. Don't make a hasty decision, I beg you!"

Laura squeezed her hands into fists. *Why* wouldn't he listen to her? Between clenched teeth she said, "I've been thinking about this for three years, Nick. I'd hardly call *that* a hasty decision."

Nick removed his hand from his eyes and stared at her, his gaze expressionless now. He got up from the chair and stood looking down at her. "I won't agree to a divorce, Laura. And whether you wish me to or not, I'm not going to leave you until I'm satisfied that there really is no chance."

She stared at him, aghast. "Do you mean you intend to follow me from city to city?"

He gave her a rueful smile. "Yes. That's just what I mean. I had hoped that you would be more forgiving, that you would take me back; but I can see now that at the moment at least, I can't expect you to let me stay with you. Since I am a bit short of funds, I suppose my only hope is to go to the manager of the circus, tell him that I'm your husband, and see if he has a job for me."

He was looking at her speculatively, and Laura had to struggle to keep her expression from revealing her despair. He was very clever. With a con man's expertise he sensed where she was most vulnerable—she did not want it known around the circus that he was her husband. If she had entertained any doubts about Nick's lack of honesty, this laid them to rest. He was going to use his silence as a club to hold over her head.

Looking him straight in the eye, she let him see her contempt. "I imagine that you know I would rather you didn't do that. To simplify matters, I have told everyone here that my husband is dead."

Nick smiled slyly. "So it would be a surprise to them to have your dead husband turn up very much alive, now wouldn't it?"

"You know it would," she said tightly.

Nick placed his thumbs in his vest pockets and rocked back and forth on his feet. "Then I'll tell you what I'll do. You get me a job with the circus under a different name. You're surely important enough to manage that. Then agree to let me see you, and talk to you. If, after a month or so, you still wish to be rid of me, I'll go quietly."

Laura looked at him skeptically. Was he lying? Quite probably. "And the divorce?"

He shrugged and raised his eyebrows. "I'll have to give that some thought. But what do you say? Do we have a deal?"

Laura thought frantically. What choice did she have? She could see no way to avoid doing what he asked. Will, of course, knew that Nick was still alive; but James Bailey would think it very odd to have Nickolas Orlando request a job of him, and there would be a great deal of explaining to do. It could make things very awkward for her, particularly since they would not be living together. She had no desire for the whole circus to know of her personal life.

Either way, she would have to accept having Nick around. She doubted the sincerity of his promise to leave in a month if she remained adamant, but she thought that perhaps, when he realized that she really meant what she said, he would grow tired of working at a lowly job, and leave. He had never been able to endure routine and boredom. At any rate, as she saw it, there was little else she could do.

"All right, Nick," she said finally. "I'll ask Mr. Bailey to give you a job under another name. What name have you picked to use?"

Nick squinted his eyes in thought, then grinned broadly. "Nathaniel Oliver, I think. I don't want to give up everything, and this way my initials will match."

Laura stared at him coldly and thought of Will. What was he going to say about all this? She had to tell him—he would certainly recognize Nick, who had not changed all

that much. And what would Will do? He was a forceful
man, used to taking charge, and he had never made any
secret of what he thought of Nick. She must prevent him
from doing anything impetuous.

And what about their own relationship? How would it
be affected by Nick's constant presence? Nick was still
legally her husband. He could make things very difficult if
he wished, and he probably would. How was she going to
handle the situation?

Nick left James Bailey's office with a jaunty step, feeling
reasonably satisfied.

Laura had introduced him to Bailey—an oddly bookish
sort of little man—as an old friend, and Bailey had put
him on as a ticket taker.

Of course, it was not quite what Nick had hoped for. It
was a lowly job, and the pay was not much. The best
possible outcome would have been for Laura to have been
moved by his tender pleas for forgiveness and taken him
back to her hearth and into her heart. Although he had
not really expected this, he had hoped that it was not out
of the realm of possibility.

But Laura had changed more than he had imagined
possible. She was by no means the innocent, unworldly
girl he had left, but a grown woman, a stranger, grown
somewhat harder and sharper with the years.

And she had changed in other ways as well. She was
more beautiful than ever, partially because she now knew
how to dress and arrange her hair.

Seeing her again had brought back memories of their
time together, and he remembered how pleasant making
love to her had been. Yes, he had been right to look her
up. She was beautiful, desirable, and evidently making
good money. If he could worm his way back into her good
graces, life could be very good indeed.

And he wanted her—God, how he wanted her! It had
taken all his self-control not to take her by force when he
had been alone with her in that railroad compartment.
But he had realized that he could ruin everything by such

an impetuous action. No, he had to use patience and guile, and win her over.

Of course, that was not going to be easy. He had his work cut out for him. There might even be another man—after all, it had been three years. Well, if there was, he would just have to be eased out. After all, Nick was her husband.

Nick smiled to himself and headed toward the sleeping car, where he had been assigned a berth. He felt reasonably certain that he would not be bunking there long. He prided himself on his gambler's intuition, and his intuition told him that his luck was on the upswing. Yes, with a little luck, a considerable exertion of charm—and perhaps a little eating of humble pie—he should soon be sharing the comfortable living quarters of Mrs. Nickolas Orlando, his beautiful wife.

"I'm so upset!" Laura cried. She stopped pacing to look at Will. "I just don't know what to do!"

Will was furious about this turn of events, but he did not want to vent his anger on Laura. He moved to her side and took her into his arms. "We'll work it out. I just wish that you hadn't gotten him a job with the show. It will only make it harder to get rid of him in the end."

Laura put her head against his chest, feeling the comforting beat of his heart. "I told you, darling, if I hadn't, he was going to ask for a job using his real name. I just couldn't go through all the explanations that would have been required. Everyone would want to know why I had lied about being a widow and why we weren't living together. This at least seemed a temporary solution, sorry as it is."

Will's arms tightened around her. "If he had come to me, I would have told him a thing or two. I still think I should go and have a talk with him, point out to him that you don't want him here and that he'd be better off elsewhere."

Laura shook her head and raised her face to his. "I know how you feel, Will, but that would be a mistake. Whatever else Nick is, he's very clever. If you threaten him, he'll find some way to turn it to his advantage. After all, legally he's still my husband. Even the law would probably be on his side. Although he's the one who deserted me, the law gives the husband most of the rights. No, we must wait him out, keep calm; he'll finally get around to telling me what he wants. When we find that out, we can handle it. Maybe he'll agree to settle for some money, and leave, letting me sue for a divorce."

Will cupped the back of her head with his hand and pressed her face close to his chest. Perhaps she was right, but he had a dreadful feeling that Nick Orlando wanted more than just money. As Laura had said, he was clever, and a clever man would certainly recognize that it was more desirable to have Laura herself, *and* her money, than to settle simply for what she was willing to give him, and go away.

Chapter Twenty-One

THE next few weeks were very difficult for Laura, and there was no sign that things would improve.

She had tried to be patient and cool, tried not to let Nick see that his presence was disturbing her, but he was too clever and too experienced not to recognize his advantage. And he was always around. He would often show up at her compartment in the evenings, begging her to let him in so that he could speak to her, reminding her that she had agreed to let him see her and talk to her, until finally, angry and frustrated, she would reluctantly let him in.

She knew that the other circus employees were talking about her new "romantic interest." Circus folk, she had found, thrived on gossip. They were a closed community, and everyone knew what everyone else was doing. The fact that Nick was often in her company had not gone unnoticed.

The thing that bothered her most was that Nick's presence made it very difficult for her to be with Will. Nick had soon found out that Will and she were seeing each other and had quickly added it all up. He had then, smiling all the while, pointed out to her that legally he was still her husband, and that if he made this fact known, the affair between her and Will would not appear in a very good light.

Furious, but not wanting to precipitate a fight, Laura

had told Will that she would not be able to see him as often and that they would have to be more secretive.

Will, of course, had been very upset; she had never seen him so angry. It was all she could do to restrain him from confronting Nick immediately.

"That bastard!" Will said explosively. "He disappears for years, leaves you penniless, and now he has the gall to show up and attempt to destroy the life you've made for yourself. Hanging's too good for him. I'd like to break his damned neck!"

Laura tried to soothe him. "I know, Will, I feel the same way. After waiting all that time for you, just when we're finally together and everything is wonderful, he comes along and spoils it all. But it won't be for much longer, I'm certain. He promised that if after a month or so I still don't want to take him back, he'll go away and leave us alone and, I hope, agree to a divorce, so I'll be free of him forever."

Will clenched his fists and turned away. "I wouldn't place any credence in any word of his. It's been almost a month now, and he certainly doesn't show any signs of leaving. In fact, he seems to be settling in more every day. I'm getting sick of not being able to see you when I want to, of having to sneak around to be with you. And the others are talking. I think they're even making wagers on which one of us you will choose."

Laura embraced him fiercely. "If they only knew that there was no contest about that!" She tilted her head back and gazed into his eyes. "I'm hoping that the whole thing will work itself out, that Nick will get tired of beating against a closed door and just go away."

Will gave a discouraged sigh. "I'm afraid that will never happen, Laura. I think that he's determined to wear you down, to put so much pressure on you that you'll agree to live with him again simply because it will be the easiest thing to do."

Laura said strongly, "That will never happen. No matter what he does, even if he tells Barnum or Bailey that he's my husband, I will never do that. Nothing will make me live with him again, darling. I swear!"

* * *

But the weeks had become a month, and one month had become two; and although she reminded Nick of his promise, he kept pressing her for more time.

At the end of the second month, Laura stood before the dressing mirror in her compartment, staring disconsolately at her reflection. Something had to be done. She was growing too thin, and her nerves were so taut that she flared up at the slightest provocation.

So far, despite the sleepless nights and hectic days, she had managed to keep her unhappiness from interfering with her work, but she did not know how much longer she could keep functioning efficiently.

She felt as if she were being pulled at from all sides. On one hand there was Nick, reminding her that she was still his wife, begging her to forgive him, saying that he still loved her; on the other was Will, growing angrier and more frustrated every day, telling her that she might as well let Nick do his worst, for he was not going to give up and go away, as he had promised, and reminding her that she was supposed to love *him*. Asking her if she was certain that she had no feeling left for Nick. And on top of all that there were the pressures of her demanding job. Sometimes she felt that she would just blow up, scream, pull her hair, create a terrible scene—anything to relieve the pressure. At other times she just wished she could run away and hide someplace peaceful and quiet, where she had nothing to do but sleep for a week.

From the beginning she had avoided Nick as much as possible, but now she found herself avoiding Will as well. She felt that she simply could not endure any more contention.

Since to stay in her compartment meant to risk having Nick pop in on her, she took to spending as much time as possible with other people, Milly and Lionel in particular.

Milly had stuck to her plan and was making a concerted effort to convince Lionel that she loved him. Laura, in an attempt to forget her own problems, tried to help her as much as possible. It was clear to Laura that Lionel was flattered by all the attention and that he was weakening;

however, he still seemed to be keeping a wall around his feelings. Laura thought he was afraid to let Milly, or anyone, inside that wall; but that only made Milly the more determined, and Laura had high hopes that her friend would succeed.

People were so strange, and so complex, she thought. Here was Lionel, wanting love, needing it, hungering for it; and yet giving his own love and devotion to the memory of a cold, heartless woman who was dead, while pretty, warm-natured Milly was offering him happiness and the comfort of her love. Why was he so blind, so stubborn?

Often, when she and Milly went to Lionel's wagon, they would find Benjy there.

Benjy had, during the past months, renewed his friendship with Lionel—or perhaps that was putting it too strongly, for Benjy still seemed like an entirely different person from who he had been before Diana's death. Perhaps it would be more appropriate to say that he went to Lionel as a lost dog might go to a stranger when his master was gone, in simple need of human contact.

Although Benjy did not contribute much to the conversation, he seemed content just to be there, and occasionally he would show a flash of his old nature. He seemed to obtain some comfort from listening to the others talk, and Laura was pleased that at least he was showing signs of coming out of his shell.

These evenings after the show with Milly, Lionel, and Benjy were good for Laura, for they were the only ones with whom she could discuss her problems. At first she had told them nothing, not wanting to put a damper on their social times together; but Milly, perceptive as always, and Lionel, sensitive to other people's moods, knew something was troubling her, and they finally persuaded her to confide in them.

It had been a wonderful release to speak of her troubles to someone who was uninvolved, and she felt that talking things over with her friends was the only thing that was saving her sanity.

Milly, in particular, was very loyal, and her anger against

Nick was almost as great as Laura's. "There must be something we can do!" she kept saying; but so far none of them had come up with a solution to the problem.

And then, on one hot, summer night when heat lightning washed the sky with sheets of crackling white light and filled the air with a sense of expectancy, two things happened—Laura's problems came to a head, and Milly achieved at least a portion of her dream.

As she did every time she knew that she would be seeing Lionel, Milly had taken particular pains with her dress and her hair. She felt encouraged, for it seemed to her, and Laura agreed, that Lionel was at long last taking some notice of her as a woman. The only problem was that he appeared to be resisting it. Milly was growing impatient and had reached a decision: she intended to seduce Lionel at the very first opportunity.

Perhaps it was a risky thing to do. It would change their relationship forever, one way or another, but that was a chance she would take.

Studying her image in the looking glass, Milly examined herself critically. She looked as good as she was ever going to; and if she could get Lionel alone tonight . . .

Her spirits lifted as she headed toward Lionel's wagon. It was a strange night. Clouds had been piling up all afternoon, and the air felt heavy and full of electricity. It was late, but the circus people were accustomed to late hours.

The door to Lionel's wagon stood open, a golden swath of light spilling down the steps and onto the ground. When Milly rapped on the door frame, Lionel appeared at once, a smile on his face.

"Milly! It's good to see you."

He ushered her inside, then leaned forward and kissed her cheek. As he greeted her, she deliberately leaned into him, so that her breasts brushed against his chest, and heard him draw in his breath as he quickly stepped back. Her resolve hardened, and she smiled at him sweetly. "Is Laura coming over?"

He nodded, and she felt a slight pull of disappointment.

Much as she loved Laura, Milly had been hoping that this evening she and Lionel would be alone together.

"Anyone else?"

He shrugged. "Benjy perhaps. I never know when he's going to drop in, but I don't press him. I'm just glad that he's beginning to make an effort to socialize.

"You look pretty tonight," Lionel added. "Pink is a nice color; it becomes you."

She gave him what she hoped was a provocative smile. "Why, thank you, Lionel. It's nice of you to say so. You know, sometimes I wonder if you ever really see me."

Lionel looked flustered. "What on earth do you mean, Milly?" he said in a low voice. "Of course I notice you! What a thing to say!"

Milly smiled secretively. She knew that she was making him uncomfortable, and that was just what she wanted. She intended to keep him off balance until she could put her plan into action.

At that moment Laura appeared in the doorway. As Lionel hurried to usher her in, Milly noticed how pale and thin Laura had become. Her heart ached for her friend; she had been racking her brain for days to find some way to help her.

Milly wondered how Laura had ever been taken in by Nick Orlando. Of course he was handsome, she supposed, if you cared for his type, and she had seen for herself that he could be charming; but it was clear that his easy charm and good looks were all that there was to him. There was nothing underneath. Men like Nick thought only of themselves and what was best for them. It was plain to Milly that Nick now thought that Laura would be a comfortable and attractive meal ticket, and that he meant to reestablish his right to her. She knew that the situation was tearing Laura apart. Something *had* to be done before Laura broke under the strain.

Laura smiled palely at her, and Milly could see that she was making a great effort to be cheerful, but her face was wan and her eyes looked strained.

Milly moved over on the settee to make room for her friend, as Lionel poured Laura a glass of punch. They chatted until Benjy arrived, and then Lionel read to them from *David Copperfield*, by Charles Dickens. They had started this practice at the beginning of the season. Lionel had an extensive library and enjoyed reading aloud. He had a beautiful speaking voice, and he read with such expression that when listening to him they could almost imagine that they were seeing it all, as upon a stage. At the end of a busy day, it was very relaxing to close their eyes and be carried away to another time and place.

After he had finished the chapter, Laura sighed and got to her feet. "Well, I'd better get to bed. Another busy day tomorrow."

Benjy stood up as well, and paused to cough, the spasm racking his small body. Laura and Milly exchanged worried looks.

"Are you all right, Benjy?" Laura asked, bending over the little man.

He looked up at her with a hint of a smile, and Milly thought that at least Laura's problem was good for something: Benjy, in worrying about Laura's troubles, seemed to forget, for a moment, his own.

"I'll escort you back to your quarters, Laura," he said in a gentlemanly manner. "I'd best turn in, too."

As Milly watched her two friends leave the wagon, leaving her alone with Lionel, a heady excitement seemed to grow deep inside her. She felt reckless and strong.

A distant roll of thunder sounded in the distance, and she heard the patter of raindrops on the wooden roof of the wagon. Good! She had a legitimate excuse for lingering.

She turned back to Lionel. "It seems to have started raining. Will it put you out if I stay awhile longer? It's only a thundershower, I'm sure, and it shouldn't last long."

Lionel gave her a rather strained smile. "Of course not, Milly. You know that you're welcome to stay as long as you like."

At that moment the wagon was shaken by a tremendous roll of thunder that sounded as if a cannon had gone off, and Milly, with an instinct as old as womankind, gave a small yelp and flung herself against Lionel's chest.

Lionel instinctively closed his arms around her, and she nestled happily against his chest, pressing her body close to his. She could feel his heart begin to pound, and he attempted to draw back. Milly clutched at him and said pitifully, "Oh, don't let go, Lionel. I'm terrified of thunder. I have been since I was a child." She looked up into his face, her lips parted. "That was so loud. It sounded as if it would split the wagon in two!"

Lionel gazed down at her, his eyes slightly glazed. He cleared his throat loudly. "Yes, it was very loud. It startled me, too, Milly."

But not as much as I'm startling you, Milly thought, pressing closer against him than before, and feeling not the least bit of shame at her performance. Such a fraud she was! She had never been afraid of thunder in her life; she was only doing what they both wanted her to do and, except for the fact of Lionel's peculiar notions, would have done much sooner.

To her delight, the thunder rolled again, giving her the opportunity to cling tighter still—so close that she could feel his body responding to her closeness.

Emboldened, she turned her face up again to his, lips open and inviting, and let her love for him shine in her eyes; and this time she spoke from the heart. "Oh, Lionel! I feel so safe with you holding me like this. I've wanted you to hold me, you know, for the longest time."

Lionel's eyes fixed on hers with a hypnotic intensity. He heaved a great sigh, as if in surrender, and he seemed to relax. His arms tightened as he lowered his mouth to hers.

Another boom of thunder rolled over the wagon, but they did not move.

Milly, feeling that her very soul was pouring out through her lips, felt a wild rush of happiness as Lionel's hands began to move over her body, at first tentatively, in exploration, and then with more surety.

Taking his mouth from hers, he leaned away for a moment to blow out the lantern, then he returned to her arms.

A tremendous flash of lightning illuminated the interior

of the wagon as they moved toward his bed; and in a few short moments, Milly found out what it was like to have the furry body of her lion man next to hers.

It was strange, and beautiful, and the most wonderful thing that had ever happened to her.

Laura just beat the rain to her compartment door, and she lifted her head as she heard the first drops strike the car roof. She gazed down at Benjy, who stood by her side. She was very tired, but the little man looked so depressed that she did not have the heart to send him to his quarters.

"I love the rain," she said, smiling down at him. "It will make me sleep well, and it should cool things off."

Benjy nodded seriously. "Yes, and it should settle the dust, too."

"Would you like to come in for a drink, Benjy? I have some good brandy. It will help you sleep."

Benjy nodded. "Thank you, Miss Laura. I'd like that."

Opening her door, Laura lit a lamp, as a loud roll of thunder rumbled overhead and a sheet of lightning flickered outside the compartment window.

She had just poured out two healthy tots of brandy when she heard a low, sneering laugh from the open doorway.

Her body stiffening, she turned slowly and saw Nick slouched against the doorframe. His face was flushed, his eyes bloodshot, and she could smell the liquor on him even from where he stood. Despite the heat, she suddenly felt cold. She had been afraid of this. She knew that when Nick was drinking heavily, an angry wildness could overcome him. Since he had joined the circus she had not seen him drink to excess, but it was clear that tonight he had overindulged. She would have to get rid of him. She was too weary to spend the rest of the night arguing with him or attempting to evade his overtures of what he called "love."

"Nick!" she exclaimed. "It's very late. Would you mind coming back at some other time?"

Nick chuckled, but it was not a happy sound. "Yes, it's late, and getting later, but I see that you still have company, Laura. What's the matter? Couldn't Mr. Adams keep you company this evening? Did you have to settle for short rations?"

There was a cruel, mocking tone in his voice, and Laura, glancing down at Benjy, saw the little man stiffen.

"Benjy is a good friend of mine," Laura said coldly, "and is welcome here anytime, which is more than you are, Mr. Orlando. If you don't mind, I will thank you to leave!"

"Oh, but I do mind." Nick ambled into the compartment. "I mind very much. Here I come calling on my beautiful wife, and she wants me to leave. Now I ask you, is that friendly?"

He addressed the last remark to Benjy, leaning down exaggeratedly to do so and thrusting his face close to Benjy's. "I said, don't you think so, little man?"

Benjy's face had gone white, and his jaw was set. "I think you had better do what Laura requests, Mr. Orlando. I think that would be the best for all concerned."

Nick loosed a roar of laughter. "Oh, you do, do you, my tiny friend? That's your advice, is it? And if I don't choose to take it, what will you do, attack me viciously about the knees? Oh, I tremble at the thought, indeed I do."

Benjy's face went paler still, and his tiny fists clenched. When he spoke, his voice trembled. "I may be small, Mr. Orlando, but don't underestimate me. We dwarfs are very strong for our size, and you are very drunk!"

Nick, holding his sides to contain his laughter, finally managed to say, "Oh, I will bear that in mind, sir. I most certainly will. And to be certain that it is a fair fight, I'll bring you up to my size. Like this!"

With a quickness of movement that belied his state of intoxication, Nick swooped down upon the dwarf and took hold of him. When Nick lifted the smaller man, he staggered, then caught himself, and placed Benjy upon the table so that he now stood at an equal height with Nick.

"I must say you're heavier than you look," Nick said with heaving breath. "Now there, my mighty warrior. Now we can go at it eye to eye, so to speak. What do you say, are you ready to begin, my little gamecock?"

Wild with anger and embarrassment for Benjy, Laura grabbed Nick's arm and swung him around to face her. "Leave him alone, Nick! Isn't it enough for you to embarrass and hurt me? Can't you be satisfied with that? Do you have to attack my friends, too?"

Nick turned to glare at her, a nasty smile barely curving his lips. "A friend of yours, you say. Well, I didn't know that, although I should have guessed it, I suppose, seeing as how you have so many strange gentlemen friends. That hairy, dog-faced boy, for instance, who's supposed to look like a lion. And then there's Mr. Will Adams, of course. Yes, I should have guessed it. But I am curious, Laura. How does he satisfy you, this little person? I mean, he's only half a man, after all, and you were always the type of woman who required the services of at least a whole and energetic gentleman. Or have you changed? Has Will Adams accustomed you to less than that? Yes, I should imagine that may be the real answer!"

Laura's temper exploded. She lashed out at him with her open hand, catching him on the side of the face with enough force to snap his head sideways.

Nick merely laughed, and seized her arm in a cruel grip that made her wince and cry out. At that moment, Benjy launched himself from the table top with a hoarse cry, landing astride Nick's shoulders. Nick staggered back and released Laura's arm.

For a few moments Nick struggled with the little man, who was indeed heavier than he appeared, and extremely strong for his size; but in the end Nick's greater weight and size and length of arm prevailed, and he managed to disengage the dwarf and fling him out the door into the corridor, where he landed with a thump.

Before Benjy could regain his feet, Nick had bolted the door behind him, and leaned against it, panting. "Well, my dear wife!" he gasped. "Your little protector is out of our way now."

He fingered a scratch on his cheek, which was bleeding. "I'll be damned! The little bastard bloodied me. Well, it doesn't matter. After all, what knight worth his salt would not fight for his fair lady."

Pulling his coat straight, Nick moved toward Laura, who backed slowly away from him. She was really afraid now. Nick was at that stage of drunkenness where he would not be stopped, and she knew all too well what he was after, what he intended to do.

Behind Nick, Benjy thumped frantically on the door, but Nick only smiled smugly. "It *is* just like a fairy tale, my lovely, lovely Laura. The princess captured by the evil dwarf, and her prince came hurrying to rescue her, just in time. Now it's time for the prince to claim his just reward."

He was upon her now, his hands roughly grasping her upper arms, pulling her inexorably toward him. She tried to pull free, turning her face away from his whiskey-sour breath, fighting against his powerful grip.

"Oh, don't fight it, my princess. It will do you no good. After all, right is on my side, and I'm only asking for what is my rightful due, what you've been denying me for so long."

Laura glared into his eyes, which were streaked with veins of red. "You forefeited any rights you had with me on the day you left. If you don't get away from me and out of this compartment, I'm going to scream."

"Scream away," he said, grasping her face in one hand, his fingers digging cruelly into her cheek. He held her pinned against the wall as he stared down into her eyes.

"Scream, and then everyone will know that Nathaniel Oliver is really Nickolas Orlando, your husband, and that he has found it necessary to take by force that which should be his by right. It will make a fine scandal, won't it, my dear? I wonder if your Mr. Barnum will put it in the papers, as he does everything else that happens in his circus?"

Laura suddenly felt dizzy. Benjy had stopped hammering on the door, and the night suddenly seemed very still; and then Laura jumped as a loud roll of thunder rattled the compartment windows.

As she stood there, weak and disoriented, she felt Nick's hands move, one to her breast and one to her buttocks, as he placed his mouth next to her ear.

"Don't fight it, Laura. Don't you remember how much

you liked it once? Don't you remember how you begged for it? It will be that way again. Wait and see!"

His voice had thickened with passion; and Laura felt a strong repugnance as he pushed his lower body against hers. Summoning all her remaining strength, she shoved at his shoulders. "Never!" she said loudly. "Can't you understand? I don't want you, Nick! I'll never let you touch me, willingly!"

He gave a short bark of laughter. "In that case, I'll dispense with the amenities. I mean to have what's mine, Laura, with or without your cooperation."

Laura gasped as his fingers hooked in the neck of her dress, and the breath left her in a rush as he yanked the fabric downward until it ripped.

She was so startled that she thought the sudden crash of the breaking door was only in her head, and it was not until she saw Will's angry face looming over Nick's shoulder that she realized what was happening.

Will grabbed Nick by the shoulder and spun him around so that the two men faced each other, and Laura, freed, fell back against the wall.

"I've been waiting for this moment for weeks, Orlando," Will said through gritted teeth. "I knew you would go too far, sooner or later."

"How could I go too far, Adams?" Nick said jeeringly. "Just because you've been enjoying her favors for so long doesn't mean that she still isn't mine."

"Shut your filthy mouth!"

Will struck him across the face, and the next few minutes were a confusion of violence and sound as the two men fought savagely.

Out of the corner of her eye, Laura saw Benjy in the doorway. Leaning against the wall, feeling weak and shaken, she could only scream at the fighting men to stop. She might not have existed for all the attention they paid her. She had never seen men fight like this, with such anger and ferocity. She could scarcely recognize Will's face, so contorted was it by his emotions. It looked to Laura as if he wanted to kill Nick, and the primitive and violent scene shook her to her core.

Nick's face was twisted in anger, but there was also fear beginning to surface now. Although the men were of approximately the same height, Will was more muscular and much heavier. Laura knew that Nick did not stand a chance; and as the fight progressed, she was afraid that Will *would* kill him, for he kept hammering him again and again, although Nick was now barely able to stand upright. Will seized him by the shirt front and held him upright against the wall with one hand, and beat him about the face with the other.

Panic gave Laura strength, and she ran at Will and attempted to pull him away, at the same time calling to Benjy to help her. At last, between the two of them, they managed to make Will stop. Nick, his face smeared with blood, slid slowly to the floor.

Will's arm, where Laura held it, felt as hard and rigid as a column of oak. He was panting, his eyes were glazed, and his face looked frightening.

"Will," she whispered, "you've got to get him out of here. Take him to the medical tent and call the doctor."

Will stared at her, his eyes like flint. "Did he hurt you? If that bastard harmed you . . . !"

Laura shook her head. "No, no, Will, I'm fine. He didn't harm me."

Staring past Will's shoulder, Laura saw that Betinna Brouder and Madame Mystic had gathered in the corridor. She lowered her voice. "You must get him to the doctor, Will."

Will blinked dazedly. "After what he tried to do to you, you still worry about him?"

"No, Will, no." She shook her head wearily. "I'm worried about *you*. If Nick should die, it would be *you* who would be in trouble. And besides, we have an audience."

Turning his head, Will stared at the white faces looking in at them, and a measure of sanity returned to his eyes. "Yes, I see what you mean."

Laura was thinking frantically. "I'll tell them that Nathaniel got drunk and attacked me, and that Benjy brought you to my rescue. It's the truth, after all. I just won't tell them that Nick is my husband. What he'll say when he wakes up is another matter. I'll handle that when it happens. Now please, get him to the doctor. I'll see you in the morning, Will."

She saw him swallow hard, as some of the tension went out of his body. He moved as if to kiss her, then stopped, shooting a glance at the people outside the compartment. He nodded to her and stepped over to where Nick lay crumpled and still on the floor.

Stooping, he hoisted Nick none too gently over his shoulder and started toward the door. As Benjy closed the door behind them, Laura could hear Will telling the people in the corridor that everything was all right and that they should return to their beds.

Slowly, feeling bruised and unutterably weary, Laura went to the door and bolted it, wondering what good it would do since Will's violent entry had left it shattered.

She made her way to her bed and collapsed on it, without bothering to remove her clothes. She desperately longed for the oblivion of sleep; she needed a respite from her troubled thoughts and emotions. She had never felt so defeated, so low in spirits; not even on that day when Nick had deserted her had she felt such bleak despair.

With a great effort she removed her shoes and her outer clothing, and sank back onto the bed again. Her last thought before sleep came was that right now it seemed as if nothing could ever possibly be all right again.

Chapter Twenty-Two

THE next morning, for the first time since she had started to work for the circus, Laura did not report to her office. Despite the fact that she had fallen into a heavy sleep, she felt fatigued almost to the point of helplessness, and her body ached all over from the struggle with Nick. She simply did not feel like working, and she doubted that she was capable of thinking clearly.

She had yet to see or talk to anyone, so she had not learned of Nick's condition, or how the circus community had accepted Will's explanation, and she felt too beaten to care. Perhaps she should give up her job, pack up and leave it all behind her. She had money saved, a fair sum. She could always find another job.

But of course, she realized, that was merely her depression speaking. She would never find another position that would offer her what she had now. Positions of the sort she held were not usually available to women, and she knew that now that she had tasted success, she could not settle for less. And why should she let Nick drive her away from the life she had worked so hard to achieve? She had to hang on, no matter what it cost her emotionally.

And there was Will. She loved him so much, and they were on the verge of such happiness. If only Nick could be persuaded to leave them alone and to consent to a divorce. She and Will could be married then, as soon as she had met his son and mother-in-law. She knew that he was only waiting for her to meet his son before asking her.

The summer was drawing to an end. Soon the season would be over, and then they could go back to New York. Men were so odd, Laura thought. Sometimes Will seemed unduly concerned over how she would react to meeting his family. Why had he thought that she would mind that he had been married and had a son? Such a situation might be a disadvantage to a woman, but not to a man. It was unfair, but there it was.

It had all seemed so simple, so inviting, and so soon to be attained, but now, this thing with Nick. . . .

She sighed, pushing her hair back from her face. Her head ached, and she felt dirty clear through to her bones. She must have a bath, but first she had to send word to the office that she would not be in today. She headed toward the door, just as it resounded to a firm knock. She paused, dreading to find out who awaited her on the other side. The knock came again, louder.

Pulling her peignoir more tightly around her, she unbolted and opened the door to see James Bailey standing in the corridor, his expression concerned.

"Laura! I was worried about you. Are you all right?"

Stepping back from the doorway, she nodded. "More or less. I don't feel too well at the moment, but it will pass. Won't you come in, Mr. Bailey?"

Bailey examined the door with a critical eye. "I'll have it repaired today." He strode briskly into the compartment. "I heard about what happened last night, Laura, and I'm terribly sorry. You're just fortunate Benjy was with you and went for help. There's no telling what might have . . ." He flushed a bright red and lowered his gaze. "But no matter. You weren't badly hurt, and that fellow will be out on his ear as soon as he's in good enough condition to walk. I'll see to that!"

Laura swallowed. "Is he all right? I mean, he wasn't seriously hurt, was he?"

Bailey looked at her strangely. "No, I don't believe so."

Laura tried to smile. "It's just that I wouldn't want Mr. Adams to get into any trouble for coming to my defense. You do understand?"

Bailey's eyes brightened as he got her meaning. "Oh, yes, of course. I see what you mean."

As he was speaking, Laura was thinking that Nick might very well spring his surprise now, letting it be known that he was her husband; but she found that she just did not care. Whatever trouble such a disclosure might cause could not be any worse than what she was going through now. *Let him do his worst,* she decided; *and if he does, then he will no longer have any hold over me. My friends will understand, and those who don't—well, they're not really my friends, and so it doesn't matter.*

Deep in her own thoughts, she did not quite catch Bailey's next few words; and then, as they penetrated her consciousness, she became alert. "I'm sorry, Mr. Bailey. What did you just say?"

Bailey stared at her with a worried frown. "I said that I hope that you aren't feeling too badly, because Phineas wishes you to join him in Maine."

Laura shook her head bewilderedly. Maine? Barnum wanted her to go to Maine? It made no sense to her. "Whatever for?"

Bailey shrugged. "Well, you know Phineas, or you should by this time. Although he's getting on in years and doesn't travel with the circus proper as much as he once did, he still likes to keep his hand in, so to speak. He and Nancy are visiting their friends the Harpers, who have a summer home in Maine; and someone there told Phineas about some kind of preserved monster that someone had discovered in a cave on their property.

"Phineas wired me that he's been to see it, and he's pretty well convinced that it's authentic. He wants you to come up and see it so that you can start an immediate publicity campaign the moment he buys it."

Laura slowly felt herself come alive again as excitement stirred in her. A trip! A chance to get away! This meant that she would not have to face the curious stares and the questions; and by the time she returned, much of the novelty of her situation would have worn off.

She took a deep breath. "I suddenly feel a hundred percent better. It sounds fascinating."

Bailey laughed lightly. "Well, Phineas can make almost anything sound fascinating, you know. I only hope that he's not letting his enthusiasm get away from him, as he is prone to do. I'll count on you to exert a steadying influence, Laura. I want you to look this object over carefully, and if you even suspect it's not genuine, let me know. I don't want to be involved in a fraud."

"Of course, Mr. Bailey." Laura's mind was racing, all her lethargy washed away by her excitement. "Will you make the arrangements for me?"

Bailey nodded. "Certainly. We'll get you on the one-o'clock train, and I'll wire Phineas and let him know you're on your way. I'll let your staff know that you will be away. Or perhaps, if you have any special instructions for them, you'd better drop in at the office after you've packed."

"Yes, I'll do that. And thank you, Mr. Bailey."

Bailey flushed, and adjusted his glasses. "Why, whatever for? I simply relayed a message."

"But thank you for bringing it in person. I really do appreciate it."

"I was happy to do it. Now, you have a nice trip, Laura, and I'll take care of things here."

As soon as Bailey left, Laura bathed and dressed. It was still early, and she wanted to see both Will and Milly before they became involved in their day's work.

She found Will in his compartment, looking somewhat the worse for his fight with Nick. His left eye was swollen almost shut, and discolored, and there was a cut on his lower lip.

"Laura!" he exclaimed, taking her into his arms. "Are you all right? I wanted to come to see you this morning, but I thought you might still be asleep after last night, and I didn't want to wake you. I told the doctor, and anyone else who asked, just what you suggested I say. Although they seemed to find it interesting, no one was terribly surprised. Incidents like that are fairly commonplace, and it appears that Nick is none too popular. He's going to be all right, by the way. He's going to be laid up for a few days, but maybe that will give him time to think things over."

His face tightened. "I swear to God I would have killed him if you hadn't stopped me."

Laura hugged him. "I know," she said softly. "But that would only have made matters worse."

He bent his head and kissed her lips, but drew back quickly with an exclamation of pain. "Drat! I forgot about my lip."

Laura laughed shakily, and he held her away by the shoulders, looking down into her face. He said, "Do you think now he'll tell everyone who he really is? It strikes me that's the kind of thing he might do."

"I don't care." Laura shrugged. "I really don't. I've had just about all I can take of this situation, and I'm beginning to think that almost anything would be better than going on like this. Mr. Bailey told me that he's going to fire Nick, and without a job I don't see how he can afford to follow the circus. I don't suppose he will agree to a divorce under the circumstances, but I'll get a good attorney and go ahead without his consent. I want to be free of him, once and for all, so that you and I can be married."

Will grinned, grimacing at the pain it caused him, and touched her cheek. "Is that a proposal, Mrs. Orlando?"

"Yes, it most certainly is. I'm getting tired of waiting for *you* to ask *me.*"

Will pulled her into his arms. "Oh, my darling, darling Laura. You must know how much I've wanted to ask you. But there was the fact of your marriage to Nick, and I wanted you to meet my family first."

"Just like a man." Laura shook her head. "Always putting things off. Why must we wait until I meet your family? You know I will love any child of yours, and from what you've told me, your boy's grandmother is a wonderful woman."

A slight shadow crossed over Will's face. "That's true enough, she is," he said softly.

"Well then, it's all settled. As soon as I get back, you can help me find a very good attorney, and I'll start a divorce suit."

"Wait a minute! What do you mean, as soon as you get back? Where are you going?"

Laura sighed. "Where is my head this morning? The reason I came over so early was to tell you that Mr. Bailey has had a wire from Phineas; Phineas wants me to come to Maine at once to start a publicity campaign for some marvelous monster that he's thinking of buying for the show. That's why I'm in such a good mood this morning. This will give me a chance to get away from Nick and from all the gossip about what happened last night. By the time I get back, I'm hoping that Nick will be long gone." She gazed at him expectantly.

The initial look of surprise on Will's face slowly became one of approval, and he nodded. "Well, this is all rather sudden, but the more I think about it, the more I believe this may have come along at just the right time. The only thing is that I will miss the hell out of you."

"Don't swear, Will!" She laughed, and hugged him fiercely.

"How long will you be gone?"

"I've no idea, but I shouldn't think it would be too long. Maybe a week, but not much more than that."

"Well, you be careful out there in those Maine woods. Don't let this monster get you." He grinned. "What time does your train leave?"

"One o'clock, Mr. Bailey said."

"Shall I accompany you to the station?"

She shook her head. "Mr. Bailey is making all the arrangements; and until Nick is gone, I think it's better if we're not seen together too much."

He leaned toward her. "To hell with the lip," he said, kissing her deeply.

As she reveled in the emotions aroused by his kiss, Laura thought that at last everything was going to be all right again.

Telling him goodbye, she left Will's compartment and headed for the wagon that Milly now shared with Madame Costa. Madame was up, making coffee on her spirit stove, but Milly was not in sight.

"She didn't come home last night," Madame said with a knowing smile, "but I was not worried, for I knew where she had gone. I knew she was in good hands."

Laura stared. "You mean . . . ?"

Madame nodded. "Yes, I think that at last our Miss Milly has gotten what she wanted for so long, and I, for one, couldn't be happier. Will you have some coffee, Laura?"

Laura shook her head. "No, thank you, Madame Costa. Will you tell Milly for me that I have to go away for a few days, to meet with Mr. Barnum up in Maine concerning a new exhibit he may have found for the circus? I should be back within a week or so."

"Surely," Madame said with a nod.

Suddenly Laura grinned. "And tell her congratulations from me!"

Madame's smile was equally wide. "I shall do that, too. I would be most happy to do so."

Barnum referred to the Harper house as a "lodge," and Laura found it very intriguing. Large and built of logs, it looked very much like the pictures she had seen of chalets in Switzerland.

The interior of the house was furnished in what Laura thought of as a masculine fashion, for there were hunting trophies on the walls, and the furnishings, while comfortable and quite serviceable, were massively scaled. The whole place had a warm, rustic feeling. It was the kind of a house in which you did not have to be fussily careful not to spot the rugs or dirty the furniture.

That night at dinner, her hostess, Anne Harper, asked Laura, "Has Phineas told you anything yet about his 'wild' man?"

Laura shook her head. "Just that a nearby farmer found some kind of preserved creature in a cave on his property, and that the body seems to be that of some sort of wild man, or woods man. Have you seen it?"

Wilbur Harper nodded. "We certainly have."

"And you think it is genuine?"

Harper leaned back in his chair. "Why, yes, I would say so. Of course, I'm no expert in such matters, but it is the body of a large, bipedal creature, who evidently walked upright, and was shaped rather like a human, except for the hair."

"The hair?"

Nancy Barnum spoke up. "Yes, Laura, it's all covered with long dark hair, like some great ape." She shivered. "I'll tell you frankly that seeing it gave me quite a turn."

"And the people who first found it, are they reputable people?" Laura asked. "I mean, are they the sort who would manufacture a hoax, do you think?"

Harper shrugged, "I don't know them that well, but their family has been farming in this area since 1774, and they seem to be well enough respected in the community."

Laura glanced at Barnum. "And you, Phineas? You haven't told me yet whether you think this creature is genuine."

Barnum wiped his mouth with his napkin and settled back in his chair. Laura could see the excitement shining in his eyes. *He's like an old firehouse horse,* she thought; *he hears the bell, and he's ready to gallop.*

"I haven't finished my examination yet, but at the present time I am more or less inclined to believe that the creature is what it seems to be."

Nancy smiled. "But, Phineas, my dear, just *what* is that? It resembles no known species that I know of. It is surely not a man, and would appear not to be an ape!"

"The Indians have long had a name for the kind of creature whose remains we have discovered," Barnum explained. "Their legends tell of a woods creature who walks upright, like a man, but has fur, like an animal. The stories say that the creature is secretive and seldom seen, although many claim to have seen his tracks."

Laura could not suppress a slight shiver. "It has a frightening sound. Is the creature ugly?"

Barnum laughed. "Well, let's just say that he's not the handsomest specimen of life I've ever seen. When he was alive he must have been about eight feet tall, with a face that looks to be a cross between that of a man and that of the great ape. Long arms, rather short, straight legs, and entirely covered with apelike hair."

Laura shook her head. "The whole thing sounds incredible. How was it discovered?"

"The remains were found in a cave in the woods on the Mercer place," Wilbur Harper said. "It was the two Mercer boys that found it, Hiram and Jacob. They were out hunting in the woods, and they came across a fox. Jacob shot at it but only wounded the animal, and it ran limping away.

"They knew they had to find the fox and put it out of its misery, so they followed the trail of blood to a small cave that neither of them had ever noticed before."

"And the boys went in?"

"They did. They went in and found that the cave was large enough to stand upright in, and it extended a good way into the hill. They were surprised, because they had thought they knew every inch of their father's property.

"At any rate, they made themselves a torch of pine wood and dried grasses, as one of the boys had some lucifers with him. They found the fox dead, incidentally, just inside the entrance. In the back of the cave, on a sort of ledge, they found something very strange indeed. I guess it frightened them out of their wits when they first saw it, for they didn't know that it was dead. They ran out of the cave, in fact, and stood around outside waiting for it to follow them. When it didn't, they finally ventured back in, and discovered that it had evidently been dead for some time, since the body was rather dried up—mummified, so to speak."

Barnum took up the narrative. "The cave is, fortunately, very dry, and stays quite cold even in summer. It was these conditions that evidently preserved the body so well. From my examination, the body appears to have been laid out on the slab for burial, as there were a number of artifacts placed around it, as if for burial offerings."

"But that would mean that the creature was intelligent," Laura commented.

"Exactly!" said Barnum, his eyes aglow. "Just think what a sensation this creature would be as an exhibit! A physical proof of a legend. A scientific marvel!"

"If it *is* real," Laura said cautiously.

"Of course, we must make sure of that," Barnum said. "Despite my hope that this thing is genuine, I intend to make no hasty decisions. I'm having an anthropologist look at the creature tomorrow. Laura, be sure to dress for hiking, as the terrain is rather rough."

"The body is still in the cave?" Laura said. "Why haven't you moved it?"

"Mr. Mercer has refused to let me move it until I have bought and paid for it," Barnum said with a grin. "He says that it is the cold and the dryness that have preserved the body, and he's afraid that moving it out into the heat will cause it harm. I do not think so myself, for it appears to be quite solid, although desiccated, but then I'm no scientist. If Dr. Whitney declares the thing to be real, then I shall make Mercer an offer. If the offer is accepted, I shall pack the creature in ice and seal it in a metal box for transport."

"Well," said Laura, "I shall certainly look forward to seeing it." She turned to Nancy, "Are you coming with us?"

"Oh, yes," Nancy said with a smile. "I am very curious to see what Dr. Whitney will make of it."

Laura was enjoying the evening very much—the pleasant company, the good food, and the promise of an exciting day tomorrow. She did miss Will, and felt guilty about leaving him to face Nick and the talk that would be going around, but this was balanced off by the relief she felt at being away from the circus. A person can stand only so much, she thought, and she knew that she had reached her limit.

Under her breath she whispered a short prayer that Nick would be gone and the situation resolved by the time she returned to the circus.

To Nancy she said, "It *is* exciting. I don't imagine that there are any two other women in the country who will be doing something tomorrow that is any stranger or more unbelievable."

Nancy laughed heartily. "If they are, you can be sure that Phineas will find them, and set them up as the next attraction for his circus!"

Chapter Twenty-Three

T HE entrance to the cave proved to be as well hidden as Wilbur Harper had reported, and Laura could understand how it had remained undiscovered for so many years.

The men entered the cave first, and Nancy, a bit out of breath from their hike, giggled as excitedly as a schoolgirl. "Isn't this thrilling, Laura? I feel like a character from one of those books for young girls! 'Nancy Barnum, Adventuress.' "

When it was their turn, first Nancy, then Laura bent over into a low crouch, and lifting their skirts they entered the cave.

Inside, Laura straightened up in the yellow glow of lantern light and thick, black shadows. The interior was fairly large.

A draft seemed to be coming from somewhere deep inside the cave, bearing a strange, cold scent, and she shivered, thinking of the man-thing that was supposedly resting on its stone shelf in the darkness.

"This way," Silas Mercer said in his odd, twangy voice, moving deeper into the shadows. "Hiram, you bring up the rear so's the ladies won't be afrighted. And, ladies, mind you walk careful now, this floor ain't as smooth as it might be."

Laura's pulse began to quicken as the procession moved toward the back of the cavern, which soon narrowed until she could touch a wall with either hand as she walked. Everyone was silent; the only sound was that of their footsteps, making a hollow, echoing clatter on the rocky floor.

At last the passageway began to widen again, and the lanterns threw crooked, dancing shadows against the stony walls. In such an eerie atmosphere, Laura found herself almost ready to believe in the strange woods creature, even without having seen it.

"There he is!" said Mercer, his voice echoing off the cave walls.

He held his lantern up high, and Hiram, passing Laura, moved to his father's side. He placed his lantern on what looked, to Laura in the wavering light, like a rough, naturally formed stone shelf.

She found herself hanging back, reluctant to see what the light might reveal. She heard Dr. Whitney draw in his breath and then expel it with an exclamation.

And then Barnum's booming voice made her jump. "Examine it thoroughly, Doctor. Remember, in the end I will be relying upon your opinion."

The anthropologist stepped forward and leaned over the dark figure now evident in the lantern light.

Laura, filled with a strange dread, moved to get a better view of the proceedings.

The figure over which the doctor leaned was very large, very dark, and was covered with fur. It lay in a semicurled position, as if sleeping. She could not see the face at all well, but it seemed to bear at least a crude resemblance to a man.

She crept closer until she could see more clearly. This was the head of a human anomaly, disproportionately large and crudely fashioned. There seemed to be little or no neck. The eyes were closed, but the mouth was slightly open, and Laura could see the gleam of long, sharp teeth. The body appeared desiccated, and the skin looked sunken in upon the bones. It was a frightening-looking object, and yet, to Laura, it did not look quite right, quite real. There was something in its proportions, in the awkward position of the limbs, that did not ring true. Of course, she had no idea of what such a creature was *supposed* to look like, but her first, instinctive feeling was that the thing was a fraud.

"Well, what do you think?" Barnum's voice, raw with excitement, came from over her shoulder.

Laura hesitated. She knew how much Phineas wanted this discovery to be a bonafide wonder. It was as if he had to keep proving to himself that he still had the old talent, and this was a wonderful opportunity to do so.

"I . . . I don't really know what to say, Phineas. I would want to see it in a better light before I drew any firm conclusions."

She turned, and saw in the wavering light that Barnum's expression was one of disappointment. Then he brightened. "Well, we'll let the doctor take a look at him and see what he thinks, eh? Dr. Whitney?"

Dr. Whitney, who had been poking and examining the creature under the sharp gaze of Silas Mercer, glanced up. His expression was thoughtful. "It's difficult to say, under these conditions," he said slowly, tapping a forefinger against his right cheek. "I should like to continue my examination under a good light, and to be really certain I would have to perform some exploratory surgery."

Barnum looked quickly in Mercer's direction; no doubt, Laura thought, expecting the man to object. Oddly, the wiry little man only looked thoughtful.

"Surgery?" Mercer said. "You mean you want to cut into him? Why, I don't know as I could let you do that. After all, if people are going to pay money to see this thing, they want to see him whole, seems to me."

"Of course," Dr. Whitney said soothingly, "but I didn't mean that I wanted to thoroughly dissect it. Only make some incisions so that I can see what's inside. If it is a real animal, I would expect to find bones, internal organs. As it is, although the creature looks real enough, it could possibly be simply a very clever construction of some sort."

Mercer looked more thoughtful still, and his narrow little eyes flicked briefly in the direction of his son. "Hmmm. I see. Well, in that case, how about if you opened up his stomach? That way you could see whether or not he had a liver and all the necessaries, and once you've seen that, you can sew him up again, good as new. With all that hair on him, no one would even notice."

As Mercer talked, Laura observed him closely. It seemed to her that he was altogether too willing. She felt decidedly uneasy about the whole thing.

Dr. Whitney seemed very pleased with Mercer's suggestion. "Excellent! I have the necessary surgical tools in my bag. If you will just help me turn him on his back, and hold up the lanterns so that I have a good light to work by, I'll do it at once. The sooner we reach a conclusion in this matter, the better."

Laura, watching over the anthropologist's shoulder, saw him open his black bag and take out several gleaming silver instruments. He arranged them neatly on a white napkin beside the animal's head.

She swallowed queasily, and glanced over at Nancy, who was standing on the doctor's left. Nancy's face was quite pale; and with a quick glance at her husband, she turned away and moved back into the shadows.

Laura sympathized with her, but somehow she felt impelled to watch.

As the doctor, holding a long, sharp scalpel in his hand, made a quick, neat incision in the animal's torso, starting just below the rib cage and continuing to just below the abdomen, she put her handkerchief to her mouth.

Using clamps, the doctor pulled aside the dark skin and hair, so that the body cavity was exposed. In the lantern light, Laura saw a jumble of what she supposed were organs; it was not as bad as she had feared. They were very dry-looking, and there was only the faintest unpleasant odor. Here was proof that this had once been a living creature.

Dr. Whitney's sudden exclamation caused her to jump.

"Ah! There are organs. Desiccated, true, as is the body, but still there."

"I knew it!" Barnum boomed out. "It's authentic!"

Laura heard a fierce cackle of laughter and realized that it was Mercer. "I told you all along that it was real. What do you say now, Mr. Barnum? Do you wish to buy him?"

Despite his age and size, Barnum was fairly dancing with excitement. "I certainly do, Mr. Mercer, I certainly do. Let's let the doctor sew him back together while you and I go outside and discuss terms."

Suddenly Mercer grew serious. "Not just yet, Mr. Barnum. I want to watch Dr. Whitney finish up his work. I want to be sure that he's put back together the way he was. We can talk later."

Laura peered at Mercer's face in the yellow light. His narrow eyes were flat and guarded, not the eyes of a man elated at being proven right, but the eyes of a man who was hiding something. Why didn't he want Dr. Whitney to be alone with the body?

The doctor, after peering at and touching the organs with a tentative finger, straightened up and put his hands on his lower back. "I'll sew him back up in a minute, Mr. Mercer, but first, might I have a drink of the cider we brought with us? I find that I am quite thirsty."

"Why, of course, Doctor," Barnum said, his voice still jubilant. "Hiram, would you fetch the canteen, please?"

Hiram nodded sullenly and went over to where they had piled their walking sticks and the canteens he and his father had brought with them.

As the elder Mercer's gaze turned to follow his son, Laura saw Dr. Whitney make a small, surreptitious movement with his left hand. She drew in her breath silently, certain that she had seen him palm something.

Hiram returned with the cider; as the doctor reached for it with his right hand, simultaneously he reached into his left breast pocket with his other hand and removed his handkerchief, with which he proceeded to wipe his face.

"Ah, that tastes good," he said, lowering the metal canteen cup from his lips. "And now, to fix our fine fellow up again, as good as new."

Quickly and efficiently, he sewed up the incision in the creature's belly, and in a few moments it was difficult to tell that the animal had ever been opened.

"So, what do you think, Doctor? Is the creature real?" Wilbur Harper's voice was eager as he sat forward in his chair. The group was gathered in the main parlor of the lodge, and all eyes were on the anthropologist.

Dr. Whitney, not above relishing the fact that he was the center of attention, rocked back and forth on his heels and tapped his cheek with a forefinger.

"It is not in the nature of my particular science to make hasty judgments, my friends. Before I can answer your question honestly, Mr. Harper, I must return to my laboratory and make some tests."

Barnum stared at him in puzzlement. "What tests? How can you make tests in your laboratory when the creature is here in the cave?"

Dr. Whitney smiled. "Ah, yes. That is so, at least *most* of him is in the cave."

Nancy and Laura exchanged glances.

Barnum leaned forward, agitated. "Most of him? What do you mean?"

Dr. Whitney nodded ponderously. "Yes, Mr. Barnum, I took the liberty of removing one of the mummified organs from the body cavity after performing the surgery. I hope you don't mind, but that was the only way I could get a specimen for testing; I knew that Mr. Mercer would never agree to let me remove any part of the animal from the cave. I also managed to snip off a bit of hair."

For the next two days, Laura gave herself over to pure relaxation and enjoyment. She missed Will, particularly at night; yet, she felt such a blessed relief at being away from her problems, at being able just to let go, that the days passed quickly and pleasantly. She walked in the woods, read on the wide balcony outside her room, and fished and boated on the nearby lake.

This, coupled with wholesome cooking, had already put the color back into her cheeks and was filling out the hollows in her body. She almost wished that they would not hear from Dr. Whitney for several days more; but Barnum was in a fine state of nervousness.

On the third day, Dr. Whitney showed up at the lodge. His expression was not cheerful, and Laura knew that his news would not be good.

"I think we had all better sit down, Phineas," he said. "And I would appreciate something cool to drink. It's a dusty drive out here from town, and an even longer one from the college."

Anne Harper flushed. "Of course, Dr. Whitney. I'm so sorry, but Phineas was in such a hurry to know. . . ."

"I'm sorry, Doctor," Barnum said, "but you can imagine how anxious I am."

Dr. Whitney smiled. "I understand, Phineas. But I'm afraid that my news is not good." He took a sip of lemonade. "That's why I came myself, instead of sending a wire. I thought it would be best if I explained in person."

Barnum dropped his not-inconsiderable bulk into a large wooden chair, which protested his weight. "Go ahead, Doctor. We might as well hear the worst."

The doctor nodded. "Well, it was very clever of them, really, what they did. I mean your garden-variety hoaxer would simply have constructed a man-shaped framework and covered it with a skin of some sort, but the Mercers went a step beyond that. I believe they constructed their creature over the skeleton of a human being."

Anne Harper let out a gasp, and the doctor turned to her. "Oh, I didn't mean they killed anyone, or anything like that, my dear lady. There are many ancient Indian burial grounds in this part of the country, and they could have inadvertently dug one up while plowing their fields; or perhaps they actually found an ancient skeleton in the cave, and thus conceived the idea for the hoax. We probably will never know the truth of the matter. At any rate, there were ribs within the chest cavity, so that gives credence to my theory."

"But what about the size of the thing?" Nancy asked. "It must be at least seven or eight feet tall, if it were straightened out."

Dr. Whitney nodded. "Yes, I know, but that could be gotten around easily enough by adding wood or some other firm material to lengthen the limbs. After all, they didn't intend to let anyone do a complete autopsy on the body. They just needed to make it look convincing to someone doing an exploratory operation."

"And the organs?" Barnum demanded. "What did your test reveal?"

Dr. Whitney's eyes flashed. "Ah, another clever touch! You will remember that it was Mercer himself who suggested that I open the body cavity? He knew very well what I would find—a full set of apparently humanlike organs, which was supposed to convince anyone of the living origin of the creature. And, as I said, there too he was very clever, for he used the organs of the one animal whose organs most closely resemble those of a human being. A pig!"

"A pig?" Barnum exclaimed.

The doctor nodded. "Precisely, Mr. Barnum. A pig. The internal 'plumbing' of a pig, you know, is very like that of man. The Mercers dried the organs first, then simply put them inside the body cavity. A very clever ruse. The skin they used to cover the skeleton was, by the way, that of a very large grizzly bear, as, I suspect, are the teeth."

He gave Barnum an apologetic look. "I'm sorry, Phineas. I know how much you wanted the creature to be genuine, but it's better that we found out now, before you bought or leased it, and someone else found out that it was a fraud."

Barnum sighed dejectedly. "I suppose you're right. But it would have been such a wonderful attraction." He smiled ruefully. "I'm almost tempted to show it anyway, We could make thousands before the fraud was exposed."

Nancy shook her finger at him. "Now, Phineas, you know that James would never agree; and such adverse publicity is no longer acceptable. Why, you admitted as much yourself."

Barnum leaned over to pat her arm. "Don't get excited, my dear. I was just thinking aloud. Of course I have no intention of doing anything so foolish. Well," he turned to Laura, "I guess I brought you all the way up here for nothing, my dear."

Laura smiled. "I wouldn't say that, Phineas. I've had a lovely rest, which I badly needed, and a very pleasant time."

Dr. Whitney gave a start and pulled a long envelope out of his inner waistcoat pocket. "Oh, I almost forgot. The stationmaster in town gave me this telegram to deliver as I was coming out here anyway. He said it would save him a trip. It's for you, Phineas."

Suddenly serious, Barnum reached for the envelope and tore it open. Everyone was quiet as he read the message, and Laura felt her heart begin to pound as she saw the look of distress that came over Barnum's face.

Nancy rushed to his side and took hold of his arm. "Phineas, what is it? What is the matter? Has something happened to Waldemere?"

Slowly, Barnum shook his head. "No, my love, something worse."

His gaze moved to Laura, and there was deep sorrow in his eyes. "There has been an accident at the circus grounds. No . . . I might as well tell you the truth, Laura. There has been a killing, a murder."

Laura's breath caught, and she clenched her hands until her nails dug into her flesh. *Oh, God! Not Will! Please, not Will!*

Barnum raised his right hand and then let it fall, in a gesture of futility. "I regret to be the one who must tell you this, my dear Laura, but it appears, from the identification found on the body, that the victim is your husband, Nickolas Orlando."

Chapter Twenty-Four

LAURA, supported by Will and Milly, stood before the sheeted figure on the morgue slab.

Feeling faint and nauseated, she steeled herself as the morgue attendant leaned forward to lift away the sheet, but no amount of mental preparation could cushion her against the shock and emotional pain when he did so.

Forcing herself to keep her eyes open, Laura pressed her handkerchief to her mouth as she looked down at the still, white face of the man on the slab. Moaning slightly, she swayed; Will's strong arm around her shoulders was the only thing that kept her from falling.

"Is this man Nickolas Orlando?" The attendant's voice was sympathetic.

Laura managed to nod, weakly.

Yes, it was Nick, but not a Nick that she had ever known. Death seemed to have washed something from his face, a quality that had made him uniquely him. His eyes were closed, of course, but his face wore an expression of surprise, as if he could not believe what had happened to him. She was grateful that the attendant exposed only Nick's face, so that she did not have to look at the wound they told her had killed him—a stab wound directly into the heart.

He looked younger in death; and Laura, despite the pain and mental anguish he had caused her, could not help but be reminded of the Nick she had met and loved, and of the initial happiness he had given her.

Tears thickened her throat, and she turned away, leaning against Will. "Please. Is that all? May we go now?"

The attendant drew the sheet back up. "Yes. There will be some papers you must sign, but you can do that outside. I'm very sorry, Mrs. Orlando."

Feeling like an invalid, Laura let Will and Milly lead her from the cold little room to a bench in the corridor outside.

Milly, her small face pale and unusually serious, was murmuring words of comfort, but Laura was too distraught to hear what her friend was saying; her thoughts had turned to the terrible story that James Bailey had told her and the Barnums.

During the time that she had been gone, Bailey had told her, Nick had spent most of his time under the doctor's care. He had been sullen and uncooperative, particularly after Bailey had informed him that his services were being terminated, and that as soon as he was up and around he would be asked to leave.

Those attending him had stated that he had made several caustic remarks about Will Adams, and had followed these remarks with a number of threats directed at both Will and Laura. He had also hinted darkly at some "surprise" he was going to give Laura when she returned to the circus.

Two days ago, Nick had still maintained that he was not well enough to be up and about, although the doctor had assured him that he was sufficiently recovered to be on his way, on the following day he would be turned out of his bed, and that the circus no longer considered him an employee.

Despite the fact that he stubbornly maintained that he was too ill to leave his bed, Nick had evidently gotten up and gone out onto the circus grounds, for the next morning his completely dressed body had been found in the center ring of the big tent, stabbed through the heart.

No weapon was in evidence, and there were no witnesses to what had happened. The body had been discovered by the Salieri family when they came into the tent to practice a new act they were perfecting.

James Bailey had sent word to Barnum at once, and the police had been notified.

Going through Nick's pockets, the police had found his identification showing his proper name, and soon the news that his real name was Nickolas Orlando had circulated throughout the circus community, causing a great deal of gossip and speculation.

It was a grim and terrible situation.

"Laura? Laura, are you all right?"

Milly's voice finally penetrated her bleak thoughts, and Laura turned to her friend. "I'm fine, Milly. Just suffering a bit from shock. Will you see if they have the papers ready to sign? I most dreadfully want to get away from this place."

As Milly walked over to the desk behind which an attendant sat working on a pile of papers, Will pulled Laura close and leaned down to speak softly to her.

"Laura, I can't tell you how sorry I am about everything. I know that I wanted to kill Nick that night, but in the truest sense I never really wanted him dead. Only away from us. It was a terrible thing."

Laura's eyes began to sting as the hot tears began again. "Who could have done it? And why? That's what I keep asking myself."

Will held her even closer. "I don't have the least idea, but I'm very much afraid the police think that they do."

Laura pulled away so that she could look into his face. "Who? Who do they suspect?"

Will's expression was somber. "I'm afraid they suspect me . . . and I suppose I can't entirely blame them. First, they found out that he was your husband, and that no one in the circus knew of this in the beginning, except you and he. Then they find out that you and I have been seeing each other, and that just a few nights ago Nick and I had a terrible fight, over you. . . . What else can they think?"

Laura felt her heart almost stop. Would this nightmare never end? "But, Will, what will they do? They don't have any proof!"

Will sighed. "Not any direct proof, no, but the circumstances are enough that they may arrest me anyway. I thought I had better prepare you for it, in case it does happen."

Laura had to fight to keep from moaning aloud. "They can't. They just can't! Don't you have an . . . what do they call it? Don't you have an alibi? Isn't there someone who you were with, or who saw you at the time Nick was killed?"

Will shook his head. "It was the middle of the night, Laura. I was alone in my compartment, alone and asleep."

"If I had only been here! We would have been together, and I could have told the police that." She began to tear at the handkerchief she was holding.

Will's low laugh held no humor. "All that would have done is made them suspect you, as well. No, since you were away, at least they cannot suspect you."

Laura slumped against his shoulder, the last of her strength draining away. "Will they arrest you?"

"I don't know, Laura, but it's quite possible. They haven't given any indication yet, haven't accused me directly, but they certainly asked me enough questions. The chief of police here, Chief Thompson, is a hard man, but cautious. He's kept the circus here since Nick's death, and Bailey is frantic, as we were supposed to be on our way to the next town yesterday."

She reached for his hand and clutched it tightly between hers. "What are we going to do, Will?"

He covered her hands with his and squeezed gently. "I don't know, my love. I suppose we can only wait. Wait and pray."

"And you say you hadn't seen your husband in over three years?"

Chief Thompson shifted his bulk in the rocking chair in Laura's compartment. He was a big man, with iron-gray hair and hard gray eyes. His voice was polite enough, and he had not pressured her in any way; but Laura, who had already answered this question twice, was growing tired and annoyed.

"Yes, Chief, as I have already told you," she said tartly.

"From the day he left me until he showed up here at the circus, I had not seen or heard from my husband."

"Then as far as you were concerned the marriage was over?"

Laura suppressed a sigh; there was nothing to be gained by antagonizing him. "Yes. He had, after all, abandoned me, left me penniless. The only thing I wanted from Nick was a divorce, so that I would no longer be tied to him legally."

"And you wanted to divorce him so that you could marry Mr. Adams?"

Laura took a deep breath, striving for calmness. "No, at least not primarily. I wanted a divorce for my own sake."

"But you have been, shall we say, keeping company with Mr. Adams?"

"We're friends, yes, and I have seen him socially. We are . . . very fond of each other."

The chief nodded, his gaze penetrating. "And yet, when Mr. Orlando showed up, you helped him get a job with the circus. I find that hard to understand."

Laura thought quickly. How much should she tell this man? Would telling him the truth make Will's situation better or worse? She opted for the truth, hoping that she was doing the right thing.

"Since my husband had abandoned me and I had no way of knowing whether he was dead or alive, when I came to work for the circus I told everyone that I was a widow. It seemed much simpler than explaining what had actually happened. It never entered my mind that he would find me with the circus, or even want to. It was partially pride, I suppose, that caused me to lie.

"When Nick did show up here, he threatened to tell everyone that he was my husband, if I did not agree to help him get a job with the circus and give him a chance to convince me that I should take him back. He promised that if in a reasonable length of time I still remained set against him, he would go away and leave me in peace."

Chief Thompson pursed his lips. "Hmmm. And did he also agree that in such case he would grant you a divorce?"

Laura hesitated. "No. No matter how much I pressed him, he had not committed himself to that."

"And he continued with the circus for several months, and you still had not changed your mind. Wasn't that what would be considered a reasonable length of time?"

"Nick was not the kind of man who kept his word," she said simply. "He kept asking for more time, although I told him that it was no use."

"That must have been quite a strain on you," the chief said sympathetically.

Laura thought that she knew where this line of questioning was leading, and decided to forestall it if she could.

"Yes," she said truthfully, "it was. A great strain, and therefore, after my husband attacked me in this compartment, and before I left to join Mr. Barnum, I told Mr. Adams that I no longer cared if Nick made our relationship known. However, at that point I was past caring, and had decided that I would employ a good lawyer and try to get a divorce without my husband's consent. I certainly had sufficient grounds."

The chief studied her thoughtfully. "Did you tell this to anyone other than Mr. Adams?"

Laura shook her head. "I didn't have time to do so. I had to catch the train to Maine."

Chief Thompson glanced down at his hands. "Hmmm, well, thank you, Mrs. Orlando. I may want to talk to you again before this is over. You will be available?"

"Of course. Although I no longer had any feelings for my husband, I did not wish him dead, and will do anything I can to help catch his killer."

The chief's blue eyes glinted, and he appeared to pounce without moving: "Even if the killer should prove to be your friend, Mr. Adams?"

Laura felt as if her blood had turned to ice. She raised her chin and looked him directly in the eyes. "I know the kind of man Mr. Adams is, Chief Thompson, and so I know that he could not have done this thing. If he could have done it, he would not be the man I so admire; and yes, I would then want him unmasked."

The chief picked up his hat and gave Laura a small, tight smile of what appeared to be respect. "I believe that you are an honest woman, Mrs. Orlando, and I can only pray that your faith in Mr. Adams is justified."

Laura watched him leave her compartment with a feeling of despair. It was obvious that Will was correct—the police did suspect him. *Dear God,* she thought. *Please, God, please don't let them arrest him!*

Despite her prayers, Will was taken into custody the next day and charged with Nick's murder.

The entire circus company was shocked and dismayed, and both Barnum and Bailey promised to see that Will had the best legal advice available.

Laura was prostrated, and Milly and Lionel stayed by her side constantly, attempting to give her comfort, telling her that despite Will's arrest, no one in the circus believed he was guilty, and assuring her that he would never be convicted.

The show prepared to move on to the next town. Neither sentiment nor grief could stay the fact that they had bookings, which had already been thrown off schedule, and which the circus needed to keep so that its employees could be paid.

Before leaving, Laura was allowed to see Will, and it caused her much anguish to see him behind the iron bars of the cell in Chief Thompson's jail.

Tears streaming from her eyes, Laura clasped his hands through the bars, and in turn he held hers with a desperate strength.

"Laura," he whispered. "I didn't do it, you know. I didn't kill your husband. You must believe that."

Laura nodded, unable to speak.

Then she pressed her face to the cold iron and kissed him on the lips. Experiencing their warmth only made her heart feel colder. "I'll stay behind," she said brokenly. "I'll get a room, somewhere near, so you won't be alone."

Reluctantly he shook his head. "No, darling. It will only make you feel worse. And there's nothing you can do here. The lawyer P.T. has hired will be here tomorrow, and we'll start to work on my defense. You go on with the show. Do your job, keep busy. It will help to keep your mind off things; besides, they need you. The season's almost over. If my case hasn't come to trial by the time the tour is finished, you can come back here then. All right?"

Tenderly he kissed her again, and she felt that her heart was going to break; but she nodded, then turned away to join Lionel and Milly, who were waiting in the outer office. She knew that if Will was convicted of Nick's murder, her life would be over.

The following days were, to Laura, a time to be gotten through with as little thought as possible.

Concentration on her work helped a bit, as did the hours when her friends gave her some comfort; but when she was alone, she felt weighed down with despair.

She wrote long letters to Will and posted them from whatever town they were playing, and in them she poured out her love and longing. She also spent long hours talking to Milly and Lionel, and she was encouraged to see that these two friends, whom she loved so dearly, appeared to be growing closer together with every passing day.

However, Milly told her in confidence that Lionel still would not commit himself to marriage.

"I've tried everything," she told Laura, "but he won't take that final step. I told him that we were practically living together already, but he says that it's still different than being married. He says that if we were married I'd probably want children, and that if we had children they might be like him. I've told him more than once that that doesn't bother me, but he doesn't seem to believe me. He can be *so* exasperating!"

Laura put an arm around her friend's shoulders. "Well, don't worry, Milly. He'll eventually come around. Just look at what you've accomplished with him already!"

"I know, I haven't forgotten that." Milly's smile was radiant. "Oh, I'm so happy, Laura, just to have gotten this far with him. I only wish you could be happy, too."

Laura turned her face aside so that the other girl would not see the tears that started in her eyes. "Well, it will all work out. They surely won't convict an innocent man, and it helps to have my friends rally around me. By the way, speaking of friends, have you been seeing much of Benjy? I've hardly seen him at all since I got back from Maine."

Milly shook her head. "He seems to be going through one of his strange periods again. I had thought he was getting better, and he seemed to be enjoying our little evenings together, but now he's withdrawing again. I suspect that he's drinking, as well."

"I hope it isn't because of that night that Nick attacked me," Laura said with a troubled frown. "Nick insulted him, you know. I'd hate for it to be that—for Benjy was so brave in trying to defend me. I must make it a point to visit him. I've been so involved with my own troubles that I'm afraid I haven't thought much about anything else."

But Benjy, when Laura sought him out in his sleeping car while the train was en route to Saint Thomas, Ontario, seemed disinclined to talk to her. He did not look at all well, Laura thought, and his cough was much worse. She tried to draw him out, telling him how much she appreciated his help, trying to be cheerful and raise his obviously low spirits; but nothing she could do or say roused the little man from his apathy.

Finally, leaving some fruit she had brought him, Laura left him, thinking to herself that Nick Orlando had a great deal to be responsible for; and that if there was any justice, he was burning in hell for all the pain he had caused so many people.

In Saint Thomas a letter from Will was waiting for her, and she read and reread it, memorizing every line. He said that his lawyer was optimistic about his chances and that the jail was not too uncomfortable. Despite the determinedly cheerful tone of the letter, Laura sensed that most of the cheer was for her benefit.

The mood of the circus was similar. The shows went on as usual; people performed with smiles and apparent good cheer, but when the show was over there was an obvious undercurrent of depression and discontent.

Laura had found out that there were no more superstitious people in the world than circus people, and the general feeling was that since bad luck always occurred in threes, something else bad was bound to happen before long.

Madame Costa had reminded her about what had happened after Diana Salieri's death. "You remember," she said seriously. "Only a month after Diana's death, Wee Willie, the midget clown, died of the lung disease, and then that elephant went mad and broke his trainer's leg. Just wait, something else will happen soon. It always does."

Laura, who had never been particularly superstitious, found the prediction difficult to believe, and yet Madame's words left her feeling uneasy, and this added to her depression.

On their last evening in Saint Thomas, after the final show, Laura was feeling particularly lonely and unhappy as she left her compartment to go to Lionel's wagon to talk with him and Milly, while the train was being loaded for departure.

As she strolled alongside the railroad tracks, she saw the huge figure of Jumbo outlined against the night sky; and she knew that the great beast and his constant companion, the midget elephant, Tom Thumb, were being led to their private car by their trainer, Matthew Scott.

Laura knew that this meant that she did not have much time to visit, for Jumbo and Tom Thumb were always loaded last, after the thirty-one other elephants were in their cars, and it would not be long before the train was ready to roll.

Seeing the huge elephant, Laura remembered that she had not visited him since returning from Maine, and resolved to do so at their next stop. Stepping over the tracks in the freight yard, she was startled by the sound of a locomotive coming around the bend at high speed.

Stumbling and almost losing her balance, she moved hurriedly away from the tracks, and then saw, with horror, the glaring headlights of the approaching locomotive fixed with stark brightness on Jumbo, who had stopped dead in his tracks, evidently terrified and confused by the sound and the light of the oncoming train.

Laura felt a scream rise in her throat, as she heard the loud squeal of the train brakes on the rails. The engineer must have seen Jumbo and was trying to bring the locomotive to a halt, but its speed was too great.

As she watched in numbed shock, she saw Scott leap aside just before the train struck Tom Thumb, throwing him into the air as if he were a toy. And then the heavy engine plowed head on into Jumbo's huge body, as Jumbo trumpeted in terror.

The impact was tremendous, and Laura felt the ground tremble under her feet. She clapped her hands over her ears as the sounds of rending metal and screeching brakes filled the night, to be followed by the sonorous sighing of escaping steam.

Finally regaining the power of movement, she ran headlong toward the scene; she saw others converging from every direction.

The engine and the first two cars of the train were smashed and derailed. As Laura approached, she saw that Jumbo, although still standing, was oozing blood from his mouth, flanks, and feet. Laura was now crying unashamedly, and she saw that Scott, who was also hurrying toward the animal, was weeping as well.

Before his trainer could reach him, the giant animal began to fall, first to his knees, and then slowly he rolled over onto his side. As though pleading for help, he beckoned with his trunk to Scott; and then, with a great sigh, the huge body heaved and was still. Madame Costa had been right after all, Laura thought bleakly; and now Jumbo, king of the elephants, beloved of the children of the world, was dead, along with his tiny friend, Tom Thumb.

Weeping with sadness, Laura stood for a moment staring down at the dead animal, then she turned away, unable to watch any longer.

She saw people gathered around Tom Thumb; and as she walked away, she heard a voice shout, "He's all right, he's not dead! I think he only has a broken leg!"

Through the bedlam of shouting voices she heard her name called, and looked up to see Lionel and Milly hurrying toward her.

"What happened, Laura?" Milly demanded, seizing her arm. "We heard the most awful crash!"

Laura gestured behind her. "An incoming train. It struck Jumbo and Tom Thumb."

Lionel touched her shoulder. "Good Lord! Are they badly hurt?"

"Jumbo is dead, but I heard someone say that Tom Thumb was only injured. He was so small he was just thrown aside, I guess, but Jumbo . . ." She broke down and could not continue.

"What a terrible thing," Milly said with a shake of her head. "I know how fond you were of Jumbo, Laura. And Mr. Barnum is going to be absolutely crushed when he hears."

Lionel sighed heavily. "I wonder what a train was doing coming in here at that speed, anyway. It seems an odd thing to do, going that fast through a freight yard."

It was not until the next day that the full details were known, and by then all the newspapers were full of the story.

It seemed that the train was an unscheduled freight, and the accident had brought about the death of the locomotive engineer as well as that of Jumbo.

The newspapers spared no bit of pathos, and Laura noticed that the stories were not quite accurate in all particulars. Many of the stories related how Jumbo had tried to save Tom Thumb and given his life in the attempt.

Laura was sure that she could detect the fine hand of P. T. Barnum in this, and threw down the papers in disgust. Much as she admired Barnum, she began to wonder if there was anything he would not capitalize on.

The articles and pictures filled the papers for the next few days, and even though Laura deplored the sensationalism, she was touched by the public's reaction. Letters poured in from all over the world. It seemed that everyone was saddened by Jumbo's death, and she was comforted by the fact that the public recognized that something rare and wonderful had gone out of their lives.

With the death of Jumbo, something went out of Laura, for it struck her as a kind of omen of worse things to come. She had to force herself now to get on with her work, and when she read an interview that Barnum had given to the press about the death of Jumbo, she felt more discouraged still: "The loss is tremendous, but such a trifle never disturbs my nerves. Long ago I learned that to those who mean right and try to do right, there are no such things as real misfortune. On the other hand, to such persons, all apparent evils are blessings in disguise."

Laura viewed the statement as cynical in the extreme. How could Phineas say that Jumbo's death was a blessing in disguise?

And when Barnum told her what he was planning to do with Jumbo's remains, she told him straight out that she thought he was going too far.

Barnum took her criticism in good grace and gave her his jolly smile. "Listen, my dear, I know how you feel. You were fond of Jumbo, as I was myself, but what I am doing is not callous. Entirely the contrary. Nine million Americans have seen Jumbo, but think of the millions that now will be deprived of that pleasure. My plan—to have his hide mounted—will enable those people to see him. Also, I plan to give his skeleton to the Museum of Natural History, in New York, where it will make a contribution to culture and scientific history. So, please, dear Laura, put your agile mind to work on a campaign to publicize my efforts."

Sighing, Laura gave in. Perhaps he was right, and she was being too sentimental. She recognized the fact that she was not quite herself these days—how could she be, with the sword of a murder accusation hanging over the head of the man she loved? And she knew that she was apt to be oversensitive and emotional.

She only hoped that if Madame Costa was correct in saying that bad things happened in threes, Jumbo's death and Tom Thumb's injury would be counted by the fates as two tragedies, sparing them yet another catastrophe.

Chapter Twenty-Five

AFTER Jumbo's tragic death, the spirits of the circus performers sank even lower; and if it had not been near the end of the season, many of them would undoubtedly have left the show. As it was, there continued to be a great deal of grumbling and a lot of talk about the show's being jinxed.

This did nothing to lift Laura's spirits. She felt that she existed in a nightmare, and every night she prayed that when she awakened the next morning it would be to find that everything that had happened in the past few weeks was only that—a frightening dream.

The weather was starting to turn cool now, and the first touch of autumn had begun to brush the foliage with bright color. The circus season was drawing to a close, and she began to dread that as well, even if it meant she would be free to go to Will.

Laura wrote to him telling him of Jumbo's death. Although she was sure that he must have read the newspaper accounts, she wanted him to know what had really happened. She also wrote to him about the creature in the cave up in Maine and the discovery that the whole thing was a hoax, and about how she was eager for the season to be over so that she might come to him.

She had just finished the letter and was sealing it when she heard a knock on her compartment door. She was not much in the mood for company; there was a fear lurking in her mind nowadays that a knock on the door meant more bad news.

She opened the door to see Milly and Madame Costa. Madame was carrying a small wicker basket filled with fresh sugar cookies, and Laura suddenly thought of her mother's kitchen in Sacramento at Christmastime.

The thought brought on a feeling of nostalgic sadness, for just what she was not certain. She did not have many happy or pleasant memories of her mother, or of Christmases past for that matter; her father had allowed little of what he considered frivolous expressions of celebration. Still, there had been a sort of stability in her life then, and her mother had done a certain amount of Christmas baking.

As she admitted her friends, Laura thought wryly that it was no doubt only the comparison with the complete lack of stability she was now experiencing that caused her to feel nostalgic for a time and place that she had been so eager to escape from.

Milly's cheeks were rosy from the brisk evening air, but her expression was serious, as was Madame Costa's.

"We brought these cookies along," Madame Costa said with a smile. "We thought they might go well with a nice cup of tea. I hope we're not interrupting anything?"

Laura shook her head and made way for them to enter. "Not at all. I just finished writing a long letter to Will, and am quite at loose ends. In fact, I'm glad you came by. I've been feeling very down-hearted."

Milly nodded. "Everyone is. I've never seen everyone in such a sad mood."

Laura reached for the tea kettle, which was already filled with water, then lit the spirit stove and placed the kettle on the flame. "Where's Lionel? Couldn't he come?"

Milly's cheeks flushed prettily. "He had some work to do on his wagon tonight, although he said to tell you hello."

Laura took out one of her beloved blue floral plates for the cookies. "Have either of you seen anything of Benjy? I tried to find him after Jumbo's death, but he doesn't seem to be around anywhere."

Madame Costa, having removed her shawl, took the

plate from Laura and began arranging the cookies, which were the large, crisp, sugar-sprinkled ones that Laura liked so much. She said, "That's one of the reasons we came by, Laura. We're both very worried about Benjy."

Laura turned away from the food cupboard. "Do you know where he is, then?"

"He's in the medical tent," Milly answered. "The doctor says that he's getting worse. That's the reason we're so worried."

Laura sank down into the rocking chair, feeling another wave of despair breaking over her. "I was afraid of something like this. How much more bad luck can we have? Poor Benjy. I suppose they're doing what they can for him?"

Madame Costa seated herself opposite Laura. "They're trying, but Benjy is being very difficult. He won't cooperate—refuses to take his medicine. They want to send him to the nearest hospital. They say that he needs more care than they can give him here."

"The doctor says that?"

Madame nodded. "And the nurse. They tell me that despite his bad lungs, he keeps trying to talk, and that he seems delirious most of the time. He keeps mentioning your name, Laura."

Laura did not attempt to disguise her surprise. "He mentions me? I wonder why. What does he say?"

"He seems to feel badly because he failed to defend you against Nick. It seems to be preying on his mind."

"But he *did* help me. If he hadn't gone to fetch Will, there's no telling what Nick would have done to me. Doesn't Benjy realize that?"

"He doesn't seem to consider that enough," Milly said. "He seems to be blaming himself for not being, well, big enough to defend you himself. We, Madame and I, thought that if you went to see him, you might be able to ease his mind a bit."

Laura got up from the chair. "Of course, I'll go at once. As I told you, I've been looking everywhere for him, but no one seemed to know where he was. We can go right now."

Milly smiled and touched her arm. "Not until after we have tea, Laura. Madame bought these cookies from a bakery in town, especially for you. Besides, Benjy is sleeping now. The nurse said he should be awake in about an hour, for his dinner. You can go then."

The patients lay on clean white cots in the medical tent. As she looked for Benjy, Laura thought how strange it was that unpleasant events seemed to lead to more sickness and accidents among the circus people.

Benjy was on a cot next to one of the canvas walls, his small body looking frail and childlike under the blankets. His face was turned to the wall. He had just finished his supper, but Laura, looking at his nearly untouched tray, could see that he had eaten next to nothing.

Sitting in the folding chair next to his bed, she reached for his little, stub-fingered hand. It felt hot and limp in her grasp.

"Benjy," she whispered. "Benjy, it's Laura. I've come to visit you. I've been looking for you everywhere."

He turned his head with a startled jerk, and Laura was shocked to see his face, so white and drawn, with the eyes sunken beneath the protruding brows, and the cheeks hollow beneath the ridges of his cheekbones.

"Laura," he said, his small voice sounding phlegmy and faint. "Is it really you?"

His awkward little fingers were now clinging to hers, and Laura felt tears clogging her throat. He looked so helpless, so pitiful!

"Yes, it's me, Benjy. Why didn't you let me know you were ill? I would have come sooner. After all, you are my good friend, and you've done so much for me."

An expression of pain flickered across his wasted face, and Laura peered at him with concern. "Are you all right, Benjy? Shall I call the nurse?"

Benjy rolled his head fitfully on the low pillow, grimacing. "What I've done for you? What have I done for you but bring you more suffering? I wanted to save you. I wanted to do something good for you, and instead . . ."

Laura broke in, "But you did, Benjy! You fought for

me, and you brought me help. That's all anyone could have done."

His sunken eyes gleamed with a febrile light. "But you aren't happy now, are you, Laura? I didn't make you happy."

Laura realized that his mind must be wandering. The heat of the small hand in hers told her that he was running a high fever.

"It's all right, Benjy," she said soothingly. "I'll be fine, don't worry about me."

"But you love Will." Benjy's voice was so soft and hoarse that she had to bend closer to hear it. "And Will is in jail."

Laura nodded. "Yes, Benjy. I love Will, and of course I'm unhappy that he's in jail. But he didn't kill Nick, and I'm sure that the lawyer will be able to prove that."

Suddenly Benjy sat bolt upright, trembling. "I can't do anything right! I try to do good! I try to help, but nothing I do works out right. Nothing!"

The nurse, hurrying to Benjy's side, placed a hand on his forehead, then turned to Laura. "I'm afraid that I'll have to ask you to leave now. He's getting overexcited, and he must get some sleep. You can visit him again tomorrow, before we send him to the hospital in town."

Laura watched as the nurse tucked Benjy in and gave him some medication, followed by some water.

When the nurse had moved away from Benjy's cot, Laura asked her softly, "What are his chances? Will he recover?"

The nurse glanced over to see that Benjy had his face turned to the wall. "I won't lie to you, Mrs. Orlando," she said with a doleful shake of her head. "It seems extremely unlikely that he will recover. His lungs are very bad, and he seems to have lost all will to live."

Laura turned away with tears in her eyes.

When Laura returned to her compartment and climbed into bed, she had great difficulty in sleeping. Finally, after what seemed like an eternity of tossing and turning, she was just sinking into the blessed relief of sleep, when she was startled fully awake by a terrifying noise. It was as if all the demons of hell had chosen that instant to cry out in pain and fear.

Heart pounding, she sat up in bed and pulled aside the heavy curtain of her compartment window.

Outside, she saw a number of people in night clothes, some carrying lanterns, hurrying toward the main tent, which was visible from her window. It seemed to be the source of the sound. The tent itself was lit from within, light spilling from the entrance. Something clearly was wrong.

Hurriedly getting out of bed, Laura fumbled for her robe and slippers. What on earth could it be at this time of night? It was after midnight. It did not appear to be fire. There were no signs of smoke or flickers of flame from the tent.

As she finished tying her robe and ran toward the compartment door, she was frozen into momentary immobility by another terrible blast of sound. The noise was so loud and so unexpected that it was a moment before she finally realized what it was—the big calliope, roaring into life.

In the darkness and stillness of the night, the sound seemed louder than usual and incredibly sinister.

Leaving the train, she saw more people streaming out of the sleeping cars. She hurried to join them, and questioned several as to what was occurring, but no one seemed to know.

Laura hurried along with the others toward the big tent, where the raucous sounds were coming from. She did not recognize the tune being played, but the hooting, howling sound, so incongruous under the circumstances, made gooseflesh rise on her arms and back.

Near the entrance to the tent she ran into Milly, Lionel, and Madame Costa, all looking as white-faced and shocked as she knew she must appear.

Milly clutched at Laura's hand with icy fingers. "What on earth is it? What's going on?"

Lionel took Laura's other hand. "We were awakened by

the calliope. What madman could be playing it at this unholy hour of the night?"

Madame Costa, a large woolen blanket wrapped around her, muttered through tight lips, "It's the third thing happening. I can feel it in my bones. I think it would be better if we don't go into the tent. I think it would be best if we wait and hear from the others what is happening in there!"

"I disagree," Lionel said. "We might as well see what's going on, since we're already here. Even if it means trouble, we might as well face it now instead of later."

"I agree, Lionel," Milly said vigorously. "Besides, I wouldn't be able to sleep for the rest of the night anyway, not knowing what it's all about."

Madame clucked. "I have a feeling that there will be little sleep for any of us this night. Very well, here is the entrance."

Laura and her friends were swept inside the tent with the rest of those who had been awakened by the blaring calliope. Just inside the entrance a number of people were milling about, and Lionel helped make a path through them for Laura and Milly so that they could see the interior of the huge tent, which looked even larger without the audience that usually filled the tiers of wooden seats.

Laura looked quickly around the huge area, trying to figure out what was happening. Her gaze went first to the calliope, which was roaring away, apparently all by itself, for she could see no one on the playing bench; and then, abruptly, the music died, as Alwyn Crest, the strongman, lifted a small, struggling form from the seat.

Laura's first inclination was to laugh. It was little Beppo, Wee Willie's brother, and Benjy's friend and fellow performer. He was so small that it had been impossible to see him from the angle at which she had been standing.

The tiny man kicked and squirmed in Alwyn's grasp, and the giant shouted, "Here is one of the problems! This little devil is as full of drink as a beer keg!"

Alwyn approached the group by the tent entrance, shaking the little man like a rat. "What the hell do you think you were doing?" Alwyn roared. "You got the whole circus out of bed!"

Beppo swung a small fist ineffectually at the big man, causing a great deal of laughter from the crowd.

"Needed an accompaniment," Beppo said drunkenly. "Can't have a stunt 'out accompaniment!"

"What on earth is he mumbling about?" someone demanded.

A man standing beside Laura answered, "It doesn't much matter. You can't expect him to make any sense in his condition."

Beppo stopped his squirming and glared at the speaker. "Do so know what I'm saying. Helpin' a friend, that's what. Got to help your friends. Gotta give 'em a good send-off. He'd do the same for me."

The little man turned and pointed with one stubby finger toward the roof of the tent, and everyone followed his pointing finger. Laura let out a gasp, which was drowned out by the cries of the others around her as they saw the small figure teetering perilously on the flyer's platform near the top of the tent.

Laura felt Milly's fingers bite into her arm. "It's Benjy! What in the world is he doing up there?"

Benjy, his tiny figure clad only in pajamas, swayed on the edge of the platform, as those watching gave a collective gasp. At that distance he looked incredibly small, like a little child, wavering high above them.

Laura noticed that the youngest Salieri brother, Davalo, was already running toward the ladder to the platform, and she let herself relax a little. Surely the aerialist would be able to reach Benjy before he could do himself any harm; but then the little man's voice rang out, amplified now by the ringmaster's megaphone, which he held in one hand, and cutting through the babble of the voices below. "No!"

Suddenly, all was still, the voices falling silent.

Benjy clung to the platform railing and leaned over to shout down at Davalo on the ladder, "No! No one comes up, or I'll jump!"

The aerialist stopped his ascent, the ladder swinging gently.

"I have something to say," Benjy said, "and I want all of you to listen."

"We're listening, Benjy," Lionel shouted, his hands cupped around his mouth. "Just don't do anything foolish."

Benjy's laughter was jarring and unpleasant. "Everything I do is foolish. Didn't you know? But that doesn't matter now. Here is what I want you to do. I want you to fetch the police. The police must be here."

Lionel said, "We don't need the police, my friend. Whatever it is, we can handle it ourselves. Just come on down now, like a good fellow. It's easier to talk down here."

Benjy leaned forward dangerously, the megaphone at his mouth. "I want the police here. Get them right away or I'll jump. I swear I will!"

A woman screamed in the crowd. Laura looked around and saw two men leave the tent at a run. She began to move slowly toward the center of the tent. Davalo Salieri had come down from the ladder and was talking in a low voice with his brothers beneath the ladder.

Laura stopped where Benjy could get a good look at her, then she cupped her hands around her mouth. "Benjy! It's Laura. Why won't you come down?"

Benjy waved the magaphone above his head, then put it to his mouth. "I've injured you, Laura, most of all," he said in a sort of moan. "And all I wanted to do was help."

"Come down, please," she said. "We can talk about it. Please, Benjy!"

He shook his head. "I will come down in my own time and my own way, and we *will* talk about it, but not until the police are here."

He put down the megaphone and dropped into a sitting position on the edge of the platform, putting his hands to his head as if he was in agony.

"Benjy?" Laura called again. "Benjy, please talk to me."

But he only continued to hold his head, his small body rocking back and forth, as the people stood beneath him, talking and gesturing. Everyone seemed to have suggestions about what to do, but none of the suggestions struck Laura as feasible.

During the time she had been talking to Benjy, James Bailey had arrived and was conversing with some of the men. Laura knew that he must be trying to think of a way to get Benjy down without causing the little man to jump, as he had threatened. Then two strangers, red-cheeked and out of breath and looking out-of-sorts and apprehensive, came hurrying into the tent.

After conferring with the new arrivals, Bailey escorted them out into the open, where Benjy could see them, and called up, "Benjy! The sheriff and one of his deputies are here, just as you requested. Now will you come down?"

In answer, Benjy got slowly to his feet and stood swaying on the platform. "Now I will say what I have to say," he said through the megaphone.

The crowd immediately fell silent, all staring up at the small man in anticipation.

"I did it, you see," Benjy said in his piping voice, and then he fell to coughing and held the megaphone aside until the spasm had passed.

"Did what?" the sheriff demanded.

"Must tell you," Benjy said, once more speaking through the megaphone. "It's been eating and eating at me. Eating me away . . ."

He swayed, and seemed about to topple off the platform. Then he righted himself and continued, "She was a devil! She was cruel to me one moment and kind the next." His voice grew in volume. "I heard what you all said. I knew that you called me her lapdog. I knew that you thought I was a fool for letting her use me, but I didn't care. You hear me? I didn't care, because I loved her!"

Milly gripped Laura's arm. "He's talking about Diana Salieri, isn't he?"

Without taking her gaze from the figure on the platform, Laura nodded.

"I loved her, even though she could never love me as a man. All I ever wanted from her was a little gentleness, a little caring, and so I served her and waited on her. Yes, like a little dog, I lay at her feet, but she didn't even give me the kindness she gave her little dog. It was that last day, that day when she said . . ."

He tottered again, almost losing his grip on the megaphone, then managed to recover his balance. "That day in the tent when I brought her the punch, I heard what her brother said, and I heard what she said in answer. She said that the lower orders have their uses. The lower orders—all of us who cared for her! That's all we were to her."

Suddenly he was weeping; great, racking sobs could be heard through the megaphone. Laura felt as if her heart were contracting with pain at seeing Benjy suffer so.

"What are you trying to tell us?" the sheriff bellowed.

Slowly Benjy raised the megaphone to his mouth. Now his words were strong with passion and pain: "Don't you understand? I'm telling you that I killed her, you fool! I killed Diana Salieri!"

The sheriff looked startled and confused. He turned to Bailey, and the two men conversed for a few moments.

Then the sheriff turned his attention back to Benjy. "And just how did you manage to do that?"

"With a sleeping potion," Benjy said, his voice now sounding drained. "I put it in the drink I brought her before the evening performance. I dared not harm the rigging, for I might have killed one of the others instead. I knew that the potion would make her sleepy and dizzy. I wanted her to fall, she who thought she was so high and mighty. And God help me, she did!"

Those below began to chatter among themselves, drowning out the dwarf's next words, until the sheriff shouted at them to be silent. He then called up to Benjy, "Very well, my small friend. You have confessed. Will you come down now?"

Benjy's answering laugh was hysterical. "There is more, Sheriff. Oh, yes, I could not leave well enough alone; even though I had killed the woman I loved, and ruined my life, I couldn't leave things alone. I saw that one of my friends was unhappy, that she too was a victim of one of them!—one of those greedy, selfish people who have no love in them. I wanted to help her, to set her free."

Laura felt suddenly as if she were sheathed in ice, for she knew what Benjy was going to say next.

"I only wanted to help you, Laura." The little man's voice was pleading. "I didn't mean to bring you any more grief."

"Benjy," she called out in anguish. "You didn't. . . ?"

Benjy nodded jerkily. "Yes, Laura. I killed Nick Orlando. For you, so that you would be forever free of him."

A loud, drawn-out gasp came from the crowd, and Laura heard a woman's voice cry out, "Oh, my God!"

"Yes, God will punish me," Benjy said, "not for killing such a man, but for not speaking when another man, a dear friend, was blamed for it."

Bailey's voice cut through the murmurs of the crowd. "How did you do it, Benjy? You must tell the sheriff."

Benjy put the megaphone back to his lips. His movements were jerky and uncoordinated. "I sent him a message to meet me in the main tent at midnight. I signed the note with Will Adams's name."

"But why should he come to meet Will?" Bailey asked. "Will had just beaten him in a fight. Why would he come to meet him at midnight in a deserted tent?"

"Because in the note I apologized to him," Benjy said, his voice growing hoarser and more difficult to hear. "I said that I, that Will Adams, would give him money, a large sum of money, to forget about what had happened and to go away."

"And he came?"

Benjy nodded. "He was one of the greedy ones. He came."

"And then?"

Benjy chuckled, a rough rumble of sound, which started him coughing again. "He came into the tent. I was just over there, sitting on the platform for the slack wire." He motioned with the megaphone. "My eyes were accustomed to the dark by then, but he had just come in, and his were not. I called out to him, and he came forward. When he neared the platform, I jumped on him, just like the little monkey he often called me. My knife found his chest. The knife is hidden under my bunk. You will find it there."

He started to cough again, and the megaphone fell from his hand, turning over and over as it fell. Laura found herself watching it, hypnotized by its fall, as her feelings vacillated between joy that Will would now be free, and pity for the little man alone up above them.

"Will you come down now, Benjy?" Bailey's voice was calm, as if he had not just heard Benjy's shocking confession.

The dwarf straightened up, clinging to the side support of the platform. "Yes!" he shouted, his voice sounding as thin and weak as a child's without the amplification of the megaphone. "Yes, I will come down now. I will come down once and for all!"

Laura reached out blindly to clutch at Lionel's arm as Benjy, grasping at the side support of the platform, shinnied up a few inches and seized the trapeze where it was tied off. Untying it, he shifted his grip to the bar.

Before anyone could move, or even anticipate his action, he had launched himself out into space with what seemed superhuman strength. As he swung out over the center ring, he voiced a shrill cry, a single word; and then, at the apex of his swing, he released the bar and plummeted toward the earth. There was no net below to catch him.

Laura, frozen in horror, turned her head aside the instant before his small body struck the sawdust. It was a sound she would never forget as long as she lived. And ringing in her ears was the word Benjy had screamed as he plunged to his death: "Diana!"

Chapter Twenty-Six

*I*N Lionel's wagon, Laura, Milly, and Lionel sat in somber silence over cups of coffee.

Benjy's body had been taken away, and Beppo, shocked into sobriety, had filled in the details of what had occurred prior to the rousing of the circus people by the calliope.

It seemed that Benjy had slipped out of the medical tent and had come to Beppo in their shared sleeping quarters, carrying a bottle of whiskey, which was a weakness of Beppo's. After several drinks, Benjy had told his friend what he had done and how he wished to make amends. He had also told Beppo that he was dying of the lung disease, and that Beppo would be doing him a great service if he would help him carry out his plan.

Beppo, who had some familiarity with the calliope, had agreed. Drunk as he had been, Benjy's story and request had sounded quite reasonable to him.

The use of the calliope had been to assure an audience for Benjy's confession; the dwarf had wanted to be certain that the information would get to the proper authorities, so that Will Adams would be set free.

Shaken and sobered by his friend's death, Beppo had still insisted that Benjy had done the logical thing.

"Better a quick death," he had said conclusively, "than to die of the lung disease, or to be hanged for what he'd done." And then he had added, "What he did was wrong, but he did it for the right reasons, hey?"

Now Laura, in Lionel's wagon, said pensively, "Beppo was right, you know. Awful as it may sound, Benjy killed Nick to save me, or at least he *thought* he was saving me. He had no idea that the police would suspect Will. It's all so terribly sad."

Milly's eyes were red from weeping. "Poor little fellow. I guess he never had much happiness in his life. But at any rate, he died with a certain kind of courage, so that he could exonerate Will."

Lionel pulled Milly closer to him and gazed down fondly into her face. "Benjy also did something else. He finally freed me from a ridiculous obsession. Listening to him tonight, I realized just how foolish and blind I have been. What he said about Diana and the way she treated him . . . Of course I knew all along that she was selfish and cruel, but it took tonight and Benjy's confession to make me see just how unworthy she was of anyone's love, let alone Benjy's or mine."

Milly's eyes began to shine as she looked up at him in dawning hope, and he smiled and put one hand to her cheek.

"Yes, my little Milly, Benjy has also freed me, in some strange way, from my own blindness and stubbornness. He has made me see that we should all take what happiness we can, without fear. I've been so afraid of being hurt that I've been fearful of reaching out for what has been offered me. But no more." He glanced over at Laura and winked. "Milly, I want to ask you something, right here and now, in front of your best friend, so that I cannot possibly back out. My darling Milly, will you marry me?"

With a cry of joy Milly threw her arms around his neck and pressed her face to his. "Oh, yes, Lionel! Of course it's yes! It has always been yes, but I was afraid you would never ask."

Laura, a lump in her throat, now began to cry for another, and far more pleasant, reason. Milly and Lionel would now be together. Watching the two of them, so happy, caused her to think of Will, and that made her eager for his release and return to the circus. Surely now, nothing else could happen. Surely now, they could put the past behind them and be happy.

On the day Will Adams returned to the circus, James Bailey gave a party in his honor; and despite the tragedies that had occurred, or perhaps in relief that they were finally over, everyone was in high, festive spirits.

It was something like spring, Laura thought happily. Although it was fast approaching the end of the year, it was a renewal of sorts, particularly for her and Will.

When she met Will at the train, she was filled with such joy and relief that she could hardly contain herself. He looked so good to her, despite his lean, gaunt appearance and the tired lines in his face, so handsome and so strong that she longed to fling herself upon him shamelessly, right there in the train depot in front of everybody.

But she managed to content herself with a more-or-less restrained embrace and kiss.

Will showed less restraint, and the fierceness with which he held her told Laura that his longing for her had been as strong as hers for him.

On the way to the circus grounds they clung together and kissed shamelessly in the enclosed carriage; and when they arrived at the grounds, Laura knew that her cheeks were flaming, as was her body. She ached to be alone with him, to have him make love to her, and she knew that he felt the same. However, there was the party to attend, and friends to talk to; and it was not until late that night, when they were alone in his compartment, that they could express their feelings openly.

As they lay naked on the bed, and his fingers traced their magic over her body, and his lips burned on hers, Laura found herself sobbing with relief and pleasure.

Their first coupling was fierce and avid, satisfying their long-denied hunger; and then, when they had rested for a bit, they came together again, this time less savagely, savoring the pleasure more.

Afterward, when they lay sated in each other's arms, Laura told him about Lionel and Milly.

When she had finished, Will kissed her tenderly. "I

think it's time we followed their example," he said, his voice husky with emotion. "Let's get married at once, either here or in the next town. I know that technically you're a widow whose husband has just died, but we both know that Nick has been dead to you for years. If we lived in a town, perhaps it might be different; but circus people are more realistic about such matters. No one will think badly of you, under the circumstances."

Laura experienced a warm glow of joy at his words. "Oh, yes! I want to marry you, Will, to be a part of you. But I do think we should wait until the season is over and we go back to New York. I still haven't met your son, or his grandmother, and I'm sure they would think it odd for you to get married without even telling them. Besides, we've waited this long, a few more weeks will seem like nothing."

Will was silent for a moment as a shadow crossed his face, and his glance slid away. When he spoke again, his voice was soft. "I just don't want anything else to happen," he whispered. "I want to be sure you're mine once and for all, and if we get married at once, that would be assured."

"But, darling, I'm already yours, forever and forever. I have been, almost from the beginning. No, let's wait. I'd really like a proper wedding this time, for I feel that this is my real marriage. The one with Nick doesn't count. It will only be a few weeks, Will."

Will sighed. "All right, my love. If that is what you want, that is what you shall have."

He moved around to sit on the edge of the bed, then reached for his bathrobe, which was lying across the foot of the bed. Standing up, he put it on and searched for his slippers with his feet.

"If you will excuse me for a moment, I have to go down the corridor. By the way, I have a nice bottle of wine chilling over there on the dresser." He smiled wickedly and raised his eyebrows. "I would have mentioned it sooner, but we were so busy that somehow I never got around to thinking of it. If you feel like it, you might pour us some while I'm gone."

Feeling relaxed, loved, and happier than she had been in a long time, Laura winked at him. "Why, you should have told me. I mean, the rest could have waited. After all, a nice wine is important!"

Laughing, he leaned down and kissed the tip of her nose, then left the compartment.

Laura stretched, then sat up and threw back the covers. A glass of wine did sound good.

It was a bit chilly in the compartment, and she pulled the coverlet from the bed and wrapped it around her. Padding on bare feet to the dresser, she reached for the bottle of wine. As she did so, her eye was caught by the corner of a cream-colored envelope protruding from beneath Will's cravat, where he had tossed it atop the dresser.

Curious, she pulled the envelope toward her and saw that it was addressed to Will at the jail. She put the bottle of wine back down and picked up the envelope, holding it near the lamp.

It seemed to be addressed in a woman's handwriting. Jealousy and suspicion squeezed at Laura's heart. Turning the envelope over, she studied the address on the flap. The postmark was New York City, but the only return address was a street number. Hesitating, she stared at the envelope, her face burning. Could the letter be from Will's mother-in-law? That seemed the likely answer, but why had the sender omitted her name?

With a guilty glance at the door, Laura pulled the letter, written on heavy cream paper, from the envelope, and quickly read the closing lines: "Justin's and my thoughts are with you. With much affection, Pearl."

It *was* from his mother-in-law!

Relief, like a cooling shower, dampened the fire of Laura's anxiety; she hastily stuffed the letter back into the envelope, and then returned the envelope to its place under Will's cravat.

She should not have looked at the letter, she knew. It showed a lack of trust in Will, and a lack of character on her part, but she had not been able to help herself.

How childish we humans are, she thought, as she poured the deep red wine into two glasses. *We think we are so strong, so sure of ourselves, but the least little thing shakes our confidence, and we return to the condition of children. I should be ashamed of myself.*

And yet she was glad that she had looked at the letter, for it had been somehow a vindication of Will's love for her, a proof that he was not like Nick, a womanizer and a cheat.

Placing the two glasses of wine on the nightstand, she crawled beneath the covers. By the time Will returned she was sitting propped up against the pillows and headboard, sipping her wine.

His face broke into a broad smile when he saw her. "I can't get over the fact that you're here with me. I must be the most fortunate man in the world."

He climbed in beside her and placed a kiss on her shoulder, then reached out for his glass of wine.

After he had taken a sip, Laura asked casually, "You know, Will, I'd like to know more about your son's grandmother. You told me her name once, but I've forgotten it."

Nick took another sip, frowning slightly. "It's Pearl."

"What a pretty name!" she exclaimed, almost giddy with a burst of gladness. "And what's her last name?"

Will took another sip of wine. "You know, this is good wine."

Laura shook her head in mock exasperation. "Your mother-in-law's last name, Will. Unless it's a big secret."

Will looked slightly uncomfortable, and Laura felt a moment of puzzlement so brief that she hardly realized that she had experienced it.

"Of course it's not a secret. Why should it be? Her last name is . . . Shay."

What a good Irish name, Laura thought. In her mind she pictured a plump, gray-haired, grandmotherly woman with a kind face. She said, "And you say she's very good to Justin?"

"She's been the only mother the boy has ever known, and they're extremely close."

"That's nice," she said absently. It was apparent that Will was still nervous about the future meeting between herself and his family. Was it partly because of the relationship between his mother-in-law and his son?

Since she had been a mother to the boy all these years, perhaps the grandmother looked with disfavor on the idea of Will marrying again and bringing a stepmother into the household. And yet Will had told her that it was Pearl who had insisted that he go to Laura and explain the situation about his son's illness. It was all very confusing.

She tried to frame her words carefully. "You know, Will, when you and I are married, I won't try to interfere between Pearl and your son. I mean, I would very much like to be a mother to him, but I would never try to take his grandmother's place. I just want you to know that."

Will set down his glass and pulled her close to him, almost causing her to spill her wine. His voice was soft and tender. "I know that, Laura. I know that you will show tact and kindness with both Pearl and my son."

Laura looked up at him uncertainly. "Will they like me, Will? Will they accept me?"

"I'm positive that they will," he replied, his voice muffled in her hair. "And I hope so much that you like them."

When the season was over and the last town had been played, Laura felt a growing sense of exultation. Only a few days more, and then she and Will would return to New York and make plans for their wedding. She had not broached the subject to Will yet, but she was entertaining the idea that perhaps they might be wed at his home, with a few of their closest friends in attendance. The address on Pearl's letter had stayed in Laura's mind, and she knew that it was in a good district, so it must be a fine house. Laura repeated the address like an incantation, for soon it would be her home too.

During the last few days Will was quite busy, as he and James Bailey wound up the circus affairs and prepared for the trip to the winter quarters. It was during this period that Laura received another urgent telegram from Phineas Barnum, asking her not to wait for Will but to come to New York immediately. He had, it seemed, found another wonder, and this time, he assured her, it was the genuine article—a group of complicated clockwork figures, fabricated by one of the most famous clockmakers of Europe, and in excellent condition. Could she come at once and initiate a publicity campaign for the winter season in New York?

Laura showed the telegram to Will with a moue. "What dreadful timing! Why can't he wait until we come in together? It would only be a few more days."

Will said dryly, "Have you ever known P.T. to wait for anything when he gets an idea?"

Laura sighed. "I know, I know. But what difference could a few days make? I've half a mind to wire back and tell him that I can't come."

"Don't spoil the old boy's pleasure. He loves to be busy, rushing about planning new triumphs. He was pretty set back, you know, by that hoax up in Maine. And after all, I'm going to be so busy these next few days that we would hardly get to see each other. Go ahead and let P.T. have his fun. If we stay on his good side, maybe he'll give us a grand wedding present."

"Oh, you!" she said, and then smiled. "All right. I'll wire him that I'm leaving right away, but my mind won't be on my work. It will be on you, darling."

Tilting her chin up with his finger, he leaned forward and kissed her deeply. "I hope so," he said softly. And then he kissed her again.

The weather in New York was already growing cold, and Laura shivered inside the carriage and wished that she had put on a heavier coat. Still, the sky was blue, dotted with fat white clouds that sailed across it, pushed along by a brisk wind, and it was exciting to be back in New York again.

She had just left the huge warehouse where she had met with Barnum to look at his latest acquisition, and she had to admit that it had also filled her with excitement.

A grouping of four clockwork figures, arranged on a platform that, furnished with carpet, chairs, and music stands, looked like a section of a drawing room or music room, it was a marvel of realism. Although the figures were quite old, they were in excellent condition, save for the clothing and the wigs, which would have to be replaced; they had been stored in the warehouse for some years.

Barnum already had his technicians working on the mechanism—he wished to be certain that the contrivance was operable—and although it still needed some work, the mechanism functioned well.

Laura had found watching the moving figures an eerie experience, for the figures were so beautifully constructed that they appeared very nearly human, and the music that accompanied their motions—the apparatus for which was concealed beneath the platform—seemed to be coming from the players themselves.

It would be very easy, Laura thought, to mount a campaign to publicize such a marvelous attraction.

Glancing out the window of the carriage, she noticed the street name on a lamp post. It seemed vaguely familiar.

Of course! It was the street name she had seen on the envelope in Will's compartment. It was the street where he had his home, and where his son and mother-in-law lived!

Filled with a sudden excitement, she began to scan the house numbers, looking for the number that was so firmly fixed in her mind. It was only a few doors down.

Her excitement spiraled. Should she? It would be most improper, for she had never so much as spoken to Mrs. Shay, and certainly she had no appointment. She made up her mind quickly.

Sliding open the window that separated her from the cabdriver on his seat, she called to him to halt.

He brought the carriage to a stop almost directly in front of the house she was looking for, and she gazed at it avidly. It was a respectable, solid-looking house—a narrow brownstone with neatly painted windowsills and a large front door with a handsome brass knocker.

"I'll get out here," she said, reaching into her change purse, and then found herself explaining her sudden change of plans: "I have a friend who lives here."

The driver nodded in a disinterested manner, and accepted his fare and a trip with a touch of his cap.

As the carriage clattered away, Laura turned to stare at the house, and wondered again if she was doing the right thing. But the question did not matter, since she felt compelled to follow through now that she had started.

It was not such an odd thing to do, actually. She would simply present her card to the housekeeper, or maid, and ask if Mrs. Shay was receiving. If the housekeeper said yes, she would ask her to inform her employer that Laura Orlando was an old friend of Mr. Adams, and to ask if she might call on her. If Mrs. Shay was not in, or was not receiving, then Laura would simply leave her card.

Holding her back ruler-straight, Laura marched up the neatly swept steps, raised the heavy brass door knocker, and let it fall.

She heard no sound from the other side of the door, and had about concluded that no one was home, when the well-oiled door swung open.

The woman who had opened the door was not at all what Laura had expected. Small, slender, and dressed in a long, straight dress of black silk, with a high neck and long sleeves, the woman was obviously Oriental. She wore her hair in an unusual and intricate style that was unfamiliar to Laura. She appeared to be in her late forties, and was quite beautiful in a strange and exotic way.

Thinking of the Chinese that she and Nick had seen in China Village near Pacific Grove, Laura could not help but stare. However, it was clear that this woman was of a different class from the women she had seen in China Village; her skin was much paler, having the faintly yellow tint of old ivory, and her features and frame were much more delicate. Also, her dress, while rather severe and not at all in the American or European fashion, appeared to be of expensive silk and was well cut.

What an odd sort of servant for Mrs. Shay to have, Laura thought, and handed her card to the woman, who took it silently.

"Would you please present this to Mrs. Shay," Laura said politely, "and inquire whether or not she is receiving?"

The woman gave a very slight smile, a slight curving of the lips, but her dark eyes glowed with an amused light. Looking down, she read the card before replying. "Ah, yes, Mrs. Shay is receiving. Most certainly."

The woman's voice was very soft, and her accent strange, but Laura found her way of speaking most intriguing.

"Please to come in," the woman said, stepping back from the door.

Disconcerted, Laura took one step forward and then halted. "But hadn't you best present her with my card first? I am a stranger to her, you see. A friend of her son-in-law, actually."

The woman smiled demurely. "Oh, she will be most happy to see you, I know, and you are not completely a stranger, for her son-in-law has spoken of you to her. Do come in."

More confused than ever, Laura stepped inside the entryway. It was not surprising that Will had spoken of her to Mrs. Shay, but it *was* surprising that the housekeeper should know of her as well.

The woman opened the door from the entryway into a wood-paneled hallway and beckoned to Laura, who followed a bit hesitantly. *This is all indeed strange*, she thought.

The woman glided ahead to a door off the hallway, as Laura curiously looked about. The entryway had been very attractively decorated, with a small table against one wall, bearing a delicate arrangement of dried flowers and branches, and a collection of what appeared to be newly arrived mail, and the hallway was hung with a number of Oriental prints and scrolls.

Strange, she thought; *I never knew that Will liked Oriental art*. He had certainly never mentioned it.

She followed the woman into a beautifully proportioned room that at first sight looked rather bare and sparsely furnished by the standards of the day. The furniture was of dark wood, carved with strange and unusual designs, dragons and other beasts that Laura did not recognize. There was a lovely carved and inlaid screen standing against one wall, and here and there were placed beautiful porcelains and carvings in the Oriental manner.

"Won't you please seat yourself?" the woman said, motioning to a low, carved chair softened with satin pillows.

Laura sat down rather self-consciously, watching the woman uneasily as she stood in front of her, hands clasped, looking at Laura with an amused and curious expression.

"Is anything the matter?" Laura finally asked, wondering if her face had become smudged or her hair disheveled.

The woman gave a strange half-smile and slowly shook her head. "To the contrary, my dear. You are very lovely. A beautiful young woman. I can easily see why Will fell in love with you."

Laura felt her eyes widen in surprise. What on earth did this woman mean? Had Will discussed her with the servants? It was all quite incomprehensible!

The woman smiled again, showing white teeth like a row of small pearls. "Ah, but you are confused. It was cruel of me to tease you, and I should have made things clear at once, but it was so delicious that you should think that I was a domestic, and I became quite carried away playing the part."

A terrible certainty began to dawn on Laura, and her horror must have mirrored in her face, for the woman's expression changed to one of sympathy. "I am Will's mother-in-law, my dear, and I do apologize for not making that clear at once. Our housekeeper is not here today. Her daughter is very ill, and I excused her so that she might be with her. I hope you will forgive me."

Laura felt her face flame with embarrassment, and with anger at Will for keeping her uninformed.

The Oriental woman shrugged her slender shoulders. "I gather that Will did not tell you of my . . . ethnic background?" She was frowning. "That was very remiss of him. I can understand how you were caught unawares."

Laura, her mind whirling, could only stammer, "But— but your name—it's Irish. Were you married to an Irishman?"

The older woman's laughter was soft and lilting. "Oh, you thought it was Shay? A reasonable confusion. No, my dear, my husband was Chinese, like myself. The name is spelled H-s-i-e-h, but when pronounced in English it does sound like *Shay*. But let us forget our rather odd introduction and proceed to the business of getting acquainted. Would you like some tea? I was just preparing some when you arrived."

Laura nodded, still feeling stunned and at a decided disadvantage. Anything to give her time to regain her composure!

Mrs. Hsieh smiled. "I shall return in a moment. We shall have our tea, and then I shall introduce you to Justin, who should be home from school by then. Meanwhile, make yourself comfortable. Perhaps you would like to look around the room? Most of the furnishings were brought by my husband and me from China."

Mrs. Hsieh took very tiny, gliding steps, walking as gracefully and fluidly as a swan gliding across a pond.

When the woman had gone, Laura slumped in her chair and pulled her handkerchief out of her handbag so that she might wipe her forehead, which was dewed with perspiration.

How could Will not have told her something as important as this? The fact that his mother-in-law was Chinese was entirely out of the ordinary and not something that he could simply have overlooked.

Looking up, Laura's eyes met the eyes of a painting hanging above the fireplace, and she gave a soft gasp of recognition. The painting was of a beautiful, delicate woman, in modern dress, but with an exotic and foreign face that strongly resembled that of Pearl Hsieh.

Laura knew at once that the portrait was of Lily, Will's wife, and she felt a pang of jealousy, and something else, something darker and as yet unnamed. There was not even the saving grace of an Irish father. Will's wife had been a full-blooded Chinese! She felt a vague sense of betrayal.

Laura felt her heart beating erratically. She must not think about this now; it was making her too upset. She must concentrate on putting up a good appearance; she must think of pulling herself together so that she should not make more of a fool of herself. Later, when she was back in the privacy of her hotel room, she could try to sort things out.

She heard a movement outside the door and straightened up as the door was pushed open, and Mrs. Hsieh appeared carrying a beautifully lacquered tray with a graceful Oriental teapot and two fragile, high-sided bowls, as well as a plate of cookies of some kind.

Mrs. Hsieh placed the tray on the low, carved table and seated herself opposite Laura. "I hope you like the tea," she said in her soft voice. "It is jasmine and very fragrant. I have it imported from China. The biscuits are almond cakes, rather like your shortbread in texture, and rice cakes."

Gracefully she poured two bowls of the steaming tea, and Laura wondered how one was supposed to grasp these handleless cups, which she took them to be.

"And now, my dear, tell me of Will, and of yourself, and of how you happen to be in New York."

Laura, striving to appear at ease, nevertheless found herself unable to speak fluently. In the presence of this sophisticated, exotic woman, she stammered, and felt herself reduced to bumbling awkwardness. She managed to answer most of the older woman's questions, although it embarrassed her to do so, even though Mrs. Hsieh was obviously trying to put her at ease. When a rap sounded on the door, Laura breathed a heartfelt sigh of relief.

Mrs. Hsieh smiled, showing again her small, pearly teeth. "Ah, that must be Justin. Now you two can meet. He is a lovely boy." Turning, she called out, "Justin?"

A boyish treble answered, "Yes, Grandmother. May I come in?"

"Of course, my dear. We have company."

Laura felt her leg and back muscles tightening as she braced herself to confront Will's son.

The boy who came into the room was handsome, and Laura judged his age to be around eight. She felt her heart catch as she noticed that he had his father's figure, large-boned and broad-shouldered; and then her heart caught again as she saw that he had his mother's and grandmother's thick, black, straight hair, and pale ivory complexion. She noticed that he walked with a slight limp, which had to be an aftereffect of his long illness.

His features, while more delicate than Will's, were more masculine than his mother's and grandmother's, and his black eyes, while showing a distinct tilt, were not as obviously Oriental as the women's.

He stared at Laura with frank interest and executed a short bow, as Pearl Hsieh said, "This is Mrs. Orlando, Justin. A good friend of your father's. She has come to town on business, and has graciously stopped in to visit, and to bring your father's greetings."

Laura felt her cheeks go hot. Graciously stopped in, indeed! She had made an utter fool of herself; and as for bringing greetings from Will . . . Well, she could only wonder what he was going to think when he learned what she had done.

The boy's eyes lit up, and Laura could not help noticing that he was a very handsome boy, despite his foreign looks.

"How is my father?" he asked eagerly.

Laura managed to smile. "Why, he is fine, Justin, and he sends his love and best regards."

"Will he be coming home soon?"

"Yes. Very soon. Within a few days, I should imagine."

The boy smiled brilliantly and turned to his grandmother, who returned his smile and took his hand. It was apparent to Laura that there was a strong bond between these two.

Studying their alien, dark-eyed faces, she felt entirely the outsider. Putting down her tea bowl, she dabbed her napkin to her lips. "I really must be going," she said in a rush. "I must get started on the promotion campaign that Mr. Barnum wishes me to do."

She got to her feet. "It was so kind of you to receive me."

Mrs. Hsieh stood also, and put her arm around her grandson's shoulders. "It was my pleasure, Mrs. Orlando, and I hope that we shall see much more of you in the future. When Will returns, I should be very pleased to have you join us for dinner."

"Why, yes," Laura said quickly, eager to be away. "That would be very nice."

"Come, Justin," Mrs. Hsieh said. "We shall see Mrs. Orlando to the door."

The boy, in a courtly fashion, offered his arm to Laura, who awkwardly accepted it. At the door they all said goodbye again, and Laura hurried down the steps, waving to a cab that was just then coming down the street.

Embarrassed, angry, and shaken to the depths of her soul, she directed the hansom driver to take her to her hotel as quickly as possible. Perhaps there she could sort out the conflicting feelings raging through her, not the least of which was a mounting fury at Will and his deceit.

Chapter Twenty-Seven

*I*N her hotel room Laura removed her clothing and drew a hot bath. The hot water, she thought, might help her relax and free her of the painful tension that felt as if it were drawing her muscles into knots.

Once immersed in the steaming water, which she had scented and softened with oil and fragrance, she let out a great sigh as the heat and water began their subtle work. She felt her body relaxing, bit by bit, but her mind was still as active and confused as ever. Why hadn't Will prepared her? Why hadn't he told her that his wife and child were not Caucasian?

Of course, to be fair, he had had no idea that she was going to barge in on his family by herself; but he had said that he was going to introduce them, and it certainly could not have remained a secret after that!

Thinking back over the times that Will had discussed his family, she could recall a certain evasiveness. And then there were the times that he had said that he hoped Laura would like and accept his son and his son's grandmother. Laura had not thought much of it at the time, but now it was all too clear that he had been worried about her meeting them; and that implied that he was self-conscious about their being Oriental and was worried that she might not find them acceptable.

Sighing again, she leaned her head back against the rim of the tub. And how did she feel about Will having been married to a Chinese woman and having a half-Chinese son?

She would have liked to be able to say that it did not matter, but she was still too shocked and startled honestly to say that, even to herself. Somehow it *did* make a difference, no matter how much she wished to deny it.

Although she had never thought of herself as a prejudiced person, the idea that Will's wife had been a nonwhite, and his son a half-breed, bothered her. It also troubled her that Will had not told her about it.

If she married him, would she ever fit in, in that brownstone house decorated in the Chinese style? Would it ever feel like her house, or would the ghost of Will's dead wife, in the corporeal form of her mother, still preside as mistress?

Will would be in New York in a few days. What would she say to him? What would he think when Pearl Hsieh told him that Laura had blithely come calling?

Restlessly she turned her head back and forth. She simply could not face him in the condition she was in now. She had to get away, to be by herself to think things through. She would have to tell Phineas that she could not work on the new promotion; she must have a vacation, some time off. She would tell him that the cumulative pressures of the tragedies that had occurred had left her unable to work. She knew that this was true to a certain extent, and surely Phineas would see the logic of it.

She would go . . . Where? Where could she go to be alone, to think?

And then the answer came to her—Pacific Grove. But if she went there, would she see her father and mother? It had been so long since she had thought of them, and she examined her feelings for her father, testing to see if her hatred of him had abated over the years. *It has a little,* she thought; *and yet I do not want to see him again.* She knew in her heart that he would not have changed—some people never did. She would like to see her mother, though; even if her mother had not defended her from Samuel Purcell, there was still an emotional tie there, and some happy memories from Laura's childhood.

Of course, it was October now; and even if they had spent the summer at the Grove, they would probably have returned to Sacramento by now.

It would be nice to see the Pacific coast again, feel the wind in the pines and watch the sea otters at play in the bay. And the butterflies should be there, as they always were, at this time of year.

Yes! It would be Pacific Grove. She would not stay in one of the hotels, but would rent one of the vacant cottages and be entirely on her own for however long it took to get her thoughts in order; for she knew that she could not face Will, or make a decision about their marriage, until she did. She would tell no one but Phineas where she was going. And Will? What would she tell Will?

In the end she decided that she would leave him a letter, stating simply that she was feeling unwell and confused after all that had taken place, and that she found it necessary to be by herself for a time. She would end the letter by saying that she would contact him as soon as she returned. He would be upset by such a letter, she well realized, and would wonder why the tone of it was so remote and lacking in warmth, but she could not help that. Right now, feeling as she did, it was all she could offer him.

The wind coming off the sea was salty and fresh and evoked many memories in Laura.

Sitting on the rocks at Jesus Lover's Point, she looked down into Sandy Cove, which was deserted except for a lone fisherman in a small boat.

How many times had she sat here in the past, thinking her private thoughts, dreaming her dreams? Simple dreams, really; for she had wanted only to get away from the narrow, circumscribed life that her father had arranged for her. She never could have imagined, at that time, the things that she had now experienced.

When she had arrived at Pacific Grove she had immediately rented a small charming house. It was of a simple, boxy construction, and the small yard surrounding it was filled with lovely plants. It was furnished with simple but comfortable furnishings, and Laura had immediately felt at home there.

The first thing she had done, after getting settled into the house, was to go to the lot where her father and mother had their tent. She had approached her former home warily, not certain what she would find there.

At first she did not recognize the place, since several of the tents had been replaced by houses. It was with mixed feelings that she realized that her family's tent was one of them; where the tent had stood was now a small yellow cottage.

Was it her parents', or had they sold the place? The house did not strike her as something that her father would have approved.

Well, she might as well find out. At least whoever lived there might know something about her parents. Squaring her shoulders, she knocked on the door.

In a moment it opened, and her mother stared at her with widening eyes. "Oh, my goodness! Laura! Dear God, it *is* you!"

Laura concealed her own surprise behind a weak smile. "Hello, Mother."

"I thought I'd never see you again." Her mother blinked back tears, made a motion as if to hold out her arms, then stepped back. "Do come in, Laura."

As Laura entered, her mother became oddly formal. "I was just about to make myself a pot of tea. Perhaps you'd like to join me?"

"Of course, Mother, I'd be happy to." Laura stepped inside. "I just got here yesterday. I . . . I came out here for a few days of rest."

"Why didn't you come directly to . . . ? Oh, your father." Mrs. Purcell looked somber. "You haven't heard, of course."

Laura's heart skipped a beat. "Haven't heard what, Mother?"

Her mother sighed heavily. "Your father is dead, dear. He died about two years ago. Oh, you aren't going to faint, are you? You've gone awfully pale."

Laura, the blood draining suddenly from her head, did

indeed feel as if she were going to fall. Despite what she felt or did not feel for her father, it was still a great shock.

She felt her mother take her arm. "Oh, you poor child! I shouldn't have blurted it out so sudden like that. Do come into the kitchen and sit down. A nice, strong cup of tea will help."

Laura let herself be led into the kitchen, where she sat down gratefully on a brightly painted wooden chair in the small but cozy kitchen.

Her mother bustled about with the kettle and teapot. There was a brisk, competent air about her that surprised Laura.

"I know how you felt about your father, Laura, but still, any death is a sad thing."

"Yes, of course it is. What caused his death, Mother?"

"He had an apoplectic fit. The doctor said his heart just burst." Mrs. Purcell darted a quick glance at her. "You know how he was."

"Oh, yes, I know how he was."

"I'm sorry, Laura." Her mother stopped her bustling and faced her, her hands locked tightly in front of her.

"Sorry, Mother?"

"Yes, for not standing up for you all those years, for not standing between the two of you. It was wrong of me, I know, but all those years with him just wore me down, took the spirit right out of me. It was terrible after you ran away. Oh, not that I'm blaming you, dear," she added hastily. "But your father raged and raged, blaming me for everything. . . . Oh, I shouldn't be saying this, with the poor man dead."

She turned away and busied herself with the teapot. In a moment she set a cup of steaming tea and a plate of fresh cookies before Laura.

Laura took a few sips of the tea and felt its warmth reviving her. She stared at her mother. "You look very well, Mother."

The woman flushed, her hands fussing with her hair, which was almost wholly gray now. "Well, you know, with Samuel gone . . ."

"I think I understand, Mother," Laura said, remembering how she had often thought that her father was the cause of his wife's various ailments. "This house . . . it's very nice." She gestured around. "Did Father build it?"

"Good heavens, no! He would never . . ." Mrs. Purcell took on a sly look. "After his death I sold the house in Sacramento and had this one built. It did turn out rather nice, didn't it?"

"Good for you, Mother," Laura said heartily.

Her mother sat down with her own cup of tea. "And you, Laura? What's happened to you all this time? That man you ran off with—did you marry him?"

"Yes, but he's dead, Mother." Laura glanced down. "There was an . . . an accident." She looked up, forcing a smile. "I've been working for a circus."

Her mother touched her hand tentatively. "Oh, I'm sorry, dear!"

Laura shrugged. "We were separated. We had been, for some time."

"And you've been working for a circus? My, that *is* unusual! Do you like it?"

Laura began to tell her something of the excitement and glamour of her life with the circus; but she soon realized, from the glazed look in her mother's eyes, that the woman grasped very little of what she was talking about.

"Anyway, that's what I've been doing," she finished. "After Nick's death, I had to get away for some peace and rest. And what better place than Pacific Grove?"

"Where are you staying?"

"I rented one of the cottages."

"But you're more than welcome to stay here. There's plenty of room."

"No, I'd rather not, Mother," she said hastily. "But thank you. I need some time alone, away from all distractions." She drained the cup of tea and rose to her feet abruptly. "And I must really be going now."

Her mother's face assumed a look of alarm, and she stood up, too. "Going? You mean you're leaving Pacific Grove so soon? I thought we could . . ."

"Oh, no. I'll be here awhile yet. I just want to walk

around while it's still light, and see what changes have taken place in the Grove. I'll be back to see you, I promise. Every day, if you like."

Mrs. Purcell brightened. "That would be nice, Laura."

Laura said gently, "Mother, are you lonely here?"

Her mother shook her head. "Oh, no! It's so nice, being by myself after all these years."

"Well . . ." Laura said uncertainly.

Tears suddenly sprang to her mother's eyes, and she said brokenly, "Oh, Laura, I thought I would never see you again, and I've had to live with the thought that I helped drive you away. Can you ever forgive me?"

"There's nothing to forgive, Mother. It wasn't you—never you."

And then her mother's arms opened, and Laura went into them, her own tears starting. They clung together fiercely, and her mother murmured fervently, "My daughter come home to me at last! I love you, Laura. I always have, even if I didn't always show it."

Will, staring down at the brief note in his hands, found himself trembling.

Wadding the piece of paper in his fist, he leaned against the hotel desk, letting its oaken bulk support him.

What in the name of heaven did it mean? When he and Laura had parted, just a few days ago, she had been full of plans for their future. What could have happened in this brief period of time that could have turned her into the writer of the note:

> *Dear Will;*
>
> *I am sorry not to be here to greet you, but I now find it necessary to get away by myself for a short time. I realize that this will seem abrupt to you, and my only explanation is that the dreadful things of the past few months have taken their toll on me, and that I must be alone to think and recuperate.*

> *I will contact you as soon as I return to New York. I hope that you will understand.*
>
>   Sincerely,
>   Laura

Will almost groaned aloud. *Sincerely, Laura?* No expression of love? This from the woman who had shared her bed and her body with him, who had vowed that she loved him and wanted to be with him forever?

Wheeling away from the hotel desk, where the message had been left for him, he strode out into the street. He hailed the first empty hansom cab and gave the driver the address of his home.

In the cab he pressed his hands to his eyes. Could it be that she was taking her revenge on him for his leaving her so abruptly three years ago? Was it possible that her letter, so cool and distant, was meant to echo his letter to her? Surely she was not that vindictive, that cruel! If she were, she would not be the woman he so dearly loved.

Perhaps he should show the letter to Pearl. She had great wisdom and had always given him good advice in the past. Perhaps she could tell him what to do.

Arriving home, he attempted to put his gloomy thoughts aside, for he knew that Justin would be eager to see him, and he must not spoil the reunion with his son.

Opening the door, he was met by a furious bundle of boyish energy as Justin jumped into his father's arms, ignoring his grandmother's plea to "behave like a young gentleman now," and for a moment Will thought only of his son.

It was only after the presentation of gifts and the exchange of news were over, and the excited youngster was sent off to bed, that Will settled down for a long talk with Pearl, which culminated with his telling her of Laura's sudden disappearance and her strange letter to him.

As Pearl read the crumpled note, Will was dismayed to see her slender face turn pale, and he leaned forward with a worried frown. Did she see something in those few words that he had missed?

Pearl dropped the letter into her lap and looked at him

with tears in her eyes. "Oh, the poor girl. And much of it
is your fault, Will. If only you had told her, warned her. I
am very much afraid that it was a shock to her, coming
unexpectedly as it did."

"What do you mean? *What* came as a shock?"

Pearl looked at him steadily. "I am afraid that *I* did, and
your son. It was obvious that she had no idea that your
wife and son were Chinese. You should have prepared
her."

"You mean she was *here*? She came to the house?"

Pearl nodded. "Oh, yes. She simply appeared last week
at the door, presenting her card. She said that she was in
town on business, and that she was in the vicinity and
decided to call. Of course, I knew who she was, and was
most delighted to meet her at last. However, I am not
certain that she felt the same." Pearl gave a small, sar-
donic smile. "I answered the door myself, you see. Mrs.
Orlando assumed that I was the housekeeper."

"Oh, my God!" Will said, shaken.

"Yes, it was most awkward for her, and that was partly
my fault. I found the situation amusing, and did not
disabuse her of the notion immediately." She sighed
dolefully. "I realize now that this was a grave mistake, for
she was embarrassed when she learned the truth, and, I
suspect, thereafter felt very ill-at-ease in my company."

Pearl paused and gazed down at her slender, long-
nailed hands. "I also suspect that she found the fact of our
race rather difficult to accept. Many people do, you know."

Will stiffened. "Laura's not like that! She's very fair
and open-minded."

"I'm sure she is," Pearl said with a melancholy smile.
"Even during our brief meeting I could see that she was a
superior young woman, very modern and intelligent in
her ideas. But even those who think themselves open-
minded sometimes find it difficult to adjust to foreigners
when they are confronted by them as neighbors or friends.
And this situation would demand that she accept a stepson
who is only half-white, and a live-in grandmother and
mother-in-law who is not white at all.

"But I am not criticizing, Will. In my country it is the

same. My people are also convinced of their uniqueness and superiority, and consider the white race barbarians. You married Lily in France, so you were not subjected to the pressures and prejudices you would have experienced if you had courted her in China." She raised her gaze to his with a look of sympathy. "You should have told her, Will. Why didn't you? You certainly did not think that you could keep it a secret once you were married?"

"I meant to tell her. I tried several times, but could never seem to get the words out." He struck the arm of his chair with his fist. "I . . . I suppose I wasn't certain how she would take to it. I guess I also felt that I shouldn't have to explain. I mean, I was never ashamed of being married to Lily! I was proud that she loved me, that she was my wife. She was a woman, and a person. What did it matter what race she was?"

Pearl sighed. "An admirable feeling, my son, but naïve in the extreme. In the real world it *does* matter, and although it might not be pleasant to have to admit it, it is only practical to do so."

"And you think that her visit here upset her enough to cause her to flee from me?"

"It would appear so. I think that on top of all you have told me that has happened to her recently, this last surprise was perhaps too much. I think that she probably did feel it necessary to get away, to be by herself so that she might arrange her thoughts and feelings, I do not think that this letter, terse as it is, means that she no longer loves you. It only means that right now she is confused and shaken and embarrassed. Angry as well, perhaps, because you did not trust her enough to tell her the truth. Do you think you could find her, Will?"

He hesitated. "I'm sure that she must have told P. T. Barnum where she was going."

She looked at him intently. "Then I suggest you give her a few more days to think things out, then go to her, with your hat in your hand, as they say."

* * *

The day was clear, brisk, and a bit windy; one of those days that showed the coastline and the sea to best advantage.

Laura, clad in practical clothing and walking shoes, wandered through the streets of the Chinese fishing village, much as she and Nick had done that day in the past.

The village had changed little, as far as she could ascertain; there were still the same rickety, stilted houses, still the fisher people in their odd clothing, still the children flying bright, birdlike kites, and the women playing mahjong and cards, all accompanied by the strange, singsong chatter and occasional laughter.

Ever since her return to Pacific Grove, Laura had felt drawn to the village, although she was not sure why. Perhaps it was simply because these people shared a common heritage with Mrs. Hsieh and Justin. For whatever reason, she had finally ventured to the village, after a week's stay in the Grove.

As she walked slowly down the street, a group of children came her way, running and laughing happily, chasing a rolling metal hoop that bounced and rolled down the incline ahead of them.

As the children passed her, Laura stared hard at their laughing faces. They were attractive children, with their neat, straight black hair and round cheeks, but they did not look at all like Justin. Their skin was much darker, and their faces much rounder and somehow flatter. Still, they were children, much like any others.

And the men working with their nets, and the women laughing and gossiping, were, despite their alien looks and strange language, men and women for all that.

Thinking back to that day she and Nick had spent here, she tried to relive her feelings of that time. Had she felt then that these people were any less worthy than she or her family were? She could not recall feeling so. They were different, true, but did that make them less in any way?

It was obvious that Mrs. Hsieh came from a background of privilege and distinction, while Laura's own family could certainly make no such boast. So why then did she feel uncomfortable with the idea of having a half-Chinese step-son, or of living with his Chinese grandmother?

Standing on the shoreline, she watched as a bright, fish-shaped kite dipped and soared against the blue of the sky; and as she did so, she realized suddenly that the feeling of tension and anger she had been carrying, like a heavy yoke across her shoulders, was gone. She felt relaxed and at peace, despite the fact that she had come to no conclusion as to what to do about Will. One thing she did know was that she loved him very much. The question was, did she love him enough?

After spending considerable time at the village, she walked slowly back toward Pacific Grove, relishing the physical contentment of healthy fatigue, and enjoying the wind against her face.

It was growing late, and the sun was dropping slowly in the west, giving the afternoon sunlight a golden glow that glinted off the sea and clouds—the promise of a glorious sunset. Washed across the sky were tints of rose, yellow, and orange. It was a beautiful and peaceful sight.

Laura was quite weary now; and since she was near Jesus Lover's Point, she walked out onto the rocks and sat for a time, watching the colors change and darken as the sun sank lower.

As she sat there, a feeling of sweet sadness stole over her, and suddenly she experienced Will's absence with a deep ache of pain. She felt that if only he were here beside her now, sharing this moment, everything would be all right again. Beauty was always wonderful, but it was most wonderful when shared.

Getting up from the cooling stone, she turned to head inland toward her cottage. As she did so, she saw two figures coming toward her through the beginning dusk.

Her eyes were partially blinded by the brilliance of the sunset, so she could not see the figures well, but they appeared to be those of a tall man and a boy.

A strange flutter disturbed her heartbeat as she walked slowly toward them, and they toward her.

As they drew closer together, she felt herself trembling

with a growing excitement. It could not be, of course, but the man looked very much like Will, and the boy . . .

Hurrying her steps now, she walked in the last rosy glow of the dying sun. Then she saw the boy's limp. It was! It was Will and his son, approaching slowly, tentatively, as if unsure of their welcome.

Suddenly, the final bit of doubt was gone, as a last ray of sunlight struck Will's face, and she saw the question there. Feeling as if a constricting band had dissolved from around her heart, she knew that these two were the most important people in the world to her, and that she loved them both with her entire being. Everything else was unimportant.

A cry was wrung from her: "Will! My love!"

Holding out her arms, she began to run toward them, as the sun sank in a final blaze of glory.

ABOUT THE AUTHOR

A few years ago Patricia Matthews was office manager for The Associated Students, California State University at Los Angeles, and a part-time writer who dreamed of making her career writing.

Married and the mother of two sons, Patricia had to struggle to find time to turn out her poems, short stories and novels which were published under her prior name, Patty Brisco. But the success of her first historical romance, published in 1977, changed all that, and Patricia Matthews' own true life story has proven to have a Cinderella ending. Today she is America's leading lady of historical romance with fifteen consecutive bestselling novels to her credit and millions of fans all over the world.